masterfully creates a narrative that is both enchanting and profoundly moving. Fans of the atmospheric storytelling found in Kristin Hannah's *The Nightingale* will be enthralled by Brock's ability to evoke a sense of place and time. *The Fabled Earth* is more than a historical novel; it is a deep dive into the power of legends and the strength of women who seek the truth, no matter how buried it may be. This is a must-read for anyone who enjoys the transformative power of storytelling."

—Angela Jackson Brown, author of *Untethered*

The Lost Book of Eleanor Dare

"You do not need a deep grounding in colonial misadventure to appreciate Kimberly Brock's graceful work of speculative, historical fiction. This ambitious, indelibly Southern novel is told from three points of view—Eleanor, Alice, and Penn—in two timeframes. The storytelling is rich, lyrical, and garlanded with Spanish moss, with jewel-like passages that beg to be re-read. Brock, however, is just elliptical enough, and deft with her pacing, to keep the pages turning."

—*Atlanta Journal Constitution*

"Brock weaves a multigenerational story based on the supposed descendants of the real-life Eleanor Dare. I appreciated that the story was well researched as I read the pages from Eleanor Dare's viewpoint as she flees from Roanoke Island to points unknown. The characters are unique and carry their own human flaws that make them come alive and feel believable. I rooted for each of them as they strove to find their place in a complicated family history. Highly recommended."

—Historical Novel Society

"*The Lost Book of Eleanor Dare* is an intriguing, dreamy story about the impact of one unhealed woman who has yet to reconcile her past in such a way that lends itself to transparency with her young daughter . . . Author Kimberly Brock delicately balances mystery, family lore, and honoring one's forebears in sonorous language throughout a sweeping story with three points of view, two timeframes, and remarkably steady pacing. Weaving myth and legend with historical fact pertaining to an age-old American mystery, *The Lost Book of Eleanor Dare* is a spell-binding, beautiful story written by a graceful hand with just the right amount of mysticism."

—*New York Journal of Books*

"A beautiful keepsake of a novel that is at once historical and speculative . . . The empowering tale of nearly 20 generations of women surviving, thriving, and sometimes vanishing, by virtue of their abilities to shoulder the weight of their pasts, to discover and learn the lessons of their present, and to pass on their wisdom from mother to daughter through the inheritance of their stories—some of which might even be true."

—*The Post and Courier* (Charleston, SC)

"Amid the atmospheric backdrop of the Lowcountry, Brock stirs up a beguiling blend of family legacy, historical mystery, and generational connections, examining the unbreakable ties of mothers and daughters, the power of stories told and stories hidden, and the unquenchable need to understand those who came before us. A beautiful tale to curl up with and contemplate the intertwining of lives past and present."

—Lisa Wingate, #1 *New York Times* bestselling author of *The Book of Lost Friends*

"In this complex, compelling, and beautifully crafted novel, Kimberly Brock explores not only the enigma of the Lost Colony of Roanoke, but also the boundless mysteries of love, family, and the human heart. As Alice Young and her daughter, Penn, settle into Evertell, the crumbling ancestral estate they've just inherited, they discover secrets long hidden in the shadows there, keys to understanding their own veiled pasts. This is a story filled with many charms, both literal and figurative, and I guarantee it will captivate readers from the first page to the last."

—William Kent Kreuger, *New York Times* bestselling author

"From its haunting first line, *The Lost Book of Eleanor Dare* transports the reader to a mysterious land, time, and family. Kimberly Brock's trademark whimsical storytelling shines in this Southern-soaked tale of family legacy and the magic of female history as she imagines what might have happened to the Lost Colony of Roanoke. With only an engraved stone and a book left behind, the captivating women of the Dare legacy must find their true inheritance hiding behind the untold secrets."

—Patti Callahan, *New York Times* bestselling
author of *The Secret Book of Flora Lea*

"Compelling and immersive, *The Lost Book of Eleanor Dare* is the story of Dare's descendant Alice, who pushes away the pain of the past until her daughter, Penn, holds her accountable to the family story. Brock's lush narrative is rich in American and Virginia history with deep roots in the mysterious disappearance of the Lost Colony on Roanoke Island. As Alice and Penn seek answers, they rely on the enduring strength of their foremother Eleanor, who was determined to leave the truth behind so generations might walk in its light."

—Adriana Trigiani, bestselling author of *The Good Left Undone*

"Kimberly Brock has crafted a luminous story, multilayered and shimmering with beautiful prose, that deftly ponders the way of sacrificial love."

—Susan Meissner, bestselling author of
The Nature of Fragile Things

"A richly atmospheric, distinctively Southern story of mothers and daughters, family secrets, and what it means to find home."

—Elizabeth Blackwell, bestselling author of *Red Mistress*

"*The Lost Book of Eleanor Dare* is a beautiful exploration of the bonds between women; the stories they pass down to one another through grief, adversity, and triumph; the secrets they keep; and the inner worlds they share. Brock has crafted a keenly observed, heartfelt tale that will linger with readers long after they finish reading."

—Megan Chance, bestselling author of *A Splendid Ruin*

"Kimberly Brock should be on everyone's Southern fiction auto-buy list. *The Lost Book of Eleanor Dare* is an absorbing, lyrical love letter to the magic of the South and to the almost supernatural tie that binds one generation's life song to the next. Brock's Evertell—the presumed homeplace of the mysterious Eleanor Dare and her heirs—is important not because of the names and dates etched on a rock long ago, but because of the triumphs and heartaches, joys and stumbles that whisper through the ages to caution and encourage each Dare heir—and us, too—to strive for better, to love bigger. Only in doing so will we settle into ourselves and step into who we were made to be."

—Joy Callaway, international bestselling author of *The Grand Design*

"Kimberly Brock's *The Lost Book of Eleanor Dare* is an immersive, engrossing tale about the Lost Colony of Roanoke, but even more significantly, about the relationship between a mother and daughter whose lives have been irrevocably altered by loss. Brock's writing is lush and captivating, and her characters are rich and complex. A masterful work by an expert craftswoman, *The Lost Book of Eleanor Dare* is not to be missed."

—Aimie K. Runyan, bestselling author of *The School for German Brides*

"For readers of Patti Callahan and Kate Morton, this harrowing exposition on history and loss is a juxtaposition of love, hope, and the wisdom that binds women across centuries. *The Lost Book of Eleanor Dare*'s plea that we learn from each other, grow from each other, and empower each other is wrapped in an arresting, urgent voice that reads as much a rallying cry as a tract on the burden of women to suture the cracks of history. A magnanimous undertaking steeped in impeccable research, Brock offers a feast of a narrative that crackles with a resonant, binding echo of sisterhood across the centuries."

—Rachel McMillan, author of *The Mozart Code*

THE
FABLED
EARTH

ALSO BY KIMBERLY BROCK

The River Witch
The Lost Book of Eleanor Dare

THE FABLED EARTH

A Novel

KIMBERLY BROCK

HARPER MUSE

Published by Harper Muse, an imprint of HarperCollins Focus LLC.

This book is a work of fiction. The characters, incidents, and dialogue are drawn from the author's imagination and are not to be construed as real. Any resemblance to actual events or persons, living or dead, is entirely coincidental.

Any internet addresses (websites, blogs, etc.) in this book are offered as a resource. They are not intended in any way to be or imply an endorsement by HarperCollins Focus LLC, nor does HarperCollins Focus LLC vouch for the content of these sites for the life of this book.

Library of Congress Cataloging-in-Publication Data
Names: Brock, Kimberly, author.
Title: The fabled Earth: a novel / Kimberly Brock.
Description: [Nashville]: Harper Muse, 2024. | Summary: "Inspired by the little-known history of Cumberland Island, The Fabled Earth is a sweeping story of family lore and the power of finding your own voice as Southern mythology and personal reckoning collide with a changing world"--Provided by publisher.
Identifiers: LCCN 2024016337 (print) | LCCN 2024016338 (ebook) | ISBN 9781400234226 (hardcover) | ISBN 9781400347544 | ISBN 9781400234257 (epub) | ISBN 9781400234264
Subjects: LCSH: Cumberland Island (Ga.)--Fiction. | LCGFT: Novels.
Classification: LCC PS3602.R62334 F33 2024 (print) | LCC PS3602.R62334 (ebook) | DDC 813/.6--dc23/eng/20240415
LC record available at https://lccn.loc.gov/2024016337
LC ebook record available at https://lccn.loc.gov/2024016338

Printed in the United States of America

24 25 26 27 28 LBC 5 4 3 2 1

To Amy Sue Nathan

There were fish in the rivers of Eire, there were animals in her coverts. Wild and shy and monstrous creatures ranged in her plains and forests. Creatures that one could see through and walk through . . .

I ranged on the tides of the worlds. Green and purple distances were under me: green and gold the sunlit regions above. In these latitudes, I moved through a world of amber, myself amber and gold; in those other places, in a sparkle of lucent blue, I curved, lit like a living jewel.

—*James Stephens, "The Story of Tuan mac Cairill"*

Folklore is the boiled-down juice, or pot-likker, of human living.

—*Zora Neal Hurston*

Chapter One

CLEO

THE EAST RIVER, SOMETIMES SHINING, A MIRROR TO THE LUCENT blue firmament above, was laid out for Cleo Woodbine's sharp green eyes, with nothing moving over its calm surface on this morning but her, a reeling seabird, a passing fishing boat. She knew the nature of barrier islands and the mysteries that swam beneath the changing waters, the paths cleared through maritime woods by deer and wild horses, the nests of the loggerheads buried in the dunes, even the trails of the damn hogs. She hated the wild hogs and feared them. The truth was, she would be glad to never see man nor beast again, if she had to look on the bright side today.

She paid attention to the color of the water and the current as she made her way. She knew to be careful of the depth. She'd been traveling these waters in her flat-bottomed johnboat almost thirty seasons now, since the summer of 1932. As with life, the river bottom was always changing. The depths could surprise people, even those who knew every bend in the salt creeks through the Georgia marsh as she did. And even Cleo had to admit that there were some changes she couldn't see coming, like the news that had arrived with the basket of produce she exchanged on the regular with the inn on the mainland, her name scrawled across the envelope in letters a child might have written.

It was rare for a piece of mail to find her. And Cleo didn't properly know any children. The ones she was aware of were more likely to throw a mink pelt at her door on a dare than to send her a letter. It had occurred to her that the handwriting had not been made by an unpracticed hand but an unsteady one. She'd opened the mail to find a sympathy card, and from it, a clipping of an obituary had fallen into her lap. She'd sighed, expecting the passing of Dr. Marius Johnston, who would be nearing eighty by now. But it had been a different name she read there. Cleo had been so affected she'd passed out. The shoals had risen up like something biblical and she woke to find herself contemplating a world that had changed so drastically that she'd ended up at the bottom of the steps.

Joanna Burton had been dead and buried almost a month.

There'd been a girl, alive in Cleo's memory all these years, in an iridescent green swimsuit that glimmered like scales, like light on the river on a grand summer day. Cleo had barely known Joanna, but their stories had intertwined, theirs and those of the young men who came to Cumberland that season. Two of them had drowned and the rest had scattered to the four corners—but to Cleo, the end to Joanna felt like the end to all.

———

In the wake of that news, Cleo left Kingdom Come. Situated with water on all sides, it had never been more than a lick of land with the river bounding the east shore and the sea to the west, a temporary realm that would one day be joined with the greater seventeen-mile Cumberland Island. She could walk around the entire thing in thirty minutes, and she'd been measuring out her remaining days before it was an island no more. For the last few seasons, the silt that rose from the riverbed with every tide meant she'd had to navigate more carefully through the waterways so she wouldn't mire her boat or drag the hull over a sandbar. She knew that locals liked to lay bets on how much longer her cottage would stand against the shifting foundation, and on the day Cleo Woodbine would come walking back into town. Farther east and north of Cumberland lay the mainland and Revery, a sleepy little fishing community known for its own long history and picturesque main street, where she'd been born. On a clear night, she might see the lights twinkle there like a few more stars from the sky, miles up the coast, still a quiet little place in 1959. That was as much as she'd cared to see of the larger world in a long while.

Taking her usual route, Cleo meandered south to moor her boat near Dungeness, the largest of the old Carnegie mansions, before she'd turn around and head north to pass the other summer homes still standing their ground against the passage of time—Greyfield, Stafford, Plum Orchard. She liked that they had names like grand old gals and often felt she could almost count herself among them. A few still housed family, either visiting or living there for parts of the year. Others were completely abandoned. But after a century, the Carnegies' strange kingdom by the sea was going to seed, crumbling beautifully, like everything eventually did on Cumberland.

Cleo herself was a small, strong, practical woman. Not yet fifty, she was most comfortable wearing a pair of denim pants with plenty of pockets, a cotton button-down worn soft, and muddy Red Wing boots. Her auburn hair was a thicket, snipped at with kitchen scissors to keep it chin-length. She was not stylish or modern or relevant in any way. She had made a life that was far from sensible as an artist and a forager. No one would miss her, she supposed, aside from the heirloom fruit trees and shrubs scattered between the estates, from which she gathered produce in order to barter for necessities. On the whole, Cleo lived her days out the same as those trees. She answered to no one, and she honestly preferred it that way.

It had been a good year for muscadine and loquat and the Ruby Sweet, a favorite of hers. She took a plum from her pocket, had her breakfast, breathed out, then turned her face to the sun. It was the summer light that always got to her, made her hate to think of leaving this place. She'd learned you could love your prison. You could make a sanctuary of it.

Long before she took up as artist-in-residence at Woodbine Cottage, her grandfather had been the first to hold the post. The Carnegies of Plum Orchard had been his benefactors, those old gods with their wild fortune, now dwindling away. Dooley Woodbine was a first-generation Scotch-Irish immigrant whose family had settled in Kentucky. There, he'd been a childhood friend of Marius Johnston, who later married Nancy Carnegie. When he'd invited Dooley to Georgia, Dooley brought his own wife, a practical girl from Brunswick, and his favorite Scotch-Irish folktales and fables in his red head, like some people bring relatives who cling and settle too close. And while living in the cottage, he'd fathered one son, Cleo's father, and written and illustrated a book of his own stories, *Woodbine's Treasury of Glories and Grims*. There'd been two hundred copies printed and he'd kept only one, which he'd bequeathed to Cleo, along with his love of the shoals.

Cleo herself had never traveled farther than the miles that separated Kingdom Come and the place where she'd been raised by parents who had worked in the mills and canneries of Revery before both dying young. After the heartbreaking loss of their only son and daughter-in-law, Cleo's grandparents had left Woodbine Cottage and come to town to care for her. Only after all her family was gone had Cleo returned to the island, holding out just enough hope for her own future as an artist.

She'd loved to sit on Dooley's knee and listen to him intone the poetic language of ancient Irish myths and Appalachian ghost stories. He'd shown her a book of illustrations by Arthur Rackham, the artist who had most influenced him. He'd gifted her with her own pen and India ink, a set of paints, and a fresh pad of special paper, and supplied new ones every year until he'd died, when she was ten. She'd copied the illustrated characters in *Woodbine's*, filling up the pads of paper almost as soon as she received them. Then, sometime after Dooley passed, her favorites of those characters took on a life of their own and began to tag along beside her—a friendly spirit named Little Hannah, a ghostly fiddler, and a lonely graveyard guardian, a dog known as the grim. She'd only added to the canon once since she'd come to the shoals, a gentle giant who slipped through the deep forests and in and out of the light, whom she thought of as the spirit of the island.

Dooley had said that all stories were ghost stories, an exchange of spirit between the world and the human heart that rode on an inhale and an exhale. Stories, to Dooley, were elemental. Cleo couldn't have doubted that truth if she'd tried. She'd imagined all those stories he'd told drifting past her heart, slipping around the forest of her bones. It was no wonder the figments of her imagination trailed at her heels. They were good company as she loitered near Dungeness. Little Hannah stayed close as a shaft of that summer light, and the melancholy fiddle tune carried over the shoals. *A serenade?* No. A reminder she was not alone in her grief. Cleo was grateful for the ragtag bunch of childhood memories she'd dragged out here with her, and she'd continued to paint them so they might be remembered even after she was gone.

Cleo liked to think of the Timucuans when she came to Dungeness, to remember their story, a native tribe that had long ago made their home in this area and down into Florida. You couldn't find one now if you tried, although centuries ago, they'd surely never have imagined that would be the case. They'd built a shell ring right where she stood from the discarded oyster shells from their tables. Later, when the next fellow came along, the place they'd marked as sacred had simply looked like the perfect high spot to build a big house. The way Cleo saw it, there would always be somebody wanting to put his foot on this wild place and claim it. The Carnegies were the latest bunch to think they could do it, but Cumberland would never allow it. Every creature and every structure were temporary guests. So far as she could understand, Dooley had had that right: a story was eternal and, so far as Cleo was concerned, the very element that made up Cumberland.

Poor old Dungeness stood witness to some of those stories today with empty eyes that stared out at the river like it couldn't remember how on earth it got there. Kids regularly snuck around taking a piss on what had once been a grand dream. Whenever she passed this way, which was more often these days, she'd slip inside and up to the empty library with its empty shelves. Nothing stirred there now, but she liked to stand at the window and look out over the river.

"Joanna is dead, but I guess you don't need me to tell you that," she said aloud, speaking to the memory of a boy called Lumas Gray, who had loved the forsaken library at Dungeness and, briefly, been her friend. "I just needed to say it."

She let herself recall the days when it had seemed their whole lives waited beyond the horizon. But their story had turned out to be a fable, a cautionary tale.

———

Near to the dock, she hopped in her banged-to-hell pickup and took the Grand Avenue, the main road that ran down this part of the island, to where she stopped in a quiet glen of bleached bones of creatures and palmetto fronds, all tangled in morning glory vine. Cleo bent to collect the hard brown pods beneath the dying blooms, the more the better. Even the sap from the broken vine could go to your head, but today she ignored precautions like gloves and welcomed the soft glow that came to the edges of her vision from exposure to the plant's gentle poison, the first taste of what was to come. Not a test of courage, for this was surely the coward's way out and she knew it.

Cracked open, the tiny seeds inside the pods looked like the pips of an apple. Ground in her mortar, they could be made fine as cinnamon. *Add that to your drink for colorful thoughts, more for walking dreams, a lot more for no dreams at all.* Any old mountain man might tell you so. Her grandfather had taught her to use it in her paints like a blessing. Her own choices had taught her it could be a curse.

It had been almost thirty years since she'd come to collect glory from this vine, but there was no real trick to it. Morning glory seeds grew in every fencerow and in the cracks of sidewalks and in vegetable gardens. The vines were pulled up for weeds. But Cleo had knowledge she often wished she'd never learned. And so she grabbed as many of them as she could find, far more than she would need, fully intending to eat every seed she could stuff in her mouth without bothering to grind them down. She'd had years to decide that this was the way she would go; it only came as a surprise that it would happen so soon. She'd thought she might be an old woman. She'd thought by now Joanna Burton would have come to witness her misery, as was her right. But there'd be no satisfaction now, no peace between them.

Her hands were dirty and stinging by the time she had filled her pockets and she felt her head begin to ache. She didn't dare eat the seeds until she'd gotten to the place she was going. The last thing she wanted was to accidentally end up wandering Cumberland like a lunatic until some neighbor or tourist found her and somehow sobered her up. Or worse, scramble her brain only to live another day, someone's burden. Cleo did not mean to become a ruin; she meant to disappear.

She took the truck out to Plum Orchard to the sandy shore on the river where the tides met in a place called the dividings. Years ago she'd told a tale of something in the water, Joanna's story. Today, the memory was like a slippery dream with details she had started to forget. The river had been so high that night, no one could judge where the night sky began. The rushing tide, rising in the reeds, had sounded like some great creature drawing breath, sucking life. Cleo had hardly needed to convince anyone at all that some reckoning had come upon them. And she hadn't been able to stop it either. She'd lived on the shoals long enough now to know exactly what she'd seen and been ready to tell it all to Joanna Burton, but it was too late.

Cleo bent at the water's edge to fill an empty jug. She dug every hard black seed from her pockets and filled her mouth. She breathed through her nose and bit down, only to find she could not chew them. Horrified at what she was doing, she rushed before she could change her mind and tried to drink them down with a long swig of the water but choked.

Eyes flooding, she gagged until she vomited and then dropped to her knees at the river's edge, stunned at her clumsiness. Her mouth burned. The seeds had been wasted and she'd barely consumed enough of them to do anything more than make her sick to her stomach. Cleo let out a miserable howl. She'd believed in stories and things unseen when she'd come to Cumberland as a girl and longed for inspiration, but she'd been too afraid of glory to risk applying it to herself. Now, she thought, when at last she sought oblivion, if she had any courage at all, she'd walk into the river with a clear head.

But then she spied the glimmer of something golden lying nearby, just inside the stone ring where there'd once been a summer bonfire. She wiped her eyes to look again and wondered if she might be hallucinating. But Cleo knew she could never mistake the bright reflection of the sun bouncing off a broken watch's face, a watch she'd returned long ago. If it had found its way back to her here, then so had Tate Walker.

"I know you're out there, Tate Walker!" she yelled, anxious he was watching her. She coughed. Her throat felt raw.

Tate had been Dr. Johnston's man years ago, and he'd been the one to save her life. She remembered him as he'd been, the lanky young man with steady eyes who had been in charge of the hunts, always at the edge of the group, like her, both of them about to make a mess of their lives. Never had she expected to see him again.

Cleo crawled closer to scoop up the watch. She looked at the face of the old timepiece. It had stopped tracking the passing of minutes and lay quiet in her hand. It occurred to her in that silence that she'd made a mistake, maybe done something she couldn't take back.

Cleo grabbed up the water jug, filled it again, and drank it down until she'd emptied it and her stomach sloshed. She sat on the shore, catching her breath, wiping her eyes until she could see straight. It seemed a good sign to her that she still had her senses. She listened for the fiddle tune, but there was only the sound of her own heartbeat racing in her ears. She knew the river was just a river. She knew the tagalongs were only a trick of her mind. She knew Joanna Burton would never forgive her.

And she was certain now that she was not alone.

"Did Dr. Johnston drag you back here too?" she called. "Well, if you want this watch, you should come and get it."

She waited, but there was no sound. No sight of him. She dropped the watch into her pocket where the seeds had been before.

If the man had heard anything about her over the years, he might think twice before accepting such an invitation. Cleo knew plenty of stories got out about the recluse on Kingdom Come. The best was about the hogs. Trespassing men were said to disappear, that the wild hogs on the shoals sometimes favored wayward sons and drunk uncles, thanks to whatever Cleo Woodbine grew in those gardens and glens. None of it was true, but it had kept many an unwanted visitor away. Tate already knew the very worst truths about her, before he left long ago, but he might surprise her now. Other things had, like the way she turned her boat toward home again then, on this day when she'd set out to die.

Chapter Two

FABLE

THERE WERE VERY OLD FAIRY TALES THAT SPOKE OF OTHER worlds beyond this one. Anyone would have thought of them now, even in the summer of 1932. After this earth lay the Many-Coloured Land. Next came the Land of Wonder, and after that the Land of Promise. To reach the Many-Coloured Land, water had to be crossed. And there was no bridge connecting Cumberland Island with the mainland, and no one could doubt it was a storied place.

Cleo Woodbine had heard many of those stories from her granddaddy. She tried to remember them all as she was ferried across by private boat, then carried in a pickup truck over the Grand Avenue, a sandy, rutted lane so rough she clenched her jaw so she wouldn't crack a tooth. The way was flanked by a thick maritime forest, and she felt as if the day were late, although she knew it was barely noon. Saw palmettos scratched the fenders, a sound that made her skin prickle. Ancient live oaks loaded down with gray moss created an endless twisting canopy that seemed to breathe above the other trees. She quietly named them—pines, magnolias, laurel oaks, sweet gums, sassafras. Her grandfather had spent time there when the Carnegies had supported his work as an author and illustrator. Now twenty-three years old, she was coming to Plum Orchard herself, in hopes of patronage for her own work.

Situated at the midline of Cumberland Island on the banks of

the East River, Plum Orchard was one of the largest of the Carnegie summer homes—vacant for parts of the year and other times
busting at the seams with family and guests. But Cleo had only
heard of it in stories until now. She arrived, not exactly staff or
guest or family member, but something in between these titles:
companion. For courage, she held a well-loved copy of her granddaddy's book. She'd learned to read from this book, then learned
to paint as he had. His work seemed to have sprung to life on the
page. Cleo hoped it might be something like that for her.

She'd been told the other guests were a group of young men
in their twenties, heirs to various fortunes from elite families in
far-flung cities. It was to be a gathering for an annual midsummer
bonfire, inspired years ago when her grandfather and Dr. Johnston
liked to try to best one another in oral storytelling. Cleo wondered
what she would make of Dr. Johnston, if he might remind her of
Dooley, a complicated and charismatic man who had adored her
and whom she'd idolized and still missed so much.

Her knuckles were white from gripping the edge of her seat. To
look at, she was just one more nervous girl preparing to face a pack
of gentrified boys set loose on a wild island, but Cleo wasn't afraid.
Cleo was not easily intimidated. In fact, she was thrilled. It hadn't
come as a surprise when, after her flinty grandmother's passing,
she'd received kind condolences from the famous island family.
But she had been delighted when, weeks later, after she'd taken
the chance to inquire after the artist's residence where Dooley and
her grandmother had lived, the response had been an invitation to
come to Plum Orchard. She would be there for the late-summer
gathering to be a companion to a Ms. Joanna Burton, daughter of a
merchant in Asheville, North Carolina.

Cleo had been so lonely she'd accepted immediately, then

waited a month for the date to arrive. Now she worried she'd have nothing in common with the girl, but if this was a sort of test of character, then she intended to rise to the occasion and earn the family's good faith. She rode stalwart as her grandmother had ever been, confident in the belief that her life was about to change. However, with her first look at the house, she feared she had never fully appreciated the outrageous wealth.

Around a curve, the house rose from an expanse of flat lawn more than two hundred yards wide. Graced with balustrades, ornate terraces, French doors, railed porches, and arched floor-to-ceiling windows, it was like nothing Cleo had ever known. Palatial and blindingly white, the house's four columns supported a gabled roof two stories high. It seemed out of place in the wilderness of such a remote island. Animals roamed the lawns, including banty roosters, bony horses, and something large that flew low and black before folding its wings to settle in one of the oaks. The bird watched the truck's approach with a shiny eye. A buzzard. They came to a stop and Cleo took a breath before climbing out. The sandy drive was soft under her shoes. Beyond the house, the East River gleamed in glimpses through the trees that edged the riverbank. The air smelled of Spartina grass, clean and fresh, briny as the sea.

Cleo tried to imagine the people who lived there while the driver, a Negro boy, carried her single suitcase around the truck to a door beneath the grand portico. He had stayed quiet on the ride, but now he said, "Mrs. O'Dowd will have heard the car come up the drive. She'll be out to meet you."

"I won't mind a minute to take this in." She was glad it was only him there. She'd have a moment to get her feet under her.

His face was smooth and sweet and youthful. And he seemed

interested in the book she carried. "Lumas Gray," he said. "You like to read?"

"Cleo Woodbine. And yes, sometimes. My granddaddy illustrated this book when he lived here as artist-in-residence, actually. He was famous friends with the family here at Plum Orchard. Dooley Woodbine?"

The boy's mild interest remained unchanged, his expression composed. Cleo felt a bit irked. Dooley had crowed over his position here often enough that she'd had no doubt his reputation had cut a wide path. He'd made it sound like his place in this family was one of honor and so was his place out on the shoals, the cottage where he did just as he pleased night and day. He'd longed and longed for it, and he had made Cleo long for it too.

This boy's youth would be the excuse for his not having heard of Dooley, she decided. Though she guessed he was a good bit younger than her, the boy was taller by more than a head and wore slacks and a white button-down shirt that were most definitely a uniform and not what he was most comfortable in based on the way he tugged at the sleeves.

"How old are you?" she asked, just to settle it.

"Seventeen."

"Before your time, then." Her grandparents would have already been gone from the island before he was born. "But surely you know Kingdom Come? Woodbine Cottage? Dr. Johnston had that built at the turn of the century as a place for visiting creatives. That's why it has our name now, in honor of my granddaddy. I hope to be the next to make a studio there and paint."

"About the same time as they built my daddy's house. You're an artist?" He took a closer look at her and seemed doubtful.

"Ink and watercolor." He looked at her hands, and she hoped he mistook the stains there for paints. No matter how she'd scrubbed them, her fingers were still discolored from the fruit pulp she'd strained for the syrups she'd made to sell with her grandmother until a few weeks ago. "Dooley always said that the light at Woodbine Cottage was the best he'd ever seen. Things just came to life for him here. But Dr. Johnston wants me to be sure it suits me, life on an island, before any decisions are made." She couldn't seem to stop herself from driving home the point that she was not staff, and if she embellished a little, it was only because she didn't want there to be any mistake. "Some people can't stand it, you know. Others are born to it."

He nodded. The idea of being born to an island life he seemed to understand. "I wasn't born to it."

"You don't like it here? Where better could you go?"

The buzzard in the tree talked to his friends, three of them now, hanging in the limbs above them, eavesdropping, waiting to hear what he might dare say back. Lumas Gray's eyes were deep and quiet, and there was nothing cruel about him. In fact, when he looked at her there, clutching Dooley's book, wearing her only dress and her black shoes that should have been replaced two seasons ago, his gentleness made her feel sorry for being so high-handed. He could have hurt her back, embarrassed her. Instead, he was kind.

"There's sure lots of places I'd like to see. But I have my favorites here. If you want, I'll show you around. If you like books, there's a library out at Dungeness House like you'll never believe," he said. "It's my favorite old haunt on Cumberland. Nobody's lived out there a while now, except maybe ghosts."

"Really?" She could almost believe anything of this island.

He shrugged. He was teasing, but she liked him. And she was

desperate for a friend. But she was embarrassed for him to see that and reminded herself that a whole party of friends were on their way, including a girl she'd been assigned to keep company, which meant she'd likely never be alone. Sadly, she doubted she would be spending her social time with a Negro boy now or in the future, not if she was given residency at the cottage.

"I guess I don't know if I believe in ghosts," Cleo said. He took a step back and nodded.

The buzzards stayed put, glaring down at her. She imagined they wondered who she thought she was. Only hours before, she'd left the little house where she'd lived with her grandparents across from the cannery in Revery, setting out like she was some kind of Southern Anastasia that these sorts of people would embrace. Part of her wished she could follow Lumas Gray and go to see a library to beat all she'd ever seen, where no one would judge her by her worn shoes or the freckles already popping out on her fair skin. But she held the book tighter, remembering why she'd come.

The door opened and a middle-aged woman stood there, Mrs. O'Dowd, Cleo assumed. "You must be Ms. Woodbine," the woman said. "Welcome to Plum Orchard."

The boy tipped the little driver's cap on his head and set off. And Cleo turned to set foot inside the grand house, clinging by her fingernails to every tall tale Dooley Woodbine had ever told her about himself and the Carnegies. She tried not to listen to the little voice in her head that reminded her she had no idea how much of it was true.

———

The housekeeper, who seemed like a kind woman, led the way up a fine staircase. Cleo was dumbstruck by the differences between the elegant entrance and the tract house where she'd grown up. At Plum Orchard, the room she was given was neat and bright and felt luxuriously spacious. Mrs. O'Dowd was watching her take it all in, and Cleo tried not to appear as astounded as she felt. The housekeeper was likely in her thirties but looked older to Cleo, who couldn't see a friend in her but smiled when the woman laid out a smart navy dress.

"For dinner. Dr. Johnston asked me to pull a few things out for you so you'd have choices. It's not a formal occasion, but the family and guests do dress for meals. This should be a pretty good fit. You're close to the same size as one of the nieces. You'll find others in the wardrobe and the dresser. Let me know if there's anything else you need."

Cleo couldn't hide that she was uneasy with the gesture. She didn't know what she'd expected, that she'd be appearing alongside ladies and gentlemen of this class in her own shabby clothes?

"Will I meet Dr. Johnston tonight?"

Mrs. O'Dowd supplied the practical information. A few of the other guests had already arrived, along with Dr. Johnston's stepson, Morrie, but the doctor himself had been delayed and would not be joining them for a few weeks.

"The young men have been out for a duck hunt all morning. Several more are expected this evening, but your Ms. Burton's plans have also changed. I'm afraid she won't be joining until Dr. Johnston arrives. When it was clear that the doctor would be delayed, her parents felt it would be better to wait until there was proper supervision." She couldn't hide the bit of chagrin that Cleo saw creep over her expression. She added, "But I'm to let you know that you're welcome to enjoy the house and the island, to come and go as you please, until she arrives. Only, Dr. Johnston would like you to wait about seeing Woodbine Cottage. He wants to escort you out there himself."

Now it was Cleo who tried to hide her disappointment at having to wait to see the cottage.

"There are only four of us staff in the house right now, but you can find one of us day or night," the housekeeper said. "There's myself, Mrs. Butler in the kitchen, and Mr. Meeks in the garden. We live on the grounds in the cottages. And you've met Lumas Gray. He's the driver and runs the boat and any other errands, but he lives up at Brick Hill. There's a settlement up there. A lot of the colored folk once worked for the Candler hotels on the north end, but that's mostly shut down now and a lot of them have moved off the island. There're others coming and going, but they'll be out at their own work on the estate so you might meet them or not. And you'll be busy with your girl soon enough. She'll want someone to help with her hair and her clothes and maybe just be a friend. She'll be the only one here in this pack of heathen boys. I imagine you're meant to be a bit of a guard dog."

Cleo realized it must be obvious she'd never worked as a companion before, or maybe Mrs. O'Dowd had been told this. "Thank you. I appreciate the advice."

It was a lot to take in at once, but clearly there were no immediate demands of her. Cleo declined to come down for dinner, opting to take a tray in her room. It wasn't a lie when she said she had a headache from the trip. But she also wasn't prepared to face a room of unknown young men by herself tonight.

"Well, you can find me down the hall if you need anything," Mrs. O'Dowd said. She was kind enough, but she looked askance at Cleo and it made her wonder what the woman had heard about her. "For now, you get your rest."

When Mrs. O'Dowd ducked out and Cleo lay across the cotton coverlet on her twin bed, she wondered if she'd made a mistake saying she wanted to rest. Now she'd trapped herself inside the lovely little room for the whole night. She didn't feel free to wander alone no matter what she'd just been told. Her stomach complained, reminding her she hadn't eaten much all day. She waited for hours, looking through the clothing that hung in the wardrobe and trying to imagine what Joanna Burton would be like, then taking the tray Mrs. O'Dowd brought up. She nibbled at the chicken dinner, but her stomach wasn't happy with the heavy cream casserole. Not long after dark, she regretted she hadn't eaten more.

Finally, after waiting to be sure the house seemed to sleep, she gave in to curiosity and snuck down the stairs. The little clock at her bedside had said it was just after ten o'clock. Maybe she could find a bit of cheese and some crackers. She prowled through the back halls until she came to a doorway and stepped into the front hall.

She could feel her heart race when she thought of morning and the smart dress she'd been given and how it would be to explore and bide her time for the next few days. The smells of damp soot, tongue oil, mint, and leather lingered and mixed with an overwhelming sweetness, the scent of what must have been hundreds of lilies. Cleo had seen them growing in profusion when they'd pulled up to the house. Blooms seemed to fill vases throughout the space, although it was too dark to see clearly. But overall, she had the impression of a very elegant hunting lodge and thought maybe the blossoms were for her benefit, perhaps an effort by Mrs. O'Dowd to soften the more savage shadows of this place. Cleo tried to imagine Dooley in a house like this, and what eccentricities she might find in these spectacular rooms when morning came.

She knew Dr. Johnston had his main estate in Kentucky, where he raised Thoroughbreds. He'd traveled broadly, including expeditions to the Antarctic and Africa. Dooley had spoken of him as a kind man, thoughtful, brought here to serve as a doctor to the family and then marrying into it. And like Dooley, he was famous as a storyteller, beloved by the children and adults alike. Cleo was looking forward to meeting Dr. Johnston, someone else in the world with whom she might remember her granddaddy. Dooley had told her once that should she ever come to Plum Orchard, Dr. Marius Johnston would clap his hands, beg her to stay like some prodigal returned, and say, "A Woodbine is back at the cottage and all is right with the world."

"You give him that book. He'll remember those old stories of ours— the little ghost girl, the fiddler, that old black dog. He'll remember how we put that dusting of glory in those paintings and it will lift his heart. He'll be sure to fix you right up," Dooley had said, jovial as always.

She was wise enough to understand that while the glory had started as something he'd only used in his paints as a charm or a blessing, like the old magic of Appalachian superstitions he'd known as a boy, soon enough he'd had a taste of it for himself, something better than liquor or tobacco, and grown to depend upon the drink. In the end, there'd been a cost to living in that golden haze. She tried not to think of Dooley under that influence, when he'd slipped too far into his own mind, when he could not bear a moment of reality, when he'd abandoned her and her grandmother for that dreamy oblivion. Her time with him before those changes had been so brief, only a few short years, but she preferred to remember her grandfather as he'd been when he was still a vibrant man with flowing hair that had grayed at the temples and a thick beard he kept trimmed and dark eyes that danced when he talked to her.

She'd believed they'd invented the word *enthralling* purely because Dooley Woodbine had existed and needed to be described.

After Dooley died, she'd spent years alone in the care of her grandmother, a woman who had rid them of every speck of glory, and Cleo had sworn never to use it for herself. And now that she was here, Cleo could only hope she'd be judged not by memories of Dooley or glory but by her own merits.

Someone gave a soft whistle in the dark. The hall was vast and the sound small, but the person who made it was very near.

"Can't sleep in a strange bed?" a voice said. "Did you want to go outside and have a smoke before I head home?"

As if he'd stepped straight out of the floral wallpaper, Lumas Gray appeared in the shadows. Cleo was charmed, and so glad to have someone to talk to.

"It's late. Everyone's asleep. What are you still doing here?" She remembered the housekeeper saying he didn't live at Plum Orchard but farther north on the island. It was hard to know if that was any real distance since she wasn't familiar with the place, but she still thought it strange he was hanging around so long after everyone had gone to bed.

"It's not that late. Anyway, you think these people sleep? They'll be out all hours at the Casino playing cards. That's the pool house up at Dungeness. People don't watch the clock here; you'll see. You're on island time now."

She could make out the shape of him in the dark and thought of the ink outline as she would draw him, the driver's cap pulled low, the slope of his shoulders, the toes of his boots. He stepped closer to her, silent on the worn rug. He had his hands jammed into the pockets of his overalls and his slim shoulders drawn up to his ears, waiting for her answer. He was only a kid, really, like an overgrown puppy.

She felt much older, but she'd never had a cigarette in her life. Cleo might have pretended to be shocked by his smoking or by the invitation to join him had she not so desperately needed the company. He'd caught her snooping in her new employer's house, not making much of a start, and thank goodness he also offered her a sandwich wrapped in a napkin.

"You're a lifesaver," she said. In the dark, her stomach and her nerves won out and pretense dropped away.

They slipped outside and into the salty wind and let the island hide them, something they would do again and again in those first days, before Joanna Burton came. Time on Cumberland seemed, as Lumas Gray had said, to move differently. A thousand years might have passed from the time she'd left her grandmother's tidy kitchen and locked the door on that dull life. And in those first days, when she woke in her bed at Plum Orchard to the sound of the young men barreling through the foyer below and outside onto the wide lawn, Cleo felt she'd wandered into the fantastic world Dooley had painted for her after all. And Cleo felt that it was her that had come to life.

Chapter Three

FRANCES

WHERE THE MARSH TIDES SPLIT, THE WATERS OVER THE SHOALS off Cumberland Island moved in both directions. It was possible, when the water was low, to walk a quarter mile across the exposed mudflats of the river to a narrow barrier island that was slowly shifting toward the shoreline. In the summer of 1959, there was nothing mystical about this occurrence, only a natural progression. Frances Flood had read all about it in the pamphlet she'd just acquired before stepping onto a ferryboat run by the park service.

What the pamphlet didn't mention was anything about Cleo Woodbine, the woman living out on that island, the reason Frances had made this trip, the person her mother had spoken of while lying on her deathbed almost a month ago.

Shortly after Joanna's first stroke, she'd shown Frances a news clipping about a group of young people who had reported seeing something in the water near Cumberland Island, Georgia, way back in 1932 after telling tales round a summer bonfire. That night, two boys had drowned and the local myth of the Revery river siren had been born. Inexplicably, Joanna had cried over the memory and grasped at Frances and said that she and Cleo had been with that party only the day before the terrible incident.

"Cleo Woodbine still has my pearls," Joanna had said. Frances had been astonished. She knew of both Cleo and her grandfather. The latter had been an illustrator and author, famous for a single

book of folktales. All her life, Frances had loved to stare at a copy of the rare book that was kept behind glass in her family's antique store. And Cleo Woodbine's paintings, inspired by the characters in her grandfather's stories, were known for being nostalgic favorites for nurseries all over. But Frances could not imagine what any of that had to do with her mother.

"All this time, I left them with her," Joanna said. *"She'll think it's because I was angry, but, Frances, I made my choices and look what a life I've had. I've had love. I've had you. Please tell her for me."*

And then Joanna had asked one more thing, that Frances go to Cleo and commission a painting in her memory. Confused, Frances promised her mother she'd do both, wishing there was time to learn more. But a succession of strokes followed, and whatever Joanna hoped Frances would understand was lost.

There'd been everything practical to manage in what seemed like an unending stream of decisions and demands over the next few weeks. To cover the costs of the hospital and the funeral expenses, she'd accepted an offer from a local developer who wanted to purchase Joanna's house and a group of properties adjacent to it, then sold or stored what she didn't need. She'd rented a room with a kitchenette and private bath at a boardinghouse near downtown Asheville and spent only one night there before boarding a bus to the Georgia coast, the first trip of many she hoped to finally take. Frances had given herself a full week before she'd have to be back for the closing. She intended to fulfill her mother's request and also finally allow herself some rest before she'd return to sign papers. Then she'd see where the wind would take her.

She had not realized how exhausted she was until she found herself relieved to allow the bus driver to carry her along the ten-hour bus ride overnight. She slept a good part of the trip along highways and twisting two-lane roads through the mountains of North Carolina and the entire state of Georgia, until she'd finally arrived in Revery late on a hot Sunday morning, a town that felt like it sat at the ends of the earth. There, she'd immediately stepped onto a ferryboat with a half dozen tourists to cruise the deep green waterways and then landed at a dock off Cumberland Island, a place that felt like it existed entirely out of time. Only then did Frances realize that she'd planned poorly.

Having no other means to cross the mudflat from Cumberland to reach the slip of land and the artist who lived in a strange sort of exile there, Frances now found herself walking the quarter mile across while the tide was out.

"It can be done," the boat captain had confirmed when she'd asked after any other options. His lined face seemed to favor the terrain, darkly tanned and craggy. *"Kids do it on dares all the time, or used to when I was growing up. Just stick to the lighter mud where it's solid and dry. You'll sink up to your knees in the dark stuff, where it's soppy. You'd better make it quick. You've got to beat the tide coming back in. And don't stay long. Figure on getting back here before we pull out. This is the last boat for the day."*

The hard gray pluff mud was as foreign to her as the face of the moon. The salty sea air dried like starch on Frances's skin. Her sundress was more suited to a trip to the grocery, but the breeze eased her along. The sun glittered over the narrow streams that spread like a silver web over the landscape. She wondered at cockleshells and gnarled pieces of driftwood. She had her field notebook, her binoculars, and new boots wearing blisters on both heels. Her mousy brown hair, which she always kept fastened neatly at the nape of her neck, had come loose and flew around her face. It was not Joanna's beautiful blonde hair but favored her father's side.

Also like Owen, she wore glasses. She pushed the cat-eye frames back up each time they slipped down her nose, and she could feel her fair skin start to burn.

She thought this was the kind of place that would inspire people to imagine the most outlandish things. Sightings of impossible creatures in the sea could usually be explained as migrating right whales in winter or calving manatees in summer, yet the myths persisted. Frances's theory, what she thought might one day become her dissertation, went like this: Humanity needed to believe in something as fantastic and terrible as they could stand. Or perhaps blame. Something they could love. Something that might choose them. And so a siren almost always appeared in their stories. Female. Something other, but what? The same seductive dread that swam the world over, the mythological consequences of risking everything for love. She ought to know; she'd spent plenty of time thinking about it.

Thanks to a familial love of a particular German myth, "The Lorelei," Frances was well versed in water-siren mythology, an obsession that had begun in her childhood and left her always scribbling notes and theories into a notebook. If anyone asked, which they rarely did, she had received her master's degree in English with a concentration in folklore from the University of North Carolina at Chapel Hill and had been entertaining the thought of continuing on for her doctorate. It seemed a charming and artsy preoccupation for a twenty-seven-year-old woman. But certainly they would have been troubled by her scribbles about scales and teeth, seduction and drowning. Love and grief.

As she stepped onto the unfamiliar shore, Frances felt at that moment she'd been asked to take this journey at a risk she barely understood. She knew the way these stories would always go, and here was how this story began: Beyond the dunes lay the maritime forest. There lived a recluse. A woman who had claimed to see a river siren. A woman who had kept her mother's heirloom pearls, and maybe her secrets, for almost thirty years. What Frances wanted to know was why.

———

She'd polished off the salted pecans in her bag. The sea breeze had picked up, so she raised her face to it, eyes closed, and tried to steel her nerves when a voice spoke to her. "You're on private property."

Frances pushed up her glasses and shielded her eyes to get a look at a very small figure standing a few yards from her in clothing so like a man's that Frances had to look hard to realize it was a woman. She came directly toward Frances in a way that made her reach for a hand, expecting help to stand, but then she felt silly when the woman only snatched up the empty bag. She gave it a brisk shake to free it of sand and tucked it beneath her arm.

"Don't be a litterbug," she said. She was gruff, but Frances was intrigued. This woman's face was darkly tanned from the sun; not old, only formidable. Her burnished hair was cut at chin's length in a haphazard sort of way. "Usually it's only little boys who try to walk out here in all that mud without a boat and get stuck so somebody has to go to the trouble to haul them back home. You look old enough to be smarter than that."

"Looks can be deceiving. And I didn't really have a choice."

"I don't agree with either of those statements. What do you want?"

Frances swallowed hard. There were a million questions she wanted to ask, but she started with the one Joanna had sent with her. "I've come to ask about your artwork."

"If you want a painting, you've gone to a lot of trouble for nothing. You'll have to get one like everyone else over at the Gilbreath House Inn. I don't sell them out of my home."

"I'm asking for my mother. She sent me." Frances paused.

Cleo frowned. "Who are you?"

"Frances Flood. You won't know me, but I hope you will remember my mother. Joanna Flood? She would have been Joanna Burton then. She was here the summer you saw the river siren. My mother told me you kept her pearls. She told me she regretted never coming to get them back from you. She wanted you to know that."

The woman did not answer right away. She looked out over the water for a time and scanned the horizon as though she expected to find something there, turning until she no longer faced Frances before she said, "I'd heard Joanna passed. I put the pearls in the mail. I sent them to that antique shop her family owned. It was the only address I had. I'm sorry for your loss, and that you've come all this way."

There was real sympathy in her tone. And Frances didn't think she imagined that Cleo Woodbine was holding on to as many questions as she'd brought with her today.

"Thank you. I'm still trying to get used to it, to make sense out of any of this," Frances said. "She tried to tell me about you, but the strokes came one right after the other. It happened fast. She wanted me to come here, I know that much. I just don't understand how you knew one another."

It felt to her that Cleo might have leaned toward her then with her own need to know about Joanna. But Frances felt herself withdrawing, unsure what she wanted to share. She didn't know what to think of this person. She didn't know what to think about anything. Joanna had kept too many secrets for this to be simple. Cleo must have felt Frances's hesitation. She looked away, giving Frances time to collect her thoughts before getting down to Joanna's request.

"She wanted a painting, a kind of memorial."

A noise of disbelief came from Cleo's throat. "What? Why on earth would she want that from me?"

"I wish I could tell you." Again Frances paused, making room for Cleo to jump in with anything she could offer to help Frances understand. Frustrated, Frances finally said, "That's fine. I think I'm going to have to get used to not knowing things." She couldn't help the exhaustion that had crept into her voice. Cleo looked sorry for it. "Can we just work out whatever it would cost, a painting?"

"Twenty-seven years."

"I'm sorry?"

"That's what it costs. Twenty-seven years." Cleo Woodbine ran a hand roughly through her hair. "Joanna sent you to me?" she said, as if it were still unclear.

"She did."

Cleo Woodbine had striking green eyes, and Frances watched them smartly sizing things up as she came to some decision. "I guess if we're going to talk about this, we ought to do it out of this sun. You'll want something to drink before you dry up." She turned decidedly to march back the way she'd come. Frances got to her feet and struggled to keep up.

Ahead, they stepped out of the dense forest that crowded the west edge of the scant island and onto a scrubby lawn. A small tabby structure huddled against the dunes encroaching from the eastern side where the sea was hidden from view. With windows open so sea breezes could waft through, the house was almost completely obscured by live oaks, but through their limbs, light and shadow cast their play across the exterior. The roof peeked out from the trees. Frances loved the house immediately. She imagined it would be like living inside a shadow box. Once inside, her assessment was confirmed and she discovered it was outfitted comfortably with running water and power from some unknown source. A little TV sat in one corner and a transistor radio was tuned to a news channel on a shelf in the kitchen. Cleo switched that off. The smells of dried herbs and fresh fruits and coffee blended around them, comforting Frances. And she saw that the main room was dedicated to a long, wide table where the artist worked with her watercolor paints. Cleo put a few jars to the side, then put clean jars in front of them.

"You like sun tea?" she asked. Frances nodded and Cleo filled their glasses.

The tea tasted of iron from some deep well.

Cleo said, "This is something, Joanna sending you to my door so I can answer for myself. She didn't do the work for me, did she?" She smiled a sad smile.

"I'm sorry if it seems that way." Frances drew a breath and dove in. "I don't understand any of it. What was she doing here? She wasn't some society girl. Was she here for a job? Is that how you knew one another?"

If people came to this river to search the waters for signs of a great mystery, surely she and Cleo Woodbine searched one another in the same way now. And the other woman clearly saw something when she looked at Frances, although she was doing her best to hide it. She threw back the rest of her water in one long gulp.

"Joanna was a guest at Plum Orchard. That's one of the Carnegie summer homes over on Cumberland. She was my job, actually. I was there as her companion so she wouldn't be alone in a group of young men. She'd been promised to a boy named Ellis Piedmont."

Frances was truly shocked. "Ellis Piedmont? The boy who drowned? She was here for a husband? Is that what it was all about?"

"It was for her. I came here because I wanted a benefactor for my art. I wanted to live in this cottage and become a renowned painter, like my granddaddy had been before."

"So it worked out for you." Frances felt bad for how sour the remark sounded. She added, "Your paintings are beloved. People put them in their nurseries, for heaven's sake."

Cleo let out a laugh like a bark.

Frances only felt more confused. "It's true. And Dooley Woodbine's illustrations are considered a masterwork. There were so few of them and they're collectors' items. We keep a copy in a locked cabinet at our antique store. But your work improved upon his. It's an honor to meet you." Frances flushed, trying to calm herself. "Until now, I had no idea that you and my mom knew one another."

Cleo's brow smoothed as she began loading a basket with fruits. She settled her gaze squarely on Frances. "I never knew about you either, if that makes you feel any better." Cleo took a breath as if to ground herself for what came next. "We were living in our own little world down here that summer. It was a long time ago. I guess I'm not surprised your mama didn't tell you."

"Well, she told me I'm supposed to forgive you. It was the last thing she said, actually. She didn't say why, but I guess it's not really my business, is it?" Frances felt herself listing to the side and put her hands flat on the table, then realized it was the room that was off-kilter, not her.

"Is that what she said? Forgive me? I think it's more likely she wanted me to have to face you because she knew it would be so much harder than facing her."

Frances considered what a strange thing that was to say and

the pain in Cleo's expression. She wanted to grieve for her mother, and instead she worried she'd never known her. She felt tricked somehow, even used. And something else was taking shape, a terrible suspicion about Ellis Piedmont and Owen Flood. Frances was counting up the months from that summer in 1932 to her birthday later that year. She'd come here hoping what she would learn would finally help her feel a stronger connection to her mother. Joanna had been so hard to know.

Frances saw Cleo almost reach for her, but Frances moved her hands to her lap. At this point, her teeth were on edge. She wanted out of the little house that had seemed so comfortable only minutes ago. "When do you think you'd be able to finish the painting?"

Cleo shrugged. "I don't know. I wouldn't even know where to start. Or that I ever could."

Frances felt bereft in a way she hadn't since Joanna's passing. Something about this conversation made her mother's death suddenly seem real. She didn't have the energy to argue with this woman. "I plan to stay in Revery at least until the end of the week. I'll be at the inn you mentioned, actually. But will you do it?"

Cleo nodded. "When it's finished, I'll mail it to that same place in Asheville, save you the trip back out here."

Frances realized then that she'd let the time get away from her. "I guess I've missed the return ferry by now."

There was sorrow in Cleo's eyes as she pushed the basket of fruit toward Frances, and a thousand secrets, an inner world not unlike her paintings. "You'll be all right. Take this. Head down behind the house to the river. You're going to come up on a man with a boat pulling in traps; he's the owner of the inn. He'll be waiting around for my basket. He'll carry you back to Revery."

———

The conversation had lasted less than thirty minutes, but she felt as if days had passed. She made her way behind Woodbine Cottage to the water, disoriented in space and time. She could understand how a group of young people around a bonfire might conjure up monsters on these wild shores. The same fables meant to keep children safe from the water seemed to draw them to it.

When Frances was young, the myth of the Lorelei had been a sort of bond between her and Joanna. But when she became a sullen teenager, the distance between her and her mother only grew. She'd read every book in the local library on sea serpent myths and legends, and when she'd gone through them, she sent away for other volumes. She'd built an extensive collection on a bookshelf in her room, safely away from the children in the day care her mother ran out of their home, called Mother's Helper. She thought of that collection now, boxes and boxes of books, papers, research, art, all ready for storage. And she imagined all those creatures and characters of folklore shut away, conversing, working out a plan for their escape. It made her smile, even if it was silly. The truth was, she truly had no idea where she would go from here. She could go anywhere. And oh, that was risky.

Now Frances's imagination really did run away from her. It seemed her mother had likely married Owen Flood, a much older Irish immigrant who had come to work for her father that spring, in a shotgun wedding, perhaps carrying another man's child. But Owen had raised Frances and loved her as his own, and the thought made her ache for him even all these years later, right alongside the complicated grief for Joanna. And that meant there was every possibility that the real myth might turn out to be what she'd believed about her own family.

Frances trudged down to the dock, exhausted and relieved to see a man pulling in his fishing line as Cleo had promised. He'd seen her first.

"Hey, hey," he called.

She lifted the heavy basket in greeting. "Cleo Woodbine sent this. She said to give it to you and you could get me across to Revery."

This boat was just big enough for two people, an aluminum vessel with a motor attached to one end. She could see where it might have had a bench at its center, but that had been removed. There was a cooler and some fishing gear and a banged-up tackle box. The man running it was young, shirtless, wearing tattered shorts and boat shoes, maybe a few years older than Frances, and squinting in the sun. He was strong-shouldered and tattooed on one bicep, an inked mermaid with vivid blue-black hair and scales. She figured him for a sailor and maybe a soldier. He ran a hand over his hair, cropped short, black and dense. He had a nose that hadn't gone unbroken, but he was clean-shaven.

"When folks ride with me, I get to ask them one question," he said. "That's my going rate."

"One question? Who are you? Billy Goat Gruff?" she asked.

He laughed, raising a hand to shield his eyes from the light.

"Sorry, that came out wrong. I didn't mean you look like a goat," she apologized. "I'm a folklorist. Bad joke."

"I've been called worse," he said with good humor. "But technically, I'm a tour guide. History during daytime hours. Ghosts after dark. You're here for the Revery siren, then, I imagine."

"And other things."

"I have to say, you've really got a look about you. You'd make a fine specter." He said this as if he were paying her a great compliment.

"I'm not sure how to take that." Frances laughed.

"Take it from me," he teased. "An expert."

"Cleo also said you own the inn. Is there anything you don't do?"

"I own the movie theater too. It's air-conditioned."

She laughed but was impressed. "Well, I'll remember that. But what I'd really like is to see Cumberland Island and the river basin, hear all of the local lore. Can you do that sort of tour?"

"To cover that sort of ground, it's out at dawn and back by late afternoon. To see everything, you'll want to take two or three tours, and I'd need to book that sooner rather than later." He had the voice of a good barker. "I've got a full day tomorrow. How about the day after to start? Will you be staying that long?"

"At least till the end of the week."

"All right, then. I'll meet you at the inn at 10:00 a.m."

"Consider me booked."

He helped Frances step aboard and settle on the floor. He winked at her and her heart stuttered. She rarely got that sort of attention from a man her own age. "Nice to meet you, Booked. I'm Ambrose Devane. Call me Rosey."

"Frances Flood."

"Flood, you say? Irish?"

She nodded, but it was hard not to start imagining, hard not to think of a summer romance gone wrong and what it had been for Joanna to come here, a young woman looking for her future in this outrageously beautiful place with these wildly wealthy people.

They watched the landscape pass as they cruised slowly along the western edge of Cumberland with its awe-inspiring maritime forests like some Paleolithic world. The mainland lay two or three miles distant as they traveled north on the river, skirting the broad expanse of salt marsh where Spartina grasses waved, bright green, then turning west, pulling away from Cumberland's shore and that Georgia hinterland into the wider water, bearing toward Revery, as yet unseen. Seabirds rode the wind currents overhead, following the boat with an eye for a meal, and the air was fresh and sweet. Frances turned her face up to the sun. The water was a calm gray beneath an azure sky, and her heart settled with the thrum of the boat's motor and the easy crossing. She thought she could believe any myth about this place.

"I don't believe I'd ever get used to this," she said.

He shook his head, eyes cast over the terrain as though he were regarding an old love. "Been here forever but it changes every minute. Kingdom Come will connect with Cumberland one morning, the world made new. One more good summer storm ought to do it."

"Kingdom Come?"

He pointed back to where they'd been. "Used to be called Little Marsh Island, but Cleo's granddaddy renamed it and folks have called it Kingdom Come ever since." His words now sounded rehearsed. Frances could imagine him saying the same thing every time he carried someone back to Revery, timing it so the islands were just a mirage behind them. Frances took a closer look at him. Every fellow to take this trip must have imagined himself Rosey's new best friend. Every girl he'd carried back must have imagined herself half in love with him by the time he took her hand to help her out of this boat.

"How do you know Cleo?"

"I don't. I came to commission a painting."

"I bet I know what she said to that." Clearly, he knew Cleo.

She wasn't ready to share anything more about what had brought her to Revery or Cleo Woodbine. She simply waited and watched them draw nearer to the mainland. "Could you point me in the direction of the inn?"

"Sure. Where's your luggage? I can help with that."

"They kept it at the bus station for me, but I only have the one bag. I can manage."

"Ah, well. You won't have to go far from the waterfront or the bus stop to Gilbreath House. Whole town's only a two-block affair, three main roads. And as I say, everything leads to the sea or it's leading the wrong way." She saw he had a crooked eyetooth. It did not make him less handsome. "My mother opened the house for lodgers when I went off to serve in Korea, but I grew up in that house. Now my little cousin's taken over since my mama passed."

"Oh, I'm sorry. I lost my mother a few weeks ago."

"Condolences," he said sincerely. "It's been almost a year for me. It will get so you can stand it. My cousin's a sweetheart. Had some tragedy herself a few months back, up in Macon where she was married and her folks still live. Barely wed before she was widowed. Guy tried to beat a train on his motorcycle. But she's got lots of folks in this town looking out for her while she gets back on her feet." He steered them back toward the lighter mood. "I'll give you a tip. Ask Audrey for my old room. It's the nicest. Top floor, east corner, looks out on the river."

She pushed her glasses up and tugged at her hair, hoping he didn't see her color rise. She had no idea how to flirt, but when he looked at her squarely, she felt bashful.

He said, "I'm going to make you a proposition."

A gulping sort of laugh jumped out of Frances.

"You misunderstand me," he said, gesturing apologetically

with his hands. "It's just, you've got an old-timey look to you. While you're in town, you really ought to come out and be a part of the ghost tour in the evenings, just for the fun. There's nothing special you'd need to do. There's an outfit. I'll show you the ropes in five minutes, tops. And during the day I'll take you out for your tours, no charge. It's only a thirty-minute gig each night around nine o'clock. No big commitment."

"Where have I heard that before?"

"You'd truly be helping me out," he said. "Audrey's turned me down and I'm short a Wandering Merry for the ghost tour."

"What happened to the last one? She wander off?"

"They always do," he lamented with a grin. He tied off at the dock and she tried not to think of other girls taking his steadying hand to step out, the rasp of his skin against theirs, causing some foolish reaction that made their hearts hitch. Frances held on too tightly. Rosey Devane did not let go. "I'd hate to think of you sitting at the inn every night, sad."

"I am sad," Frances said. "I miss my mom." And she did dread the idea of nights at the inn, alone. She thought, too, of what he said about his cousin having people in this town who were supporting her. Frances had no one like that, just her studies. But here, there was nothing to do to pass the time, and this was a harmless way to keep busy. "If I say no, do I have to pay for the ride? When I got on the boat, you said you get to ask a question of anyone who gets a ride."

"Well, in your case I think I'll save that one up." He gave her hand a squeeze before releasing her. "But I'm telling you, you'll regret it if you let this chance slip by. You were born for this role."

Chapter Four

AUDREY

THIS HOUSE WASN'T HER HOUSE AND THIS TOWN WASN'T HER town. And she didn't owe anybody the truth. That's what Audrey Howell kept telling herself for so many reasons that she was losing count.

On a quiet night a little less than a month ago, Audrey had snapped a photo of a boy named Jimmy Walker. She'd been hired by her cousin Rosey to take the portrait, her first paid job as a photographer. He wanted an example of her work to put on display, another service to offer patrons at his recently reopened movie theater, and to sell to those on his local history and ghost tours. People had taken to stopping through Revery since the interstate to Florida came through years back, and Rosey was single-handedly reviving the tourism in the sleepy little town. He was also trying to draw her into that community. He sincerely wanted her, and everyone else, to be happy here.

Audrey had been the photographer for her school yearbook, and Rosey had encouraged her to set up a darkroom of her own in the stalls of the old carriage house behind the inn. It wasn't much more than a fancy little barn with a loft with dormer windows, dark and cool, but she loved it. He'd put the old Brownie camera into her hands, explaining it had once belonged to her mother, and it was the first time Audrey had felt alive in weeks. Audrey knew so little of Mimi's childhood in Revery, it had felt like a clue to a great mystery. There was a framed photo in the front room of two teen-age girls standing on the steps of a great house, and Audrey had recognized one of them as her mother, shocked by the difference in her demeanor. She looked so happy, like some kind of wild child, tanned and barefoot and wearing a scarf knotted around her head like Audrey had seen fortune tellers do in storybooks. Something Audrey had never seen Mimi do, instead always so buttoned-up and conservatively fashionable. No wonder Audrey had spent ages staring at that photo since coming to the inn, trying to imagine her mother so carefree, her arms inexplicably full of books.

When she'd asked Rosey about it, he'd told her that the other girl had been his mother, Audrey's aunt Shirley, and the photograph was taken out front of Dungeness mansion over on Cumberland Island where the girls had loved to play and borrow books from the Carnegie family's private library. She'd been too excited, still distracted by all of this new insight into her mother, when she'd agreed to take the photograph of Jimmy Walker, which probably explained her embarrassing mistake, one that had now taken on a life of its own.

When she'd taken the photograph, twelve-year-old Jimmy had smiled a twinkly-eyed, gap-toothed grin. Jimmy didn't attend school and spent most of his time at the movie theater. He was young for his age—some might call him simple-minded—but he could quote films at the drop of a hat. Audrey liked him. His father was another story.

Rosey's oldest friend since childhood, Glenn Walker was a handsome widower. Even the married women in town still blushed when he spoke to them. Once, he was a star football player, but now he had a chip on his shoulder in regard to just about everything. He seemed to think that he and Audrey had an understanding, having suffered the same grave injustice of losing their spouses young, and it made Audrey nervous of him from the get-go. But she'd given him the benefit of the doubt as her cousin's friend, a man alone and raising the sort of son any other parent might have institutionalized. But she hadn't been seeing things clearly for months, which explained how she'd ended up in this mess with the photos and Glenn both.

Audrey was only twenty years old and had not learned how to say no. Or to say nothing at all. Or when best to do either one. In this case, she'd mixed up the two.

To start, there was the photo of Jimmy. Of course Audrey knew a double exposure when she saw one. She'd only neglected to advance the film and exposed it again so one image was overlaying another. But she'd not been thinking straight when she squinted and leaned close to the film in the developer. The sight made a cold sweat break out on Audrey's brow. For that split second, the mistake had looked to Audrey like poor Freddie, her recently deceased husband, and she'd gone running to tell somebody.

The old Audrey, the hopeful girl, not the tragically widowed one, would have known what she was looking at. She never would have shown anyone her silly mistake. But she'd been confused and hoping someone else would see Freddie there too. She'd raced to the theater to find Rosey. Instead, she'd first run into Glenn, who had looked at that photo like she had performed a miracle, or a magic trick, and it didn't matter which because both would pay. He recognized the specter as a boy, long gone from this world, a legend in the town—a young Negro kid named Lumas Gray who had once worked for the families on Cumberland and drowned in the East River in 1932.

"Do you know what people will shell out for this? A photo of a ghost?

This is genius, better than anything Rosey could have thought up. Can you do it again?" he asked, working up a sweat in his excitement.

Glenn had her explain the process by which she'd created such an image and that, yes, she could repeat it as many times as he liked with the old negatives she'd found. She really hadn't understood where it would lead until he'd let out a whoop—and then she'd regretted every word she'd said but couldn't take them back. Before she knew it, he was calling her *partner*, like they were old cowpoke pals.

The truth was, she could have said no right there. But she hadn't been thinking only of Glenn. This feeling had come over her when she'd believed it was Freddie in the photo, and it had seemed possible he'd somehow found a way to reach her from wherever he'd gone. The part of her that believed she'd done it once wanted to do it again, with the hope that it might really turn out to be Freddie the next time. So she'd gone along and told herself that there was some good in giving that feeling to others, even if it was only a little game for broken hearts.

Now visitors stood in line to pose in front of Audrey's camera, thrilled to be bamboozled by the phony ghost photography at the Marvel. There were six different negatives with Lumas Gray, presumably from before 1932, and she used them over and over, developing them as an overlay with the photos she was taking, positioning the old images of him so he appeared as natural as possible when he made an appearance alongside the faces of folks in 1959 Revery. Lumas Gray, the spirit of Revery, like everybody's long-lost friend. A stand-in for everyone they'd ever loved and lost. So far Audrey had made it so he'd materialized in more than three dozen photographs.

The new Audrey, the girl with nothing to lose, too tall and curvy and ripe in all the right places to go unnoticed by lonely men like Glenn Walker, understood what those sad old folks were looking for in those photographs, because she was looking for it too. They wanted that ghost to smile and make them feel less guilty that he was gone in the prime of his youth while they were living out their years, taking them for granted. Even if they all knew that none of it was real. Even if they were just fooling themselves for a moment of comfort. That didn't stop her from hoping for Freddie to appear sometime, so she'd feel that he'd forgiven her for the fight they'd been having the morning he died. Forgive her for living her stupid life, for all the days and years he was supposed to have been living right alongside her.

She could have said nothing. She could have said no. But if anything was true about the new Audrey, it was that she was alone in this new place because she'd wished she was alone. Those were the words she'd hurled at Freddie's back when he'd walked out the door for the last time.

———

The new Audrey was cooking and cleaning to beat the band. Nobody had mentioned before she came to this house that it had not been modernized since the dinosaurs walked the earth. She had running well water and a water heater, thank goodness. But the stove was ancient, fed by fire. And the smell of the creosote from the train tracks that ran perpendicular to the inn had soaked into the furniture and the curtains, along with the sickening aroma from pressure on brake pads and hot steel as the trains slowed through the crossings. Sometimes she tried to see how long she could hold her breath before she was forced to inhale and start the countdown all over again.

"You'll get used to it," her mother had promised just after Audrey arrived—the last time, in fact, they spoke on the ancient telephone that jangled like a dairy cow's bell when it rang and looked like it had been installed about the same year the *Titanic* sank. *"Those tracks are three blocks away. You'll have the view out to the river. If your daddy wasn't so needed in Macon, we'd come down there and take over the house ourselves. But you'll have plenty of company once you have paying guests and plenty to keep you busy. You're going to find your place. It'll feel like home in no time."*

They hadn't come down and Audrey didn't want them coming down and worrying over her. But she'd have killed for a Westing-house washer and dryer like they'd had at home in Macon. She'd been doing her laundry in the sink with Woolite, afraid of the contraption on the porch. She'd have loved to have a Hoover to replace the squeaky old carpet broom. But at least there was a small electric fan and a large refrigerator and a huge deep freeze on the back porch, where she'd found the old film in storage. And she did like that there was a little spring house. Some days she went out there to hide in the cool. But to be honest, she was bored out of her head.

Luckily, already she had her first two guests at the inn, one a former resident of Revery, Tate Walker, Glenn's estranged daddy. He had shown up three days ago, the first to take a room since Audrey had taken over, and he'd paid up front to stay a full month. The other was a young woman, Frances Flood, who had arrived the afternoon before with plans to check out the following Sunday. She'd come in on an overnight bus, and so far as Audrey knew, today Frances was still sound asleep.

It was already noon, and Audrey had no desire to stay in the house once she'd served brunch. And since there was no sign of either of her guests, she decided to take the one o'clock ferry out with the tourists to see Cumberland Island, all of them given a map of the island and surrounding waterways.

They docked near Dungeness mansion, and she stood in front of the massive house to look at the steps where Mimi had stood for the photograph and to take a few shots of her own. Then she took a bike like the rest, shooting pretty landscape photos along the shifting, shimmering tidal creeks, trying to imagine the childhood her mother would have known there. She'd made sure to load a new roll of film so there'd be no chance this time of raising the dead.

She wanted less people and more peace. And she had one other place in mind that she wanted to see: Woodbine Cottage. Rosey had told her about the place and the woman who lived there when Audrey asked out of curiosity about a room that was never rented at the inn.

"Just leave it. Give it a dusting now and again, but it's not for rent. Mama always kept that room ready for Cleo Woodbine, and it's likely she might need it sooner than later with that old house she lives in sitting on a spit of land that could shift out from under it any day," he'd explained. *"Mama always felt sorry for her out there by herself. Cleo was friends with Lumas Gray back in the day, and my mama and your mama grew up with that boy."*

"When they played on Cumberland?" Rosey had nodded and Audrey wondered if Lumas Gray had been the one to take the photo of her mother and Shirley that day.

Rosey said, *"I guess Lumas was why my mama had a soft spot for Cleo. Why they all grieved him. She wanted her to know there was always a place waiting for her if she decided to come back to town."*

The story of Lumas Gray was common knowledge in Revery, and it appeared to Audrey it had touched everyone there one way or another. But it was Cleo, in particular, who interested her, the woman who had lived on the shoals for almost thirty years since that fateful event. Audrey's aunt had been a kind woman and she'd traded with Cleo Woodbine for produce. She sold Cleo's watercolor illustrations at the inn, and they were famous these days. People paid a pretty penny for them. Audrey wondered where all the money went.

Rosey had further explained the basics about the wild events of 1932, when people said they'd seen something in the river and then two boys had drowned (one of them Lumas Gray), and how Cleo had been part of it all. And how Cleo had lived as the artist-in-residence in the Carnegie cottage ever since, with lots of rumors cropping up about her, like she was some old island witch. Especially that she made some kind of poison she used on trespassers and poachers. Some said it made you hallucinate, made you see anything she wanted you to see. Some said it could turn men into hogs so they ran wild all night until the dawn.

"She's not old. Probably no more than fifty. And she's not a witch," Rosey insisted. *"She just doesn't want to be bothered."*

Audrey had not been able to stop thinking of a woman like that, who had lived on her own terms. She didn't want to go knocking on Cleo's door, but from the sounds of it the house might not stand much longer with the shifting tides, so Audrey had the excuse of taking a photograph or two to justify being nosy. Maybe she'd make a picture as a gift to Cleo, send it in the weekly basket of produce after she'd developed it.

She'd have just enough time to make the trip there and back before she missed the boat, if she hurried. She set out on the Grand Avenue, pumping her legs and enjoying the freedom of the bike's wheels spinning down the sandy lane.

The island was surprisingly busy with boats coming and going.

There were plenty of people still inhabiting homes, some of the grander ones and some just shacks. The more recent batch of Carnegies were tearing around in cars that looked like they belonged in another century, dodging skittish horses and an odd assortment of other animals that had gotten loose to roam after decades in barnyards or being fed as wild pets. Audrey had recently heard tell of drunken hunters with shotguns. The Carnegies had always been battling trespassers, but Rosey said it was getting worse.

Audrey had read a report about a growing problem between the Carnegies of Cumberland and trespassers on the island in the local paper delivered to the inn for guests. People who had raised their families and worked on the water and on the islands for generations were getting edged off their land by development. Fishing wasn't what it used to be. Jobs at the nearby paper mill were the only way to make a good living, and there'd been layoffs of late. And come fall, the local high school would be integrated, which really had people riled up. As in every place across America in 1959, things were changing, and crumbly old Cumberland was one big scenic backdrop for all that small-town drama.

When she came upon Plum Orchard, she saw that the photos she'd seen in the paper hadn't done justice to the magnificent monstrosity. Audrey left her bike, bringing the Brownie camera to her eye to frame the shot, not wasting an exposure until she could get the light and the angles just right. She took her bike around it to see it from all sides, then took the trail down to the river's shore to stand where the salt marsh began. She'd timed her visit to this place knowing the tide would be out, leaving the creek bed exposed. She was careful where she stepped, keeping to the hard, light gray pluff mud and avoiding the lower, darker spots where things got murky.

Ahead of her, she could see the little island called Kingdom Come where Woodbine Cottage stood, but the house was hidden behind a maritime forest.

She held the camera to her eye and scanned the mudflats until she'd turned herself all the way around and was startled by something close. Her grip clenched and snapped a shot. It was a boy stretched out in the marsh grass only a few yards from her, his face turned up to the sun.

She froze where she stood, debating whether to speak to him, when she heard a soft, sad moan escape his lips. Jimmy Walker roused as if waking up, barely able to lift himself up on an elbow in the mud, his face a terrible grimace, teeth showing.

"Jimmy? Are you all right?" she called, alarmed. "You need me to get somebody?"

But there was nobody. She knew Plum Orchard was empty, and she saw no sign of anyone else with Jimmy. The boy turned on his side, his right arm still fully extended, obviously caught in something. Even from this distance, Audrey could see his panic and exhaustion. She felt a charge of fear and urgency when the boy began to cry.

She hurried to reach him. "Hush," she said. "Let me see."

He wailed. Audrey was on her knees, leaning over, trying to understand what had hold of him. He gasped when she touched him. She sat back on her heels. Jimmy's hand was caught in the metal teeth of an animal trap. She saw the whites of the boy's eyes as they rolled in his head. He was having trouble staying conscious. "No, don't fall asleep."

He gulped a deep breath. His head jerked back. He was doing his best to stay awake. Clearly he'd been trying to get loose for some time. There were prints from his boots and deep ruts in the mud where the trap was mired in the riverbank. She tried not to look at his injuries. She could barely make out the shape of things in all the mud.

With one foot on each side, putting all her weight on the trap, she would have to try to force the jaws open. Audrey positioned herself but hesitated. "It's going to hurt." Jimmy only looked away.

There was no point putting it off. But when she stood on both levers, nothing happened. She gave a bounce, then another, sweating through her shirt and feeling nauseous in the heat. She knew she would never forget the sounds coming from the boy. Then, like a miracle, the spring retracted. Jimmy screamed.

Audrey lost her balance and landed next to him in the mud. He curled into a ball around his hand, moaning. She wrapped herself around him, holding him there for a moment and making soothing sounds. He felt thin underneath the fabric of his shirt. He shook like his bones would come apart. When Audrey got to her feet and helped him stand, she dared take a look at the hand as he held it drawn up to his chest.

"Can you move your fingers?" she asked, as if she knew anything about such injuries. He gave it a tentative try, nodded, and winced.

So maybe not broken, not mangled, but there was a deep puncture where the trap had caught the edge of his hand. She knew she wouldn't be able to get him onto her bike with her. There was only one place she knew to go for help. She looked across the mudflat to Kingdom Come.

———

The painstaking walk across the tidal creek took longer than she'd dreamed, requiring all Audrey's strength to keep her footing and hold Jimmy Walker up too. She'd never been so relieved when they climbed up on the stoop of the cottage. Audrey didn't even have the chance to knock on the door before she heard a voice from the inside.

"Go away."

"I have a boy here. Jimmy Walker. He's hurt," Audrey said.

When the door swung open, Audrey couldn't help feeling a thrill at seeing the lady standing there after all she'd heard about Cleo Woodbine. But Cleo barely spared a glance at her. She looked at Jimmy and grimaced, her lips a hard-pressed line. "Jimmy Walker, what have you done to yourself?"

"A trap got me." Jimmy's teeth chattered in a way that alarmed Audrey, and she felt weak with relief when Cleo pulled them inside. Jimmy was leaning heavily on her, and Audrey was glad to let him sit down on a small sofa in the dim little space.

"Well, come on in. Everybody else has these last two days. What are you doing out here, anyway?" Cleo demanded, but she was gingerly inspecting the boy. She filled a small cup and he drank it all down. She looked him in the face, expecting an answer.

"We're tripping traps so the mink don't get killed. Nobody needs to kill those mink. They don't need to hunt them; they're just being mean."

"Not me," Audrey said. "I was just out on the riverbank with my camera."

Cleo kept her eyes on Jimmy. "We?"

"Me and Harl," he said.

"Harl Buie? Well, where is he? Did he leave you like this?"

Jimmy shook his head. "He was hiding."

"Hiding?"

"From her," Jimmy said, looking to Audrey.

Audrey listened to all of this. "I never saw anyone else."

Cleo went to jerk her door open, and a Negro boy maybe a few years younger than Audrey stood at the edge of the yard.

"Well, this is a mess," Cleo called to him. "You know Jimmy's daddy is going to have your hide when he sees he's hurt."

"Yes, ma'am," the kid agreed. Audrey watched from where she stood inside the house. He was taller than Jimmy and his voice was deep.

"There's no point in it. Whoever's setting those traps will be right behind you to reset them. Then they'll come looking for you, you know that."

"Yes, ma'am." He wasn't going to argue, but Audrey could tell he might not agree with Cleo that it was a good enough reason to change what he'd been doing.

"Do you have your boat?" she asked. The boy nodded. "Good. I'm going to wrap Jimmy's hand up. Then you're going to take him straight to Rosey. You can go wait out there or come in here and listen to more of what I have to say about this."

"No, ma'am. I'll wait in the boat." Harl shook his head and went back in the direction of the river where Audrey knew the water was rising.

Cleo shut the door and came back to Jimmy, but he'd closed his eyes and started making a little whimpering sound, so Cleo let him be. "I know it hurts. Now, lay your head back and rest. Is your daddy at work? Does Rosey know where you are?"

Jimmy said that yes, Glenn was at the mill, and that no, Rosey didn't know where he'd gone. He was fading and Cleo reached to ease his head down on a throw pillow. She grimaced over his bloody hand. "All right, you be quiet now. We'll take care of you." She sucked her teeth, then looked to Audrey, who was eyeing that cup and the drink she'd given Jimmy. "Can you speak for yourself?"

"Yes, ma'am. I'm Audrey Miller. I mean, Howell. Audrey Howell." She added her married name like you might spit tobacco. She hadn't gotten used to it and now she wondered if she'd have to keep it.

"You look like a skinny blackbird on those legs. You're one of the Gilbreath girls, aren't you?"

"Shirley was my aunt. My mother was Mimi Gilbreath. I'm working at Gilbreath House now."

"What business do you have out here?"

Audrey almost laughed. "None. I mean, I wanted to come out and take some photos, that's all."

Cleo cocked her head. "Rosey tells me Glenn Walker's got you making pictures."

"Yes, ma'am."

"Not the kind you're taking out here, I hope."

"No, ma'am."

"Don't ma'am me. I can't stand it. It's Cleo."

"Yes, ma'am," Audrey said again before she could stop herself.

Audrey's stomach threatened to heave and she wished she could step outside. She wished, in fact, that she hadn't come. She watched as Cleo went about her little kitchenette gathering things to wrap the boy's hand. Audrey realized she'd been expecting the cottage to be a grim sort of place. Maybe a hearth and a caldron, not this neat little house that smelled sweet and warm. There were shelves lined with jars, a whole canning operation with a pressure cooker. Cleo's paints set out on a long table. She craned her neck to try to see what Cleo Woodbine might be working on, but the woman came around and tossed a bedsheet over everything without so much as a word to her.

Jimmy moaned as Cleo gently wrapped his hand and placed it atop his chest. "You're going to ride back with Harl. Get Jimmy straight to Rosey and let him take care of this. I can't do much for it here. He's going to need a few stitches."

Audrey's jaw hung open. "You want me to take him back to Rosey?"

Cleo shook her head as if she'd never seen anybody so stupid. "Unless you want to be the one to work out what to say to Glenn about the boy being all the way out here."

Audrey did not relish getting caught up in any of this with Glenn or Rosey or anyone else. "His granddaddy's at the inn. What if he could help?"

Cleo glowered at her. "How would I know? Go to Rosey."

Audrey nodded. Jimmy shuddered and she asked before thinking, "Did you give him something? Just then, in the drink?"

"I sell fruit syrups and the like and there's nothing more to it. Don't believe that nonsense about glory."

Glory. That must be what locals called the drink made from morning glories.

"Everybody says you can make people see what you want. Make them believe what you want."

"Who's them?"

"Just people, I guess. People who come out here. Rosey said it. I never said I believed it."

Cleo shook her head sadly. "People dream up all sorts."

Audrey drew a breath and tried to think clearly. "I just meant if you gave Jimmy something, they'll want to know about it if he goes to the hospital." Audrey turned back to Jimmy. "He'll be okay, won't he?"

"Harl Buie's the one to worry about if Glenn gets hold of him and knows he let Jimmy come out here and get hurt, messing with mink traps." Cleo's mouth was grim.

"And Nan too," Jimmy said quietly. Cleo and Audrey both looked at him and he blinked like an owl.

Cleo sighed. "Nan's here too?"

Jimmy nodded.

"Nan is Harl's sister," Cleo said flatly to Audrey. "Lord in heaven. What a day this has been. Jimmy, you can't be coming out here with those Buie kids. Harl's already crossways with your daddy, raising tempers over who ought to be out on Cumberland or not these days. You just got a hole in your hand for your trouble. Let this be the last I see you out here."

Jimmy looked sorry as could be and wiped his runny nose with the back of his good hand. Audrey didn't know Harl Buie or his sister, Nan. She barely knew Jimmy, but Jimmy's worried expression was enough to make up her mind. "I'll say Jimmy was with me and we'll just leave the Buies out of it. I came on the ferry to take photographs and Jimmy came with me. I should have been paying better attention."

Cleo took a better look at her, then gave a short nod. "That sounds exactly right to me. Don't that sound right to you, Jimmy?"

Jimmy nodded. Audrey wasn't sure he could tell the lie, but they walked out of the cottage with the boy between them. They took the same path through the stand of oaks and down to the river where the tide had come in, and they found Harl and Nan Buie waiting in a little johnboat with a motor.

Audrey piled in with the kids. The boat was barely big enough to hold them all. Jimmy sat next to Nan, a girl a few years younger than her brother, with darker skin and the same dark eyes, never looking directly at Audrey. It seemed obvious to Audrey that the Buie kids were afraid of what trouble she might cause for them. Cleo gave them sharp instructions to get back without drawing attention and then to take themselves home before anybody had any reason to start talking.

"This is Audrey Howell," Cleo said. Their eyes darted to meet hers and then quickly went back to Cleo, whom they clearly trusted. "She's Rosey's cousin. You don't need to be worried." This seemed to mean something to them, and Audrey was relieved they appeared to think a little better of her. "All you're doing is giving this girl and Jimmy a ride back because they missed the tour ferry. Jimmy was with Mrs. Howell and that's it." She looked at Audrey while the others nodded. "You let Rosey do the talking to Glenn."

She did as she was told and left the Buies at the dock as soon as they reached Revery, delivered Jimmy Walker to her cousin, and made the trip with them to the hospital in Fernandina before coming back to Gilbreath House. She cranked the film to the finish and stored the roll away in the freezer. Then she went out to the carriage house and tried to cry. Audrey suspected it said a lot about her that her eyes remained dry. But she was going to have to figure it out soon. She'd felt a quickening when she'd least expected it. But expecting was what she was. Expecting life even after death.

Chapter Five

CLEO

><e

"TROUBLE COMES IN THREES," WASN'T THAT THE SAYING?

It seemed to Cleo that Joanna's passing had kicked off a parade of characters right through Cleo's solitude, and these were the living, breathing sort, bringing all sorts of complications and feelings and expectations with them. Not simple storybook illustrations that sprang from her own imagination, easy to predict from beginning to end.

For three days, visitations had come upon Kingdom Come. First, Tate had shown up, spying on her and leaving that watch for her to see so it nearly stopped her heart. A day later there'd been Frances Flood with her mother's message from the grave, asking questions Cleo could not answer. Just thinking of Joanna's request made Cleo's hair stand up—a painting in memory of what? She'd been sitting in front of her watercolors with a blank paper ever since and still could not make a start. Then yesterday that sad little Audrey Howell had interrupted her concentration, barreling up onto her stoop with Tate's grandson, who was bleeding no less. If the two had been guileless children lost in the deep wood and she'd been the crafty crone ready to throw them in her oven, she'd have made an easy meal of them. Instead, it felt an awful lot like the universe was trying to warn her of the past repeating itself.

Seeing Harl Buie standing in her yard had been like seeing a ghost. He looked so much like Lumas Gray waiting there that

Cleo had had to blink twice. Cleo knew he was getting himself into trouble, tripping traps that other boys had set along the river so they could catch a mink and throw the dead pelt at her front door on a dare. But what Harl was doing would raise hackles with the boys, which would raise hackles with the daddies over more serious matters. What had her worried was how Harl was working for the Carnegies as a woodsman, which meant reporting signs of poachers on the island. That put him square in adult territory. And territory was the bigger issue, as it always had been on Cumberland, the beef with Georgia boys who had grown up running all over these islands, who still liked to believe the whole wild coast was theirs and wouldn't be told otherwise by an outsider with a property deed. Much less a skinny colored boy barely getting his whiskers.

That's what Audrey Howell and Jimmy Walker had brought to her door. The damn world.

Cleo had minded her own business while those tensions grew, stayed out of it until yesterday. She couldn't have cared less if the Carnegies had a turf war with the poachers, so long as they left her out of it. Only a few days before, she'd been at the end of things, glory in hand, ready to leave Kingdom Come on her own terms. Now she felt she was being dragged back into the land of the living with all its troubles. She was on edge, waiting for the next knock.

She was disgruntled by the idea of looming interruptions, thinking of Frances Flood waiting on her painting, and figured if anybody was headed her way to take up her time on a fine Tuesday, it would be Tate Walker, come back to get his watch. No wonder she couldn't settle to paint.

She could not stop pulling that old watch out to look at it, eaten up by the desire to know what Tate had come here to say. But also to tell him his son and grandson were about to get caught up in a holy war over the island. She'd have to make up her mind what to do, maybe put a note in her basket to the inn, although the last thing she wanted to be to Tate Walker was a pen pal.

She made her morning rounds, foraging while sweat popped out on her forehead and across her upper lip, though it wasn't even noon yet and a good breeze was coming over the water. She was making her way south, past Plum Orchard, when she saw him there, just near the site of the old bonfire.

She hadn't laid eyes on him in almost three decades. From a distance he appeared nothing more than a little plover on the shore. But she'd remembered the shape of him. He had not changed so much. Tate would be somewhere in the neighborhood of fifty-five now. He'd been a few years older than the boys in the party that summer, working for Dr. Johnston to manage the hunts at the gathering. The only one in the bunch who was married, Tate had already had a little son, Glenn, back then. That made Tate Walker sweet Jimmy Walker's granddaddy now. Though who would have known it for all Tate had to do with those boys? He'd left for the railroad, then left his family somewhere along the way. Cleo knew because Rosey talked of it. Shirley Devane had stepped up to watch out for the man's wife and child, which was why Rosey and Glenn had grown up so close.

It was an irony that the Devanes had been her single connection to the outside world all this time, and also to Tate. She thought of that as she maneuvered the johnboat, cutting the motor while she was far enough away that he would not have heard it, pulling ashore in a cove she knew so she could walk out and have a look at him before he saw her coming this time.

Every week for almost as long as she'd been out on Kingdom

Come, Cleo had packed a basket with whatever she'd gathered from the wild—the surprising, the strange, the wonderful. She made a simple fruit syrup for flavoring drinks or cakes or what have you, which she'd adapted to whatever fruit she had available. She'd traded at random for a few years until Shirley Devane sent her husband, Henry, to offer Cleo a partnership with the Gilbreath House Inn. Cleo became the sole provider of fruit flavoring for signature drinks and fresh fruits for the guests. Henry came once a week and collected a basket, which Cleo left at the dock. It had been an ideal arrangement, and there had been joy in it.

Cleo walked, sometimes swam, as far as it took to find what she wanted and sometimes made more than one trip. She sent jelly jars filled with jewel-colored jams, pickled beets or cucumbers, freshly pressed olive oils, and spiced pastes. In return, Shirley sent back vegetable soups, string beans, okra, and corn, all canned and labeled neatly. In the summers there'd been a back-and-forth of surprise pies, and in autumn there were cobblers. In the winter there'd been cornbread and biscuits, bacon and sausage, and sometimes even venison. And then one day Cleo had included one of her paintings. Shirley sent word asking for more.

Certainly Cleo could have gotten any of the things she needed over the years from the people living in the communities on Cumberland. But this was more than an exchange of goods; it had been a conversation of sorts, interrupted only once when she'd found little Rosey Devane half-drowned, too far out on the mudflats after the tide began to turn. She'd pulled him in, and when he had enough sense to talk again, she'd sent him home no worse for the wear.

"You take this basket back to Shirley," Cleo had said. And she had let the boy continue to visit while he grew up and chatter on about news from town, people she didn't know, a movie theater

where he'd seen his first film, the pies Shirley would make. Rosey had been her most regular visitor out of a string of other lost souls over nearly thirty years.

She had not lived these many years a prisoner or an exile, as people believed, but time could get away from a person out here. Still, Cleo would argue she had known contentment and satisfaction, without the stupid everyday concerns most folk endured. She had never worried over keeping a house. She'd never had to consider a neighbor dropping by. She did not tend to a man. She'd worn what she chose and she chose what she needed, not what was fashionable. If she brushed her hair or her teeth, it was to keep them from falling out of her head.

All of this set up a kind of deep thrumming in her mind as she walked through the edge of the marsh to where Tate was bent forward, scanning the ground. Cleo watched a long while, guessing what he was out looking to find. She felt a rush of emotion at the sight of him, an overwhelming connection to that faraway summer that had come to seem more like a dream to her than reality. But there he was, a solid man, and it made her suddenly solid too. It made her consider how much time had truly passed and what she'd done with it, and what she had not. She was dizzy with the collision of the past and present but realized her confusion was made worse from having had nothing to eat all morning.

Maybe that explained the disorientation that came over her as she stepped out onto the shore at the edge of the rushes, a few yards north of Tate. Like the day she'd gotten the obituary, a dark curtain swung over her vision and she had the wherewithal to be appalled she was going to pass out. She was going headfirst into the mud and water, but if she was out, it was only for a second before she heard splashing and then felt herself being grabbed up under her arms. She was being hoisted out of the water, one arm under her hind end like she was a calf being hauled out of a dip bath.

It was Tate who had her, of course, carried her through the rushes, then dropped her in the sand and joined her there. She kept her eyes closed, humiliated. The memory of the last time they'd been together like this on this shore came roaring into her head. The hard knot of scar tissue inside her chest burned and she pushed her fist into the spot and could feel her heart beating wildly there. This was not how she'd wanted to meet the man again.

"I guess you're glad to see me again," she said. He stared at her and she could see the young man again after a moment when he chuckled. They both sat there, clothes soaked and in disarray. She was missing a boot and he was muttering that he had lost his glasses. After he'd pushed himself to stand and found them, he settled them on his nose, then leaned down to take her wrist, thumb pressed on one side of it. He looked her square in the eye. "Your pulse seems fine. No irregularities with your pupils."

She pulled her hand away. Her head had not really stopped spinning. "My pupils are just fine. Sometimes the glare off the water blinds me. Makes my head sick."

"Migraine. My wife used to get those. Said it looked like angels appearing to her. The doctors said there was nothing for it but rest and quiet for her nerves."

"My nerves are steady." But they weren't.

"It's likely you're dehydrated. Sun's high. A spell like that can come over you fast."

"I am plenty used to the sun." She was not coming down with the vapors, the diagnosis for all woman problems. And so like what they'd said about Joanna Burton that she was sure they both must be thinking of her then.

"Appears you and I are not the spry young things we used to be. Although you look about the way I remember you."

"Well, I'm not that girl. Haven't you heard? I'm the old island hag now."

"You'll turn me into a hog. That's what I've heard."

"I have never had to lift a finger to do that to any man. They do it to themselves."

He did not seem bothered by any of this. She supposed he'd lived long and hard enough he was comfortable with his hog ways. He stood over her in his Blue Bell overalls with his big hands hanging at his sides. She was eaten up with curiosity about him. She did not get to her feet but looked up at him as if she were comfortable right where she sat.

"It's been a hundred years since I've seen you. Or at least it feels that way. You still a railroad man?"

"Recently retired. I'm looking to stay in one place these days."

"This place, you mean?" She wondered how his son would feel about that. "Will they have you?"

He shrugged. "Won't know until I try. I'm over at Gilbreath House just now. Got to Revery a few days ago. Looking around to see what I can see. Not much has changed."

"Some things have. That why you came now?"

He nodded. "I got tired of riding that train one place to another, never getting anywhere. Seemed like I needed to put it to rest while I still had time. I was just putting it off, but then Dr. Johnston sent the obit."

"I saw you'd been back to this beach. Figured as much."

"And what about you?"

"What about me?"

"Don't you know this is the year for the next storm of the century? The old folks are talking about it, keeping watch. They say this season's will be the one to lift that shoal in the river so Cumberland takes your little island back."

"That storm's nothing but superstition." But she did not say whether she believed any of it. "I'll tell you what I know for a fact. There's other storms brewing I'd be more concerned about if I were you. Your boys are right caught up in the trouble with the Carnegies and the poachers, or they're about to be." She knew she had his attention now. "You heard what happened to Jimmy, getting his hand hurt in that trap? It was just boys catching mink to try and get a rise out of me, but Archie Buie's grandson's been hired to report poaching and there've been rumors that Glenn is one of them, running boats over here at night, making some cash. Tempers are high. People aren't being careful. Jimmy's going to get hurt worse than a torn-up hand, running around without anybody keeping an eye on him. He don't know the difference between these grown-up boys and his games."

Tate had a frown while he listened. "I know about that trap and what you did to help my grandson. Thank you for that. I'll be keeping an eye on him from here on out. Can't answer for my son."

Whatever he did with the information was on him, and at least she felt some relief of the responsibility.

He had some deep lines cut in his forehead now. He was tall, if a little soft around the middle, and he blocked the sun where she sat. Cleo decided it was time to go and shoved herself to her feet. She avoided taking the hand of help he offered. She still listed and leaned a little, to her embarrassment.

He said, "I have a little pole boat. We ought to be able to float our way back to your place with nobody the wiser. I know you're worried, but I won't say a word about any of this. Reputation's safe with me."

"When did I ever care about my reputation?" She looked where he was gesturing to the boat up the beach a few yards past the tide line. She'd been too out of her head to notice. A nice, shiny aluminum skiff with a little motor at one end. "I have my own boat and I don't want to trouble you."

"Well, that's good news. But you ought not be out on the water by yourself just now. And I was hoping to ask a favor of you, if I'm being honest."

"Well, I shouldn't be surprised. Every day there's somebody new out here asking me for something." She had expected they'd talk about why he'd come back, about Joanna's passing and their memory of that summer, maybe what they'd done together then or how their lives had gone since. But a favor had never occurred to her. What could she do for Tate Walker?

"I might need you to let me carry you in my boat so you can hold something on your lap while we get you home. Seems like I'm about as much trouble as my grandson."

"Hold something?"

He'd brought her something? She was trying to put the pieces together when she remembered she had something for him, too, then noticed the missing weight of the watch in her pocket. It must have gone into the water with her tumble into the creek. Now she glanced back to the spot, uncertain where she'd landed, seeing only the smooth surface of the rising tide sparking sunshine. She'd lost his watch. That's what he'd come back for, not her. And as stupid as it made her feel, she wanted to keep him there a little longer. Again, the sick headache came on hard.

Tate Walker put a steadying hand under her elbow and she felt herself swinging between reality and some old memory of this place and the people they'd once been.

"Here, chew on this. It'll make you feel better." He reached to pull a thin stem of sassafras from the pocket of his fishing vest. Her throat closed and she clamped the sassafras between her teeth, but the sweet gesture was bitter as an aspirin on her tongue. "Dooley Woodbine taught me about sassafras. That man was a legend in his own mind."

"People forget," she muttered.

But not Tate, it seemed. When she thought back, she couldn't recall they'd ever had a conversation long enough for her to realize that as a boy, he might have known her granddaddy from that time he was living at the cottage. "Did you know Dooley or just hear tale of him?"

"Shoot, yeah," Tate Walker said. "We all knew Dooley. Long before you came that year. Used to chew the fat over at Plum Orchard with him and the Johnstons. Always had a stick of sassafras in his pocket for us kids, didn't he? To tell you the truth, I was just wishing I could listen to Dooley tell one of his tales again. A talent he sure enough handed down to you. I remember that too."

She could remember Tate with a cowlick and the same sad eyes. She wondered again what happened that kept him away from his wife and family. "What's this favor? Let's just hear it straight out."

"I'm sorry to say that what I've got on my hands today is a life-and-death situation. I don't know if it might be beyond us both to do anything about it."

This alarmed Cleo more than the loss of the watch. "What on earth do you mean? It's not Jimmy?"

"No, no. Jimmy got twelve stitches—one for every year of his life, he says—but he got lucky with that trap. It only grabbed the meaty edge of his left hand. He's walking around like a prizefighter with a bandage like a boxing glove. Ought to come off in a few weeks. I'll need to bring him out here to thank you proper. Rosey told me you helped him and Mrs. Howell out."

"Nobody owes me a thank-you. I didn't have much choice in the matter. The girl showed up ready to blow my house down if I didn't let them in."

Tate laughed at that, and Cleo was surprised how the sound knocked around deep in her belly. But it annoyed her too. He'd alarmed her, and nothing he said was making sense. "Well, you can't say it's life and death and then stand here making small talk," she snapped. "It's not Glenn, is it?"

"No, no."

It occurred to her that Tate himself might be sick, and she demanded, "Well, what's wrong, then? You look like you're doing fine to me."

Tate walked a few feet and bent over the high tide line where the usual flotsam and jetsam would get stranded. He reached to lift something gently from a bit of seaweed. Cleo watched as he revealed a small mink cradled in his huge hands. The animal wasn't struggling and might have been dead except that she could see its chest barely rise and fall with rapid, shallow breathing.

"Not you too," Cleo said, both relieved and dismayed by the sight.

"I came up on another one of those damn traps in the riverbank. I worked the jaws loose in the nick of time, but he's gone pretty limp now."

"I can see that." Cleo didn't want it alive any more than she wanted it flung up dead on her stoop. Like it or not, she now found herself receiving the poor thing from Tate Walker.

"Surely there's something you can do for it."

Cleo clenched the fabric of her empty pocket, knowing she

should tell him about the watch but unable to admit her careless mistake. And wondering if they could really stand here and pretend that Tate had not seen her on the shore that day, that he didn't know what she'd been about to do had she not seen that watch.

"I think you're asking me to do the impossible. I thought you knew better than to believe what people say about me. I can't turn you into a hog any more than I can raise the dead. I can barely keep my own self alive."

"That animal's not dead yet. Surely you can try."

Cleo's resolve wavered. "I guess I owe you as much." She owed him more. "But I can't make any promises."

She doubted the mink would survive the next hour or two even as she climbed into his boat and took the limp creature on her lap. She felt a warm stream of urine from the mink trail down her pant leg and a foul odor burned her nose, scent glands defending a life even as it was ebbing away. Cleo yelped, offended. "The little SOB pissed on me!"

Tate Walker laughed, showing all his nice white teeth, pretty as pearls.

When he left, he promised to be back, and Cleo knew then he'd used that mink as an excuse to come see her again. She couldn't say she was upset about that.

Chapter Six

FABLE

THE YOUNG MEN WHO HAD COME TO PLUM ORCHARD WERE UP AND out every morning going on their predawn duck hunts, stalking deer, and even tracking a bobcat they'd heard at night. In the evenings they lay about eating mountains of food or hauling in sheepshead or flounder or shrimp or crab, leaving all their fishing gear in tangles on the porch. They went swimming in the indoor pools, and just as on that first night, there was gambling long after dark. Mrs. O'Dowd liked to say that while most of the country struggled with the economic depression, Morrie Johnston, John Oliver, and Ellis Piedmont—with fathers who had amassed fortunes in oil and steel—never felt the mildest pinch where they lived in upstate New York and Philadelphia. Morrie Johnston was the youngest, not yet twenty, and the other two were only a few years older. Richard Flemming and his brother, Wally, were sons of a fellow Kentucky horseman, both in their late twenties, and they lived seemingly unaware of the want all around them up in their Appalachian haven.

But it was the sixth of them who drew Cleo's attention. A grown man of thirty, Tate Walker, who was the only one with a rough edge. Like her, he'd grown up in Revery. He was only at Plum Orchard for the summer gathering, in charge of hunting, although he knew the family. He was a childhood friend of many of the Carnegie kids and a favorite of Dr. Johnston's. Already married and a father about to embark on a job with the Southern Railway, he struck Cleo as a hanger-on, perhaps reluctant to give up his youth. He wore a shiny new railroader's watch, which they'd all pretended to admire but laughed at behind their hands.

Each morning, during those days before Joanna Burton arrived, Cleo pulled on something from the borrowed clothing in the armoire and pinned her hair back and told herself she was not a novelty, not a hanger-on. She had her own purpose, her own plans. She wouldn't give the others the opportunity to make a joke of her. She avoided introductions and haunted the huge house and grounds, spying on the others to entertain herself. She walked the grounds, sat on the riverbank, perused the library, looked out from the many verandas, and painted in her room. And it turned out that she did, indeed, befriend Lumas Gray.

There were dozens of old sheds and hunting and fishing camps that dotted the Carnegie properties, and when he'd finished with his duties, they took bikes and flashlights and rambled far and wide. And she learned that Lumas's tale was an oddity to match her own. Years ago, a boat had washed up on the shoals with only a toddler aboard, this nut-brown boy who could not speak a word of English to say what had become of his fellow travelers. The best that could be guessed was that he'd come as a refugee from Cuba, blown off course. He could not even say what name he'd been given at his birth. The Carnegies were the ones who had named him.

"What would you have named yourself?" she asked.

He wrinkled his nose as if he'd never thought of such a thing. "Who picks their own name?"

"But you could have been anybody."

"Or nobody." The suggestion sent a shiver through her. "I like being Lumas Gray."

As promised, he'd taken her out to Dungeness, the largest

Carnegie mansion eight miles south on the Grand Avenue, now going to seed. They'd climbed stairs and smoked cigarettes in the cavernous, moldering library. He'd told her about one of the fishermen's daughters, a girl named Mimi Gilbreath who used to roam around Cumberland with her sister, Shirley. The three had been childhood friends, and Mimi had taught him to read from the books in the Dungeness library.

"Did you love her?" Cleo teased.

"She was about like my sister," he said. "Except she's a white girl."

He'd chuckled at that, but Cleo thought she could hear that the memory of the girl made him a bit melancholy. There'd been no sign of Mimi now, who had grown up and no longer came to run wild on Cumberland, and no sign of a ghost either. But Cleo had loved the library and Lumas's stories all the same.

"One day I'm going south," he said. "Down to a place in Florida where there are cigar factories run by Cubans."

He talked of catching a ride on a train that came through every year. "It's a circus train."

"You're making that up."

"They come north in the early summer to make their tour and then they come back through on the way to spend the winter in Sarasota."

"So you'll be a carny, then?" she asked.

"I'll be whatever I need to be to get a ride out of here. Sarasota's close to Ybor City. That's where I'm going."

"Maybe I'll go with you if I don't like it here."

She'd expected he would beam at the idea, but he'd looked at her askance, like it was a crazy suggestion. She wasn't even sure why she'd said it when it was far from her plans in any real world.

He was right. Outside of this island, just like Lumas and Mimi Gilbreath, they never would have been friends, a grown white girl and a Negro boy. Certainly they would never travel together unless he were driving her someplace.

She'd snatched a dusty volume from one of the shelves, one of the few books still scattered about, something so dull no one had stolen it yet. Inside the front cover, she looked at the embossed stamp on the title page: *Dungeness Library*. She ran her fingertips over the words.

"Do you want to be one of them? Is that it?"

"Who? The Carnegies? No, I don't want to be one of them." Cleo sighed. She had never considered wanting to be a Carnegie or a Johnston or anything like them. She was a Woodbine. She wanted to be *more* than them, the way Dooley had led her to believe he'd been, a sage and artist. The Carnegies were only a means to that end for Cleo. But she wasn't going to say that to this boy. He'd never known Dooley or been loved by him, inspired by him. "Everything will change when they give me the residency at Woodbine Cottage and I start to paint. I'll be somebody people are watching and talking about, Lumas. They'll want things from me. They'll want to know what I think and what I have to say. And you can't come out there. You know that, right? It won't be like it is now. So I think we just shouldn't talk about it."

She hurried out of the room and down the stairs, and since it had gotten dark, he walked her back. He was not afraid of the island at night. She didn't think he even used the flashlight when he turned around to head toward his own home, miles north.

Another day Cleo took out her watercolors and introduced Lumas to the characters that had trailed her in her younger years. She painted for him and Lumas told her a myth about giants who once walked the coast of Georgia and north Florida, a tribe that had disappeared, the same natives who had built the great mound where Dungeness stood. He swore their long bones could be found in a quiet glen called the bone orchard, proof those men had been nine feet tall. Cleo knew about the place called the bone orchard. Dooley had spoken of it. But she didn't say so then.

Instead, on the back page of Dooley's book Cleo painted that giant, ambling through the enormous oaks of the island, making him smile.

Cleo felt the sky above like a great dial cranking the summer away. While they walked beyond Plum Orchard to the river, Cleo said, "I can't imagine my grandmother here. She never wanted to come back to Cumberland. And she wouldn't like it that I've come here. She'd say I'm here for a handout. But she grubbed for every little thing we had. She made fruit syrups that she sold and that's what I did, too, for a long time. She didn't grow the fruit or any-thing. She just bought it cheap, whatever was passed over at the market in Revery because of bruises or because it had gotten soft, and she'd cut it up and make these jars of flavoring syrup. Over and over again. I don't even think she liked it. But she made me learn how to do it. She told me that no matter what, I'd always be able to pay my bills without depending on somebody else. How is that any kind of life? She hated it, I'm sure of it."

"You mean you hated it."

"Of course I hated it. Why would anybody want to live like that when they could be here?"

"That's why your fingers were stained?"

Cleo nodded. "She didn't like me either. I know that. I was al-ways more like Dooley. She said you can't feed a family on flights of fancy."

Part of Cleo still couldn't believe that Lumas Gray had not heard of Dooley, and she pressed him. "You're sure you never heard of him? They never talk about him or his book at any of the Carnegie houses? If you've heard something bad, you can tell me."

"I swear I never heard his name," Lumas said.

Cleo believed him and it stung, the first crack in the story Dooley had told her of himself and his importance here. The first reason to doubt she had some inherent claim to a stint at the cottage or some real talent as an artist and to believe that her grandmother had been right to steer her toward a practical means to support herself instead of these castles in the air on Cumberland. But Cleo hated to doubt Dooley even for a minute and felt desperate to hold on to the dream version of him, so much so that her thoughts turned to a way she might be able to believe it all a little longer, or at least convince everyone who mattered.

She thought of what he'd taught her about glory. That was why she finally said, "He told me something special about that place here he called the bone orchard. Something that grows there." She felt her fingertips tingle at the thought of those tender vines run through with sap. And she saw that Lumas did know something of that plant.

"It's not a place I'd go if I could help it. Archie never wanted us anywhere near there. June believed it was cursed." A Negro man named Archie Buie and his wife, June, had taken Lumas in when he was found on Cumberland, and he still lived with Archie now in a cottage north of Plum Orchard.

"Cursed? You can't be serious."

Lumas shook his head. "That's how I was raised. June grew up here. She knows all about what grows out of that glen." They walked along a few steps farther before he stopped. "I can't take you out there. I think you ought to leave that place alone."

She thought of Dooley and how at first he'd only used the crushed seeds in his water to paint, giving her a wink, enjoying the little ritual, a holdover from when he'd lived on the island and gone to gather the glory from the bone orchard. But later he'd talked of the careful use of the plant's seeds for gentle inspiration, a calming sense of well-being for the nerves, to bring about a spiritual experience, even. She'd believed every word, but when she'd grown older, she'd understood that morning glory vines were common along every roadside or fencerow, the reason for Dooley's constant supply. And that her grandmother had been right when she threw out all the glory Dooley had hidden away and blamed it for making her granddaddy forget himself. He'd died in his sleep, but nothing could convince her it was a natural departure rather than the consequence of what had become his habit.

If it hadn't been for the last memory Cleo had of Dooley—she'd seen him in the bed, slack and soulless, a husk robbed of life—she might have gone straightaway to find the vines that grew in the bone orchard when she'd first arrived on Cumberland, to gather the dried seedpods for herself. It was insecurity that drove her to take the risk now.

"You don't have to go with me, but I want to see it for myself. I've heard stories about it all my life. I want to know it's just a place like any other place. I don't believe in curses."

"Like you don't believe in ghosts."

"Ghosts are just stories," she said. "If you're scared, I can find my own way back."

"Don't go poking at that place; it's a mistake," he said. "Promise me."

When she didn't answer, he left her there to find the glen on her own, which was impossible, of course, in the deep maritime forest. Finally, she'd taken her bike and made her way back to Plum Orchard. She could not have known then that young Ellis Piedmont, a guest she'd barely noticed before, would turn an eye on her, lonely and desperate to be special to someone. And unlike Lumas Gray, he'd be all too eager to lead her down every crooked path.

———

The following day, after the guests had bounded out of the house and piled into the car, engine running high as they shot down the sandy drive, startling a mare and her new foal born only the night before, Cleo stepped onto the second-story front porch instead of going to find Lumas. She didn't see the boy seated in the rocker at the far end of the wide veranda until she stood almost directly in front of him. He was so still, a book balanced on his knee, that he startled her and she embarrassed herself by letting out an undignified word.

"Bless you," he said. He didn't smile, although Cleo felt he was making fun. Ellis Piedmont's eyes were round and dark, and if he'd not been so cold, he might have been handsome. Instead, she got the feeling she'd come upon something hiding in the grass.

"I'm sorry. You scared me."

"I'm scary. I've been told so."

Cleo seriously doubted that, although she did find him unsettling. "No, I just didn't see you there. I thought the party had all gone."

"I'm not much for a party. But you could entertain me."

Cleo didn't know what to say to this. In fact, she wasn't comfortable talking to the young man. Cleo frowned. He was rude.

He liked seeing her uncomfortable. He had a pout and she wasn't sure she trusted him. His hair was lank and sandy blond. His skin was sallow. She couldn't imagine how he had spent days in the sun and still looked like some sick Victorian child. She thought carefully before responding, working hard to keep her expression as impersonal as possible. "I don't think I'm very entertaining."

"Oh, please. I was hoping you'd be more interesting. Can you try? At this rate you're not going to be very successful as anybody's companion."

Cleo felt the remark land like a slap, an insult meant to bait her. He looked at her as if she were on display, taking in her plain shoes and the stiff cotton skirt and blouse that now felt more like borrowed clothes than ever. She was embarrassed by the way her hair was loose, leaving pieces of the wiry auburn nest to wave upward where the breeze caught it. She curled her fingers into her palms, making fists so he wouldn't see the paint staining her nails. It didn't matter. He was already bored of her, as bored as Cleo herself. She resented his disappointment.

She dropped her gaze to the book in his lap long enough to note the embossed title on its cover. *The Great Gatsby*. She imagined his grip on the book tightened. With as much disinterest as he'd shown in her, she said, "I know better stories than that one."

He laughed. Not just any laugh but a guffaw that startled the birds from the trees. Anyone else who might have heard the boy would have been offended. But the shocking and complete lack of pretense made Cleo cover her own mouth to stop herself from doing the same. Just as his disappointment had dropped her low, now his approval raised her high. He should not have had such power, this scarecrow of a person, and maybe that was what made him so interesting. Cleo was rarely interested in anyone.

"Will you tell me a story, then?" His tone was overly eager, and Cleo flushed. "Make it a good one I can use for the bonfire. We're all expected to sit around and scare the wits out of one another, you know."

"I don't think so," Cleo said, surprising herself by teasing him back.

"Ah, come on. Tell me something awful. Rattling chains and dressing gowns. Something I could tell to turn everyone's hair white. What do you know?"

Cleo knew plenty of stories. It pleased her to hold on to them. Finally she had something that might be wanted. She kept silent.

"You do know something good. I can see it. Why will you not tell me? Or do you think you'll win the night for yourself?"

Cleo opened her mouth but he shushed her and stood, brushing his pants, thrusting the book into her hands as he walked past.

"Don't try to act like you don't want to do it. But what if we were a team? Two is always better than one, don't you think? We could shock them all. Oh, you're very entertaining, after all."

Clearly he believed it was settled. And though she'd meant to refuse him, hearing him state plans as though they were suddenly co-conspirators was too enticing. At no point since she'd put her feet on the floor this morning had she ever dreamed she would be standing on this porch with one of the boys from the party, made into someone with something to say. But Ellis Piedmont had declared her so.

"It might not be the kind of story you think," she said. He was expecting ghouls and graveyards.

"Don't be silly," he said. "Sad girls like you always know the most truly horrible tales."

Chapter Seven

FRANCES

ON FRANCES'S THIRD MORNING IN REVERY, AN EVERLY BROTHERS ballad poured out of a turntable on the credenza in the front room at the Gilbreath House Inn, where tables were already set and ready for brunch in a few hours. Yesterday, Audrey Howell had been gone for most of the day and Frances had slept and read the hours away. She'd found a box of old *True Romance* magazines in the closet in her room, something she never picked up when she passed them on the stand at the grocery store. It had felt decadent to sit in bed and pore over the sensational stories with headlines like "I'd Die for Love" and "I Started Deadly Rumors."

In the evening, she'd come downstairs to the empty rooms of the main floor and helped herself to a glass of sweet tea and a sandwich, then sat on the back porch overlooking the river until it had gotten dark before going right back up to her room. It had been heavenly. From her window, she'd seen the light of a lantern on the street below as Rosey Devane had passed the house with a group of five or six people, leading them along one of his ghost tours, she supposed. Frances had concluded that she'd take him up on his invitation to play the role of a ghost. Whatever she did or did not discover about her mother's time here, Frances did not want to spend her days haunted by it, too angry or afraid to make the most of her opportunities while she had them.

This morning she felt ready to see all of Revery and whatever she might learn there. To start, she was glad to see there was no wait for the bathroom at the end of the hallway. There was currently only one other guest at the inn, a man who appeared to already be out for the day. The door to his room had been left open, the bed made. The sight brought to mind Owen Flood, a fastidious man like that, tidy and up early. The memory of her father, mingled with the loss of her mother, produced a feeling she was starting to understand came from being orphaned.

Since talking to Cleo Woodbine and beginning to sort through the puzzle of the past, Frances didn't relish the thought of walking the streets of this town where the Piedmont name was carved over the library door and printed on the paychecks of the mill workers. She felt partly a stranger to herself, looking in the mirror for signs of unknown genes in her face before she pulled on a practical blouse, a pair of jeans, and good loafers for walking. She had her field notebook and a pair of sunglasses and looked prepared for a day of sightseeing in town like any other tourist, she hoped.

This morning customers waited on the front walk and porch, eager for a meal. Revery was surprisingly busy with foot traffic, and she could see Rosey's tours would be in demand. From the entrance to the kitchen, she noticed men milling about in the side yard, colored men. She watched as Audrey Howell gathered up a half dozen paper sacks and opened the door to them, handing the meals out with a nod, taking coins in exchange. The innkeeper was only twenty, tall and tanned like she spent time outside in the sun, with glossy black hair that swung forward to hide her face. Frances took advantage of the moment to take a look at her. She wore pedal pushers and sandals and a cotton top with little daisies on it that seemed far too cheery to suit her.

Frances couldn't help thinking about the terrible loss of Audrey's husband. The girl had barely graduated high school, but there she was, managing a kitchen and a house that wasn't even hers like some kind of Betty Crocker. Frances doubted it was the life she'd expected to be living right now. It struck Frances that this might not be so different from Joanna's experience, rushed home to marry a man a decade older than her and start an instant family. It made her take a closer look at Audrey and appreciate what the girl was facing.

Frances wasn't hungry. She hadn't really regained her appetite since losing her mother. Instead of joining others at the brunch buffet, she walked through the house to see Cleo Woodbine's folksy watercolor paintings where they hung in frames, each marked with a modest price on a little tag. She wondered now what that woman would choose to paint for her mother's commission. These illustrations appeared deceptively simple and innocent. But while Dooley Woodbine's original characters were present, they had evolved under Cleo's hand. Their expressions were harder to read, their eyes more alive, and Frances had the impression they might speak to her at any instant. Moreover, Cleo's characters did not stand against the stark background of the page; they were embedded, tangled, stepping from the shadows of the forests and glens and shores of Cumberland.

Frances felt herself on the verge of tears. She blamed it on the cloying sense that the furniture in the inn appeared to have been sitting just as the former owner had left it and the sound of a grandfather clock in the foyer marking time so steadily. Frances wondered how the young innkeeper could stand it. No wonder she played her music day and night.

A rising breeze from an open window swept over her face,

and Frances was grateful as she stepped outside. She waited on the porch swing out front, but when it was time for the tour, it wasn't Rosey who appeared on the sidewalk. From a distance, she watched a thin boy with a bandaged hand coming up the street. He loped along on his toes as if the calm wind off the water were a gale force. Frances sat up in her chair with the impression that any minute he might lift off the ground. He arrived at the foot of the steps and stopped there. She was stunned by his beaming smile and responded in kind. He spoke deliberately, as if he were orating from a stage.

"Uncle Rosey invites you to meet him down at the marvelous Marvel Theater to begin your tour." His teeth were a bit of a jumble in his mouth, giving him an overbite that made his chin appear very narrow. "Would you like for me to walk there with you? Or do you feel happy to walk on your own?"

Charmed, she said, "I think I can find it."

She judged that he must be close to twelve years old, but slight for his age. His nose was tipped upward, as were the corners of his eyes. He gave her another gap-toothed grin. "Have a glorious day! I hope you see everything!"

He set off around the house to where the workmen picked up sack lunches for their day. When she stepped down off the porch and onto the front walk, she could see the boy talking with them. The men slapped him on the back.

Frances found her mood vastly improved by the encounter, and five minutes later, she stood in front of the Marvel Theater, the centerpiece of Main Street. The marquee announced two films, one for prime time and one for the matinee hours: *The Hangman* and *The Hound of the Baskervilles*. Rosey was on a ladder, at work on the lights.

"Jimmy find you?" he called, seeing her there.

"If you mean that kid who came to charm my socks off, yes. He asked if I was happy to walk over."

Rosey laughed. "Yep, that'd be Jimmy. I'm running behind. Had a couple of bulbs go out, and we can't have that. Got to light up the night—otherwise this town would roll up the carpet and go to bed as soon as the sun goes down." He turned back to the second-floor open window beside the marquee and spoke to an Indian man leaning out there. "Can you get this ladder down for me, Will? Merry's here for the tour. She's the new spirit in town."

"My name is Frances, and I haven't said yes to anything yet."

Whatever the man inside said to Rosey, they laughed. Frances pulled her shoulders back, pretending she hadn't noticed. Rosey climbed down and jumped to the ground before reaching the bottom rung, dusting his hands on his pants.

"Watch it or I'll raise your rent," Rosey called back to the man upstairs. Then he said to Frances, "You two will get along great. Couple of college-educated wise guys. Will thinks he's smarter than me, but I'm older by two months and I put a roof over his head, so that makes me the big brother." He winked at Frances. "He rents the room above the theater."

Will called after them jovially, "You're not the boss of me, old man. Hey, don't listen to anything he tells you." He gave a salute before pulling the window shut.

"He works for you?"

"With me. It's me and Will and Jimmy, that's the crew at the Marvel, so you've met us all. When we came home from Korea, I convinced Will to come to Revery and partner up running the Marvel. He's from Oklahoma, some reservation out there. He's

Cherokee. But he was scouting around after we were back state-side, deciding where he wanted to settle down. He's taken that projector apart and put it back together a couple times now. I'd be dead in the water without him, so he got the view from the room over the marquee. I moved out to my dad's old houseboat."

"Really? A houseboat?"

"Floats, but it doesn't run. Been sitting there so long it's grown roots. But every night she gives me dreams of saltwater creeks."

Frances couldn't help imagining the berth beneath such a boat, a tiny bed for this larger-than-life man. She hurried to change the subject. "I grew up in the mountains."

"Ah, but all rivers lead to the sea." He had a quick answer for everything. "Anyway, if we're gonna start a history tour of Revery, might as well start with the Marvel Theater. This place sat empty a good few years. We had our work cut out for us. But now look at her." He was obviously proud of his investment. "Originally it opened in 1929. The first theater in the Southeast built for talkies."

"Incredible. And dangerous work?" Rosey looked confused. Frances could tease too. "What's wrong with Jimmy's hand?"

"Ah, you saw that? He's part racoon. Couldn't resist sticking it where it shouldn't have been. He got bit by a mink trap out on Cumberland," he explained. "Just a couple of stitches. It'll heal."

"Yikes." She was grateful when he didn't make her ask the other obvious questions about the boy but explained as if Jimmy were only another part of the tour, something she thought he might have done many times based on how the words rolled off his tongue.

"It's rare, what Jimmy's got. They call it elfin face syndrome, but they don't know much about it. He's got a weak heart. Doesn't slow him down much, although he doesn't go to school anymore.

But he loves the movies. Very dramatic. Will reads to him a lot. And you ask him any song, he knows it. He never meets a stranger. Honestly, he's part of the reason I bought this place."

"What does he do at the theater?"

"Well, one day maybe he'll do more. He's learning. Right now he does what a lot of kids do for their first jobs: Stocks candy. Changes reels. Earns some spending money. But if you stick around long enough, you'll see he's more or less busy just being Jimmy. People come to the Marvel to see movies, sure, but sometimes they just come to see Jimmy. He's different from most people in a lot of ways, but the thing about Jimmy is that he is a person with purpose and he lives like it. If God took everything good about Revery and made one person out of it, that'd be Jimmy. And I figured that's where I wanted to put my money."

One thing was clear: Rosey Devane was devoted to the boy and to his friends and to his town. It showed on his face when he talked about them. When she asked if he'd always lived in Revery, he said, "Hard to leave a place where the tide runs both ways; you just end up carried back where you started from. The draft's about the only way you'll shoehorn most of us out of here. Glenn's the only one of us who volunteered—Jimmy's daddy. But they didn't take him on account he's a widower with a dependent. He's forever looking for some way to make up for it. I remind him he's had his glory days. He was the biggest football star Revery ever knew. No surprise he's a Piedmont man now, to the core."

Frances stiffened, hearing the name, but tried to keep her tone light. "Piedmont man? What's that mean?"

"That's what we call the fellas who work out at the paper mill. There's the fishermen, there's the folks in town, like me, and there's Piedmont men who make their living pulling shifts out at the mill."

"But not you."

"No mills for me. I'm in movies and tours."

"And ghosts."

"Well, yeah. Ghosts. Honestly, I thought the novelty would wear off by now. It started out as straight history tours. But less people are going to the movies now everybody's got a boob tube at home, and history can be a little dry. Throw in a haunting or two and watch them line up out the door. Ghost stories pay the bills."

"Sounds to me like you're a Revery man."

Rosey's delight was evident. "I believe I'm going to use that."

She saw something play across Rosey's face, a thought he didn't share, and then he gave her that razzle-dazzle smile she'd seen that first day on his boat.

———

It was hotter than Hades and the heat bugs droned in the tall grass between the buildings in downtown Revery, but Frances was charmed by the sleepy streets of the historic town and she listened with interest as Rosey pointed out landmarks like old friends. He rambled on about the history of the Spanish missions of the 1500s and the Timucua Indians, about the town's early days in the 1700s when the Spanish and British clashed, and about a group of oppressed French Acadians who suffered and died from an outbreak of yellow fever. He pointed out oaks planted to commemorate the death of George Washington and memorials for every war and talked of Kings Bay Army Terminal downriver, established by the army at the start of the Cold War to allow for rapid movement of forces and supplies in a national emergency.

"It's pretty quiet out that way now. But you can't convince folks around here to stop looking for Russian subs in the water," he said, looking out on the water from where they strolled along the river-walk. "Or commies on land."

He ticked off facts about the industry over the years—fishing, lumber, canneries, the railroad. He pointed out examples of architecture, the oldest homes and churches that had survived Sherman's march. She nodded and smiled with interest, but none of it was really what she'd come to see in Revery. They stopped inside a pharmacy with a lunch counter that stood near the Esso and the bus station at the other end of the street from the riverfront, and he treated her to a Coca-Cola. They were circling back past the theater when he pointed to a building next door. She'd walked right past it earlier; now she could see if she'd been paying attention, she'd have noticed the Piedmont name etched into the stone above the door.

"See that little place there? The Piedmont family founded that, same year as the paper mill. You'll find everything that was ever written up about our river siren sightings. They keep a little folder and call it an archive to make it sound official."

Frances stared at the neat tabby building. "It's not very big, is it?"

"Well, it's just a dusty little place for a dusty little story. They've got a board of old gray heads that likes to approve everything inside, so it's pretty limited, as you can imagine. Lucky they don't have their mitts on the theater too. You've got to go over to New Canaan for a real public library. The thing about this library is it's a memorial to Ellis Piedmont. Only Piedmont I know of to actually set foot down here. The rest live up in Philadelphia someplace."

They stood on the walk while he told the story, some of the details filling in the cracks of the story she knew.

"Back in the summer of '32, the Carnegies—specifically, Dr. Marius Johnston, husband of Nancy Carnegie—had guests out to Plum Orchard for shooting and fishing. There was a long-standing tradition of bonfires and storytelling. You can take the Scots out of Scotland, but you can't stop them telling stories round fires. The season Cleo got hired on, she took a mink stole from a closet and joined the party. She had them convinced they could see something out in the water, a river siren, and two boys drowned. The way I've heard it, it had been a wild week already and everybody stayed pretty liquored up. There'd been an incident the day before at the Dungeness pool that got a girl sent to the hospital. She was the intended for one of the guests, Ellis Piedmont, the original Piedmont man."

This was what Frances had been waiting to hear. She felt her pulse quicken, knowing the girl must have been her mother. And she knew how Piedmont's story ended, of course. "I read some about this. He was one of the ones that drowned," she said.

She'd had time to get used to the fact, but she wished just then that she felt something more than anger at having been lied to her whole life. It seemed cold not to grieve an unfortunate young man just a little, even if she'd never known him. But when she thought of Ellis Piedmont, it was with detachment, and inevitably she then thought of Owen Flood and she missed her daddy.

Rosey nodded. "Yup. It was an accidental drowning, but the liquor played a role. And somebody had a gun. The others said it was hard to tell exactly what happened, but Cleo got shot. Put a hole straight through her middle. She spent a long time recovering at Plum Orchard. Piedmont blamed Lumas Gray, a Negro boy who worked for the family. That's what Ellis was screaming about when it happened. Both of them went into the high water in the dark."

Frances shivered, even in the heat.

"That's when everybody went crazy for the siren, reporting

sightings. Now, it's been years since anybody saw anything. But you never know," he teased, taking a lighter tone after the morbid story. "Gotta keep your eyes peeled for water monsters and commies, you know." He grinned. "The building itself, though, now that's interesting. If the walls could talk, they'd tell you some scandalous tales, I'd bet. It used to be the old courthouse; an office, a courtroom, and a couple of jail cells. And the books in there, most of them came straight out of the library at Dungeness mansion, the grandest old house over on Cumberland. That was Lumas Gray's favorite haunt, so he's followed his books over here."

"You're joking." He could sell anything, she thought.

"Oh, it's true. These days people report seeing lights moving inside the Piedmont Library after midnight." She admired the agility with which he'd brought his story right back around to connect to his ghost tour. "Good old Lumas, still watching over those books he loved."

"Convenient for you."

He noted Frances's expression. "I didn't mean to upset you. It's only a ghost story."

"I know that. But it's my mother's story. She was Ellis Piedmont's intended." He looked surprised. "See, that's how I feel about it too. I had no idea. When she died recently, she told me. She sent me here to commission a painting from Cleo Woodbine."

Rosey's brows lifted. "Well, then." He took a closer look at her as if he might see something he'd missed. "Talk about burying the lead, lady."

Frances sighed. "Story of my life."

He was good enough to let it go. It couldn't have been hard to see that she didn't want to talk about it anymore, and Rosey Devane was nothing if not a man who understood timing. They continued to the final stop on any history or ghost tour, the cemetery at the edge of town, near a grove of oaks.

Rosey stopped several yards away from the neatly tended graves and gave her a wry smile. "Everybody who's anybody is over there," he said, pointing behind a delicate iron fence. "But over here we have Merry. You ready for this one?"

Rosey worked hard to lift her mood, and Frances let her interest shift to the unremarkable little stone. "So who was she and why is she wandering?"

"Merry's a restless soul, buried in unhallowed ground with just this little marker that says her first name. Who she was, nobody knows. Some say she was an Indian princess who lived here long before Revery. Some say she was a wife to one of the boys who fought in the Revolution; sometimes he's a patriot, sometimes a redcoat. Some say she was an immigrant from the first days of the town and her child died from yellow fever and was buried at sea. I've also heard she was a Civil War Southern belle with a favorite brother who went off to fight Yankees. You can pretty much substitute any war, but the boy she loved never came home. Any way you tell it, she's never to rest on account of lost love."

"Give me a break." Frances rolled her eyes. "That sounds like one of those sad records Audrey Howell plays at the inn. Or the Lorelei myth. Why are women always trapped, cursed, or grieving in these kinds of stories?"

He'd stopped, hands on hips. "How's that?"

"Maybe she just stays here because she loves it."

She hesitated and he blinked at her. He began to nod as if she'd confirmed all his convictions. "You're hired."

They agreed he would take her out to tour Cumberland on Thursday, leaving the dock at seven in the morning. He offered to provide lunch. Frances didn't know if it was standard for the tour, but she was too shy to ask and take the risk of embarrassing herself.

When night fell and again she saw Rosey Devane carry his lantern to lead his ghost tour through town, she donned the frothy white nightdress, hair loose over her shoulders, and walked to the dock. She stood quietly gazing over the water as Rosey had directed her to do, then wandered farther away and into the shadows of the oaks. The tenderhearted on the tour found themselves weeping. And Rosey Devane put a hand to his heart.

Chapter Eight

AUDREY

EVERY MORNING SINCE SHE'D COME TO GILBREATH HOUSE, Audrey hurried past the empty room at the end of the upstairs foyer. It was silly to avoid a pleasant, well-lit space with a pretty bed and curtains on the window. She didn't believe the room was haunted any more than she believed in spirit photography or that Frances Flood in a white nightgown was fooling anybody on Rosey's tour last night. But the sight of that room always seemed sad to Audrey in a very real way. When she looked through the doorway, Audrey felt she might have something in common with Cleo Woodbine, who had never come to take that room. There were reasons some people couldn't accept comfort.

By her count, today she was six months along with the baby. Anyone might have seen the truth if they'd caught her at just the right angle, even though she was barely showing. And although most days now the grip of nausea had finally turned her loose, it might still come over her without warning if she was tired or hadn't eaten enough. But even if she could have continued to hide her pregnancy from everyone in town right up until the day she went into labor, Audrey knew she should have already seen a doctor. When she'd been at the Fernandina hospital with Rosey waiting for Jimmy to have his hand treated, she'd almost revealed the truth about her situation. She might have done it, had Glenn Walker not shown up.

She was grateful that Glenn had accepted the story they'd told and that he'd tried to comfort her about Jimmy's accident and the twelve stitches that resulted, assuring her that he did not hold her responsible. But she had kept her mouth shut about her pregnancy, lest he try to swoop in to the rescue. He'd been so nice about everything that she'd felt like she couldn't just quit the ghost photography right then. By the time she got back to the inn, she felt like she was the ghost in town, dragging a chain behind her. When she thought about her life in Revery, she realized the real Audrey was disappearing day by day. There was nothing true about the girl she was becoming. About the only time she felt like herself was when she opened the side door in the mornings to the colored men waiting to buy sack lunches on their way to their labor.

With dust on their faces and grease under their nails, they'd frightened Audrey at first. But they spoke softly, thanked her or paid her a compliment on what a good job she was doing. On occasion one of them might mention he thought her aunt would be proud of how she was running the inn. She'd started adding a bit of extra to their meals. She didn't say anything if they sat in the garden out back to cool off.

Her mother never would have approved of Audrey continuing with that arrangement. She'd have been shocked her sister had started it in the first place. Had she known anything about it, Mimi would have shut it down right quick. Likely, she had in mind that Audrey was weeding her flower beds religiously and serving everything up on fine china, the way she'd watched her mother do all her days. But Audrey was learning every day that she was not like Mimi. And what Mimi didn't know wouldn't hurt her. Besides, if her mother had wanted to know about Audrey's life in Revery, then why hadn't she ever asked? Audrey tried not to think too hard about that. Or the fact that as much as they had their differences, avoiding a problem was something they very much had in common.

Audrey could say this: if running Gilbreath House was good for anything, it was good for distractions. She enjoyed feeding kindling into the woodstove each day. The smells of biscuits baking in Shirley's oven and ham warming in Shirley's pan filled Audrey's nose. She could breathe easy while that fire burned. She cranked up Freddie's records, playing Johnny Cash and Elvis Presley loud enough to wake the dead (which was about what needed doing since all the regulars at brunch seemed a hundred years old). She was on a Patsy Cline kick lately, especially "Walkin' After Midnight."

This morning Frances Flood had come down to eat and then Audrey had watched her go out to settle on the back porch with a stack of magazines. Audrey had left her to it, glad to see her out of her room. She was curious about the other young woman, and maybe lonely for a friend. She reminded herself to give her guest privacy even if what Audrey really wanted was to sit out there with her and talk about anything normal. Instead, Audrey tried to focus on her own work. After all, these visitors would come and go. Audrey had to make a life here.

Staying busy was the key. That, and the air-conditioning at the Marvel. By afternoon, she decided to slip away. Her guests were out for the day, and Rosey had given her a free pass for a matinee. If she hurried, she could have herself some popcorn and a box of Boston Baked Beans like any regular twenty-year-old, even if she wasn't roller-skating or smoking behind the gym or out on the beach getting her summer tan.

The Hound of the Baskervilles was playing, which suited Audrey, who didn't want any sappy romance in her face. Gothic horror soothed her soul. Bring on the strange inheritances, the grisly murders, the howling wolfhounds, the tragic overacting. Bring on the missing portrait, the stolen dagger, the webbed fingers. She'd seen the movie twice already.

The theater was crowded with local high school kids roughhousing in the seats in the back. She still felt like one of them, but she could see that when they looked at her, they did not see a girl close to their own age. Freddie being dead so soon had been a shock, but maybe more so was how his death now defined her life. Freddie had gone on to some place, some life after this, she hoped, but Audrey had no idea where she belonged.

She took a seat near the front and tried to think of something else. Inevitably she thought of Jimmy. Now, that kid was a great distraction. His hair was nothing but a sable cap over his skull, buzzed off. She'd noticed that first off when she'd seen him, the way he ran his hand over the top of his head like he was calming a soft animal. He had large brown eyes that gave her a dreamy impression, and underneath his clothes he was slim and vulnerable. Puberty was still on his horizon, although he had that coat-hanger look to his shoulders that boys get before their muscles catch up with their broadening bones to fill in the outline of a man. Glenn was looking for a mother to help with that boy, but he was wasting his time looking at Audrey. She felt closer to Jimmy's age than his daddy's. Or maybe she just wished she could stay a kid and life could stay innocent.

When the picture burst onto the screen, she sat back in the dark and finally relaxed. That was why she nearly jumped out of her skin when a finger poked her upper arm. Jimmy had appeared in the seat next to hers as if she'd conjured him up. He practically glowed in the dark, his fair complexion lit by the light from the movie screen, his expression one of happy anticipation. She was ridiculously pleased to see him too. He leaned close, although he was looking straight ahead and not at her at all. She could see the bandage on his hand gleaming in the light from the movie screen, a white boxing glove. He took her hand with his good one, warm and sweaty. His breath smelled of cherry candy.

She didn't withdraw. His touch was so light and trusting, and she waited to see what he would do next. She let him lead her up the side aisle and out of the auditorium while the movie played. The lobby was empty, but they didn't stop there.

"How's your hand?" she asked.

"I'll have a scar," he said. He was pleased.

He held on to her and pulled her along through a side door that opened to a narrow hallway. They could hear the soundtrack, and Audrey realized they'd come around to the back of the movie screen to a sort of stage area. When he turned to really look at her for the first time, she was surprised he frowned, and she felt uncomfortable. But he seemed to immediately decide something. Tucked into his armpit, she saw he held a book, and now that he'd let go of her, he pulled it out. Smoothing the cover, he offered it to her without raising his gaze to meet hers.

"What's this?" Audrey asked. She squinted in the dim light to make out the title of the thin little paperback book he'd handed to her. *Our Town*. It was a script. "Where'd you get this?"

"Do you want to be friends?"

"Well, sure."

"Do you want to sneak candy?"

Audrey smiled. "I don't think we should do that."

"It's not stealing. Uncle Rosey says if I'm hungry, I should eat."

"Okay, but is that all you eat?" The kid was growing up in a fantastic bachelor pad, she realized. But one look at him and it was obvious he could use a proper meal. "If you want, you can come to the inn. I have so much food there. So much fruit." She was thinking it might do him some good.

"I come there all the time," he said.

"Oh, I've seen you in the yard. You can come inside, you know." She was about to ask after Harl and Nan Buie, but the Indian guy who worked as an usher, Will Tremmons, stepped out of nowhere. He was Rosey's friend. They'd served together and come back from the war and bought the theater. She'd seen Will plenty when she'd been taking photos. He wore little round wire-framed glasses and Glenn made fun of him, calling him a wise old owl, but Glenn was three years older than Rosey and Will, already in his thirties, and he seemed like a different generation to Audrey. Rosey and Will seemed like teenagers, maybe because they were still free and single.

Today Will had on his theater uniform, all buttoned up, and carried a little broom and dustpan. She thought he looked like somebody's butler, not like he ought to be sweeping up after teenagers. But what did she know? She didn't look like an innkeeper either, did she?

"Hey, buddy," he said to Jimmy. "Rosey'll be after you to get sweeping up. He'll put your girlfriend to work."

"She's not my girlfriend, she's Audrey," Jimmy said, giggling at the teasing. Audrey smiled at him. "She's a girl and my friend. She said I can come eat all her fruit. She's going to be in our play."

"I never said I'd be in a play."

Will smiled. His dark eyes shone behind his glasses and Audrey found herself smiling back. "Well, it's not really a play, but you're welcome to join. It's not a full-on production, only a read-through."

"We're reading it together after the matinee," Jimmy said. "You're here and you can be all the girls. Will's all the boys. I'm the stage manager."

"No auditions, then?" Audrey relaxed a little and thought how she'd rather be at the theater with Jimmy than back at the inn, alone. "Okay, sure."

"Come on. We need to rehearse." Jimmy grabbed her hand and pulled her behind him.

They went up a set of stairs to the rooms above the theater that Rosey rented to Will. Audrey would have protested, but she was curious to see the space where the Indian man lived, and when she did, she was further surprised to see all the stacks of books and newspapers on the floor, on tables, on shelves all around the living room. Classics Audrey recognized, like a big volume of Shakespeare, a worn Bible, but also a copy of James Baldwin's *Go Tell It on the Mountain,* which was splayed open on top of these other books as if it had only just been put down by the reader. And beside it, she was a little shocked to see a copy of *The Boy Came Back* by Charles H. Knickerbocker. A kid at her high school had written an entire essay about the book's banning and why it was vulgar and communistic.

Glancing at a corkboard, Audrey saw Will Tremmons was interested in more than reading. There were pamphlets and flyers of all sorts, mostly about meetings in New Canaan to do with integration, and she saw a few about the water conservation efforts and concerns of runoff from the Piedmont Paper Mill. There'd been talk that the mill needed to clean up the river. Glenn had been going on about it being political, about it costing jobs because the mill was having to cut shifts. She was unclear on any actual facts. She'd honestly stopped listening to him.

But she knew if he saw all of this, it would upset him. Now she was rethinking being upstairs.

She stood, not willing to move anything aside to make space to take a seat on the sofa or a chair. Even the little dinette table had books on it. "Will won't care if we're up here without him?" she asked Jimmy.

"Nah. He doesn't care," Jimmy said, bouncing on the balls of his feet. He poked a finger at the script she was still holding and Audrey smiled at his enthusiasm. "Okay. Where do you want to start?"

"At the beginning?" Audrey said. "But shouldn't we wait until we're all here?"

Jimmy began to orate, projecting loudly and dramatically without referring to the script. It seemed he'd already memorized large parts of it. Audrey followed his lead but only read the female characters. She'd read the play before, in school, but she'd paid so little attention to it then. She'd been bored by it, in fact. Now she was hearing the lines differently as understanding dawned. The play was about death, about small towns, about her own life.

They'd been at it like that, never sitting, on their feet in the center of the room for at least half an hour before Will joined them. The matinee had ended and the next show wouldn't be until the evening at seven. He stepped in mid-scene and Audrey was so entertained as he played the roles, encouraging her to mime and move around the room as if they were onstage, that she soon forgot to be nervous. He was taller than her, but only by a few inches. His dark hair was cut short, still looking very much like he was in the military. But there was an elegance to Will Tremmons, and she was curious about him. She'd never really known an Indian, and he was not at all what she'd imagined. It embarrassed her to consider that she'd only ever thought of them as people being marched along the Trail of Tears or riding horses in Western films. And she realized the three of them were not what Thornton Wilder had had in mind for his cast. It made her feel a little rebellious, but also a bit grateful that no one would ever be the wiser of their play.

They laughed and grew serious, too, when the play called for it. And soon act two had her standing opposite Will Tremmons for the wedding of Emily and George. She was enjoying herself so much that she didn't notice the point when they were no longer alone until Glenn spoke from the doorway.

"What the hell? Jimmy, get downstairs and wait on me."

Jimmy shot out of the room like a bolt and Audrey blinked, feeling as if she'd been jerked back to reality and given some sort of mental whiplash.

"We're reading a play," she said. "Jimmy's really good. He already knows most of the lines." Her voice sounded weak even in her own ears.

Glenn glared at her and she felt herself shrink, although she wasn't sure why. "What are you doing in this man's rooms? Does Rosey know about this?"

"We're just reading *Our Town*."

"Didn't look like any kind of reading to me."

Audrey felt her temper rise, but Will stepped back from her purposefully and said, "I'm sorry for upsetting everybody. Maybe we ought to call it a day."

"Call it a day?" Glenn bellowed. He pointed a finger at Will. "If I ever get wind of you having Jimmy up here by hisself with you again, I'll have you run out of this town. Reading who knows what kind of thing."

"What kind of thing?" Will asked calmly.

"I heard enough to know you're over in New Canaan every chance you get, pushing all kinds of ideas, Red." Audrey cringed at all the implications of the slur he'd used. Will's expression remained calm. "You're with that group that's about to cost us our jobs out at the mill. And I know how the ones like you came back from Korea."

"A veteran?"

"I'm a patriot and that's better than a veteran. I don't want you selling any socialist ideas to my kid."

"You've gotten hold of some misinformation," Will said, his voice steady and low.

Audrey felt it provoked Glenn all the same. Her head was spinning. She couldn't even remember how she'd gotten herself into the middle of this standoff, then remembered Jimmy. "Somebody should go check on Jimmy," she said. She could tell Glenn wasn't listening.

"Rosey's done you every kind of favor and look how you're doing him. Up here with this girl. Knowing what people will talk like if they hear about it."

"Why would they talk?" Will asked. "Her husband just died. She's being friendly to your little boy. They're both lonely."

Audrey was mortified. She felt the heat of embarrassment rush through her, but she couldn't move from the spot where she stood. Glenn blocked the exit.

"I saw what I saw when I came in here. I saw you grabbing her," he said.

"Excuse me, I'm going to be sick," she finally blurted and hurried down to the lobby and through the front doors until she was standing on the street. All she wanted was to put a cold cloth on the back of her neck. She didn't see Jimmy anywhere, and she was grateful for that, at least, as she retched into some shrubbery. She didn't realize until she was back at the inn that she still had the script clutched in her hand.

Chapter Nine

CLEO

AFTER TWO ATTEMPTS TO WASH OUT THE SMELL, CLEO DECLARED her favorite pair of pants a lost cause and tossed them outside to keep the lingering stench of mink urine well away from the house. Meanwhile, the mink itself was holding its own since she'd brought it back to the cottage, tucked comfortably into a towel in a peach basket. Tate had not been by to check in as he'd promised, but Cleo had done her best for the animal, salving up the broken skin around its back end where the trap's jaws had fastened on it, even knowing the effort to try to save it was a fool's errand. She'd be setting herself up for heartache to think differently.

"I'm sorry those nincompoops have done this to you," she said to the little soul in the corner while it trembled and clung to life. She wondered if and when she finally did leave Woodbine Cottage whether this nonsense would stop. Or if boys would go right on killing things and throwing them at this place, just finding some new excuse to do it.

Cleo stood looking at the crack in her foundation. For a long time, the crack had been thin as fishing line, but it was steadily snaking up from the ground, inch by inch. She didn't need Tate Walker or anybody else to tell her the shoals were shifting. She didn't have to believe in the superstitions of old sailors about a storm of the century bearing down on them this summer. Change was coming for Cleo one way or another, just like the bed of the river had grown shallower with every tide, just like that little crack had crept as high as her windowsill on the east side of the house and grown as wide as her thumb. She marked its progress by what she could see, measuring by the oyster shells embedded in the wall, by her own height, and by the other cracks that had begun to appear in the ceiling. Invisible progress was revealed by new leaks in her roof caused by shifts in the eaves. No, there was no denying what was going on.

Boom, boom, boom. The footfalls of that invisible Timucuan giant walked her dreams, the spirit of the island itself mixed up in her imagination with the memory of Lumas Gray since that day she'd painted that giant in the back of Dooley's book, telling her she'd overstayed her welcome.

The problem was, Cleo couldn't imagine what she'd find beyond that far horizon she'd been staring at all these years any more than she could seem to put paint to paper for Joanna's commissioned memorial. This was for her daughter, a girl Cleo had never known. Never once had Cleo considered such a person existed, much less how that changed the story of that summer. For all she'd pondered while she sat here with her own guilty conscience, she'd learned not one lesson on life that helped her know what to do for that girl now.

And so, until she could think of something, there was nothing to do but what she always did. For certain, she was not going to continue to wait around on Tate Walker to show back up.

Cleo wondered if she ought to put anything out for the mink before she left the cottage. She'd only be away for a few hours, but now there were things to consider that had never crossed her mind when there'd been only herself to think about. She peeked at the little ball of fur and didn't think it was going to leap up for a snack, but at least she could leave a saucer of water. The best she could manage was a screw-top lid from a coffee can, and she set it close enough to the basket that the animal ought to be able to reach its skinny neck and take a drink. She felt better having settled that question, but no sooner had she made it down the front step with her empty basket than she stopped to debate whether she ought to have left the door open for the thing to escape or if it was a worse risk that it might be eaten up by some passing creature.

She closed her eyes to try to clear the worry in her head. She'd never kept a dog or even fed a tomcat. The closest communion she'd had with animals on the island was with the ones she'd brought to rest in the boneyard. Of late, she'd enjoyed hearing the coyotes and bobcats at night. But when she opened her eyes this day and glanced out the window, she'd only seen the grim as Dooley had painted her, there at the edge of the yard. She was glad it was this figment her mind conjured today. That black lab was always the most comforting of the tagalongs.

She seemed to smile at Cleo, if dogs could smile, with her whiskery chin feathered white like a beard. For the mink's sake, Cleo decided the door ought to stay closed.

The dog sat near her in the boat like a shadow, and when Cleo made stops along the way, the old girl traipsed around but was ready to rejoin Cleo when she moved on. They traveled through Cleo's favorite inlets, working their way south again and into the marshes that branched off the East River below Dungeness, stopping to trip more of the mink traps, glad there were no signs along the shore of Jimmy Walker or the Buie kids out taking chances. She thought of returning to the place where she'd lost Tate's watch but made herself pass on by. It was no use sifting through a thousand years of silt.

Daylight was already getting away from her by the time she'd collected the loquats and muscadine from near Dungeness. Her basket was heavy. The island was giving up such a bounty as Cleo had never seen, or at least it seemed that way to her. It didn't need her. That was the underlying truth she'd learned about Cumberland. She often wondered if Dooley had ever realized it. Had he understood his insignificance while the river rolled on into the future, ever shifting, ever the same?

She paused at a little statue—like a banty rooster, the god Mercury with his horn perched atop a pedestal—near the old rose garden at Dungeness, out of place as anything else the Carnegies had built. She'd learned once from Rosey about this cupid-looking boy, a messenger of fortune and gossip, one foot in this world and one in the next. Just then he put her in mind of Tate Walker. He'd left out on those trains for all these years and come back to tell the tale. Maybe he'd teach her the trick to it. As soon as she thought it, she grimaced, irked he'd come to mind again.

She was anxious about the mink and didn't know if she hoped to return to find it had expired or miraculously healed. That was a thing she'd forgotten about hope, how it only serves to remind you there's so much to lose.

She'd been lost in her thoughts when she came to the dock to leave the basket, but when she approached the edge of the forest, she was stopped by the sounds of men arguing. She crept forward, out of sight, drawing only close enough to overhear the conversation. It carried easily on the breeze. One voice belonged to Tate Walker. The other she didn't know. She could have stayed there to eavesdrop, but even Cleo had her scruples. Also, she felt the pressure to get back to the cottage and her basket was exceptionally full. She decided to make herself known and get about her own business. She set her load down with a loud thud at the end of the dock. Both men looked up.

"You two are disturbing my peace," she said. The second man seemed familiar, but then, all the outdoorsmen who showed up on the shoals looked the same to her. The thing that caught her attention was the small rifle he held at his side. "Doing some shooting?"

"That's what we were just discussing," Tate said, keeping his tone easy. "Seeing as small game's not in season till this winter, I said I was surprised at seeing him."

The other man spoke up. "We're on island time on Cumberland. Seasons work about the same, wouldn't you say? There's a little wager going on to see who can get that old bobcat. Did you know it's the same one been out here nearly thirty years? They say those cats can live that long in captivity, but I never heard of one."

Cleo felt the blood rush into her face, furious at another one of these jackasses. But she didn't recognize the sound of him.

Tate said, "I was admiring his .22 but told him I think it'd be a shame to take a life like that one."

Cleo narrowed her eyes as she watched the stranger shift his weight and lift his gun to rest in the crook of his arm. "I'd listen to him," Cleo said. "There're mink traps being set all down the creeks and I've had a mind to report it. That wouldn't be you, would it? I thought that was little boys, but now I might think again."

The man had the gall to laugh at her. "Cleo Woodbine, as I live and breathe. I figured you'd be long gone from here by now."

"You know the Carnegies keep a woodsman to watch out for such as you," she said, hoping if he knew enough to know her name, he'd know to heed the warning. "The Carnegies aren't feeling much like taking prisoners lately, I hear."

He let out a sharp laugh. "I don't believe Harl's gonna give me any trouble."

She squinted, trying to place the craggy face of the man, and she might have made a further point, but then she saw that black dog lope down the dock and take a seat at his side. She had believed all day long that the animal on her heels was one of her imaginary tag-alongs. Now she watched, goggle-eyed, as Tate laid a hand on top of the dog's head and she leaned heavily against his leg, real as real could be.

"Is this your dog?" Tate called to her.

The other man was grumbling something about that and reached to grab the dog by the scruff. She couldn't hear him well enough to understand. But to her dismay, there was that buzzing in her head, that feeling she'd gone all woozy. Cleo couldn't even answer him.

She swayed a little on her feet, feeling the same as that day on the creek when she'd pitched over and lost that watch. What was she losing now? Her mind? The sand of her good sense was slipping out from under her, same as the shifting of the shoals. She sure as hell had a crack in her foundation if she couldn't tell what was real anymore.

She gave the men a wave and turned to hurry away while she still stood on her feet. Somehow she managed to get all the way back to the cottage without giving out. Back on the cottage steps, she yanked her muddy shoes off her feet, sitting spraddle-legged until she could calm down. She couldn't stand the thought of somebody shooting that cat out of pure meanness, but she was about as likely to stop it as she was to control the tides. Mink were one thing, she thought, but that cat had been here for decades, perhaps as long as her. And recently she'd seen tracks, sets of twelve. She knew there were kittens. By the size of the prints, nearly grown, but it didn't make Cleo feel any better about what she'd just heard. If they'd kill one, they'd kill them all. She thought of that gun and she thought of Harl Buie and she wished she'd kept her mouth shut.

Chapter Ten

FABLE

IN THE MONTH OF JUNE, WHEN THE WATERS OFFSHORE TEEMED with mysteries and migrations, almost nothing slept through the muggy nights on Cumberland Island. Loggerhead turtles, some weighing over three hundred pounds, crawled ashore from the deep to secretly lay their eggs by dark. Come dawn, the unlucky would likely be found and plundered by wild hogs or careless boys. This summer, a bobcat began to be heard in the maritime forests each night, its unsettling screams so like a woman's that they wrenched the guests at Plum Orchard from their slumber before they'd even begun to dream, making them grumpy, leaving their thoughts muddled, and throwing off their aim for the next day's hunt. Their hatred for the cat became the focus of most of the conversations Cleo overheard, their plans to shoot the animal for a prize. She doubted any one of them was the kind of shot to be a threat, and she enjoyed hearing the animal while she lay in her bed, if only because she had riled the young men. She'd smiled, watching them march away from the house, then back again, defeated.

Over the next four days, Cleo spent no time with Lumas Gray. Instead, she met Ellis Piedmont on the second-story porch. He'd lied and told the others he'd rather spend his time reading as they set out on their hunts. Plum Orchard became a playground for Ellis and Cleo. They had games of squash on the courts, chased each other through the gardens and rooms, wondered at Dr. Johnston's collections from his safaris—heads mounted on walls, flotsam he'd collected from the island. And in between all of that, they'd lounged away the hours. No one paid attention to them or objected to the way they passed their time.

Almost immediately, Ellis had talked her into coming to the table for meals. Introductions were so offhand Cleo wondered why she'd ever been nervous. She might as well have been another piece of furniture in the room for all the interest the others showed in her. She enjoyed Ellis smiling behind his napkin at dinner or touching the side of her leg. If Mrs. O'Dowd disapproved, she didn't dare speak to Cleo about it.

One by one, she recounted Dooley's folktales just as he'd told them to her, but he was not so charmed as Lumas had been. Once she brought the book with his watercolor illustrations. Ellis thought they were hilarious, especially the most recent one, her own original work, the painting of the Timucuan giant. Ellis said he'd never met a girl who made him laugh like her. She hadn't meant to be funny, but she only heard a compliment.

One afternoon they swam in the indoor pool at Plum Orchard, or rather, she swam while Ellis watched her from his place on the steps that ran the side of the pool. He'd never learned to swim and would not be persuaded to try. All of the big Carnegie houses on the island had pools such as these, she'd learned. But the one at Dungeness in the building called the Casino was the favorite. With sets of gymnastic rings strung across the middle of the pool, it was a great place for pranks in the dark. Guests on the island loved to go home with stories of high-flying feats on those rings, another of the many traditions the Carnegie family liked to keep. There were plans for the group to swim there nearer the end of their stay, with Ellis acting as judge of their games.

But for now, the games were only between Ellis and herself, with all of his attention on her face, her voice, her hands. It was all she could do to wait out the hours at night until the next morning when she could get back to their secret world.

He'd grown handsome to her eye in an unlikely way, with his milky skin and soft hair and eyes that were a deep brown so that in the dark they looked like bottomless holes. Ellis Piedmont was her first boy in so many ways, although their love remained chaste, and she believed it spoke to his character. She saw possibilities in him that the others did not, and she saw, too, how she could help him put himself forward within the group. She taught him all of the tricks to telling a good tale, but Ellis's confidence always faltered around the table. She saw so clearly what was needed. She remembered Dooley's insistence that glory was only for good, and she talked herself into believing it. After all, her grandmother had been the one to fear it and she'd had no imagination at all. Cleo could be both practical and full of fancy ideas. She believed a life worth living required a bit of both. The kind of life she wanted for herself. And for Ellis.

Before the week's end, she'd wheedled the location of the bone orchard out of the gardener, Mr. Meeks. The glen was not so far from Plum Orchard, where the bones of wild things rested beneath a quiet, mossy canopy and the cool green of resurrection ferns. She went there, not for herself but for the boy she was starting to love. She took what she'd gathered to her room and made the glory, crushing the seeds until she had a powder like the one she'd seen Dooley keep. Nervous she might miscalculate how much to use, she dropped only the lightest dusting over Ellis's plate the first night. The effects had been exactly as she'd hoped: a brighter countenance and a quicker smile. She wasn't the only one to notice. Thereafter, every time she administered the smallest sprinkling, it seemed a blessing.

She watched him at dinner, transformed from the rude young man to a charismatic golden boy, well liked, easier.

She enjoyed watching him seated close to Morrie Johnston at the dinner table or seeing Wally Flemming slap his shoulder when he told one of Dooley's old tales, even if the telling lacked the sparkling life to be truly remarkable. Cleo was sure he would only improve with practice. She swelled with satisfaction. She was the reason Ellis was rising in the estimation of his peers, even if he was none the wiser. It was a heady drug, her pride in him. And, too, she felt she'd proven Lumas Gray's fears of glory, and her own, unfounded for a girl who was careful and motivated by good intentions.

The days were slipping by so quickly that she barely noticed. In a blink, she'd passed two weeks at Plum Orchard, and with only one more before Dr. Johnston and Joanna arrived for the bonfire, she began to dread the end of their idyll and dream of more than summer days with Ellis, of marriage and a home. Woodbine Cottage and Kingdom Come were no longer her singular ambition. She wanted more. She could paint anywhere, and she said as much to Ellis, expecting he was dreaming the same.

But as the days passed, Ellis grew moody as a storm cloud and she spent a lot of her energy coaxing him back to high spirits. He kept secrets, but that was part of the reason she'd been drawn to him, the puzzle she couldn't work out. Cleo couldn't read Ellis's thoughts, and it only made her try all the harder for his approval.

He was nothing like Lumas Gray, who had been easy to trust. Ellis had caught them smoking a cigarette together as they'd done every night since that first one, behind the smokehouse. He'd made a joke, but later he made it clear he was disgusted that she had spent any time alone with a Negro boy.

"You know he's only after one thing," Ellis said. *"You're lucky it was me that caught you and not one of the Flemmings. Just give them an excuse and they'll make sport of him. It'll be his head hanging on Dr. Johnston's library wall, another safari trophy."*

It was a poor joke, but she knew there was enough truth behind it. She agreed she wouldn't see Lumas again, feeling a tightening in her stomach. She tried not to think of him alone in the library at Dungeness looking over the river basin and dreaming of that circus train. She reminded herself that she barely knew Lumas and he wouldn't give a second thought about her, just another guest to come and go from Cumberland. And even if she knew she owed him an explanation, it wasn't hard to distract herself. Ellis's attention had turned to her body and his hands roamed. When they stood on the steps of the pool at Plum Orchard, Cleo let him draw her close so their legs moved softly against each other. He said he loved her for her stories. Cleo wasn't sure if that meant he loved her for herself. She rested her hands on the tops of his shoulders. She thought he might kiss her, but he said he was a gentleman. Still, he made her believe it was a struggle to resist her beauty. She'd felt triumphant to have held his interest, until the evening he said to her, "Joanna will be here tomorrow, thank God. I've written and told her all of your stories. She's furious she's had to wait while we've been here ahead of her. She'll be determined to best you."

"Best me?" Cleo held very still, willing herself not to pull back at the mention of the other girl's imminent arrival. Realizing Ellis knew her. The girl she had almost completely forgotten. The one who would need a guard dog. The one Ellis seemed elated to welcome.

"She's going to fall in love with you. She'll be dying to work it all out."

"Work what out?"

"I'm making her guess how we'll win with our story at the bon-fire. I've convinced her that we'll have the best. You won't make me a liar, will you? You'll tell a terrific, terrifying, unforgettable tale? She can't stand not knowing the details. There are no mysteries in our circles, you know. All of us paired up before we could even walk. Arranged. Promised."

Ellis watched for her reaction, reminding her of that first day on the porch when they'd started playing this game, and Cleo couldn't do anything to hide her feelings as he continued to talk.

"We have to find our entertainments, don't we? Oh, don't worry, the fun's just beginning. Believe me, when she meets you, Joanna will wear you like a crown. She'll have you for her maid of honor at our wedding if you're not careful."

———

They were not yet engaged. The correct word was *promised*. Joanna Burton arrived wearing a little ring to show for it, but as soon as she was away from Ellis, Cleo watched as she poked her finger in her mouth and sucked on it until the ring loosened. She tossed it into a dish on the dresser in her finely appointed room. The girl with the cupid's bow lips looked at it and pouted.

"This was not my idea. They're auctioning me off like they do everything else. That's what my father does. Burton Antiques, Fine Art and Collectibles." Her round face lacquered with boredom, rouge, and powder, she threw herself across her bed on her belly in her underthings, ankles crossed behind her and swinging in the air while she told this to Cleo and complained of the heat.

Nothing had been announced of the arrangement between the Burtons and the Piedmonts. This was the thing that kept Cleo from flinging herself into the pond at Plum Orchard where Cleo had heard an old alligator lurked.

"I don't know how you can stand it down here." She observed Cleo for a moment, then said, "Ellis said you were keeping him company until I got here, so hopefully you're fully trained now. What I want to know is, what the hell is there to do in this place besides sweat and swat mosquitoes?"

Cleo stuttered, something she wasn't prone to do, but Joanna Burton was an intimidating kind of girl. "Wh-why did you come if you didn't want to?"

"You think what I want has anything to do with it? Really? It's a trial run before the Piedmonts make our engagement official. Well, what if I don't like Ellis? Did anybody think to ask that? I thought of it, I promise you that. And you know what I'm thinking? Maybe I'll see something I like better while I'm down here."

Cleo almost felt sorry for her. And what she'd said gave Cleo hope that the whole arrangement might fall apart. Surely everyone would be happier for it. But she watched for the next few nights as Joanna Burton took the seat next to Ellis at dinner. When Joanna reached her hand to touch Morrie Johnston's arm, her laughter tinkled like bells and every eye in the room turned to her. She was not beautiful in the way that deserved such attention, but she was the only woman other than Cleo, and it made her glow like an ember among them, transformed. It made Ellis edge ever closer, seeing the growing interest of his peers, how they vied for her attention. She was a gravitational force. She was a moon.

But when the evening grew late or when the men went off on a hunt or somewhere else they didn't disclose, which was often, Ellis did not stay behind anymore, not with Cleo or Joanna. They were left alone, so Joanna turned to Cleo, seemingly delighted and also as if they shared a plight that made them sisters. Cleo was annoyed to have lost Ellis's attention and to have become the other girl's babysitter. All morning long, here came Joanna needing her to brush her hair, asking her to go for a walk, whispering silly gossip and asking if Cleo could believe it.

"Scarcely," Cleo said, distracted. Honestly, Cleo almost never had the faintest idea who or what Joanna was talking about.

The day before the bonfire, Joanna went through everything in her wardrobe and made Cleo watch her try on outfits and then made Cleo try them on as well, but it had only taken up an hour and she'd flopped back on the chaise lounge in her room, bored.

Finally, Joanna convinced her to take the bikes to the east side of the island and the impossibly wide, deserted beach. Cleo protested when Joanna wanted to swim.

"But we'll be going out to the Dungeness pool in only a few hours."

Joanna knew this, of course. They'd talked of nothing but the pool and the acrobatic daring they anticipated on the gymnastic rings. In fact, Joanna had been the most excited of them all and crowed about the shining green swimsuit she would wear. Cleo had been annoyed. She didn't want to prance around in a swimsuit in front of the young men, especially not alongside Joanna, and she especially didn't want to dangle from suspended rings to be ogled or teased or both.

"Exactly. I want to work on my tan," Joanna said. "I'll be perfectly baked to a crisp, just the way I like it. I'm going to put on a show. You know they think they'll embarrass us on those rings, but I took gymnastics classes when I was younger. We'll go at night and Ellis already told me they like to let people get out to the center of the pool, especially girls, and then they turn off the flashlights so they can't see. When they fall in, the boys are there to grab them and get a handful. Ellis can't keep a secret to save his life."

Joanna seemed excited at the prospect. She stripped down to her skin.

Cleo didn't want to be naked in front of the other girl. "We shouldn't go in the water out here by ourselves."

"Well, that's the whole point, isn't it? To do what we shouldn't. Who's going to see us? Come on, Cleo. Accompany me. Isn't that your job?"

Cleo stalled. "Ellis told me that Dr. Johnston used to sit out here with a shotgun when the kids swam in the sea because a shark took a chunk out of his leg one time."

Joanna only laughed. "And you believed that? If everything Morrie says about his stepdaddy is true, the man must be a regular Frankenstein's monster. I'm terrified to lay eyes on him when he finally turns up. Half a face, half a leg. It's too much."

Cleo could almost agree. Joanna made Cleo feel silly for swallowing Morrie's tales whole. Dr. Johnston had apparently accumulated many scars, not just from the shark but also from an accident with a shotgun when he was a boy. With every new anecdote she'd heard of him around the dinner table, her anticipation of meeting the man in the flesh only grew.

"Come on," Joanna squealed. "Let the sharkies try and get us. They won't like the taste of bitter girls."

Slowly Cleo removed her clothing, folding it neatly on the shore until she'd shed even her underthings, then hurried into the surf and up to her neck in the briny water. Bobbing in the warm Atlantic waves, Joanna was in full bloom, rounded and pink and without the least inhibition, while Cleo kept her small, sturdy self submerged, careful to stay in deeper water and praying it hid her inadequacies. All the time, she thought how she compared to Joanna and that Ellis must have been laughing at her all along.

It was Joanna who finally brought up the bonfire, bragging that she'd been practicing the story she would tell, reciting it in the mirror at home. "I had to learn this when I was small, in German, actually. It's my mother's favorite old myth and she made me recite it. She grew up on the Rhine River, and it makes her cry for home. She always feels so sorry for Lorelei. I feel sorry for the boys she drowns. At this bonfire, we're supposed to tell a story that's unforgettable, right? So I figure when these boys here are all drunk as skunks tomorrow night, I'm going to tell this little story in a way that will turn their hair white."

"Tell it to me now," Cleo said, truly more interested in Joanna than in any old German myth.

Joanna flipped over so she floated on her back and her breasts rose above the water, and Cleo could not take her eyes off the other girl. Her hip bones peeked out, and her toes were tiny islands drifting. Her hair fanned out behind her, and Cleo could find no fault in her. This was what it must be like to be dusted with glory, she thought. Joanna had some power of another order, not derived from a weed she'd grubbed from the ground, not from a fruit she'd crushed and boiled. Something Cleo felt certain she herself did not possess.

"Poor little Lorelei was the daughter of Old Father Rhine. She was a mermaid in some stories, or a water spirit, but always a tempting little siren. She liked to sit at the top of an enormous rocky cliff overlooking her father's river and tease the boys. Her favorite thing to do was to sit up there and comb her golden hair while singing mesmerizing songs so they echoed off that rocky old wall, captivating the sailors until they crashed their little boats and drowned."

Joanna tutted at that. "But finally, of course, one of them turned out to be a prince. Though not charming enough to survive Lorelei. Poor guy. His daddy sent a whole army after her to avenge his poor, silly son." Joanna saw Cleo was listening intently, and she laughed. "What? Did you think she'd just get away with it?"

"What happened to her?"

"Well, she'd been getting away with murder for a long time and didn't think something like a little army would change that. She was the daughter of Old Father Rhine, after all. She wore a string of priceless pearls from her old man, which he'd given to her as a way to call to him should she ever need him. One by one, she dropped them into the sea, *plop, plop, plop,* thinking her daddy would get the message and come to her rescue. And sure enough, here came his chariot to whisk her away, and she jumped right in! But do you think she had any say in where she went after that? Daddy sent her off to the deepest, darkest depths of the sea. The end."

The ending was too abrupt. Cleo felt let down.

"Why didn't she just use her voice on her daddy or his men?"

"Because they weren't all stupid. By then, they had her number and all had their ears stuffed full of something. Nobody was listening. But every man who heard her story thereafter was haunted by it, always swearing they could hear her song in their dreams, always feeling her luring them to the water." Joanna hesitated so the water lapped quietly around them before she giggled. "Moral of the story according to my mom: she should have kept the pearls and sold them and got her own damn sea chariot and gone where she wanted." She clapped her hands. "Now, you, little mystery. What bone-chilling story will you tell at the bonfire?"

Cleo had no way to compete with a murdering siren. Dooley's

folktales and fables suddenly seemed childish and would not do against seduction and savagery. Raggedy little tales of fiddlers and little girl ghosts seemed unsophisticated when Cleo stood them up in her mind against the romance of the Lorelei. And so she told Joanna a true story instead. A tragic, terrible tale, just the kind Ellis had once predicted Cleo would know. Not a flashy myth about some water nymph banished to the bottom of the sea by her daddy, but the story of a girl who walked away from death on her own two feet. A story that would win the admiration and respect of any listener.

"It was 1917. My father surprised my mother with a Model T. He'd saved enough money from work at the lumberyard. My mother was seven months pregnant and I was eight and we stood on the street and watched him pull the shiny black car out front of the house and cheered. Not only us, but neighbors cheered too. It seemed like a dream when we climbed inside. I remember Daddy came around and helped my mother step up and shut the door behind us just like a coachman for ladies.

"My folks were young, so young. They weren't rich, but they were in love. And I was in love with them being in love. It was my favorite fairy tale, their story. I watched my mother let her hair down to catch the breeze when we drove and it was falling over her shoulders. It was the same color as my hair. It had copper threads running through it. I thought I was seeing the woman I would be one day, like I'd developed the sight."

Cleo felt she'd never grown into that sort of beauty and she could see that Joanna pitied her a little. But Joanna was a good listener. Her eyes never left Cleo, and she did not interrupt. When Cleo paused, she didn't interject. While Cleo allowed the silence required for a story to form in the imagination of her audience, she could hear the sound of the waves rolling onto shore, yards away, and the high calls of seabirds in the air, soft, rhythmic, a sort of seduction. When the waves swelled, they lifted the young women off their feet and then they would land again on the velvet sand, one soft reassurance after another. They'd forgotten the sharks. They'd forgotten the golden chariots that might whisk them away. They felt safe.

"It was dusk. We might have heard tree frogs and cicadas, but the motor was loud in our ears. It was only a dirt road that ran through pastures and forest, running along the back side of Brunswick. There was no one else going that way. We were only doing a short tour and back home. My daddy was worried about bouncing Mama too much. He made a joke about it and took it slow. He was holding her hand. She was laughing. There was no reason at all to be worried, and we weren't."

Joanna drifted closer, only a few feet from Cleo, her head and shoulders visible above the water. Facing one another, they might have been mirror images, but Cleo knew that was not the case. It might have been truer that they were two parts of a whole, two parts that had come together at just such a time, just such a way, to change one another somehow. But Cleo could not yet guess what that might be.

This time she'd waited too long before going on with the story. Part of her hoped she could let it end there with her family happy together, the road still before them.

"What happened to you?" Joanna asked, her voice like a tether that Cleo reached for, feeling it bind them together. In all the years since her parents had died, whenever the essentials of that day were related to anyone, it had always been her parents' story, what happened to them. Always them. No one had ever asked Cleo what happened to her. The answer seemed obvious. She'd lived, and it never failed to astonish her that those simple words could mean something entirely different to the person hearing the story than what they meant to the storyteller.

"There was a deer. A doe with a white tail. I saw it come from my mother's side and dash across the road in front of the car. I saw my mother's hair. I heard the car's motor. Daddy jerked the wheel and the car juddered sideways, and then it was sliding and spinning. We tipped and the car landed on its side. We'd stopped in a ditch. No more than a minute passed, but the deer was gone when I crawled out of the back. The door wouldn't open. I climbed over and stood there in the road."

Cleo shuddered. Joanna had surely guessed how the rest of the story would go.

"Daddy was still partway in the car, partway under it."

"Where was your mother?"

"In the road. Her dress was covering her face, but I saw her hair."

She could see that Joanna waited for a conclusion, but Cleo fell silent. Cleo had thought this story would win her the night at the bonfire. What could be more bone-chilling than to come face-to-face with the truth that life was not promised, that sometimes you lost everything you loved and had to keep breathing and all there was left to do was tell the story? But now she found she couldn't finish the story for Joanna as she'd planned. Neither could she embellish for dramatic effect to bring the whole thing around to some comforting moral. There were grizzly details she'd kept locked away, a catalog of injuries she went over nightly, a debt against which she'd always weigh her every breath, and she did not share those now. It didn't matter. How the tale ended would never change. And so all she could say was, "I didn't have a mark on me. They were dead and I left them there. I walked all the way back. To look at me, you'd never know."

The real ghost of the story was Cleo herself.

Chapter Eleven

FRANCES

FRANCES SHOWED UP FOR THE TOUR OF CUMBERLAND FEELING
energized, more like her old self, curious what she'd see and hear
and trying to ignore the twitch of nerves in her stomach but thrilled
to be busy again. She was learning she wasn't very good at being
idle. She liked her days to have a plan.

She'd spent the better part of Wednesday consumed with the remaining *True Romance* magazines from the box she'd found. She'd
taken them out to sit on the back porch overlooking the river this
time and kicked up her bare feet and read and watched the world
go by. She'd been enjoying herself until she thought of how hard her
mother had worked every day with the children at Mother's Helper
and wondered if she'd ever once taken a day like that for herself.
Frances honestly couldn't remember but found it hard to imagine.
So, after unsuccessfully attempting to take a nap but distracted by
her thoughts, she went downtown to grab dinner at the pharmacy
counter and then to the dock, dressed as Wandering Merry. By that
time, it hadn't been hard at all to work up a good and loud moan.
Rosey Devane had laughed.

This morning she was out of bed before her alarm clock could
even sound, to meet him at the dock while the fishing boats and
shrimp trawlers set out. She smelled diesel and heard the men calling to one another in greeting. All of them called to Rosey. They
exchanged dire warnings about some colossal storm of the century,

each one with a different prediction for when it would come. Rosey only chuckled. Clearly this was some joke among the seamen.

"Don't believe a word of it," he said to her. "They do this every year. It's the same thing, summer after summer. 'Oh, it's bearing down on us any day now,' they say. 'See the signs gathering round? Batten the hatches.' It's just old wives' tales."

"Red sky at night, sailor's delight. Red sky in morning, sailors take warning," Frances said.

"For certain. But today's blue skies and clear sailing," Rosey said.

Still, one of the fishermen called, "I seen a halo round that old moon last night, Devane. Rain'll be comin' soon."

Frances smiled, but by all accounts, Rosey was right and it looked like this would be another clear morning. Their crossing was serene, the water smooth, the air filled with seabirds, the skies vast and cobalt.

On Cumberland, she looked in awe at the incredible live oaks all around as they climbed into an old truck near the dock and Rosey launched into the script for what he called the Old Gods Tour.

"The Timucuan Indians—remember those guys I mentioned on the town tour a couple of days ago? They were here first, before the upstarts came along."

"Upstarts?"

"Starting all the way back in the 1500s and rolling right through the centuries up till where we are today, there've been upstarts come ashore on this island, little men declaring it made them big to stand on top of it, over and over again. *Since the beginning of time*," he said, loudly orating for effect before flashing a wry smile and quietly going on, "they got shut of the Indians. Or put them to work. When they needed more people for the labor, they bought them some, slaves to plant indigo and rice and cotton. When they weren't buying and planting and selling, they fought wars. They cut down the oaks to build their boats. And then everybody got pretty comfortable for a spell, for that old Gilded Age. The old gods over here got rich and fat, got self-righteous, but before they knew it the financial tide had turned, as it always does, and now here we are, looking at that decline. But just give it a minute. They're already scrambling to see who's going to be the next to stand on Cumberland and try to call it his own."

"So that's what you mean by old gods? The old families here?"

Rosey smiled. "My dad was always calling them the old guard. He'd say the *old guard* this and the *old guard* that. But it sounded to me like he was saying *old god* with that drawl. And once I called them that, it's all we ever called them. Seemed to suit."

"So who do you think the new fella will be?"

"Likely the government. But that'll be a war too. The Carnegies are fighting an outside war with the poachers who plunder this place like it's just a big playground, but they're fighting an inside war, too, amongst themselves, trying to figure out how to hold on to the island. Some want to sell, some want to stay, some want to protect it, some want to develop. If the government gets their way, maybe it'll be preserved in some way or other. Only time will tell."

He enjoyed relating more information about Spanish forts and missions and legends of early settlements of Brits and Scots, but her ears truly perked up at mention of a myth of a water beast.

"The Indians called it the Altamaha-ha, named after the Altamaha River, which runs north of here. They said the creature moved through the rivers and estuaries and rice fields. Maybe that's your siren."

"My mother told me the myth of the Lorelei when I was little. She could recite a poem. It was the only time I ever heard her speak

German," Frances said, surprised she could smile about it. "My grandmother came from a place on the Rhine River. She lived in a region called the Palatinate. I think when she left Germany, no other place was ever entirely home. My mom remembered her trying to fit in with the neighbors in Asheville. She made dishes for the potlucks and bake sales knowing they mostly got scraped into their trash."

"Tough crowd."

"Yeah, I didn't get any of the recipes. But I got the story. I wonder what she'd think, my grandmother, to know she brought that Lorelei story from Germany for it to end up down here."

"Did you ever want to go back to that river in Germany? See it for yourself?"

It was funny, but when Rosey asked about that old river across the sea, that's what brought a tightening to her throat. Another reminder she'd been left adrift and how alone she felt in the world. It hadn't occurred to Frances that once she'd fixated on the Lorelei as a child, she'd neglected to learn much else about her family history. It was obvious to her now that she'd been trying to root out Joanna's story, that she'd instinctually felt something was wrong, even if she hadn't known it back then. In the myths Frances studied, the stories often began with a lie, and the endings were not always happy ones.

She tried not to let her mood turn morose and instead listened as they traversed the island and Rosey explained the purposes and ownership of houses, barns, sheds. There was still a little airstrip where a steady stream of famous visitors had come and gone from over the decades. Rosey listed them by name, including Charles Lindbergh. He rattled off the names of the Carnegie houses built up and down the Grand Avenue and the Carnegies themselves and their multitude of offspring who had inherited, all of their names a jumble in her head as they often repeated, passed down over several generations. From his stories it seemed everything was always being built only to burn down. Now the Carnegies worried that would be the fate of Dungeness, the largest mansion that now stood abandoned. Frances was eager to see it, along with Plum Orchard, where Joanna had once stayed.

She knew she'd never remember all the sprawling history. She felt overwhelmed. "Talk about an extensive mythology. They were mostly the same deities and myths as the Greeks and Latins, just rehashed and renamed to suit the next bunch who were in charge. It will make you crazy trying to sort it all out."

Rosey grinned and nodded, and she knew he liked that she shared his fascination. It was a new and unexpected experience for Frances, who felt she'd forever been trying to share the memory of a fascinating dream when she talked of her love of folklore but no one had particularly cared to listen.

"Here we go," Rosey said when they pulled to a stop. "Just up this way. Dungeness. Creepy old gal, sitting out here empty. They've tried to sell it, argued night and day over the expense of keeping it up. The Carnegies are worried somebody will get hurt one of these days, kids or hunters, or it'll catch fire and burn up the whole island."

They strolled through an opening in the trees and Frances drew her breath. "I read about it. I even saw pictures. But I didn't know it would be like this."

Splendor was the word that came to mind when she beheld the mammoth house, the wide veranda, the high walls, the graceful tower. But a sense of loneliness pervaded the place. A trio of rangy horses grazed only feet away from them. Rosey winked at her, leading the way past them.

"Just give them a wide berth. They won't bother with you."

Frances followed him, noting the neat white cottage near the main house, a near replica of the one where Cleo lived, and a long arbor beyond that was covered in vines. The entire scene was too romantic to believe, mysterious and strange. He pointed the way to a terraced area at the back of the house, facing the river.

"What's left of Dungeness gardens is down that way," Rosey said. "One of the places Cleo forages for the produce she provides for the inn. She pretty much scavenges the whole island; lots of native plants and heirloom ones are still hiding out. That's what Audrey's feeding you, a steady diet of the last four hundred years."

They walked the barren terraced area where once there'd been vegetables and found only a few wild herbs in tangles. But it was easy for Frances to stand beneath the hulking structure and imagine what it would have been like when it was full of life and family, guests spilling onto the porches and out onto the lawns, lovers lingering beneath the arbor or strolling along the banks of the river. The wind off the water blew over her face, and she thought she'd never felt herself so carried away by a story before. When Rosey talked of the coming of the robber barons after the Civil War, just at the turn of the century when they'd made all their money, each story became more outlandish. She felt as distant from them as she did from any of the names on the tour, but there had been a time when her mother had walked among them here.

"This house is actually the second Dungeness to stand on this spot," Rosey was saying. "After the first burned, a new one was built here. I think about that," he said. "How I bet people stood around after that fire and thought everything was lost. And now look, here this is. And we're still talking about what's passed here for centuries."

Again, Frances was amazed at how the man seemed to read her thoughts. She had stopped writing in her notebook an hour ago. She wanted to remember for herself the colors, the smells, the sound of Rosey Devane's voice, the way the sun lit his face, the way he moved and how his eyes never stopped roaming over this place and over her. "It does feel like it somehow all still exists here. I think it's how you're telling it."

"Damn if it doesn't tell itself," he insisted.

Another building stood near the mansion, more of a Victorian cottage by comparison.

"That's the infamous pool house," Rosey said. She considered the pretty pool house; all shingles and turrets, it was friendly as any cottage ought to be to lure a child or young woman inside, but she couldn't bring herself to approach it. "They called it the Casino, where the boys brought their friends from the mainland. I've been told it smells like the depths of hell in there. It's from the sulfur water in the pool."

Somewhere wrapped up in this story was the heartbreak out of which Frances had been born.

"Afraid they keep it locked up tight," Rosey said decidedly.

For the first time, she suspected he wasn't being entirely truthful, but she was glad to go along with it.

Frances's eye caught some movement above them in the turret at the top of the main house. Maybe it had only been a reflection, but it sent a chill up her arms. She saw Rosey glance up with a grin.

"Don't say it's a ghost," she said. "I mean, it's obviously the most haunted house on the planet. But I don't believe in ghosts, remember?"

She saw a twinkle in his eye. "Frannie, there're so many ghosts up in that house you can barely elbow your way inside. For sure there's one in that tower. Used to be, the lady of the house would take a boat out by herself and make a boy stand up there as lookout to keep an eye on her, in case she fell asleep and went floating out to sea."

Frances rolled her eyes, though she'd felt a zing inside her when he called her Frannie.

"If you don't believe that, you won't believe most of what I tell you went on around here. But you're right this time. That's no ghost. It's Harl Buie up there, Archie's grandson. The Carnegies hired the kid this summer to keep a lookout."

"Not exactly a summer lifeguard job at the Y."

"Oh, not so different, really. Except for the shotguns. There're plenty of idiots who are out here up to no good." Rosey waved and the boy in the turret waved back. "Come on. Let's get some wind in our hair."

———

Having seen Dungeness, Frances was somewhat prepared for the expanse of Plum Orchard. Eight miles north, they pulled the boat ashore at a sandy little beach only about fifty yards long and walked a trail through the forest that hemmed the riverbank until she could see the house from the lawn. The austere white mansion, palatial from a distance, sat there like an aging beauty queen trying to keep up appearances. Paint peeled in big flakes; balconies appeared to be near collapse; banisters rotted. If Dungeness could be described as soulfully derelict, this house simply felt neglected. Strangely, it didn't spook Frances like the pool house at Dungeness. But the walk down to the river's shore was solemn, and when Rosey stood at the edge of the water near a firepit and explained that this was the site of the famous bonfire, Frances tried to imagine the scene as Cleo had described it.

"This is it. The place where Cleo spun her wild tale."

The rest they left unspoken, but Frances thought the words in her head. *Two boys died here.*

She searched the horizon, the sparks on the river's surface, as if there'd be something to see there. It was somehow sadly anticlimactic to see only a river like any other, beautiful as it might be. It occurred to her then that she'd never seen a photograph of Ellis Piedmont. And she turned to leave the shore, knowing she would not find anything for herself there.

———

Along the shallow creeks north of Plum Orchard, Frances watched the waters as they made their way to a man named Archie Buie, Rosey explained, to trade for the oysters Archie frequently harvested from a nearby bed. Frances asked if or how the man was related to the boy in the tower with the same surname.

"Oh, sure. Archie is Harl's granddaddy. Buies have been up at Brick Hill long as that little community's been up north of here. Started out as part of a freedman's colony. Buies are third and fourth generation on Cumberland. In fact, Archie and his wife, June, fostered Lumas Gray. That was before my time, but used to be Archie's uncles had a sawmill up on the Satilla River and my dad worked out there some in the winters. They all fished together when they were boys, and then their boys did too."

"Did you?"

"Oh, sure. Mostly when it was summer and we were kids. We were turned loose over here. Those were good days. Long as we didn't bother Lucy Carnegie's cattle, we could traipse all over the island and fish any creek we liked all the way up past the bluff and Brick Hill— that's where Archie's still living—and back down to the other end too. Ran all over together like puppies until we got sent back to school in the fall. Then it was like we'd never known one another, some of us. You get separated out into your groups and grow up to find your place, your job. Some go to the mill, some go to the rails. Some stay on their boats, although making a living on the water's harder than it used to be with all this commercial business. Some of the kids go off to school nowadays and they don't come back here to make their homes. They move out to the cities."

She didn't say what she was thinking, that Rosey had gone and come back. He spent his days preoccupied with the past and his evenings walking with ghosts, dug into this town extra deep. "And these are the guys Harl is paid to report to the Carnegies now for trespassing and poaching?"

"One or two of them. I believe most aren't local. They run up the water from Florida, bringing boatloads of them when they can get on the island in the dark and go after the wildlife or just lay up and drink. It's a way to make a buck if you've got a boat and you know the shoals, running one of those outfits. They've cut back hours at the mill. You might hear some about that. Glenn's been knocked back to two days on, three days off."

Frances didn't ask him to confirm what was obvious by Rosey's face, that Glenn was likely one of those runners.

The fish camp turned out to be little more than a shack on the creek. Archie was a man with a white beard and gnarled hands with knobby knuckles. There were two kids with him, a teenaged girl and Jimmy Walker. Frances was surprised to see him there, but it didn't seem to strike Rosey as at all unusual. While they filled the coolers with fish and oysters, Frances stayed in the boat. Archie looked her way and threw up a hand. Frances waved back. The girl scowled while Jimmy smiled broadly and waved until they all turned and disappeared inside.

When they'd pulled away, Frances asked, "Do Archie's grand-kids live over here?"

"They live over in Revery with their folks. Harl will be part of the first integrated class at the high school over in New Canaan this fall."

The sun dipped lower as the afternoon grew late, but Rosey was in no hurry. They had to shield their eyes as they quietly cruised the salt creek through the marsh grasses. Near a bluff he showed her where an ancient canoe had been found decades before. "Folks claim they've seen long bones over behind Plum Orchard that prove the Timucua Indians stood nine or ten feet tall."

"I can't take any more." Frances laughed in spite of herself.

"You sure? We haven't seen Little Cumberland or the lighthouse."

"I only meant no more tall tales."

"I thought you might've changed your plans in a rush to get back to somebody in the Blue Ridge."

Frances shook her head, embarrassed by the insinuation and thankful her face was already flushed from the heat. She was twenty-seven and still living with her mother. An academic with a head full of cautionary tales. A social life hadn't happened. She was being silly. Rosey was only being friendly and she was paying for the entertainment. Probably too many of those *True Romance* articles about desperate, lonely girls. "I don't leave until Sunday. I have time."

They took the boat out into the part of the river that Rosey called the dividings and then north on the East River, past all the old Carnegie homes and Brick Hill and finally swinging past the point of the island, an area called Little Cumberland, where a solitary lighthouse stood and the river met the sea. Where the news clipping had said Ellis Piedmont's body had come to rest.

"They deactivated the light in 1906, but she's still a lovely old gal, don't you think?"

Frances agreed. Rosey sat quite still in the boat and she saw his gaze search the waters in a way that was all too familiar to her. He had a story to tell her, and for once it was about himself.

"My dad used to bring me up here. We'd spend the day out on the river and come all the way up to the point, to the sound, and he'd tell me about the slave ship *Wanderer*. He always told it the same way. It was the history that haunted Henry Devane, my dad. Haunts me now. Can't shake it. Seems like we're doomed to repeat it, different time, different men, same story. And I can't help thinking there's got to be some end to it. I come out here like Dad did and I wonder about that."

"Wandering Rosey?"

"The *Wanderer*'s not my story, no. But I look at that lighthouse and I think maybe Merry knows. Maybe she saw what happened here. Later, the Confederates removed the Fresnel lens down to Brunswick for safekeeping. But that night, I wonder if Merry was standing there, if she and the lighthouse were witnesses."

He cut his eyes toward Frances, but the bright spark she'd grown accustomed to had been tamped down.

"In November of 1858, the *Wanderer*, carrying illegal cargo—more than four hundred slaves from Angola—steered toward the lighthouse beacon here and anchored in the sound. They'd been forty-two days at sea and provisions were gone. Some say eighty Africans had died, some say closer to two hundred. The ship was infested, full of rot, a horror. The ship's owner feared a storm, and the fellow spearheading the scheme to smuggle slaves into Georgia wanted to get his investment ashore, so they brought them to Jekyll. But once that happened, word got out about the ship's arrival and the men were caught in the act. And still, none of them paid for their crimes."

Rosey's tone was pure disgust. She didn't know how many times he'd told this story. Maybe a hundred. Maybe never. He dusted his hands, then spread them over his thighs and stretched his fingers while he finished the telling.

"The *Wanderer* was one of the last ships to bring slaves into the United States. It made national headlines. The smuggler crowed over that. Considered it a success for emboldening those in favor of secession from the country. He was known to be the last Confederate officer killed in that war. Died leading a charge against the Union seven days after Lee surrendered. Still fighting that battle. Some people don't know when the war's over."

For a long time they stayed as they were. Frances wondered why he'd told her the history of the *Wanderer* in this way, as if it were personal, as if it were happening this very day.

"I'm going to tell you something else," he said. "You're leaving here in a few days and it won't matter to you, but I need to tell you. I want you to know this."

"Okay."

"When I was a boy, Glenn and me got into all kinds of trouble for sneaking around Revery. We'd break in places, trespass. We'd sneak into the movies. Glenn always got caught."

"You didn't?"

"I knew where to hide." He almost smiled, but his chagrin was clear. "I nearly forgot about it. It was years after that when I thought about it again, when I was gone, when I didn't know if I was ever coming back. I thought a lot about those marquee lights, the way they lit up everything when we were kids. I decided if I got home, I wasn't going to work at the mill. I was going to buy the Marvel. I asked Will and Glenn to go in as partners. Will took me up on it, but Glenn turned me down, liked where he was down at Piedmont, he said. Truth is, he didn't have the money to go in with us and he didn't want to be working with no Indian. And I was glad about it, if you want to know. It seemed better for everybody." Rosey took a deep breath and set his eyes on the horizon. "I thought about Korea. Troops were integrated there. I saw what that could be like and what it should be. I figured it was maybe a place to start. But there's some that just can't stop fighting an old battle."

Frances sat very still. There was only the sound of the seabirds and the lull of the ocean lapping at the boat.

"I didn't see that right off. I was feeling like a big shot. But now I'm seeing just about every day is a kick in the teeth for Will. I said I'd be front of house and he'd be back of house, where folks would be more comfortable with an Indian. Already, right there, I was pushing him down and I didn't ever think one thing about it, not for a long time. Not till Glenn started yukking it up about me getting myself a Tonto or a Geronimo or whatever else he thought made a good joke."

"That's not your fault," Frances said. She wanted to say more about her thoughts on Glenn Walker, but it seemed like Rosey didn't need telling.

"Glenn started saying this or that about Will being Red, liking Red—about colored men in Korea getting indoctrinated by the Reds."

"Is that true?"

"It's all just talk. No more truth to that than there is to the talk about this doomsday storm. But Will got on Glenn's bad side from day one, and then a couple weeks ago, Will went to that conservation meeting about the mill's runoff. He said some things to some people about cleaning up their own mess and Glenn got wind of it. There's a lot of fear that mill's going to get shut down until they take care of that business, and Glenn's job would go with that. And it's giving him the excuse to lay into Will extra hard. So I told Will last night he needs to think about moving on sometime soon."

"Because of Glenn? Surely he'll listen to you if you've been friends that long."

"It's not just Glenn. Ever since Will got here, he's made good friends with the colored people, been going to New Canaan to support the integration at the high school this fall. I never once went with him. I told him he needed to steer clear, that he didn't know people here, he wasn't from here, and all it was going to do was get him hurt or run off himself."

He leaned forward, elbows resting on his knees. Frances reached to take his hand where it hung heavy. He was right. But she also saw that wasn't what he wanted to hear and she kept quiet. Frances felt certain this was not part of his usual script for his paying customers.

"I'm about to figure out who I am in this story, Frannie. And it's not who I thought. And I've been wondering what Merry would say if she's watching."

He was asking her something very personal, she realized. At least here, Frances knew what to say.

"You're a Revery man, remember? Their boatman. You carry souls through the dividings, ferry them safely both ways. Take it from me, I know about these things," she said. "I'm an expert."

"Geezus, I should hire you for ghost tours."

She was glad to hear him tease again. "But you know, there's a danger to the boatman who spends all his time on the water. If he listens to a false voice, the one telling him it's the end of the story, that all his choices have been taken from him, that there's nothing ahead but the rocks and the waves and the depths, where nothing can change . . . that weight will drag him under."

"I guess I'll have to think on that."

Frances thought the mermaid, inky blue on his arm, was lovely and obviously besotted, appearing to gaze up at Rosey as if she waited to hear what else he would say.

"I hope you don't mind I told you."

"I asked for the full tour," she said.

He did laugh at that, some of his old confidence returning, although it wasn't the ringing sound she'd gotten used to and it made her heart squeeze. Finally he pulled in the anchor and started the motor, and they set out over the beautiful estuaries and twisting creeks, a complicated maze, back toward the town and the people he loved.

Later, she walked the dock again in Merry's white nightdress and then they sat on Rosey's houseboat until it was far too late, this time listening to the radio. It was easy to sit beside Rosey without talking, something that made her content in a way she wished wouldn't end. Frances felt the gentle tug of the water on the boat and thought of the roots growing down beneath them, holding them in place. She wondered if that was really even true, or just something he liked to say.

When she left, she thought about kissing Rosey Devane. She was imagining herself falling in love, something that would have seemed as impossible before she left North Carolina as most of Rosey's stories of Cumberland.

Chapter Twelve

AUDREY

REVERY WAS A TOWN WHERE GHOSTS WALKED THE STREETS, and tonight that included Audrey. Being out after dark was easier. By daylight, she had taken up the habit of learning shortcuts through alleyways and backyards to dodge anyone who might want to strike up a conversation that carried the risk that they'd get a closer look at her. Today, after Frances Flood had gone out with Rosey to Cumberland, Audrey had hidden in a closet beneath the stairs, pretending to be busy organizing the hats and coats her aunt had left there, reading *Our Town* until the customers from brunch emptied out. She thought of Glenn's accusations and the books and pamphlets on Will's shelves. It was obvious he was jealous of Will's friendship with Rosey and that they owned the theater together. He was jealous that Jimmy liked Will too. She was afraid that now he'd gotten the idea they were friends, he'd be looking for any reason to go after Will. She'd decided to give the script back and keep her distance for everybody's sake.

On the walls inside the closet, she'd found the names her mother and her aunt had carved into the beadboard, something they must have done as children. Seeing it made Audrey even more heartsick for a friend, but she'd left all her girlfriends behind in Macon, separated herself out when she'd married and then again when she'd been widowed. The distance was too far to cross in so many ways she couldn't even name them all. Even if she somehow managed to befriend the young woman who was a guest at the inn, she'd only be in Revery a few more days.

She traced Mimi's name with her fingertip and wished she could call her mother and tell her what she'd found, tell her about the camera and the negatives and everyday things, too, about running the inn. Although she'd have stopped short of asking advice on men. Mimi had chosen a life that Audrey didn't want for herself, moving in polite society after marrying a much older man for money. She had left this house a long time ago and hadn't come back for reasons she'd kept to herself, like she'd kept so much of herself from Audrey. They'd never understood each other. Audrey could not imagine Mimi hiding under the stairs, a girl who would carve her name into the wall.

The longer Audrey was in Revery, the more she realized it felt more like home to her than she'd ever felt in her mother's house. She was beginning to believe that what she missed was not Mimi at all, but the mother she wished she'd been. That picking up the phone now meant risking too much disappointment for them both. Above all of that, Audrey wasn't ready to share her biggest secret, that she would be a mother herself very soon.

So she hid.

Later in the evening, after taking the photos for the tour group, she'd lingered around the Marvel, hoping for the opportunity to return the script to Will instead of slipping out to head back to the inn. Given the choice to head back to another long evening alone or find better ways to amuse herself, she'd decided to snoop around in the basement storage room and there discovered a true secret at the Marvel Theater: an actual tunnel.

She shouldn't have stepped one foot inside the dank corridor, but once she'd seen it, she couldn't resist. It ran the distance of several yards before ending at another door. She'd imagined that it was probably some remnant of Prohibition or, less likely, an old pirate tunnel. But when she'd stepped through, she found it led to the janitor's closet inside the Piedmont Library next door.

Audrey knew she was too old to be sneaking into places after hours, but that didn't stop her as she touched everything she wanted to touch and lounged in reading chairs. She kicked off her shoes and propped up her sock feet on tables. She pondered the intricate plaster moldings on the ceilings and the smooth finish of the polished wood floors. It felt good to be a girl who could break a few rules in the dark when it seemed all day long all she did was follow them. Audrey whispered, thinking of Freddie's last insult the day of their fight, "How about this, Fredrick L. Howell? Who says I'm dull now?"

"You're not dull," a voice answered, causing Audrey to startle. The beam of a flashlight suddenly shone on Jimmy's gleeful face just a few feet away as he laughed. She shushed him in case someone might hear them. Maybe Will Tremmons, who worked the janitorial job.

"We shouldn't be in here," she said. He uncrossed his legs, getting up from the reading chair where she'd been sitting only half an hour before. It occurred to her that he'd been here all along, watching her. "You're a sneak and you should have said something. This is a bad idea. Come on, I don't want to get blamed for one more thing with you."

Jimmy only giggled and flicked off the flashlight so the library was thrown into darkness. "Come hide and see." Audrey was about to argue, but then she heard someone approaching through the tunnel. Jimmy grabbed her hand in his soft, sweaty grasp and they wedged themselves under the reading table, crouched far beneath the bench seating. There were whispers and she could hear the sounds of several bodies moving through the tunnel.

Audrey wrapped her arms around her legs and gathered them close in the crammed space. She still held the script and didn't dare put it down. She tried to recognize the voices, but they were only whispers. There were two of them. She could see their shoes. They used their own flashlight to browse the stacks until finally they were satisfied and left the same way they'd come, back through the tunnel. Even after she could no longer hear them, Audrey remained still a long time. Only when Jimmy unfurled did they crawl out. They peered carefully out a front window. Crossing the street like long shadows, the Buie siblings carried stacks of books in their arms.

Audrey tried to think what to do, whether to leave through the front door or go back through the tunnel, afraid of being seen following the Buies either way. The sign at the front window of the library was clear from the streetlight outside, even in the dark. *Whites only.*

"Jimmy, this is not a game. This is not like mink traps, do you understand? If they get caught, there's going to be a lot of trouble. You can't be in here like this."

He shrugged again. She was starting to realize this was something he did a lot. Jimmy Walker was sweet as pie, but he had his own opinions. "They come in the back way at the pharmacy, the Marvel, everywhere," he said.

"That tunnel is not exactly the same thing as the colored entrance, Jimmy. There is no entrance for them here. They're not supposed to be in here at all."

But he wasn't listening. "Harl's getting integrated. He's going to high school. Will says he's going right in the front door there.

All he's got to do is read up so he's smarter. So I showed them the tunnel."

Audrey was shaking. "You showed Will this tunnel? Or this was his idea?"

"No. I didn't show him. It's a secret."

This time she was the one to take Jimmy's good hand. "All right. Well, I'll tell you who needs to get smarter. Me and you, Jimmy Walker. Come on. You need to go home. Where does your dad think you are?"

He shrugged. "He's not home. He's working. Three days off, two days on."

"Okay. What time does he get home?"

"Eleven."

It was only just after ten o'clock. Jimmy was old enough to be home alone. But old enough to be sneaking out and getting into trouble, too, unfortunately. "Look, I need something to eat before I fall out. You can listen to my records. Want to do that?"

She led him back to the Gilbreath House Inn and fed them bowls of chicken casserole out of Shirley's freezer. He ate like he'd never seen food. He walked through the house, quietly having a look at Cleo Woodbine's paintings, but was especially delighted with Freddie's record player.

"We have to keep the volume low. People are sleeping upstairs." She'd almost mentioned his granddaddy, but then realized she didn't know if Jimmy even knew Tate Walker. He was quiet and seemed kind, but family could be complicated. Best not to wake him, even if only because Audrey didn't want to have to tell another lie about where they'd been a half hour before.

Jimmy chose a record and started it playing, keeping the volume just above a whisper. She watched him dance in the front room, helpless against his jubilation as he wore himself out to "The Battle of New Orleans." He knew every single word to the lyrics and sang them quietly but with gusto. To see him dance was to see a boy in ecstasy. Audrey felt a surge of affection toward him. Maybe this was something like motherly love, she thought. Maybe she had instincts that would kick in after all.

When Frances crept up onto the porch and stepped inside as she'd done for the last couple of evenings, still wearing Wandering Merry's white nightdress, Audrey and Jimmy both turned and she looked surprised to be met at the door. The grandfather clock in the foyer announced the hour: eleven o'clock.

"Time to go!" Jimmy lit out into the night as if he'd been waiting for the door to open.

Frances looked after him. They watched him head in the direction of his house and turn the corner. "He shouldn't really be out by himself like that, should he?"

Audrey lifted the needle from the record, tired but wide awake. "Lots of folks shouldn't be lots of places." Frances pulled at the nightgown and the fabric billowed like a sail, far from anything revealing, but a blush crept up her neck. Audrey had tried hard to act like a professional and leave this young woman alone, but just now she didn't care if Frances was leaving soon. She needed a girlfriend. She said, "Good thing we don't have chaperones. Want to sneak out with me?"

———

They took a jar of pickles, slices of ham, pepper jelly, and a jar of peanut butter out to the carriage house and Audrey showed Frances her darkroom. There was electricity there, too, and she carried the oscillating fan from the kitchen so they wouldn't burn right up. But they'd forgotten utensils and so they sat there eating with their fingers.

"Who needs glory when you've got Skippy?" Audrey said.

"Glory?" Frances said.

"That's what Rosey said. What people call it, whatever Cleo makes from some weed to control people's thoughts or something. I don't think it's real, do you?" Audrey was glad to gossip about Cleo Woodbine. It took some pressure off.

"I don't believe half of what I hear from anybody in this town about anything. You should've heard all Rosey was telling me to-day about the people on Cumberland. It just gets more and more outrageous."

"You mean the water monster? I kind of like that story. But you know there was no Wandering Merry before you, right? Rosey made that up."

Frances ate a pickle and licked her fingers. "Maybe. But do you want to know who I really am?"

Audrey thought she was teasing. "Oh, do tell."

"There's a good chance I'm Ellis Piedmont's love child."

Audrey looked at her to see if she was serious and Frances nodded. "As in Piedmont Paper Mill and Piedmont Library?"

"And my mother was his jilted fiancée, the one with the story about the siren. I just found out. I don't actually know if I'm his, but it's certainly possible. And the best part is, I'll probably never know. But she sent me to commission a painting from Cleo, so that's why I'm here. Besides that, I don't know anything, really. What I'm doing down here, what I'll do when I leave. So maybe I really am Wandering Merry."

"Wow." Audrey laughed at Frances's expression as she sat there still wearing the ghost's nightdress, until Frances laughed too. It felt amazing. Everyone expected Audrey to be so dour.

"All right. That's awful," Audrey finally said when their laughter died down. "But do you want to know how to make a ghost from a dead boy's picture?"

Audrey gave her a full demonstration. She had it down to an art now, if that was what you could call creating a double exposure. The process wasn't rocket science.

"And Rosey suggested this?"

"It wasn't exactly his idea that there would be ghosts."

"If you don't want to, then why are you doing it? For Glenn?"

Audrey made a face. "I've been trying to quit for weeks, but something always happens before I can. Usually it's something to do with Jimmy and I end up wrapped up in it. I don't know how." Audrey paused. That wasn't entirely fair, to blame Jimmy. "I just chicken out and don't say anything. Rosey gave me this job at the inn and he asked me to take the photos and I know Glenn is his friend. It seems like he really wants to help Glenn and Jimmy, and Glenn was so excited about doing this. I don't know. I don't want to give Rosey any reason to change his mind about having me here. I can't go back home. Everybody knows it's my fault my husband's dead."

Audrey hadn't said the words out loud until now, but they'd been running in her mind the whole time, she realized, like one of Freddie's records, constantly playing. Here was the reason she couldn't say no to Glenn Walker. Here was what she truly thought of herself. "We were fighting. I wouldn't go for a ride on his bike. I was afraid of it and he was sick of me because he said I was so dull. We'd gone to Daytona Beach for our honeymoon, but as soon as we were back, he started working at the pharmacy with my father and he said I didn't have to work. He wanted me to stay home. We were renting this tiny house and he was gone all day and we didn't have a car. I was bored. He said we never should have gotten married. I told him to leave. I told him I never loved him. I didn't want to be married. I didn't want to stay in Macon." Audrey drew a breath. "I didn't want to ride on his stupid bike and I told him he was going to kill himself and then I'd do whatever I wanted."

"This is not what you wanted," Frances said.

"Does that matter?"

That put a real damper on the mood. For a moment, Audrey thought the night was over, but then she remembered she still had the copy of the play. "Are you tired?" Frances shook her head. "Good. Because I have the perfect thing."

Frances smiled. "What?"

Audrey pulled out the flashlight she always used to cross the lawn and the script for *Our Town*, and they took turns playing the different roles with outrageous accents and flamboyant personalities, a couple of midnight hoodlums, snorting and squealing with pleasure. Maybe it was that neither of them could stand one more minute of grief or that together, facing down death didn't seem so scary. But it was a wonder Tate Walker didn't flip on the porch light at the back of the house to tell them to knock it off.

Audrey was so relieved by what felt like a normal evening with a girlfriend that she'd almost forgotten Frances would leave any day and she'd be alone at the inn again. But then Frances yawned and closed the script and handed it back and the spell was broken. When Audrey thought about life running the inn, she wondered if this was what the rest of her friendships were going to be like, always saying goodbye to people after only a few days. She felt like her chance to confide in someone was slipping away.

"This is Will Tremmons's script," she said. "But this is definitely not his town. He has a lot of books of his own, books they don't have at the Piedmont Library. And even though he's the janitor there, it's whites only. Do you think that will change now the schools are integrating? Do you think Rosey will change the theater? The inn doesn't rent rooms to colored people. Who would stay here if they had to sleep in a house that was integrated?"

"I don't think anything's happening that fast where the owners have a choice. And even when they do, it's like you said. Would they put themselves out of business if they decided to integrate?"

"Will reads to Jimmy. Isn't that sweet? He's really good to him. Glenn found us upstairs yesterday, reading the play. We were just goofing off. But Glenn didn't like it. He doesn't like Will."

"You should say something to Rosey," Frances said. She seemed confident that Rosey would take Audrey's side. "He'll surprise you, Audrey. He's not going to make you leave the inn. You're his family. And you should tell Glenn to make his own silly pictures. You said yourself it's not rocket science."

Frances was a problem solver. She wondered if Frances had an answer for the one thing she really needed to tell someone about, the thing she'd been working her way up to since they'd come out to the carriage house.

Frances sighed. "What do you think Cleo Woodbine will paint for the commissioned piece? All her regret in living color, dumped in my lap? I don't know what I'll do with it."

"How do you know it will be regret?"

"You're right. Maybe it will be revenge." Frances rolled her neck as if she were getting a tension headache.

Audrey didn't have any idea what Cleo Woodbine would make, if she made anything at all. Audrey thought of the first day she'd come to the inn. Then she thought of that empty room. And strangely, it made her consider how it had felt to discover the tunnel underneath the theater and take those first steps inside when she'd had no idea where it might lead. She thought of playacting in Will's rooms, of those Buie kids sneaking books out of the library in the dark, of watching Jimmy dancing out into the street. She thought of finding the names of her mother and her aunt on the wall under the stairs, two little girls sharing secrets. Cleo could paint anything. Life was unpredictable.

She said, "When I think about all the things I could have said or done differently, I realize it doesn't matter, does it? I can't imagine things turning out any other way. Freddie just always ends up in front of that train. I end up right here. It's inevitable, like when you have your photo made. What you see in a picture may surprise you, but usually you're the only one who's shocked. Everybody else has always seen the things about you that you're finally just noticing."

Audrey was thinking of the photo of her mother with the scarf tied around her head like some gypsy woman, tanned and barefoot in shorts, showing off her long legs, smiling so widely on the steps of Dungeness. That girl was a mystery to Audrey. She wondered what Mimi would say about that photo now, and the girl she'd seemingly left behind when she left Revery.

Audrey didn't know what Frances Flood might think of her, but she suddenly felt desperate to be seen. She blurted, "I'm going to have a baby and nobody knows."

For a long while, Audrey could see Frances thinking. Finally, she said, "Well, now we both know. How far along are you?"

And with that, Frances took hold of her hands and Audrey felt her shoulders drop as if she'd been carrying two tons on her back.

She answered every question and Frances quietly promised to go with her to a doctor.

"I can even help make the appointment, if you want. I don't have to be back to sign papers to close on the sale of Mother's house until Tuesday, and I was planning on taking the overnight bus anyway. It's easier to sleep through part of such a long drive. So I can stay until Monday. Unless you've already rented the room to somebody else."

Audrey's throat tightened. She could only nod in agreement.

When the girls slipped back across the dark lawn in the early hours before dawn, it seemed to Audrey that they were both reluctant to leave the cocoon of the carriage house. They stood inside the front foyer of the inn to say good night, and Audrey said, "Rosey's got a truck. We could steal it and run away."

"I think we both already tried that," Frances said. "And I'm not sure you can outrun this baby. But maybe he'd let us borrow it for your appointment. I can ask."

"Yeah," Audrey admitted. "But don't tell him that's what it's for."

Later, as she lay in the soft bed, Audrey rested her hands on the small mound of her belly and stared at the ceiling. She listened to the early train when it rumbled through. For the first time since she'd come to town, instead of trying to plug her ears and block out the sound, she was glad of something certain, something she could count on to be the same each day, and she wondered where it might be going.

Chapter Thirteen

CLEO

CLEO WAS UP TO HER ELBOWS IN WATER AT THE SINK, WASHING vegetables, when Tate finally knocked on her door.

"Took your sweet time. If you came to see about the mink, he's slipped this mortal coil, as I told you he would three days ago."

"Ah, no."

"Ah, yes. Yesterday."

Tate's face was so crestfallen at the news that Cleo actually felt bad for delivering it right off. She wouldn't have admitted it to a living soul, but she'd cried a little into her pillow before getting up to make her coffee. She hadn't been so softhearted over a wild thing in years, and she blamed it on all these recent human interactions.

"I'm sorry to hear we lost that little fella."

"Well, he wasn't something we owned, was he? Not ours. But that animal went out with the comforts of a house cat, thanks to you."

"And you."

"Where's your gun-toting friend?"

He acted like he didn't hear a word. "I bring news of the world. Bad weather coming in."

"You can stop that right now. I've lived on this spit in this river for nearly thirty years. They talk about that storm every damn year and I've long stopped believing a word of it. Weather comes, weather goes. You ought to know well as anybody. Now, really, why is it you're set on convincing me to come into town? I'm not that sort, Tate. You ought to know it." She had waited long enough to ask what she wanted to know. And after that last run-in on the dock, Cleo wasn't feeling particularly patient.

He took up a dish towel beside her to help dry and stack the produce. For a long while, they didn't talk. The man was jittery, as though he'd had too much coffee. It gave her a little charge, knowing she made him nervous.

"You make a pretty painting," he said.

"That is not an answer."

He noted the usual watercolor illustrations of tagalongs laid out to dry around the room. She hadn't thought of putting them away.

"Apparently these old things are beloved. Can you believe that? It's what that Flood girl said. *Beloved.* I never laughed so hard."

"I wouldn't know. Don't see much art on the railroad." He cocked his head, searching the watercolor images like he was hearing something far off.

Cleo said, "All I ever did was copy Dooley's little pictures the same as I remember them. If I knew how to paint anything else, I'd already have this damned commission finished and put to rest."

Tate followed her gaze to the blank paper where she'd sat for hours at a time, trying to figure where to start on the commissioned work.

"Is that the trouble, do you think?"

Cleo ground her teeth. "Every time I think I'll sit down and get started, I haven't got any idea where to begin and that paper's just staring back at me, white as it can be. If I thought being out here all this time would make me crazy before this, well, I had no idea what crazy felt like. Dr. Johnston should have asked me to paint him a picture all those years ago. That would have been punishment enough, I can tell you that."

Tate chuckled and Cleo threw her dish towel at him. He bent to snatch it up and said, "Seems like if you want to paint something new, maybe you've got to do something new."

"Aren't you the great philosopher? Where'd you come by all your wisdom?" Cleo said. But he was right. She knew it. "I'm not leaving this cottage. Not yet. Not until I'm ready."

"And when will that be?"

"I don't know, but not now."

He went to peer at the empty basket where the mink had been and she swore he was just like a kid, heartbroken over death when it only happened every day. "What did you do with that little friend?"

Cleo put down her towel, finished with the work at the sink. "If you want to come with me, we'll put this thing to rest. Then maybe you can work up the courage to tell me whatever it is you've really come here for."

"Maybe I just want the company. Did you ever think of that, Cleo?"

Cleo had thought of it. But she said, "I keep my own company. It's been a lot less trouble."

———

She had wrapped the animal in a flour sack and put it on her woodpile behind the house. Now Tate carried it and walked at her elbow. She could hear the high, thin notes of a mountain fiddle on the breeze. Tate didn't seem to notice it. Given she'd recently mistaken a very real black dog for one of her friendly figments, she was careful not to react to the soppy tune of the fiddler on the air, lest Tate realize how truly off her nut she had become. *What is this one, anyway?* she wondered absently. *"Some Enchanted Evening."*

Tate Walker was awfully close, or maybe it was only that she wasn't used to living company on her walks. She could smell him and hear his steps lining up with her own. "Could you back up and stop breathing down my neck?"

"Well, excuse me."

Cleo tried to put some space between their strides. Unlike so many of the men her age, the fishermen and the ones who worked for the Cumberland families or down at the Piedmont mill, he had not lost all his hair or grown a paunch around his middle. He was still tall and lean, if pleasantly softer at his edges than he'd been as a boy. He still had a head of sandy-blond hair that had grown long at the collar, streaked gray in a way that only accentuated the flat plain of his forehead and sharp nose. Looking at him, she wondered if maybe they weren't so old after all. She'd call him a handsome man, in fact, and the thought startled her. On its heels, she found herself wondering what he'd made of her. She couldn't recall the last time she'd looked in a mirror.

She dragged her thoughts back to the business at hand. The tide was coming in so they took her johnboat out on the water. He'd surely guessed where they were headed but kept his thoughts to himself until they stood under the shade of the sprawling oak limbs, moss draping down. The sunlight sifted through the understory to light the long white femurs, ribs, and even an eyeless skull of a pony staring up from the resurrection ferns. As always, she was struck by a sense of reverence. It was gratifying to see that feeling matched by the look on Tate's face. In a whisper, he said, "Long time since I thought of this place."

"The bone orchard. That's what Dooley called it. Lumas Gray told me there was a giant buried here."

"He told everybody that."

They smiled at the memory as they walked through the glade. Here was a great carapace she'd found on the dunes and brought to the boneyard only a year after she'd come to the cottage. There were other bones that reclined in repose, some skeletons that remained intact and many more that had been foraged by the living wildlife of the shoals, but all of it silent and festooned with the moss and ferns of the forest. All of it perpetually consumed by time and tide, returning to mineral and mud, a kind of resurrection that appealed to her way of thinking. And twining through it all were the morning glory vines. She thought about Lumas warning her the place was cursed, and maybe it was, but it was also sacred. Now she was a woman who was old enough to know how to respect this place for both reasons.

"He'll rest like a little king here," she said to Tate, gesturing toward the light bundle in the crook of his arms.

With great consideration, Tate looked about them before deciding on a spot near the foot of one of the oaks. He tucked the mink there, unrolling it from the flour sack before giving its soft body one delicate stroke and stepping back so the ferns closed over it. He surprised her by folding his hands and drawing himself up straight. He closed his eyes and said a little poem, something she'd never heard before in a language she did not know. His voice was low and melancholy, and the ends of the lines turned up like a sort of yodel. Cleo felt slightly embarrassed to be watching, but Tate didn't seem to mind. When he finished, he turned dark eyes her way.

"Cleo, I'm going to be honest with you."

"Well, thank heavens above."

"Listen, don't be that way. I'm trying to tell you what you want."

"All right, fine. I'm sorry."

He settled to it, folding his arms tightly against his chest, but as he spoke, his hands seemed to need to gesture and she thought she'd never seen him so sincerely trying to communicate a thought. "When I got that news from Dr. Johnston, it seemed like it woke me up some way. Do you know what I mean? Woke me up from some long dream where I'd just been going from one place to another all this time, never really getting anywhere."

"I guess I can imagine." She tried to sound encouraging.

"He sent us all every which way, didn't he? Thinking he knew what would be best. I guess that's why he sent that obituary out to all three of us—you, me, and Morrie. We're the last ones to remember that summer. Did you think of that?"

"I think about it every day, Tate. I never left here." A question occurred to her then. "How'd you know he sent one to Morrie? You talked to either one of them?"

"I have," he said. He looked at her a little funny, she thought, then said, "I got on that train, riding away and away from here, and my life's just gone right by me. But when I'd think about it, what happened, I'd think about you. And I'd think at least there, I'd done a good thing."

"Me?" Cleo took a step back.

"I think about those boys, of course. And Joanna. But I felt responsible for you, Cleo. What's happened to you?"

She'd never heard such intensity in his voice. It made her consider where she stood with him, with the morning glory vines all around their feet. Surely it had nothing to do with the charge in the air. It was only Tate, raising the past between them. Only a man and his regrets. But he was looking at her as if she were the answer. "You have got your head screwed on wrong."

"This is coming out wrong."

"Well, then, get it right."

"When I got that obituary, I pulled out that watch and realized I'd been living like I had all the time in the world. And I was wrong. And it scared me, Cleo. I figured it might scare you too. And if that was the case, I knew where I was going."

"I don't know what you're trying to say."

He nodded and finally looked at her straight on. "I saw you that day," he said, "after I left the watch in the ash pit. I saw you come out and pick it up. I know what it stopped you doing. You want to know why I came back? Because I knew how I was feeling to hear Joanna had died, and I worried how you would take it. And I was right, wasn't I?"

Cleo didn't deny it. She didn't feel like lying to the man. And she wasn't ashamed. "If you're worried I'm still going to do it, I haven't decided. But I'm not thinking about doing it right this second."

He let out a long breath. "I guess that makes me feel a little better." After a pause, he added, "But do you still have that watch? Could you think about letting me have that back?"

Cleo groaned and he looked alarmed. "I was going to give it to you and tell you to leave me alone. That's why I came out to Plum Orchard that day I first saw you, to tell you to stop sneaking around, spying on me. But it dropped out of my damn pocket in the water. I was embarrassed to tell you. I'm sorry about that." He was obviously disappointed. "What was the point of leaving it out there if you ever wanted it in the first place?"

"I hoped if you saw it, you'd figure I was back. Maybe it would give you a little time to get used to the idea of me while I worked up the courage to see you face-to-face." He shrugged. "I was trying not to spook you."

"Wouldn't want to push the lunatic over the edge?"

"Nobody's saying that but you."

"Plenty of people say it. You just said you raced back out here thinking I might do something crazy when I heard the news and then you saw just how right you were. If it hadn't been for that watch and how smart you are, I guess I would have offed myself. I absolve you, my son."

"Cleo, don't act like this."

"Well, what do you want, Tate? Do you want me to thank you for saving my life all over again? Do you need to be a hero to get yourself right with your boys and then you thought you'd tote me back to town over your shoulder like it was Cleo Woodbine season and you brought in the prize?" Cleo started putting the pieces together. She felt humiliated. He was only here to feel better about himself. She ought to know. It was the same reason she'd kept those pearls. She was humiliated to realize that she'd believed he'd come back because he wanted to see her, but he'd only been worried she'd go through with what she started. "Did you bring me that mink so I'd have something to keep alive?"

"It wasn't something I planned. But now I think of it, seems like it worked."

"The mink's dead," Cleo said, her voice rising.

Cleo was embarrassed and angry. She'd felt something for Tate these last few days. Now she just felt pathetic.

Finally it was Tate who said, "Did any one of us do the right thing back then, Cleo?" He shoved his hands in his pockets and turned to go. She watched him walk a few steps, then stop.

"I spent a lot of time thinking my life couldn't change. That I'd made my mistakes and I had to live with that. But I want something different. Don't you? I came back here to tell that to my boys. And to you, I guess. And now I have. So if you want to live, then get on with it. I plan to do the same."

They let that understanding settle down between them. She checked the sun overhead. The tide was high. Off in the distance, she could hear that fiddle tune picking up again.

As if it had only just dawned on him to pass the information along, Tate said, "Morrie Johnston's about as likely to get that bobcat as I am to win the Derby. Listen to him. You'd think he was playing a serenade for the thing."

Cleo only felt confused until Tate gestured in the air and she realized he was talking about the music. She kept her face turned down, feeling foolish, but not so surprised this time. And with that, each of her tagalongs had transformed so there was no denying they'd taken corporal form. Flesh and blood. Cleo felt she'd been entirely dragged back to reality.

"That was Morrie with the rifle? On the dock? That's when he told you he got the obituary from Dr. Johnston?" It occurred to her then that Morrie might have been back longer than Tate. "That's his dog?"

"He says it won't hunt a lick. He's opened up Plum Orchard again. Drinking enough wood alcohol, I don't know how he's not blind. Missing old times. Glenn's trying to get on his good side, cooking up some sanctioned hunts on the island to make some extra cash. But Morrie's shut him down. So now there's some argument about it since Glenn's taken money from a group of outdoorsmen that expect to come up from Florida sometime in these next weeks."

"I've heard some about Glenn's schemes from Rosey," Cleo admitted. "Why is Glenn so hard put for money?"

He sighed. "Paper mill's cut back hours, did you know? More than two dozen jobs were cut without any warning. That's a lot of men got an axe to grind with the yuppity-yups. You know how it can get. You need to keep informed if you're going to stay out here."

Talk about such normal things, present things, seemed to release a little pressure between them. They'd come to the place on the Grand Avenue where they could part ways. That fiddle music sounded faint now, headed away from them, when Cleo said, "You tell Glenn and any more of that bunch they'd better not come too far out my way." She set off before the tide could get ahead of her but tossed a final thought over her shoulder. "You know how I can get."

Tate heard the warning. "I do. But I'll be back, Cleo."

"You're never going to find that watch," she said, as if that was what he was really after.

Chapter Fourteen

FABLE

SOMEHOW JOANNA HAD CLOSED THE SPACE BETWEEN THEM AS they floated in the water. Her face was close to Cleo's face, her eyes blue and tipped up like a cat's, her lips slightly open as if she'd sigh, her hands resting on Cleo's upper arms. She reached to tuck Cleo's hair behind her ear and drew Cleo close. They stood on their toes in the sand and the water moved over and around them. The embrace was not so different from the way Ellis had held her. Cleo wept. She hadn't meant for any of this to happen, but that's how it was with Joanna, she was learning. She couldn't name what she felt for Joanna, only that she could not pull away from her.

"You're beautiful, you know," Joanna finally said. Cleo felt embarrassed, as if Joanna could have somehow read her thoughts.

"I'm not."

"Well, you are to me. And to Ellis. He said so." Now it was Joanna who paused for effect. "We could have any of these boys, you know? But you shouldn't tell that story. Not to anyone else. We have to keep some things for ourselves."

"I don't want any of the boys."

"You mean you want Ellis? Truly?" Joanna laughed, but Cleo could tell she really wanted the answer. "I thought he was only using you, trying to make me jealous."

Cleo felt embarrassed it was so obvious. "I didn't say I wanted Ellis."

"No, say it, please. Take him."

Cleo felt completely out of sorts. She'd opened up the door to the memory of the overturned car and she felt overwhelmed by all the old feelings, but also by her feelings for Joanna. And Ellis. And how they all seemed tangled together now. She'd come to Plum Orchard believing she was an artist, and then she'd imagined herself a lover, and then she'd been willing to take such chances with glory and turned her back on Lumas Gray. Now she didn't feel she knew herself at all. Standing naked in the water with a girl who might as well have been singing a tempting siren song to her, Cleo feared she'd lost her way. She'd surely lost her composure and blurted, "It doesn't matter. He loves you."

"Why would you think that?"

"Because we've been together so many times, but it didn't matter what I did, he never went through with it."

"Through with it?" Joanna's mouth fell open. She knew exactly what Cleo meant, and Cleo would have stuffed the words back down her gullet if there were any way. "You and Ellis? You mean he never ravished you in all those little swims you took at Plum Orchard?"

Cleo opened her mouth to deny it.

"Oh, stop. Of course he told me. But what do you think's wrong with him?"

Cleo jumped to Ellis's defense. "Nothing's wrong with him. If anything, I'm the one with something wrong. He was nothing but a gentleman. He said he loved me for my stories."

Joanna laughed. "Oh, geez. He's so strange. Ellis only really loves Ellis. He's just entertaining himself. That's why he has me here, because he's bored. He's just waiting for me to drop my pearls and that's the truth. It's a game we're playing, me and Ellis. See which one will have the upper hand. I guess this is how it will go the rest of our lives. Little entertainments."

Cleo remembered he'd said much the same to her that first day, but she'd pushed the thought aside and even now hurried to defend Ellis. "You're lucky. He's gentle. He's respectful. And he'll be Dr. Johnston's golden boy by the end of this summer if he tells the best story at the bonfire. Everyone says so. How can you say he won't have choices?"

"Maybe a golden goose egg. Which is only because of you," Joanna said. "Everything that comes out of his mouth around the dinner table is because you whispered it in his ear, Cleo. What's going to happen when he goes back to Philadelphia and you can't be his muse? I'll tell you. Everyone will see what we both know is true: he's dull as ditchwater. Whatever it is you do, I can tell you that I certainly never had that effect on him. You say he never had you? Well, then, you must have wiles I can't even guess, Cleo Woodbine. But I think you're just a liar."

Cleo was so embarrassed, she blurted, "It's not like that. It's only a seed I grind and dust over his food to calm him. He gets so nervous and it inspires him to confidence, that's all."

At this, Joanna's eyes widened. "You're serious? I was only joking. You really did something to him? You doped him? Oh, Cleo. You have to show me what it is."

Cleo had said much more than she'd intended. "I shouldn't have done it. I've already decided I won't do it again. It was wrong. It was stupid. I'm going to tell him, even if he won't forgive me."

"Forgive you? Whatever it is, trust me, little witch, as long as he's getting what he wants—all that attention, all that confidence— then he's only going to want more of it. Don't forget, that's what they're born to. More, more, more. But don't tell him. If he ever figures it out, or figures out how to get it for himself, he'll never want you. Don't drop your pearls, Cleo. Remember Lorelei. Hang on to whatever little bit of influence you have and don't give it up, not to the sea or Daddy or for the swine over at Plum Orchard."

"I don't have pearls," Cleo said flatly.

After the moments they'd just shared and all of Joanna's tenderness, Cleo still didn't trust her. She was ashamed for being so naive and unnerved that she'd revealed what she'd been doing with Ellis. She felt manipulated. Joanna's bright eyes missed nothing. Cleo could see by the hint of triumph in her face that she was well aware she'd upset Cleo. And with her next words, she loosened the invisible tether between them just enough so Cleo understood this was the end of their strange intimacy.

"Hey, do you think I'd win with my story if I recited naked?" She flipped onto her back again and drifted away.

"I think you've already won," Cleo said.

Joanna moaned. "What do you think I should do? Should I jump at the chance to move out from the apartment over Burton Antiques, Fine Art and Collectibles and up to a Philly mansion and have lots of little Piedmont babies? Should I take you with me, my dearest companion, so you can feed him whatever it is that makes him tolerable?"

"Why did you even come here if you don't want him?"

Joanna looked at her then, dropping her feet again and walking out of the water on full display, squeezing water from her hair. "Because my parents arranged it. They met the Piedmonts through some auction or other and learned they had an eligible son and thought of all that money," she called over the sound of the surf. "I'm only here because I have to be."

"So you don't love Ellis. Really, you don't want him?"

"Trust me, if I wanted him, I'd have already had him and I wouldn't have to dope him to do it. Honestly, Cleo, neither should you."

The insult humiliated Cleo. But it occurred to her that Joanna was only a merchant's daughter, and in that way, not so different from herself. In fact, Cleo realized, in one way she had the advantage. She'd come here for an independent life, unlike Joanna. She joined her on the shore and grabbed for her clothes. Joanna did not dress but stood there drying in the sun.

Cleo said, "I never came here to snag a husband."

"You could have fooled me."

"No, I came for the opposite. I never planned on Ellis."

"Do tell," Joanna teased.

"My granddaddy and Dr. Johnston were best friends growing up in Kentucky. He gave Dooley—my granddad—a place to work. It's mine now, if I want it. I'll be artist-in-residence with Dr. Johnston as my patron."

Joanna pursed her full lips and gave a low whistle. "Well, now. That is something different. Where is this house?"

"It's only a cottage. When Dr. Johnston arrives, I'll meet him and it will be settled."

"Oh, Cleo, you are hilarious. Do not tell this story either. They'll eat you alive."

Cleo's jaw tightened. "When I wrote to Dr. Johnston, he invited me up, then asked for my help with you as a favor, to give me time to decide if island life was for me."

Joanna smiled knowingly. "But you decided you'd have Ellis Piedmont instead."

"I didn't decide that."

"Well, then, you should have no compunctions if I do." She

liked this, Cleo saw. She liked seeing Cleo cornered, even out here on this wide shore. She wanted to force her to admit the truth. "Or maybe you want both? Aren't you a minx. And I thought I was the sly one. You've really stacked the deck, haven't you? What do you need Ellis for if you already have a house? I'd live under a cockle-shell out here if I could do it without having to answer to anyone. But you'll always be answering to them if you take it, won't you?"

It struck Cleo then that Joanna was perturbed. It went to Cleo's head and she twisted that little advantage.

"I guess we'll both do what we like, won't we? Dr. Johnston will be here tomorrow and I haven't even gone out to see the cottage yet. You may be right about it. It's probably nothing but a shed and I won't stay there anyway."

"I guess we both have choices after all."

Cleo walked back toward the house, taking the sandy path through the dunes and into the blessed shade of the oaks, where the other girl could not see her tears. She'd tried not to show how Joanna's words hurt. She'd meant what she'd told Joanna, that she would confess everything to Ellis and then give him the choice. She could show him how to use it, how to be careful, how they could both get what they wanted. But if Cleo had heard one thing she knew was true from Joanna, it was that glory was powerful. And she wasn't going to let Ellis go so easily.

————

Cleo took one of the bikes they'd ridden out to the beach and made her way to the bone orchard. There was no one to see her there in the late afternoon. She collected the blooms for their seeds and brought them to her room. In her mortar and pestle, she ground them down to the finest powder, enough so she'd be ready for whatever Ellis needed. If he wanted her for glory, then he would have it.

She hurried out to the porch where she knew Ellis would return before dinner with the others. "Cleo," he said when he saw her. Not like he was glad about it.

She wished then that she had taken the time to clean up after the swim, changed into fresh clothes, pulled up her hair. She tried to remember the ways she'd seen Joanna move, how she'd touched her throat or leaned her hip. "Let's go somewhere."

"What do you mean? We just got back from the duck hunt." He was already testy. He must have been dismayed with his performance. She should have found some way to have helped him along. "I need a shower and a drink."

His eyes darted from Cleo to the lawn and then swept the length of the drive, looking for anyone who might witness their exchange. It only emboldened her. She tried the tone that had always worked before when they were sneaking away by themselves. She put her hands on his arms and pulled him close. "Just for a little while." She pressed her lips to his. He tasted of sweat, but also the tang of mineral, and she was confused as to whether it might be the salt water on her own mouth.

He pushed her away from him. His eyes darted past her again. He looked almost excited, like his old self. She noticed then that his hair was damp.

"I love you, Ellis. I've loved you since that first day on the porch," Cleo said. "Joanna laughs at your harelip. She says your engagement is just another auction item on the block with her father. But I know you can talk your way past anything, be anything, do anything. I helped you when—"

"Shut up, Cleo. They laugh about you, did you know? Morrie

says your granddaddy was a hillbilly lout. Dr. Johnston kept him around because he felt sorry for him. You know that, right? You're here out of charity. And I doubt he'll keep you around very long if I tell him you've been poisoning me."

"You know?" The words struck like blows, but Cleo wouldn't give him up. "It's not poison. Never poison. I never did it to hurt you. That's what I wanted to tell you. I only want to give you what you want. Give you the choice." Some twisted pride had hold of her, the certain knowledge that she had inspired this confidence in the boy she'd found cowering that first day. Surely he knew it. She thought she would die of heartbreak if he walked away, and it was not the same pain she'd felt when her parents had died. Not even when she'd lost Dooley. Those had been a quiet blackness that left her cold and drifting. This pain was sharp and hot and alive.

He gave a sharp little sound almost like a laugh, almost like he'd been taken by some sudden pain. "You really think that? That I have a choice about anything in my life?"

"But you do. You don't have to forgive me, but I hope you will." And then she saw the truth.

Joanna stepped around the house, barefoot, her hair dried in a golden riot, her mouth wild with smeared lipstick, her blouse untucked from her skirt and open to her thin camisole. If she'd heard Ellis's awful words, she didn't seem to care. Her eyes were on Cleo as she came up the steps. She saw that Cleo understood. Still, she said, "Oh, you're not shocked. Don't look at me like that. I told you I could and I did. I hope you meant what you just said, because whatever you've been giving him, he's going to need a lot more."

Ellis shrank from Cleo now, flushed. His mousy eyes swiveled away, searched for an escape. In the time when Cleo had gone to gather glory, Joanna had been true to everything she'd told Cleo.

She had not waited. And whatever false confidence that glory had inspired in Ellis Piedmont, Joanna had scooped it out. She swept past them, and over her shoulder, she called back as she stepped inside, "I swear, this has been the worst day. Cleo, come help with my bath. It's burning the hell up in here. Don't forget we're going to the old Dungeness pool tonight for some acrobats on the rings. Better rest up."

Pretty Joanna with her lilting voice. Joanna with her arrogant heart. She didn't love Ellis or see him the way Cleo could. All Cleo knew was that she hated her for making a joke of Ellis. She thought of the bottle filled with glory tucked deep inside her dresser drawer, and as she left Ellis to follow the other girl inside, her only thought was that with Joanna gone, everything would change.

Chapter Fifteen

FRANCES

THERE WAS NO MUSIC FROM THE TURNTABLE TO WAKE FRANCES the morning after she'd shared secrets with Audrey in the carriage house. But when she threw her feet out of bed, her first thought was not to question the silence but of scheduling the overdue pre-natal checkup. Frances hoped she could find a local directory at the library when she stopped to see the archive materials on the siren sightings, something she'd been putting off.

It still made her anxious to think of stepping into the little tabby building next to the theater, walking beneath the doorway with the Piedmont family name over the lintel, knowing what she was really hoping for was a photo of Ellis Piedmont. She'd thought of it last night when Audrey had talked about such things, what might be revealed in a photograph. She wondered if it would change how she felt about her identity as Owen and Joanna Flood's daughter.

Everything was set up for brunch downstairs, but it was still hours before the buffet would open. Frances came upon Audrey in the empty bedroom opposite hers, going through boxes of what Frances assumed were the former owner's things. She observed her for a moment before Audrey noticed her there. The poor girl looked so small surrounded by the things she'd unpacked, a silk scarf draped across her shoulders.

"I'm sorry," Frances said. "Are you okay? Are you crying?"

Audrey turned to shove everything back into a box, embarrassed to be caught out. In the light of day, Frances realized that everything they'd shared the night before made her, too, feel vulnerable.

"Do you want to be left alone?"

Audrey shook her head and flapped her hands to dismiss Frances's concern. "No, come on in." She sighed. "I'm not crying. I'm trying to cry. I never do. There's something really wrong with me."

Frances apologized again and Audrey told her to stop. "Okay, I'm not sorry. But there's nothing wrong with you. And you can talk to me, if you want. Please do. It's great to think about someone besides myself for a change."

Audrey sighed. "Every day I avoid this room, so today I thought, why not just get over it already?"

"Why do you avoid it?"

"I don't know. Maybe because I didn't really have a chance to do this with Freddie's things. His mom and sister took care of most of it. But this was all here just like Aunt Shirley left it. This is the room she always kept for Cleo Woodbine, but I guess she still kept stuff in this closet. The whole house is full of her stuff. Should I pack it all up or donate it? It seems wrong to be going through everything, but it seems worse to pretend it's not even here. How am I supposed to decide what matters and what gets tossed? It was her life. Doesn't it all matter?"

Frances rested her hands on her hips and glanced around. There wasn't really that much in the room. "There must be plenty of storage in a house like this, a big attic?"

Audrey pointed to the ceiling. "Packed full. I swear. But there's a loft in the carriage house. I haven't made it up there yet. I don't like mice."

"Well, I don't mind them. Let's have a look now. See what you're dealing with."

In the carriage house, the space was rustic. Frances climbed up the open stairs first, announcing the all-clear for rodents, and Audrey followed. They peered into the murky darkness. Frances found a single bulb and pulled a string. In the hazy light, their expectations were exceeded. The loft ran the length of the carriage house with a highly pitched roof, and it felt less than haunted. In fact, Frances was hard-pressed to find a cobweb. The thin layer of dust did not seem to have accumulated for decades. It looked to her as if someone frequented the loft on the regular.

Beneath the dormer windows at the front, Frances found a blanket, a flashlight, and a stack of books. "Have you heard anything moving around up here when you're in your darkroom? It looks like somebody's made a playhouse up here. My house was lousy with other people's kids, and this is a blanket fort if I ever saw one. And comic books."

"I bet it's Jimmy Walker," Audrey said. "I should have known. He said he comes to the inn all the time. I just never thought about the loft."

Frances walked around the space while Audrey inched farther up the ladder and poked her head in. "Makes sense he would know about it. Rosey probably played here when he was younger and showed it to him. The good news is there's plenty of room up here to store away everything you want to keep. Everything I own would fit up here."

"Oh, please move in right away. Hurry, do," Audrey begged playfully, then picked up the comics with a moan. "I'm being invaded by Walkers."

They climbed back down the unsteady steps and made their way back to the inn and through to the foyer. Audrey put the comics down on the table there, then took a seat in the living room.

Frances asked, "Did you decide you'll tell Glenn you don't want to do the photos anymore?"

Audrey nodded. "If you see smoke coming from the Marvel, it's because he's spontaneously combusted."

"You realize I haven't even met him yet. If anybody's a ghost around here, it seems like it's Glenn." She ticked the evidence off on her fingers. "Everybody's talking about him, there's troubling evidence he exists, but he never actually materializes." She thought it was a pretty good joke, but Audrey didn't laugh.

"Frances, I'm serious. You could stay here," she said, sounding sheepish.

"Very funny," Frances said as if the invitation were only a joke, even though she knew Audrey was serious. She also knew Audrey wouldn't be alone very long, and that had nothing to do with the Walkers. And she wouldn't make promises she couldn't keep. "I'm going to find a doctor today. I'll look for someone in New Canaan, like you asked. In case you aren't sure what you want just yet."

"What I want?"

Frances tried to choose her words carefully. "I only mean in case you want to make choices. If you're not ready to be a mother."

"You think I'd give the baby away?"

"I just want to help."

Audrey relaxed. "I want the baby."

She looked so young. Frances's heart ached for her. "You're going to be a good mother, Audrey."

"How do you know?"

"I know because I had a good mother." Even as she said it, Frances knew it was true. "I know one when I see one. Her whole life was about mothering. The day care she ran out of our house after my dad died was called Mother's Helper, for gosh sakes. I can't count the times I heard her say, 'Good mothers do what's best for their kids, even when it's really hard,' to let those ladies know it was okay that they had to leave their children for the day. Because mothers love their kids above everything, even themselves. Like you already love this one."

Audrey said, "You're saying really nice things, but how do you know any of that about me? I've been trying to pretend it didn't even exist. I don't know if I love it, but I know I'm not ready for it."

"That's the easy part," Frances said. "They come whether you're ready or not."

"I'm serious. I have no idea what I'm supposed to be doing. Don't I need a nursery? I don't even have a diaper. I don't know how to do any of it. I didn't have sisters or brothers. I never even did babysitting."

Frances laughed. "Let's start with getting you to the doctor. The rest we can manage one thing at a time. We'll make a list." A thought occurred to Frances. "A lot of what you need is sitting in boxes from my old house in Asheville. You can have it. I was going to donate it anyway."

Audrey looked at Frances like she'd just provided the answers to life's greatest mysteries. "You really are a mother's helper."

"I don't know about that. I didn't do much of the actual helping, more of the stepping around and complaining our house was their house. It's funny now I think about it, knowing what I know now. I never understood how she could be so patient with them, these kids who were basically strangers, and their moms too. I think my mom knew what she was doing was important. What she did for them mattered. I didn't see it then, but I'm starting to."

Audrey looked around the room. "After my uncle died, Aunt Shirley started letting the rooms out here. For money, I'm sure, but

I think also so the house wouldn't feel so empty. I think she missed my mom, but we never came to visit. I don't know why. I know my mother never would have opened our house to strangers. I don't think I'm much like her." Audrey laughed, but it was mirthless.

Frances reached to help Audrey get to her feet.

"I really do wish you would consider staying here, Frances."

Frances tried to keep her tone light. "Well, how about if I promise I'll come back again? I'll have to, won't I? To meet this baby? How's that?"

"I guess I'll keep a room ready for you, like Aunt Shirley did for Cleo."

Frances felt she was disappointing Audrey, but she had a plan and it was not to go back to the same situation she'd been in before, living in someone else's house, caring for someone else's children. And that's what this would be like, she thought. She fell back on the wisdom of years of study for what she might say that wouldn't be hurtful and said, "In the stories, the heroes are always on a journey or a quest of some kind, just like in life. That's the part of the story we're at now, where you don't know where it's going to lead just yet; you're just hoping." Frances smiled. "I've got to go see a librarian about a river siren. You think about how to quit working for that ogre. Then we'll see what happens next."

She left Audrey smiling again, if not so brightly as the night before.

———

The Piedmont Library was pleasingly cool inside. It smelled of paper and water and time, exactly as a library in Revery should smell. A librarian greeted her from the circulation desk.

"Are you the girl staying over at Gilbreath House?" she asked.

"Yes, ma'am." The temptation to try out her true name right there in that place burned the end of her tongue, so she bit down on it to keep her secret before she answered, "Frances Flood."

The librarian smiled. She was a dim sort of person, faded at the edges of her graying hair and gray dress. But she was kind. "Everybody calls me Mrs. Mae," she said.

"I understand you have an archive dedicated to the local sightings of the river siren."

"Archive? It's just a half dozen clippings and such. But nobody ever comes in here for it."

"Do you think you could bring that out for me? I like to study myths and legends around the world."

Mrs. Mae smiled. "What are you looking for? Monsters or ghosts? We have both, you know."

Frances felt friendly toward her. "Well, I have a personal interest in the siren sighting here in '32. I'm hoping you have more information than I've been able to find on my own, which has not been all that much, to be honest. Just the little that my mother could tell me. She was only visiting that summer."

The librarian's small brown eyes appeared very bright with curiosity. She left Frances for a few minutes before returning from a back room carrying a thin folder. Frances could hear the swish of her pantyhose as she walked in the silence of the library.

She smiled apologetically at Frances. "Here you go. I don't know if this will be what you're hoping for, only a few short articles and some notes scratched on the backs of a few photos."

"That's exactly what I was hoping for." Her hand shook a little when she took the folder, and she knew the other woman noticed. She must seem a strange girl to be so worked up over the dusty old articles.

Mrs. Mae said, "I hope you won't mind me saying, but you look a little piqued. You need to keep your head covered out in that sun down here, honey. It can drain you."

"It's just history tours."

"Well, it will do you good to sit in the air-conditioning this morning, won't it? You've been going out with Rosey Devane, we've all noticed."

Frances searched for some way to throw the librarian off the scent of a hot new romance in a small town and remembered her other reason for coming into the library. She smiled and asked in her most academic voice, "If you have a local directory, I'd appreciate having a look at it."

"Well, sure, but it's not a big place," the librarian said, pulling a thin directory and phone book from behind the counter and offering it to Frances. "I could save you time. If you ask me, I'll likely be able to point you in the right direction of whatever you might need here in Revery."

"Thank you," Frances said without further explanation, taking the directory.

Frances hurried away to find a little reading table where she could have some privacy. She found the name of a physician's office in New Canaan, scratched the number into her field notebook, and quickly put the directory aside. It took only a moment to see that Mrs. Mae's evaluation of the so-called archive was spot-on, and her hopes fell. It amounted to exactly two newspaper articles that were nothing but nostalgia, primarily colorful quotes from fishermen or local teens who had reported their own sightings over the years since the event in '32, and one stakeout by a couple of scientists that resulted in no evidence at all of anything in the East River that could not be explained away by nature. Normally Frances would have enjoyed poring over all of it, but she pushed it aside in search of the original reports, finding one that was identical to the clipping her mother had saved, then another from a Brunswick paper. Frances read that carefully, noting the scant details of Ellis Piedmont's drowning and that of an unnamed colored boy, whom she knew to be Lumas Gray. There'd been no mention of Joanna Burton or Cleo Woodbine, either one. And no photos.

After only thirty minutes, she returned the materials and turned to leave the library disappointed. The librarian watched her go and must have truly worried about Frances when she stopped dead in her tracks only a few steps from the door to stare up at an oversized portrait of a young man hanging next to the exit. The little gold plaque screwed into the elaborate frame read, *In memoriam of Ellis Piedmont.*

Next door Rosey had just unlocked the doors at the Marvel when Frances stepped up to wave through the glass. He said, "You look like you're running from the law."

"Your librarian thinks I'm getting too much sun."

Frances had been thinking about what Audrey said about Rosey making up the ghost of Wandering Merry just for her as she barreled down the sidewalk with no idea where she was going.

Rosey smiled, but he was starting to look concerned. "Want to come in?"

"Audrey convinced me to stay an extra day," she said as she stepped inside. Rosey looked pleased but didn't tease her this time, and Frances was grateful.

She followed him through the theater's foyer, which must have once been grand, with a black-and-white checkerboard marble floor, dimly lit by wall sconces that glowed like torches. Now it was a bit scuffed and dingy. To one side was a concessions bar, encircled by plush ropes that matched the red velvet carpet. Rosey led her up a narrow set of stairs and through a door to the film booth, where the projector hummed and flashed the picture below.

"Perks of owning a theater. You can screen a movie anytime you like." He tossed the explanation over his shoulder. "Come through this way," he said, and they continued from the booth up another short flight of stairs to an apartment. She wasn't surprised to find the simple living space with a kitchenette in the back corner and the windows facing the street, the ones that looked out above the marquee board.

"It's nice up here," she said, stepping to the window. Her hands were still shaking and she clasped them tightly in front of her. "You can see all the way out to the water."

"Best view in town. But the marquee lights are my favorite. I'd leave them on all night if the power bill wouldn't sink me." Rosey looked at her in a way that made Frances want to forget the reasons she never should have come upstairs. "Want some coffee? I'll put on a pot," he said, not waiting to fill the percolator.

"Are these Will's rooms?" she asked absently, realizing this must be true even through the jumble of her thoughts after what she'd just seen. Then recalling what Audrey had told her about reading from the script and how upset Glenn had been when he'd walked in on them. "Won't he mind?"

"Will's out. And he won't mind. It's more of a community space."

Frances didn't argue as soft bubbling sounds and the comforting scent filled the room. There was another door and she assumed that led to the room where William Tremmons slept. Books were stacked on a table and against the walls just as Audrey had described it: philosophy, politics, poetry. Rosey saw her looking.

"The man will read anything. I call him the professor. Just move something if you want to take a seat. Will got two years of college at Oklahoma State University Institute of Technology and an associate's degree in engineering before he volunteered for Korea. Thought it would be good experience, being a soldier."

Frances carefully did as he'd suggested, pushing a stack of newspapers aside as she took a seat on a sofa.

"Nobody can match his skill with a set of tools. Put just about anything in his hand and he can use it to fix something one way or another. I picked the best when I needed a right-hand man."

"So I'm guessing that demotes Glenn to your left hand?"

Rosey rolled his eyes.

Frances was thinking of what Rosey had said the day before and of all that Audrey had later confided. "Audrey thinks he's jealous."

"Glenn? He's not interested in Audrey that way. She's just a kid, barely older than Jimmy."

"Audrey's a little more grown-up than you think. She married and buried a husband, and she's sorting a lot out for herself."

"She's doing a great job with the inn. I should tell her that," Rosey said.

"I'm supposed to ask if we can borrow your truck."

Rosey agreed. He didn't even ask what she and Audrey had planned. He was looking at her in a way that made her head swim. She took a steadying sip of the terrible cup of coffee, starting to regret her late night in the carriage house. She was too tired this morning to sort out her feelings for Rosey Devane or the photograph of Ellis Piedmont.

"You know, you've never said what it is you do for a living with a fancy degree in folklore," Rosey said.

He was smooth. It was a clever way to get her talking about her favorite subject. "I was saving a little money. I had thought I might start my PhD this fall. Or travel. I still might do both. But I have to close on the house first to pay for the medical and funeral bills. I'm still deciding what I want to do next."

"Oh, that's easy." A low rumble from the auditorium speakers vibrated beneath their feet, and he said, "I'll tell you. You're going to see a movie."

———

Rosey pulled the swinging door open on silent, well-oiled hinges and Frances walked through into the darkened auditorium. The smell of old wood, popcorn, and candy met Frances with a familiarity. On the screen, a battle on horseback played out between cavalry officers and Apache Indians. A boy too young to be a soldier but outfitted in uniform crouched behind a crop of boulders, a large, regal German shepherd at his side. Frances recognized the dog as the famous Rin Tin Tin.

"Hey, we've made it just in time for the best part," Rosey said as they took their seats in the center of the empty theater.

"I've never seen this one," she said.

"Oldie but a goodie." Rosey shushed her.

Frances frowned, trying to focus on the film playing in front of them and not the closeness of the man beside her. But when she peered into the flickering light of the empty auditorium seating, she felt they weren't alone. It was the one place, she realized, that Rosey did not feature on his ghost tour.

"Who else is watching this movie?" she asked.

"Besides us? Jimmy's here," he explained. "I run the old Rin Tin Tin films for him and then he sets up concessions for the day. He's never late. Even when he had a bad cold one winter. Jimmy used to love playing pretend Rin Tin Tin out at Dungeness with those Buie kids."

A small piece of ice hit the top of Frances's head and trailed, freezing, down the back of her neck into her blouse. She turned in her seat to look behind her, but the orchestra seating was empty so far as she could make out.

"Just a joke. He's upstairs." Rosey called, "Cut it out, wise guy." They heard Jimmy giggle from the colored seating in the balcony. "He likes to sit up there when the theater's closed."

"By himself?"

"Well." Rosey shrugged. "I don't see anybody else. Do you?" Even without him saying it aloud, she knew the two Buie kids were up there. "Can't hurt when there's no one around. Long as his daddy doesn't get wind of it."

Frances sat back in her seat and stared at the huge screen with the enormous German shepherd performing heroic deeds alongside his boy, guarding the army fort. And when Rosey Devane took her hand, she decided to agree with him. For just that moment in the dark, for this stolen time, she let herself believe none of it could hurt.

Chapter Sixteen

AUDREY

AS SOON AS FRANCES HAD GONE OUT, AUDREY MADE UP HER MIND
to stop putting off what needed to be done. She'd stuffed the latest
batch of spirit photography she'd developed into an envelope, the
usual method of exchange with Glenn, and left it in the foyer. She'd
take it over to the theater and that would be that.

Everything Frances had said had Audrey thinking about what
she really wanted. She hadn't thought about it the first time she'd
joked about Frances staying in Revery; it had just been something
to say. But the idea had taken root, not only because it would be
so nice to have a friend with her, someone who would be there
when the baby was born and afterward, but also because Audrey
was starting to have a feeling for what the inn could be and how she
could put her own touch on things. It was the first time she'd had
any real interest in anything in months.

This morning, before Frances had come in, Audrey had finally
found the courage to explore the waiting room. In her mind, that's
what she'd started calling the room that sat empty. But it hadn't
always been a waiting room. It had been a room in a house that had
once been a family home, a home to her family. And once she'd
started to think of the house in that way, she'd started to imagine
how that family had lived there, with a set of parents downstairs
in the main-floor bedroom that now served as a parlor. Upstairs,
where the guests now slept, there would have been two sisters. Of

course, later it would have been Audrey's uncle Henry and her aunt Shirley and Rosey. But first there had been her grandparents and their two girls, Shirley and Mimi, the girls who had carved their names in the closet under the stairs.

Audrey didn't know if they'd shared a bedroom, but she had been thinking of it that way since the hours in the carriage house with Frances. But now she was realizing there was an obvious possibility she hadn't considered. And that was simply that the waiting room had once belonged to her mother, Mimi.

That's what had made her want to cry. She'd opened the closet and found several leather belts, an umbrella, and three colorful scarves like the one in the framed photo, still hanging from hooks. The soft scents of talcum powder and rose oil had filled the space. It had left Audrey homesick for her mother, and she'd lifted one of the scarves and settled it on her head, tying it in a knot and sliding it around to hide it beneath her hair. That was how she'd been taught to tie ribbons, the same as her mother had taught her to hide every knot in their lives. Women were held together by unseen connections that made the world believe they were walking wonders. That's how Frances had found Audrey, wondering what had held her mother together.

Now Audrey was thinking of putting her mother's camera to more practical uses than hawking ghost photography. She wanted to photograph Revery as it looked today, a modern Southern town, and use the new images to make a brochure for the inn. Hopefully she'd draw customers. She'd rent every room.

Let Frances travel, but when she came back she would see what Audrey had made of Gilbreath House, and then she might really think about staying. Let her parents see what a success she could make of her life. Revery would be Audrey's town, but only if she made it so. She didn't want to spend her time conjuring the dead; she wanted to focus on living. That's what she would say to Glenn.

Downstairs, she dug out two more rolls of film from the box in the freezer. Her index finger accidentally slid over a slip of paper that had gotten stuck to the bottom. She winced at the sting of a paper cut and poked her finger into her mouth. Seeing the culprit, with her other hand she worked a small envelope free.

It was addressed to Ms. Gilbreath at the Gilbreath House Inn. It had been opened long ago. Inside, she found a newspaper clipping, only a photo with no caption, no date. If there had once been one, it'd been trimmed away. The photo showed a Negro man who struck Audrey as very familiar. She peered at the figure, trying to place where she'd seen him before. He was probably older than she was now, a young man. He was seated in profile and bent over a book he held open on his lap.

It was the sight of the book that made the hair on her head rise. She knew exactly who she was looking at. This was the same figure she'd seen in every double exposure she'd created since she'd come to Revery, only he was years older. He had the same broad sweep of shoulders, so like her young husband, but Audrey wouldn't mistake him for Freddie twice. And he most definitely was not a ghost.

———

Audrey carried the photograph in her back pocket, anxious to see Tate Walker so she could show him what she'd found, but there was no sign of the man. She managed the buffet with the usual customers and passed out ham biscuits in wax paper at the side door, impatient for Tate to come downstairs and hoping he might be able to confirm what she believed she'd discovered. But he didn't amble through the house until hours later, and by then, Will Tremmons had arrived with his toolbox. Will had come to service the grand-father clock in the foyer, which was running slow and chiming at odd hours, and the two men had put their heads together over that before she could pull Tate away.

She lingered and waited and kept poor Freddie's records playing Don Gibson—"Oh, Lonesome Me," which was kind of pathetic—and went about with her feather duster while they talked about the impending weather and the general state of things in Revery. Tate asked to hear some Tennessee Ernie Ford and the men sang along to "Sixteen Tons." It wasn't long before the topic turned to the photographs she'd been taking at the Marvel. It seemed like some kind of opportunity.

Before she could lose her nerve, Audrey said, "I don't think I'll have time for it anymore. I have ideas for the inn and I think it's going to keep me really busy. I hope nobody will be too upset about it." She watched Will from the corner of her eye for his reaction.

"Good for you," he said. "But you're very good with your camera, Mrs. Howell. I hope you won't give it up altogether."

"I had a more modern camera at school. Rosey gave me that old Brownie camera after I got here."

"But you set up your own darkroom. That's impressive."

"It was a hobby in school. It's not that hard to do once you know how. Anyway, I'm going to take pictures of the town and make a brochure for the inn."

Mr. Walker turned an eye on Audrey. "That would be Mimi's camera you've got. But I guess you already know that."

Audrey's ears pricked up. She'd never considered that Tate Walker might have known her mother, but now she realized he likely would have known the whole family, and better than Audrey ever had. "Rosey told me. She never talked much about her childhood."

"Well, that's a shame. Some folks don't like to look back. But I guess she did all right for herself."

"Oh, she did. She's president of the Junior League in Macon now."

"That's not surprising. Mimi always did have her mind set on getting out of here. Have you ever seen any of her pictures?"

"I think so."

Audrey felt her skin tingle. She thought of the clipping in her pocket and of the negatives she'd found with the camera and of the photos she'd developed of Lumas Gray and wondered if those could be the photographs he was talking about. If that was true, her mother had known her ghost, maybe very well. She itched to get back to them now and have a closer look. Mimi had known him well enough that she'd kept a picture of him hidden away. She'd known all this time what Audrey had just discovered, a truth that would change everything about the spirit of Revery.

Tate worked his jaw a moment and Audrey now had a thousand questions she hadn't even known to ask five minutes before. But then Tate changed the subject.

"Don't worry about Glenn being upset. I'm sure he's going to understand you've got your hands full with a business to run." Seemingly out of the blue, he asked, "Do you have any idea if that circus train still rolls through here in the summer on its way up from Florida?"

Audrey felt the blood leave her head. She couldn't believe Tate would be so inconsiderate as to bring up a train; then again, he was an old railroader. And maybe he didn't know the particulars of Freddie's death. Or maybe it was just that he didn't stop to think of it. One person's nightmare was another person's nostalgia. Confused by the abrupt change of subject, she said, "I don't know about that. This is my first summer here."

Tate said, "Well, it's just that I was thinking that might be a good photograph for your brochure, a picture of that train. It passes this way coming up from Sarasota at the end of every summer. Used to be that was the highlight of the year for all the kids. When Glenn and Rosey were little, we'd stand out there to wave it home. I'd like to see that again. 'The time of your life,' that's what it says on that train."

It was funny that he would suggest the idea and the motto when it was almost exactly what Audrey had been thinking of earlier, of the photos she'd like to make of the vibrant seafront town.

They were silent after that. Tate lit a cigarette and stepped nearer the open screen door as Will carefully adjusted the gears inside the clock. Audrey changed the record on the turntable.

"I'm about finished up here," Will said. He must've seen her fidgeting.

"What do I owe you?" Audrey asked, relieved.

"It's payment enough to get a minute's peace away from Rosey's yakety-yak. I'd rather sit here and listen to this."

Audrey smiled as they all paused to hear the clock ticking evenly.

"Did you ever hear of the light clock?" Will asked.

"No. What's a light clock?" It seemed to Audrey that Will was always thinking. He had a little wrinkle in his brow between his eyes just now above the place where his glasses sat low on his nose. She had the urge to push them up, the way Frances was always doing with her cat-eye rims. The feeling shocked her. A little wave of heat shot up her neck, the way she'd felt about Freddie at one time. It so surprised her that she had to look away from the man. Will Tremmons was too old for her, too everything for her. And she'd have never acted on the feeling. But as quickly as she realized the attraction was there, she felt pleased it could happen for her again. Maybe not with him, but someday. Probably it was just hormones, another wild reaction to the life growing inside her. One more reason to know that with life, you just never could tell.

Tate finished his cigarette and stepped back inside. Will talked while he packed his tools away.

"Einstein's theory of special relativity says all clocks run slow. They've all got this space between their ticks and tocks and it can alter. He proved it with a thought experiment called a light clock, this contraption with two mirrors and a pulse of light that bounced off of each mirror at the top and the bottom at a constant rate. When one of the clocks moved, the time between ticks stretched out. That's special relativity."

"Special relativity," Audrey said. It sounded like a familial term. She thought of Freddie and how there was no name for their relationship now. "What does that mean?"

"A second is not always a second."

"How can that be true?" Tate asked.

"It's entirely negligible to us while we're going about our days," Will explained. "We can only really observe the phenomena at the speed of light. That's how you catch a ghost with your camera. You catch him in time. In the space between the ticks and tocks."

Audrey felt a jarring understanding of what he was saying as he reached to set the long arm of the clock swinging again. She remembered the old tradition of the clock being stopped for death. Each time some hand had reached inside this clock to stop it ticking and later wound it back up and set the great arm moving again. Grief interrupted time, even if it would not stop for it, making just enough space for a soul to slip through.

Will Tremmons had looked inside this grandfather clock and

understood that unaccounted-for space it was marking, the special relativity of the light she was trying to catch in her photographs. She looked at him and wondered what loss he had known. And she felt ashamed she'd only ever thought of him as Rosey's charity case or the library janitor or any of the things Glenn tried to make him out to be. Whatever he was, he wasn't a Piedmont man, that much Audrey knew.

The moment was interrupted by heavy boots clunking up the front steps. Glenn swung open the screen door and let himself inside. He glanced at the three of them and frowned. His gaze landed on his daddy.

"Well, I guess it's true. I heard you'd rolled back into town, old man, and here you are."

"In the flesh," Tate said. "How are you, son?"

Tate looked like he had planted his feet hard into the floor, expecting a blow. Glenn seemed paper thin to Audrey, and it caught her by surprise. His tone was not matched by the sad expression on his face or in his eyes. But the air was charged between the two men, and she wished there was a way to edge out of the room.

Glenn ignored Tate and spoke directly to her. "Just dropping around to invite you over to the theater for the community meeting tonight. It'd be good if we're there to support Rosey and whatnot."

"Support him for what? What meeting?"

"There's been some concerns raised, what with little dustups in the news in other towns and this integration going on with the school in New Canaan. City council wants to give business owners assurances we're not going to see the same happenings in Revery. I brought it to Rosey and he's offered to let them hold the meeting at the Marvel."

Audrey could just imagine who had raised such concerns in the first place.

Will tried to excuse himself, but Glenn stopped him, holding up a hand. His tone stayed friendly as a man just dropping by to shoot the breeze, but his attention turned very deliberately to Will. "Rosey said you were over here too. I thought somebody ought to let you know that old grandfather clock never kept time worth a damn before you wasted your whole day. Can't depend on it." Will did not meet Glenn's eye but used his handkerchief to polish the frame of the clock.

Tate said, "Will was just telling us how Einstein proved that time as we understand it is a mere construct of the imagination." He laid a hand on Will's shoulder.

Glenn looked galled by Tate's familiarity with Will. "Learn that at the Indian college?" he said. "That's some fancy-sounding business. We just learn how to tell regular time down here."

Tate didn't seem to pay his ire any attention. "Audrey was just wondering when that circus train's due this year. Would you know about that?"

"Now, why would you bring up that silly thing? Audrey won't care about such as that." But Glenn's eyes darted back and forth between the three of them, all his teeth showing in a broad grin.

The unspoken implications were zinging past Audrey, but she had no idea what they meant.

"Don't tell me that's what brought you down here. Tigers and elephants and bearded ladies? You always did like that nonsense. That train never even stopped here. Never saw any carnival myself. Nobody ever took me. Probably just a bunch of dirty old railroad hobos and clowns, I guess. Didn't miss much."

Tate showed no indignation over what was clearly meant to be an insult. "That might be, but time's coming when these things will disappear. A lot of people will want to remember that train."

"Well, I suppose. Now, I've got to be getting on. Audrey," Glenn said sharply, dipping his chin in farewell and using her first name like he'd just tagged her ear. "As they say, time stops for no man." He directed this last quip toward Will as if he'd laid down some true wisdom, implying he had no time for silly things like science or circus trains.

"Waits," Audrey said.

Glenn's head swiveled toward her. "How's that?"

"I think the saying is time *waits* for no man."

"Is that right?" Glenn tried to laugh at his mistake. "Same difference, I guess."

Audrey did not agree. "I don't think I'll make it tonight. But thank you for coming by. I'm sure Rosey has all the support he needs."

"I'll be sure to be there," Tate said. "I'd like to hear what's said."

Glenn made no sign he'd heard Tate but nodded to Audrey. Then he seemed to reconsider and looked at Tate. "I wonder if you've had a word with Morrie Johnston of late."

"I did have a conversation with the man."

"Well, don't be speaking for me. I don't need anyone fighting my battles. Do we understand one another?"

Tate shrugged. "No, I can't say we ever have, son."

Glenn looked at Tate a tense minute more, shaking his head, then Audrey had a sinking feeling when she saw him notice the envelope on the table beside him. Audrey watched as he picked it up from the foyer table. He tapped it twice as if to check the weight of the photographs, and a shadow crossed his face, suggesting there were fewer than he'd like. Worse, he then saw the script lying there. Audrey had forgotten any of it was on the table. She waited for what Glenn might say or do next, but Will stepped over to pick up the script, reaching past Glenn. Audrey held her breath as he gave Glenn a nod, an acknowledgment, before he stepped out the door.

Will said, "Thanks for returning this, Mrs. Howell."

Audrey stood there, prepared for whatever Glenn was about to dish out. But Tate didn't give him the chance. "Mrs. Howell was saying she's got some new ideas for her photography."

It was a distraction, but maybe not the kind Tate had intended. Audrey felt herself shrivel.

Glenn's expression changed so fast it made her dizzy, his expression brightening. "Is that right? What do you have in mind? I'd love to hear all your ideas."

Audrey's mouth went dry.

Tate stepped up beside her. "She's going to make a brochure for the inn, take a bunch of shots around Revery. Drum up some business. But she's been worried people will be upset with her if she commits all her time to the inn."

Glenn's optimism fell away. "Well, that's the first I'm hearing about it. Audrey, is that true?"

"I guess it is," Audrey admitted. "I'm sorry, Glenn. I'm not going to make the ghost photos anymore."

"No, no. No, don't you be sorry. I just wish you'd told me yourself."

She felt like an iron band had been released from around her chest. She could see he was waiting for something from her, but she only looked at him until he gave his head a little shake, then nodded at Tate. Audrey's stomach soured, but seemingly she'd done it. She'd told him no. She couldn't help worrying what kind of mood he'd be in for the meeting tonight, but that only gave her all the more reason to avoid it.

When he'd gone, Tate cursed under his breath. The clock in the hall ticked on, steady and sure, so far as any one of them could tell if they hadn't known better.

"I shouldn't have said anything, Mrs. Howell."

"It doesn't matter. And please call me Audrey. You knew I was going to tell him and you were only trying to help. I'm glad it's done." With Glenn told and gone, she felt silly for being so afraid of how he'd react. Maybe it was only because his dad was standing there with her when she did it, but she didn't care. It was over, and she wouldn't let herself get roped into anything like it again. She might have been more upset about Glenn if she hadn't found the photo that morning and been waiting ever since to ask Tate if what she'd seen this time was real, if she was right.

"Really, thank you. The ghost photos couldn't go on. Especially not after what I just found. I wonder if you'd take a look at something for me. Tell me if I'm seeing things." Audrey placed the news clipping into Tate's calloused hand.

"Let's see here," he said to himself as if he were just waking up. As if he needed a minute to see what was in front of him. He brought the photo closer, peering at the clipping a long time before Audrey felt the need to prod him for a response.

"That man there, the one who's reading. Do you know who that is?"

He lifted his gaze to meet hers. "Where'd you get this?"

"I found it this morning, in the freezer with my mom's old canisters of film. I think maybe I've seen him before." Audrey suddenly doubted herself. She hadn't slept. "I'm probably wrong." She reached for the clipping, but Tate held on to it.

"Now, hang on," he said, like he was uncertain. "Who's this supposed to be?"

"You know who it is, don't you?" Audrey took a deep breath. "I've been making all those ghost photos from old negatives, and when I saw this clipping, it seemed like it might be the same person. The ghost, I mean. Lumas Gray."

Tate nodded and then he said, as if he could hardly believe it himself, "Yeah, you sure are right about that."

"And he's older, isn't he? That's a photo from after they said he drowned."

He flipped the clipping over, as if there'd be more of an explanation there, but the other side of the newspaper only showed part of an ad for tires.

Audrey held the envelope marked with the address for Gilbreath House and handed it to him, then dipped her chin.

Tate saw she was struggling. "What is it, honey?"

"Will you take it to Cleo Woodbine for me? She should know he didn't drown like they said. Somebody should have told her."

Tate nodded as if he was thinking hard on the task she'd set before him. "I can do that tomorrow morning. I believe she'll appreciate it. Tonight I've got a community meeting."

"Do you think I should go?"

"I think it's going to be a whole lot of nothing. You just keep doing what you're doing. I'll make sure to speak for what a good job you're doing here."

Tate smiled at her and Audrey tried not to worry. He seemed calm enough about dealing with Glenn, and maybe he knew what he was talking about. He stood next to the credenza and considered the record player and the stacks of Freddie's albums. "These belonged to your late husband?"

"They did."

"It's quite a collection. There's some good stuff here."

"He liked country. And rock 'n' roll." She knew so little about Freddie that it frightened her. Maybe that's why she said, "We were barely married. I don't even know which songs were his favorites. I couldn't tell you more than ten things about him, really."

Tate listened to the song a little longer, then said, "A man who loves music is a soulful man. When you play this music, I imagine it's like having a good talk with him. I want you to know it doesn't bother me one bit to hear it. You turn it up if you want, as late as you want. I'm an old railroader and don't have half my hearing anymore. I can sleep through anything."

It was maybe the longest conversation she'd had about Freddie since he'd died. She'd never thought of Freddie the way Tate described him, as soulful. She'd never considered why she was playing those records except to drown out her own thoughts. But maybe he was right. Maybe she could think of it that way, Freddie's music, even if it was only a nice thing to say.

She flipped Tennessee Ernie Ford over and played the B side.

Chapter Seventeen

CLEO

IT'D BEEN ALMOST A WEEK SINCE THE PAINTING HAD BEEN COMmissioned and Cleo still glared at the blank paper, beginning to believe she just didn't have it in her. In the night, she'd even entertained the fancy of collecting a little glory to see if sipping on a bit of Dooley's tea might change things. But by dawn, she'd come to her senses. Maybe that was the point of this damn request from the grave, that Joanna would have the last laugh. An artist was not some little god. The Lord made this whole world in seven days. What had she ever made?

When Cleo heard the sound of a tail thumping on the front stoop, she groaned. She knew that old black dog was out there, happy to see someone approach. Cleo opened her door, half afraid it would be Frances again, then wanting to throw herself at that stubborn mule, Tate Walker, for coming back after the way they'd left things on such a sour note.

"Seems like you've made you a friend," Tate said, nodding at the animal, who looked all too content.

"I imagine my whole house will be full of fleas."

Tate only laughed. "Can't blame me if you attract the riffraff."

Cleo tried not to show she was glad to see the dog or the man, even though they both looked at her about the same way with their big brown eyes. She reminded herself that it wouldn't do her any good to go counting on either one. Both had reputations for getting gone for long stretches, with no signs they'd come back.

"I thought you might be going out to make your rounds and maybe I'd hitch a ride, walk near about you for a while," he said. "Got me a metal detector on loan, see if I can do a little digging around and find that old watch."

"I don't need to tell you that you'll be wasting your time. What did you want a broke watch back for anyway?"

"Just miss the weight of it in my pocket, I guess." He shrugged. "Figure my grandson might like to have it. I've met a young man that knows about clocks. Might be he could do some repairs."

"Suit yourself." It seemed to Cleo that Tate had things on his mind this morning, things he wasn't saying, but she did not pry.

She knew good and well that the search for the watch was only an excuse, but she didn't run him off. If this was how they were going to make peace, so be it. She got her things together, and they left the dog lolling on the stoop and set out for the morning in her johnboat, heading down to Dungeness. While she filled her basket, he was patient and interested, waiting until they took the truck and made a stop at Plum Orchard at low tide when the estuary had emptied out and he could roam all over the creek bed with his detector on his fool's errand. Cleo figured he knew that watch was never going to turn up. Some things get lost and can't be found. But maybe she'd be wrong. She'd mistaken the black lab for the grim and then Morrie Johnston, a perfectly alive man, pickled as he might have been, for her imaginary fiddler. Life could still surprise her.

She liked the sound of Tate's voice in her ear. He rambled on about places he'd seen while he'd worked the railroad. He didn't say he'd left the job, but it seemed to be the case. So long as he was doing the talking, she didn't have to, and when he finally went quiet, she had to admit, her loneliness did ease a little with his breathing in the background. He was not a particularly handsome man, but there was an elegance to his limbs. He put her in mind of the wood storks on Cumberland, up on stilt legs, diligent.

Along their walk, another thing struck her as exceptional about Tate Walker. He seemed to respect that she knew what she was doing. He didn't ask her why she bothered with the old groves. He was learning her ways, the paths she took, how she passed the hours. And he did not question any of it. Neither did he assume she was miserable.

A couple hours after they set out, they made their way back to park the truck near the dock. He put that metal detector down and they waded into the creek to fill a net, then made their lunch over a little fire. They climbed into Dungeness and walked its grand halls and sad old steps. Up in the library, she thought of Lumas Gray but didn't dare speak his name aloud while Tate picked up one of the moldering books that had been cast aside by some other trespasser and read to Cleo. He was pretending he didn't feel her looking at him. She was making lists in her mind, memorizing details and tucking questions away, deciding if she wanted answers.

She showed him how to slip into the pool house. This was dangerous territory, opening the door to those sulfur-scented memories, remembering Joanna Burton, remembering Lumas Gray and Ellis Piedmont. They left their clothes on the side of the pool and it was easy being naked together in the dimly lit water. It seemed like a hundred years since they'd been in this pool. They did not speak of it, although there was no doubt they were both recalling those strange days, how their lives had been set on a path and how improbable it seemed to be back here.

It was the only place that ever could have brought them back together, the place in their lives where the tides ran in both directions. He slipped up beside her, his skin against hers comforting as worn bedsheets. The time they'd spent together that summer had been brief, but life had hung in the balance then, and what was between them now felt like the old scar at the center of Cleo. Something that would not shift, that had remained with her, that always would. Both of them were too old to pretend this was courting, too young to ignore the taste and smell of the other or the ache that had taken up inside them. If he thought she was brazen, she'd lost the habit of thinking on a future where that sort of thing would matter. You could fit with a person like she fit with Tate, even if it made no sense to the outside world.

It was also a fact that Cleo had not been alone the whole of her years on Kingdom Come, and she wasn't ashamed about that. There had been men, brief encounters with fishermen or hunters who had stayed a night or two, and once a geologist who had come back the next year. But they'd been transient men and she'd never asked them to stay. She'd never even wanted to know what was on their minds. With Tate, she found she had come up on a man with a pit at his center, not unlike the knot of scar tissue in her chest, like the fruit in her groves. And she wanted to know what she might tease from that hard stone. What he might tease forth from her.

Finally, he said, "Aren't you going to ask if I remember it all? That's why you brought me here, isn't it? Why you're tolerating me so well today?"

"If you didn't remember, then I'd know you've got the old-timers."

"We're not old, Cleo."

"No," she agreed. She was not yet fifty. She did not feel old.

She did not feel young either. If being away had made him a time-keeper, Kingdom Come had stolen a feel for time from her. Cleo paused to consider what might happen if she told this man what she'd never told a soul. That she was afraid she'd gone a little crazy after all. And even if she told him, what might change?

She tapped her head. "You can't know what it's like, living out here alone like this. I suppose some people talk to themselves, don't they? It's not so strange. Only I talk to those characters I paint." She shrugged. "Those tagalongs, there were plenty of times they seemed pretty real to me."

"Tagalongs? That's what you call them?"

She nodded. "It was a name for what they became when they wouldn't stay on the page, on account that's how it always felt to me, like they were just following along, staying close to me. And I've been thankful for the company when it would get too quiet, too damn lonely. It started back when I was just a little girl. I'd heard Dooley tell those old tales so many times that I could see them clear as day, clear as you here now."

Tate squinted at her, starting to understand what she was try-ing to tell him. "Do you see them now? Here with us?"

"Yes," she admitted. She watched for his reaction, but his ex-pression stayed calm as the surface of the pool's water. "But they aren't always here. Not so much anymore."

Cleo held Tate's hand and told him about each of the tagalongs she could see hovering near.

"So let's see here," he said. "We have Little Hannah, that's the little girl?"

Cleo hesitated. Tate waited. She could hear a faint giggle and looked to the window to see Little Hannah pulling faces at her. "She was a child in the story, buried in a cemetery far from the rest of her family and always floating around the graveyard looking for them. When I was a girl, I imagined we'd be good friends. Most times she's not much more than a little patch of fog."

Tate nodded. "And the fiddler? Is he any good?"

"He used to keep me up nights. He could play like he was on fire and make me laugh," she said. "And there's the black dog, the grim, that was always scratching at my door. In the story, everybody was afraid of that big dog, but he was just guarding the place where his beloved master died. He was waiting for the day he could show the man's wife where he'd been buried. Love kept him bound. Devotion. Until the wife finally came and then his soul could go on. He was a good dog."

"And there's the giant. The Timucuan?" Tate raised his brows.

"That one's mine. It wasn't one of Dooley's stories. When Lumas told me about the giant and the bone orchard, I painted that giant for him." Cleo felt a warm draft in the room. She knew it well. She always felt it when she talked to Lumas Gray's ghost. "I've never seen that one, but I've heard him, that old Timucuan out here, banging around, moving in the trees. When he walks, it makes my bones judder."

She considered what she really wanted to say. "They're all just ghosts. I was out here hoping so hard for Dooley's ghost to visit me after he died. I cried and cried, but he never did, no matter how hard I tried to see him. I guess I felt about like that old grim, bound to my beloved granddaddy. But it was only ever those silly stories that came, walking the earth the way Dooley told me they would if I looked with my whole heart.

"I'd seen them before, when Dooley first convinced me, imaginary friends after my parents died and I was just a little girl. Children have those, don't they? My grandmother didn't worry. She said one day I'd wake up and they'd be gone. *Poof.* And that's what happened. I grew up, or I thought I did, and I came to Plum Orchard. But after Ellis shot me, I dreamed and I saw those friends again. Big as life. And when I walked out to Kingdom Come, well, I guess my heart needed them again."

Tate listened and nodded as if he could understand, as if the things she said weren't the least bit unusual, a grown woman confessing to hallucinations. It was still hard, being seen after all this time. Deep in her bones she felt a stirring. *Boom. Boom. Boom.* There was a quaking, or maybe it was her heart starting up again.

"Tate, I know they're not real."

"Sounds like they're real enough."

"I mean, I'm just entertaining myself. And apparently a whole bunch of people who want to buy up those pictures and hang them on their walls."

"I'm sorry you've been out there like that. Missing your granddaddy."

Cleo lifted her face to him. "Oh no. You're wrong. He never left me. That was him every time. All of them. Every one, from the start. I just wish I'd understood that sooner. I imagine that's all you want for your boys."

She could see it surprised him to hear her say it, hit him square like a good left hook, to hear her paying him a compliment for coming home and showing that she understood he'd always loved them.

"It's a gift, Cleo. Being able to glimpse something most people can only dream of."

Cleo considered the sentimental idea and shook her head. "I'd have done a lot better to have just seen things for the way they were. That summer I said I saw a monster in that water, but really I just managed to make one of myself."

Tate might leave. He might stay. But for the first time since she'd exiled herself to Woodbine Cottage, she did not mind that time stood still. She thought of the watch. She remembered the day it had stopped in this pool, and how it had then stopped her from taking her life only a few days before, and she thought of all the little ways this man had just been trying to convince her to remain in the land of the living. And in the sulfur-scented water and the shadows, she reached for him.

Chapter Eighteen

FABLE

IT HAD BEEN JOANNA'S IDEA THAT GLORY COULD BE USED TO Cleo's advantage, after all, and Cleo told herself that it was Joanna who had taken away every good choice.

Joanna pulled on her swimsuit and wheedled Cleo about being a chicken when she declined to go for the night swim and claimed to have a sick headache. As a joke, Joanna fastened a string of pearls around her throat, her only piece of fine jewelry.

"Look," she said. "My mother's pearls. Call me Lorelei." She saw Cleo's face blanche and Cleo blamed the headache. "Oh, I never slept with him. It was only a tumble so you would see the truth about him. You don't need him, Cleo. You're free as a bird. Now, come with us. We'll swing from the rings like a flying circus act, the two of us. Two is better than one. And you don't really feel all that bad about stupid Ellis, do you? I did you a favor. You won't have to give up your island cottage and set up house, be Mrs. Ellis Piedmont and live with that little grubworm the rest of your days, sprinkling voodoo root over his breakfast. Please. And now that's done, we'll cull the herd for you tonight, find a better entertainment for you. Which goat will you take, Ms. Woodbine?"

"Stop it." Joanna did not believe Cleo could possibly love Ellis as she claimed. She thought the whole thing was a great joke between them. It confounded Cleo. Worse, it made her stomach sour because in part, Joanna was right. The minute she'd realized what

Ellis and Joanna had done, Ellis had transformed before Cleo's eyes. She saw his weakness, his petty manipulations, and it made her furious. "You go. You don't need me there. I need to rest so I'll feel all right for the bonfire tomorrow," she lied.

"Cleo. You're still thinking of that? Telling your sad little sob story? Don't ever tell people like that the truth. They'll only pity you the more for it." Joanna's eyes flashed. She basked now in having entirely put Cleo in her place.

Cleo turned to pour herself a glass of tea. Against the railings of her conscience, she dosed the remainder of the drink in the pitcher with a thick dusting of glory, stirring it in with sugar and mint, enough to make Joanna's head spin and loosen her adder's tongue. Joanna wasn't paying her any attention.

"Aren't you afraid of what Ellis will be telling them about you?" Cleo asked.

"You still don't understand how this works. Poor little Ellis won't say a peep against me unless he wants everyone to know how you've turned him from a toad to a prince of men these last few days."

Cleo cringed. "You shouldn't have told him. You should have let me be the one."

"He deserved to know. His ego was out of check, believe me. But you think I've betrayed you, don't you? Cleo, I've delivered everything up on a silver platter for us! He'll be desperate to get more of it and we're going to give it to him. I already promised him you would. And that means we're in charge for the remainder of this little gathering. And by the end, we'll both get what we want."

Joanna was so confident in her plans. She filled her own glass and turned it up. Cleo watched the tea disappear, then off she went. It couldn't have been easier.

There was a deep momentary satisfaction in knowing there would come a moment, not too long from now, when it would dawn on Joanna that she'd underestimated Cleo. She was prepared for the consequences when Dr. Johnston guessed what she'd done, dosing that beautiful Burton girl with all that glory, causing a wild scene, a scandal. If it cost Cleo the residency, at least she'd cost Joanna and Ellis as much.

Within the hour, Joanna would not be able to hide her ugly self anymore. Out of Joanna's pouty mouth would pour all the horrible thoughts she kept hidden behind her flirting and fawning. The Lorelei, indeed. Then she'd see what it felt like to be made a fool. With luck, she'd shame herself so awfully that she'd be sent home. Cleo could imagine her creating such a spectacle that the gossip mills would run on it for months. The Piedmont family would never accept such a daughter-in-law. But then the full truth filled Cleo with a sick feeling. If glory hadn't been a curse as Lumas had told her, as her grandmother had believed, now Cleo had certainly made it one.

And what did that make her?

———

Cleo had thought she didn't want to see what her choice would do, but she found she couldn't stay behind. She stole away from Plum Orchard, taking a bike to follow the others after they left, careful to stay unnoticed.

She heard them inside and slipped through the door and stayed to the shadows, breathing the sulfur in the air, feeling the humidity sticky on her skin, her hair curling, damp against her face. The young men splashed in the water and the scene was set. Cleo watched from the place where she crouched as Joanna pranced and performed for them on the side of the pool, taking hold of the first of six sets of acrobatic rings suspended in pairs by ropes, lined up across the width of the pool. In a graceful leap, she swung out over the water. The boys howled and clapped and they were wild for her, as she'd known they would be.

Cleo held her breath as Joanna's body moved in an arc, long legs flying, head thrown back, golden hair streaming. With the pearls at her throat, she was luminous, alabaster and rosebud in the moody green light. Cleo watched for signs of intoxication, lack of coordination, silliness, all the ways she hoped Joanna might humiliate herself, but the girl only dazzled her audience. They roared with appreciation for her performance. Her laughter rang out, bouncing off the walls in strange echoes. The second set of rings hung there, waiting to be grasped, and she reached for one of them and missed twice, each time eliciting gasps. Cleo held her breath.

Joanna cursed loudly and cackled at her clumsiness, and Cleo knew then that the glory was at work. When she caught the ring on her third attempt, a cheer went up. But she'd lost the momentum it would take to cross the entire pool.

She swayed her hips with urgency, trying to move forward, and the young men laughed and then booed, teasing her. She extended her arm toward the next ring, far out of reach, giggling, knowing it was hopeless. Soon she would have to let go and drop into the pool where the boys swarmed below her like they would devour her. Cleo was waiting for the scene to go wrong, willing Joanna to act out, feeling the opportunity slipping away with each second that passed. In fact, Joanna was enjoying the moment, becoming more dramatic as she played like a woman in a film desperate for rescue, whimpering for help, grinning all the while.

"Don't you love me a little? Won't you save me?" she wailed.

She made silly jokes, which began to turn crude. But nothing she did seemed to turn them against her or shame her. In fact, they only loved her more. Her swimsuit sparkled, iridescent and green. She had their devotion, or at least that was what Cleo saw. It was Ellis who called to her to put a stop to it. And he might as well have pulled the pin out of the bomb.

"Oh, Ellie, Ellie," she sang out. "Little Ellie, pitching a fit. He had me but couldn't keep me. He's a lousy lover. And not my first."

She sounded drunk, slurred her words. The boys teased her about getting into the hooch for courage, or maybe so she could stomach doing the deed with Ellis. They splashed water in Ellis's face and pulled him away from the side of the pool where he could cling, then pushed his head under until he was furious, panicked, and gasping. "Tell them, Ellis," Joanna called out, drawing the attention back to her high-flying act. "Tell them the secret to your manhood and I'll let go. I'll fall if you tell them. You can shut me up!"

She struggled to hold on, clinging to the ring with both hands like a cat afraid of the water. She worked one hand up, extending her arm through the ring. The diameter was just wide enough so she could reach up and wrap the rope above the ring around her wrist. Then pressing her elbow against the inside of the ring for leverage, she managed to remain in the air. But Cleo could see she was shaking from the effort.

Ellis protested there was no such secret. Some offered to catch her fall. Others wanted the secret and turned to Ellis. Joanna cackled. Cleo was surprised at her strength. And it seemed Cleo's plan would be less than successful. No one was upset except Ellis. No one was ruined. But come morning, when Joanna's head cleared and she guessed what Cleo had done, she'd be sure Cleo regretted the trick.

But for all the scenarios of embarrassment Cleo had imagined for Joanna, she could not have foreseen what would happen next, when Joanna lost her hold on the rope. The boys whooped, thinking it was another fantastic feat to entertain them, but Joanna howled.

It was a sound no woman should be able to make. The sound of pain. At first it was impossible to say what had happened. There was only her horrible scream. Cleo froze, unable to move to either help or flee. All of them could only watch as Joanna grappled at the rope with her free hand. She curled her body upward toward the ring, crying out. She bucked and pleaded for help, but none could reach her there or tell what should be done.

"Let go!" they called. "Just fall! We've got you!"

But she could not. And given those extra moments, Cleo and the rest of the party came to understand that Joanna's shoulder had dislocated. Cleo heard one of the men say as much. When she'd slipped, her arm had wedged, wrist pulled upward, within the ring and gravity had done the rest. She could not bring herself to wrench it out of the trap. She thrashed her head weakly side to side, hair flying, her mouth wide and red, too red. There was blood, inexplicably, covering her lips, her chin. And she clawed at her arm and her throat, breaking the string of pearls so they showered down on the boys.

"Ellis, get her down!" one yelled. Ellis only stared, helpless.

They urged one another to take action, but there was only chaos. "I'm not touching her," one said. "Damn, what's she drinking, Ellis? What'd you do to her?"

To Cleo's disbelief, the men stayed where they were, unwilling to be the one responsible for Joanna, who hung limp and silent by then, having blessedly fainted.

She'd have hung there longer had it not been for Tate Walker, who'd had the sense to climb out of the pool and cross to her on the rings. He did the horrible job of pushing her arm and wrist free so in one awful move, she screeched like a banshee and fell to the water, where no one, in fact, reached to catch her.

Cleo did not breathe. Joanna's body surfaced, floated faceup, exactly as she'd looked in the sea only hours before, but she might have been dead. It was Tate Walker who pulled her up onto the side of the pool and pushed her hair from her face and listened for signs of life, carefully arranging her arms and legs and calling for a towel for modesty. Joanna did not move. And still, Cleo thought, bloody and mangled and a horror, she was beautiful to behold.

Cleo's regret threatened to overwhelm her and her vision blurred. She could see herself in her mind's eye, the girl who had brought this awful end to pass, how far glory had taken them all, how out of her control things had gotten.

Ellis stood among the others, all of them out of the water now, dripping and fearful and something else. Guilty? Angry? No. Already whispering and entirely concerned that none of them would take the blame.

"Where's that companion?" Morrie asked. "She ought to have been here with her. She's got to say she saw it. That none of us had anything to do with it."

She saw them argue. She saw Joanna's eyes roll white and wide. Only when Joanna suddenly coughed and Tate turned her onto her side to vomit did a low hum go through the group. And then they left her; by ones and twos, they walked away from the accident. All but Tate Walker, who reached to lift her and carried her out of the pool house.

Cleo sat where she'd stood a long while, huddled there, shaking. A coward. A monster. Alone. She stared at the place where Joanna had lain, the darkness of the wet pavement, the blood and vomit, evidence that none of it had been a dream. But something caught her eye, a glint of light, and when she was able to get her feet to carry her, Cleo knelt and picked up the railroader's watch she recognized. Tate Walker's watch, no longer running. Time had stopped, and Cleo felt the worst kind of relief in that. She'd have stayed in that purgatory forever if she could have, but she felt a hand touch the top of her head. She looked up, thinking it might be Ellis, come to tell her he'd always understood that they were two of a kind. But she saw then it was Lumas Gray. She saw in his face that he pitied her. He had warned her what glory would bring. He'd said that plant was a curse and she'd known it was true. She'd seen what it had done to Dooley's life, but she'd believed herself to be special, an exception, capable of turning a curse to a blessing. Only now could she see that was glory's real power, that seduction. She'd never known such self-loathing. And when he offered her a hand to help her stand, she could not take it. Instead, she put Tate Walker's watch down and she followed the young men and ran.

Chapter Nineteen

FRANCES

ON FRIDAY FRANCES HAD MADE THE CALL AND SET AN APPOINT-
ment for Audrey for Monday morning. She would be glad when
Audrey was ready to tell Rosey about the baby, but for now she was
keeping the secret, and after Rosey had canceled the ghost tour
last night due to the community meeting, she knew he would have
plenty else on his mind. Frances had stayed in and had dinner with
Audrey, and they'd watched TV until Tate had come in to assure
them the whole thing had been nothing but a little thundercloud
that Glenn had whipped up and it would all blow over by dawn.

Frances was apt to believe him, and the streets seemed peaceful
as ever until she overheard an argument in the little pass-through
between the theater and the Piedmont Library. She stopped just at
the corner of the library building, not wanting to interrupt such an
intense exchange, but as she listened, she edged closer so she could
peer around. From there, she could see Jimmy Walker curled on
the ground, wrestling to keep away from a man who had hold of
one of his arms.

"Get up from there. You're going to listen to me," the man
roared. "Now, you steer clear of that Indian or I'll keep you home
and there'll be no more of this theater for you and that'll be the end
of it."

She saw Jimmy's arm twist. She saw the man's angry face. Frances didn't stop to think. She snapped out of her gloomy fugue and

flew at them, acting on instinct from caring for the children at Mother's Helper. "Get off him!"

The man straightened, still struggling to keep hold of Jimmy, and turned too quickly for her to see it coming. The back of one of his hands caught the side of her face, sending her sideways. Her palms and knees hit the gravel with a stinging impact.

"Oh geezus, lady," he said. "What are you doing? What were you thinking?"

Frances's ears rang. She carefully touched her bottom lip with her tongue and found it busted. She looked up and locked eyes with Jimmy beside her on the ground. The man was offering to help her stand and she slapped his hand away.

"Look, you've got the wrong end of things," he said. "I'm his daddy. This is a family matter."

Jimmy got to his feet and lit out so fast that he kicked gravel in Frances's direction. They watched him scramble through the colored entrance of the theater.

"He's been like this since his granny died. Won't stay home. Won't hear a word I say." Glenn had such a distraught expression that Frances calmed a little. "Scares the devil out of me sometime he's going to end up needing more than a few stitches."

He was a heavyset man with tired eyes, perhaps once a prize bull; now he was pork-fed and had a kind of desperation rising off him. "Come on, now. I'm Glenn. Glenn Walker? Rosey told you about me, yeah? You're Rosey's little Wandering Merry, aren't you?"

He was patting the air in her direction in an effort to calm her down. She wanted to follow Jimmy inside and make sure he was okay. Glenn glanced at the open door, too, but made no move toward it. He looked as if he'd rather take off in the opposite direction, seeming to regret that she was there to witness the conflict down to his sad core. "He gets so damn upset. Always seems to go that way with us. Now, look here, are you hurt?"

He reached out and took hold of her upper arms and gave her an awkward little squeeze, seemingly meant to be kind, appearing to check her over to be sure she wasn't hurt. He showed his teeth in a smile but looked like a sad clown. She began to understand why Audrey had a hard time telling him no but also dreaded seeing him coming. She was struck by something familiar in the look, and it astonished her to realize his fatherly concern put her in mind of Owen Flood, if only for a split second. Glenn Walker was certainly nothing like the man who had raised her, but in that instant he did seem to be a man who was worried for his child, one who was sadly running so hard from him.

"I think I just need to go get myself cleaned up," she said.

"Sure, sure," he said, sounding desperate to appear friendly. "You have a good one. You see Jimmy in there, you tell him I'll see him at home? Tell him I ain't mad at him?"

———

She could hear the previews playing in the auditorium when she stepped inside through the door where Jimmy had disappeared, a side entrance used by the colored patrons. There was no sign of Jimmy in the lobby or anywhere near the candy counter. She thought of seeing him in the balcony seating before and took the narrow steps up to peer into the darkness. Half a dozen sets of eyes turned to look back at her, shining in the light from the movie screen. None of them belonged to Jimmy. All of them looked shocked to see her, and she was thankful for the gloom or they'd have really been worried to see a white woman with a fat lip upstairs. She leaned down and in a stage whisper asked the boy seated nearest to her, "Did you see Jimmy Walker anywhere up here?"

He shook his head. All the other kids shook their heads, but they didn't make a sound. Frances clambered back down and into the wings. There was no sign of the boy there either. She made her way to a storage area in the bowels of the building. There, she found him. He stood against the wall, very still, as if hoping she wouldn't see him there.

She spoke quietly. "Are you okay? What are you doing back here?"

The way he stayed drawn up straight like a spring stretched too tightly, she didn't dare touch him. But she joined him, turning her own back to lean on the cool concrete wall.

"Your dad said he's not mad, you just scared him. Why do you think that is?"

"Don't tell Uncle Rosey."

She had plenty of reasons to wish she could agree to that. "Is this about the meeting last night?"

Jimmy nodded. "He thinks Will's got ideas that are going to lead to trouble. And if I follow Will around all the time, I'll turn out just like him." Jimmy gave a deep sigh. "Daddy seen us in the balcony and he don't like it. He said if I don't know what's good for me, he'll just keep me home from the Marvel same as he kept me home from school."

Another voice came down the corridor. "What's going on back here?"

Frances turned to see Rosey. He had a theater flashlight and he swung it toward them so the beam caught them crouched like they were waiting for the bomb to drop. She was reassured to see

Jimmy's face now, unmarked, and although she brought her hand up to shield the glare, she figured Rosey had gotten a look at her, too, because he hesitated.

"Jimmy, what's going on?" Rosey seemed uncomfortable. "Will's looking for you. Show's about to start." She could see Will coming right behind him.

"Jimmy was just telling me what good friends he has here at the Marvel, but his dad's worried about him." She didn't want to say more in front of the boy.

Will came toward the dark little corner with his own flashlight, wearing his usher's uniform. "I was looking for you. We've got a full house upstairs." The men were acting weird and Frances thought it was not the first time they'd seen this sort of episode. Will said, "Let's get out of here, Jimbo, so Uncle Rosey can give her a smooch."

Above all, Jimmy was a twelve-year-old boy. The ploy worked. He sputtered and giggled and off they went.

Rosey turned to Frances and shrugged. "Let's take a walk and you can tell me what happened."

———

"It was an accident." Frances's mouth hurt. "I'm fine. Just your Left-Hand Man caught me off guard when I stuck my nose in his business."

Rosey looked upset. "You mean Glenn did this?"

"I promise, it was just an accident." She described the scene, setting the facts straight so far as she knew them. "Maybe it just seemed a lot worse in the moment," she said, trying to remember exactly what she'd seen and heard and why she'd thrown herself into the middle of it. "I know he wasn't trying to hurt Jimmy, or me. It just got out of hand."

"If I hear somebody say that one more time when it's got to do with Glenn . . ."

Rosey was trying to control his temper. She thought of Glenn Walker's grip on her arms. She thought of Jimmy down on the ground, curled into himself. "He asked me not to tell you."

"Who did? Glenn? Or Jimmy?" Rosey frowned.

"Jimmy. Glenn said he was scared because Jimmy won't listen to him and won't stay home. Actually, he said he doesn't approve of his friends, or that's what he's saying to Jimmy. What I heard is that he's worried Will's putting ideas into Jimmy's head, that he's a bad influence on the kids here. He saw them all in the balcony together and I guess that's what kicked this off." She hadn't shared the details of what Audrey had told her about Glenn being so upset when he'd found them reading the play together. But now she added, "I guess he didn't get what he wanted out of the meeting last night?"

Rosey sighed. He shuffled his feet a little. "Well, there's town business, and then there's Glenn and Jimmy business. Glenn and Jimmy, they're like oil and water. The trouble is that Jimmy's growing up, but not like Glenn. They've got nothing in common. He's not going to be the kind of boy Glenn had in mind, is he? Glenn tries to interest Jimmy in the things he knows, and Jimmy's all in his head. He's never going to work at the mill. Never going to drive a car or a motorboat. He'd rather listen to Will read a book or sit up in the balcony and watch a film. He spends a lot of time here, and that means he's with Will a lot. So when Glenn says Jimmy's following Will around, it's true. He's picked up a lot of habits from Will, tries to dress like him, talk like him. Will encourages that and Jimmy's got a little hero worship going on."

Frances could accept that Glenn was a bully and a bigot, but also that Jimmy and his father had been fighting a battle in that alley as old as time. If she knew nothing else about parents and their children, she knew things could be other than they seemed. "I'm sorry about all of it."

"No, no. You've got nothing to be sorry about. None of it's your problem."

His tone was sharper than usual and it stung, even if Frances knew he was only trying to be nice. None of it was really any of her business. "I just came by to check if the tour was back on for tonight." Rosey's expression brightened, and Frances was pleased to be the cause. "And to be sure I said I really appreciated you showing me everything. It's been great, really."

He hooked his thumbs in his back pockets. "Nine o'clock sharp. Listen, I'm sorry you got bumped in the mouth. And I'm happy to have been of service."

She didn't know what he was expecting her to say. She probably should have let him get back inside, but they stood there a minute more.

He grinned and said, "Will's covering the matinee today. Want to take a test drive in the old truck?"

They climbed into the Chevy parked behind the Marvel, rolled down the windows, and pulled out of Revery onto the long, flat highway that had first brought Frances to town. She didn't care where they were going. It felt good to let the wind blow over her face.

"Thanks for letting us borrow your truck Monday," she said.

"Well, this truck belongs to Will, actually. Thank him. Long as I fill it up with gas, he lets me use it when I like. I sold my Oldsmobile when I bought the Marvel." Rosey squinted in the bright sun and cocked his head as he drove. "This thing between Glenn and Jimmy didn't come out of nowhere today. Glenn's scared."

"Of what?"

"Same thing he's always scared about, what's going to happen to Jimmy."

"He never seems to even know where Jimmy's at as far as I can tell."

"I didn't say he was doing a good job of it. Glenn's always been this way, always trying to make an extra buck. Now he's trying to figure out why his kid admires the Indian man working at the Marvel more than he does his old man, and this is how it goes. He's his own worst enemy, and it's catching up with Glenn today."

"How's that?"

"Those groups of men that come down here for vacation and can pay a good price for somebody to sneak them over to the island by night? Harl Buie's been naming names of the ones running them, and one of them was Glenn."

Frances could guess where this was going. "This is more of his enterprising? Like the ghost photography?"

Rosey shrugged. "Most cases, it's all been harmless. Like the ghost photography. But over on Cumberland, there've been campsites left with fires barely smothered. Animals that belong to the families have been hurt or killed, and wild things too. Hogs, deer, turtle nests plundered for the eggs. Glenn grew up like me, running all over Cumberland. He loves that island. But it gets stuck in his craw that those old gods call all the shots, and when folks are short on work, they try to get around the rules, that's all."

The way he spoke told Frances that even Rosey wasn't sure who to defend.

"What happens now he's been named? Will the Carnegies press charges? If he's so worried about Jimmy, maybe he should have thought of that."

Rosey flipped on the radio and they rode a few miles outside of town, silent. When he pulled off the highway onto the shoulder, in the distance, in the bend of the river, they could see the plume of white smoke rising from what she could only gather was the Piedmont Paper Mill.

She'd come to know his expressions and the pride that was always on his face when he looked over the waters he loved. "Did you ever see a map of this place, see these creeks like a bird sees? Curving every which way, not a through line to be found. Nothing's straightforward. Not with this river, not with people neither."

She felt sorry about the way the day was going. They sat there while a cloudburst passed overhead and the rain pounded the top of the truck, but only for a few minutes before the sun broke through again. That was how everything happened on the shoals from one moment to the next. People had to pay attention or they'd get caught in a downpour, Frances thought.

When they'd started the drive back, Frances finally dared to say, "There's nothing wrong with your houseboat, is there? You could take it out anytime you wanted. You could travel."

"I've been away from home before, remember? I fought my way back here. Some people might not understand that, but it's fine by me." His tone was bitter, something Frances hadn't heard from him before. She watched him struggle briefly with that emotion, shaking his head a little and trying to smile again before he added, "How about you go and come back and tell me all about it?"

They were dancing around all the questions Rosey wouldn't ask. She wondered if the fact was that he wanted her to go, and she felt foolish to have never considered that. Wandering Merry was never meant to stick around.

"I'm going to see the Rhine. I don't know anything else, but I know that much." She was hurt. There was an awful tension between them where it had been so easy before. If they were going to leave it like this, she decided she might as well have her say.

"You told me some things the other day, when we were out on the sound. I'm going to tell you something about me. Folklore was only a problem for me after my dad's death. Before that, the Lorelei was just a story I loved, but after his big heart gave out, fairy tales and lore became a way to escape reality. And since I was running, my mom's job was to chase me. She worried I was wandering too deep into the dark wood of my own mind, and she was right."

Rosey didn't comment and Frances continued, watching the river roll out before them, as if this was the story come to life.

"I was only seven years old that day he went fishing, something he'd often done. Once, he took me with him in a borrowed boat, and that's still my fondest memory. We floated along in the foggy morning when it was hard to tell the difference between water and air, and we imagined what it might be like to be a catfish or a redeye or some other big fish."

"Must've been nice."

"It was. Until it wasn't. That last time he left, I don't even remember saying goodbye. He never came home. And I needed something to blame. I thought of the lonely Lorelei and I believed that siren must have seen my sweet daddy and wanted him for herself. I was so young and didn't understand death. It changed me from the girl who loved the river, and instead I spent all my time hunting for its monster. It scared my mom to death that she was losing me too."

Frances turned in the seat so she faced Rosey and tried to make him understand. "Glenn's not just afraid he's losing this place; he's afraid he's losing Jimmy. Maybe not to a water siren, but to something he can't understand any better, I think. Something just as foreign to him. Something he can blame with a lot of names, but really, it's just life. It's time. It's change."

"You said it," he agreed. "The harder Glenn reaches for Jimmy with all that fear, the harder Jimmy's going to fight to get away."

"Yes. And it's not completely the same as me and my mom, I know that. But the thing is, some of it's about you."

"How's that?"

"I watched the kids being dropped off at Mother's Helper, and at first they would scream bloody murder for their mamas. But after a few weeks, all of a sudden it would go the other way. Those mamas would come to pick them up after work and the kids would grab onto my mama's legs. They'd hide. I'd have to bring them out from under our beds or our closets. One time this little girl ripped Mama's curtains out of the wall. And you think that didn't make those women mad? Some of them took their kids and didn't come back when that would happen.

"Mama was taking care of those babies just like they needed, just like their parents asked. She didn't do anything wrong. She was just there when somebody needed to be, when the other mothers were out doing the hard work of earning a living. The trouble was that they never wanted to hand their kids off to somebody else. She got to play and tell stories and share all the little everyday things with their children. They hated her because those babies loved her, even though the babies didn't know any better. And I just think maybe that's what's making things hard for Jimmy and Glenn."

Frances drew her breath deep into her chest and let it out slowly.

"You might be right. You might. But things are fine," Rosey said. "Just got to let it all play out. Let things settle. They always do."

What did she know about any of this? Only that fear and blame ended up making monsters out of shadows, and fools out of even the most well-meaning men.

Chapter Twenty

AUDREY

THE COMMUNITY MEETING HAD NOT BEEN WELL ATTENDED AND only stirred up the kind of action Glenn probably hadn't counted on. The people who came for brunch the following day were back to talking about their superstitions of a great summer storm that, if anything they said could be believed, might land any day now. Audrey eavesdropped on old men who claimed to have seen signs on the water and mothers who swore their babies were cutting teeth with the drop of the barometer. She heard neighbors advising neighbors to be ready to batten down the hatches on businesses and homes. She heard there were discounts for those in need of shutter repair. Even Tate claimed to feel there was some natural force gathering on the horizon.

But for all the talk that the weather could suddenly turn ugly, Audrey had decided it was just one big exaggeration, a way the locals entertained themselves in these longest of hot summer days. And she was glad for their good-natured banter after fearing there'd be conflict.

After brunch, she was alone in the house. Tate had gone out to see Cleo and taken the photo of Lumas Gray. Frances had gone to see Rosey. Audrey knew Frances was in love with her cousin. She saw how she had jumped at the chance to stay a little longer, and that made Audrey hopeful, but also restless.

After a passing rain shower, only the boring sort of cloudburst common on a hot afternoon on the coast, she decided there was no reason to let the possibility of running into Glenn keep her from leaving her house. She made her way through the streets, getting shots of local landmarks, trying not to think about the doctor's appointment and what it would mean to tell her family and everyone else the truth about her condition. She dreaded being alone with it all after Frances was gone. Thinking she might find her friend at the theater, she stepped into the lobby and poked around, but there was no sign of Frances or Rosey. The matinee of *The Giant Gila Monster* was already playing. A lot of people had had the same idea, to get out of the heat. The movie was a silly flick with a huge creature stomping around, killing folks left and right. Audrey slipped into the auditorium and into a seat.

For a while it worked and she was distracted, cracking up at hilarious quotes she wanted to remember for when she next saw Jimmy, but after a while she started to lose interest. There was only so much pointless fury a person could take.

She'd sat only three rows inside the swinging door, on the aisle, knowing she'd need a bathroom for her ever more crowded bladder. A rowdy bunch of teenage boys was in front of her. They horsed around and made so much noise that she got fed up less than halfway through the show. Having polished off two boxes of candy, she was feeling queasy again. She hadn't learned her lesson the other dozen times she'd done this to herself. Audrey lifted the camera from her lap and prepared to sneak out, hoping not to throw up.

It could have been that simple if not for the business behind her. Before she could get to her feet, she heard someone moving into the back row. Kids sneaking in without paying, she figured. She sat still for a minute to let them settle, not wanting to draw attention. Surely she had enough on her plate already without making a couple of crew-cut hooligans mad at her. When she finally stepped into the aisle, she made the mistake of apologizing for blocking the view, a polite habit so ingrained that she hadn't even known she was doing it until her eyes locked on Harl and Nan Buie. In that split second, they all stared hard at one another. There was no fear in their faces. If anything, they looked back completely unsurprised. She had the sense to wonder what they expected now they'd come down from the colored seating to the whites-only main floor.

That's when the worst thing happened. She caught the toe of her shoe on the edge of the seat. The camera slipped from her grasp and hit the wooden edge of the seat, making a racket the whole way down. The air around Audrey seemed to hold still. The movie had been nothing but roaring sounds, gunfire, and crashing around, but it had gone quiet, a love scene between the hero and a bimbo woman with too much lipstick. Harl Buie reached down and picked up the camera and put it back in her hand. Nobody said a word. And God knows why, but she didn't head straight out the door like she should have. She sank down in the seat across the aisle. Her knees had gone watery.

She hoped wildly that maybe no one had noticed the noise. It seemed like maybe they'd all just sit there together, those crew cuts none the wiser. She prayed it was dark enough no one would even see Harl and Nan. She prayed the kids up front were too distracted with their own stupid selves. She prayed harder that the Buies would get on up and out of there while they had the chance.

But then a piece of ice went flying past Audrey's head and hit Nan. Audrey watched. Nan didn't move, just kept watching the monster on-screen. More ice came with a few slurs. Audrey wanted to call for Rosey, but she couldn't. She wished Will Tremmons would come rushing in with his broom and settle this down, but he did not and the movie played on. Something bloomed in Audrey's chest that felt hot and wet. Not ice. Fear. Shame. Still, she did not move.

The show ended and the theater was silent as the lights came up. Audrey had no idea if that monster had died or if it had devoured the whole world. The Buies stood and filed out, dignified. A chorus of ugly shouts and threats began. Others moved into the aisle, some of them climbing over the theater seats to rush into the lobby. Audrey looked up to the balcony searching for any sign of Jimmy. She was wishing the kids had gone down to hide in that tunnel. She was shaking so hard her breath came out in little puffs as she finally made her way out of the auditorium. The crowd had spilled onto the street. She hurried toward the front doors where she could see what was happening outside.

It was nothing short of a standoff, not so different from what they'd just seen in the monster movie on the screen. Some of the kids who had come out of the show were shouting rude things. She was horrified to see folks stepping out from storefronts and onto the sidewalks in both directions, slowly gathering to see about the trouble. She recognized the faces of those who had dropped by the inn for a bite and to pat her on the shoulder or squeeze her hand and offer condolences. Now, as it began to become clear that a crime had been perpetrated, they looked angry and confused and scared, as unsure as she was of what would happen next. Ladies who had come by as part of the welcoming committee with flowers from their gardens, the barber from the corner, the pharmacist, all looked to one another as if waiting to see who would take charge. And on the sidewalk across from the Marvel were the colored kids and Will Tremmons in his usher's uniform. As silly as he'd looked to her before—and she had truly been embarrassed for him—she could see the soldier now. He put himself in front of the kids.

The air was charged and the wind off the water was picking up. And as if that were some sort of signal, the crowd on Audrey's side of the street seemed to surge. Will Tremmons spread his arms. With that, more slurs and threats flew, demands that the Buies stay in their place. And without warning, the words were joined by rocks and anything at hand, all thrown at the young figures and Will. Audrey watched in horror as they were struck.

Audrey still held the camera. On instinct, she lifted it above her head, clicking the shutter repeatedly, frame after frame, until she'd come to the last of the film. Then she shoved her way forward. She had no idea what she intended to do once she'd reached them, but she couldn't remain where she stood. And then, like Will, she put herself between the Buies and the crowd, holding her arms wide.

At the same time, a car pulled down the street and jerked to a stop. A young colored woman was driving, her window rolled down, calling for the kids to get in. They seemed stunned. Harl was bleeding from his head. Will Tremmons had taken the brunt of the assault and he limped forward, one arm still shielding his face. Audrey had a horrible idea of what it was like for him at war, then a flash of memory of him innocently playacting with her and Jimmy.

Audrey yelled at her neighbors to back off. She yelled at the kids to get into the car. She was shocked by the sound of her own voice, loud and furious. She yanked the door open to the back seat and shoved the crouched bodies of Harl and Nan into the automobile. She saw Will climb into the front passenger seat. She heard the kids urging her to join them but she hesitated. Someone pushed past Audrey from behind and climbed in and slammed the door shut just as the car began to pull away. When she saw Jimmy Walker's face and his bandaged hand waving at her through the window, it was too late to stop him from going with them. The car spun off, leaving her in the street. She turned and the expressions on the faces that stared back at her told her that she'd chosen a side by crossing the street, by standing firm, by raising her voice.

And just then, the weather broke.

Another shower poured down on Revery, a curtain of rain so thick her view of her neighbors blurred. The deluge sent some scurrying back to the cover of awnings and close to brick walls. A thunderclap startled men, women, and children.

Audrey remained where she stood. The wind whipped around, a great gust blowing up her back. And then the cloudburst stopped almost as immediately as it had started. This was not the great storm everyone had been anticipating, but she saw them looking to the skies as if the downpour and this day's events were only further proof of the legitimacy of all their dire predictions. She watched people disperse as the water on the ground rushed into the drains at the curb. None of them stepped over to see if she was okay. She might have stood there longer if not for a touch at her elbow. She nearly leapt out of her skin.

"Hey, now. You all right?"

It was Rosey. She fell into him. She let him take the camera and walk her back to the inn. Frances got a towel for Audrey's hair.

"It was Harl and Nan Buie," Audrey said. "They came down and sat in the main auditorium, and when the movie was over, people saw them. I think they wanted people to see them. Will tried to help. Jimmy got in the car. I couldn't stop him."

"We know. We saw," Rosey said.

"You're going to lay down and rest," Frances said as she helped Audrey to the living room and Rosey went to call the Buie house, then a few minutes later came to tell them what he'd learned.

"They're fine. Amanda Buie's got them all over at their house. But now, you're going to lock the inn up this evening until everybody calms down," Rosey said, a directive, not a suggestion. He looked to Frances. "Geezus, this day," her cousin said under his breath. "You're going to keep her here. You're just going to keep her here, you understand?"

Rosey was frightened, Audrey could hear. Frances heard it too. She was insisting he should go check on the Buie family in person, and he was telling her that he knew good and well what needed doing.

"Stop arguing." Audrey didn't like to hear them talk this way to one another, but when she interrupted them, it wasn't to stop the sniping. She'd started the worst headache on the walk back to Gilbreath House, her blood pounding in her ears, and now a fist seemed to knot in her belly and squeeze until she let out a soft gasp. "I don't think it's supposed to feel like this," she said.

Frances's head whipped around at that and she sat beside Audrey on the sofa. Audrey explained how she was feeling while Rosey looked on and listened, confused, until Frances said, "Don't look so surprised. She's about six months along. She should see somebody. Can we get her to a doctor?"

Rosey didn't argue with Frances this time. "The doctor's twenty minutes away. I know someone closer. I can run there. I'll be right back."

He hurried out and in barely ten minutes he was back with Jimmy and Harl's aunt Amanda. Audrey recognized this woman as the driver of the car that afternoon. Her touch was firm but gentle.

"My grandma was a midwife like her own mother and grandmother before her," Amanda Buie said to Audrey as she quickly set about examining her and then firmly assured her that she was fine.

"This baby's still tight up inside you. All you need is a little rest and something to eat," she said.

"Thank you," Audrey said. "You should stay here. You should all come stay here tonight."

"Oh, well, that's sweet of you to offer, but no." Amanda Buie smoothed Audrey's hair off her face like she was only a child and shushed her. "I think you've done enough playing hostess. How about you let Jimmy come rest with you? He's waiting out in that hall. How about that? So I can go back home and see to my own babies. You need me, you just send Jimmy running and I'll be right back. But you're not going to need me. Get yourself over to the doctor first thing in the morning."

"Do you still deliver babies?" Audrey asked, hopeful. She felt such comfort under this woman's confident care.

"No, honey. It's against the law now for anybody like me to do that. You've got to see a doctor or a nurse. Don't worry. You've got plenty of time to get it all sorted out."

For the first time Audrey admitted how she was feeling about the baby. "I'm scared."

Amanda Buie only smiled at her like she'd heard it all before. "After what I saw you do today, putting your little body out front of that crowd like you'd hold back the Red Sea, I don't believe you ought to be scared of one thing. Anybody needs to be scared, it's whoever tries to get in your way, Mrs. Howell. Now, you shut your eyes like I told you."

Audrey did as she was told, grateful. She felt the bed move and felt Jimmy's small weight beside her and then she slept.

Chapter Twenty-One

CLEO

THE AFTERNOON HAD BEEN LAZY AND SWEET AFTER THEIR SWIM. No one had watched Cleo paint since she'd come to Woodbine Cottage, but there was Tate Walker lying about all the rest of the day, stretched out on her bed while she worked. The light was waning and it seemed like they were the only two people in the world.

He said, "Did you ever think life's just one thing after another, repeating itself? People making the same damn mistakes?"

She'd thought it often enough. She wondered what he was seeing when he looked at her painting. She was putting the finishing touches on the piece and feeling as if her hair was on fire from the energy of creating something that seemed to have come through her rather than from her, a whole world fully formed.

Cleo had worked quietly then and Tate had napped and she'd thought if he'd stay like that it might have been nice to have a man come around. But in the silence, her own mind had been at work on the silence she felt from Tate, and so when he'd rolled over and sat up to see how the painting was shaping up, she'd taken a guess at what it was about. "What's happened between you and Glenn, anyway?"

Tate let his breath out through his nose, then said, "Last time he called was about five years ago. He'd got thrown in the drunk tank and wanted me to wire him some cash. I told him he'd have to dry out before he called me again. That was it."

"Maybe you should've picked up a phone on your end now and again."

"When did you become such a fan of conversation?" he said. But even when she'd provoked him, Tate was soft-spoken. He made a frustrated sound. "I believe it's too late to turn that train around."

"It's ship. You say 'turn the ship around.' And you don't believe that or you wouldn't be here."

"You and that Audrey like correcting people," he said. But Cleo could hear that he liked it. "Glenn's got no interest in talking with me, however you want to say it. I left when he was too little, making like it was all about the railroad job, sending money back like that's what a daddy's for. I knew there wasn't going to be any way I could change what I'd done when I came back after his little wife died, and he wasn't having it."

"You did? That's been more than ten years ago."

"Oh, I did. I stood at the back of that cemetery. But he had Rosey walk me out of there. Never let me see my grandson. I figured I deserved that. Kept me from being here when Glenn's mama died last spring."

Cleo understood from Rosey that Tate's marriage to Glenn's mother had ended when Glenn was only a boy. Tate had left and later they'd divorced. That had been a long time ago now. But it still made Cleo sad to see his regret over those losses.

"I knew she was the one Glenn had helping him. I should have come back then, even if he wouldn't let me close."

She could look at Tate and see he didn't believe for one second that Glenn would have anything to do with him now. He didn't believe he ought to. She understood that regret. She'd wished a lot of years that she could walk back into Revery, back into some kind of life, maybe deliver that basket to Shirley herself. Just to thank her. That little bit of trade had kept Cleo alive in a lot of ways. But anytime she'd almost worked up her courage, Cleo had thought of Ellis and Lumas. And Joanna.

Tate reached to try to level her table, throwing things off-balance, and Cleo had to grab up the water jar for her painting before it could spill. "What are you doing that for?"

"Well, I was trying to fix it for you. Cleo, you can't just keep propping things up around here. You've got to face what's what. Now, look at this place about to tilt right off into the water."

"That's not even true." It was partly true. But it had been a long time since anyone had taken such a tone with her. "And we were talking about you, not my house."

"Aren't you lonely, Cleo?" The way he said it made her wonder if he wasn't talking to himself. "I don't know how you stand it. Being so alone."

"Who says I'm alone? I've never been alone. I've had my tag-alongs to keep me company."

"What kind of company is that? These little pictures?" Tate sat back in his chair. "You can't tell me that's the same thing."

Cleo shrugged.

He said softly, "I want you to come back to the inn with me. They've had a room waiting for you over there for years now, sounds like."

"You're taking a good day and going to ruin it." She felt her resolve weaken, felt a quaking in her bones the same as when that old giant walked the shoals. She had left all good sense behind when she'd taken this man out to swim at that pool, letting herself get too close to those old memories, and now he was in her house and in her head. She'd let her guard down and he was pushing right on in.

"Look here," Tate said. "I've got something that might change your mind. Audrey Howell sent this with me, asked me to pass it along to you." Tate handed over a small, limp photograph from a news clipping. "Said she found it stuck in with some of Mimi Gilbreath's old film. You remember that girl? Shirley's sister? Audrey Howell's mama?"

Cleo choked up seeing the unexpected photograph of Lumas. "I never knew Mimi Gilbreath. She left Revery a long while back, didn't she? But when was this taken? Where?"

"I couldn't say. Nothing written on it and nothing else with it."

Cleo swiped at her eyes with the back of her hand and pushed the news clipping into the back pocket of her pants, then looked at Tate straight on. "Do you know anything about this? Don't lie to me, Tate."

He looked at her as if he couldn't comprehend how there could be any confusion in the matter. "I watched those boys go in the river, same as you. Nothing I could do."

"Then why are you standing there with your tail between your legs?"

"You see what I see, don't you? If that's Lumas in the picture, if he didn't drown that night, it changes things."

She squared her shoulders. For a few hours, she'd let herself admire the long shape of his naked feet and she'd forgotten herself and the reasons she chose to live the way she did. "I don't see how."

Frustrated, Tate raised his voice by a decimal, something sharper than the mellow tone Cleo had grown to trust. "You can't tell me you don't see what I see when I look at that picture. That's Lumas Gray, and he's not anywhere near Cumberland there."

He was right. She couldn't deny it, but she was overwhelmed to think it was true. She remembered that night. She remembered the way that river had swallowed Ellis, and then Lumas, and then the rest of her life.

"I don't see it, so why don't you leave me alone, old Mercury," she lied, said it as if she were spitting the word out of her mouth. "That's what I'm going to call you from now on." Tate only stared at her, confused. She tried to laugh at his face and put on like he was the one acting crazy. "Flitting in and out of people's business un-invited, with silly little wings on your feet and little wings on your head. Mercury. Reporting on other people's affairs when he ought to see to his own."

She watched his anger rise.

"All right, then. I've said my piece," he said.

"Good. Let's hope it will help you sleep at night."

"I doubt it very much."

"You need to go spend your time with your grandchild. You want to do me a favor, you can take that damn painting back with you and save me the trouble of figuring out how the hell to mail it to Joanna's girl. I'd say that finishes it between all of us, wouldn't you?"

She saw that she'd hurt him. He rolled his eyes, but she was pleased to see him finally get mad enough to fight. It was better than seeing him so sad. Maybe she had some power after all.

"I'm going. If you can't see what's clear as day in front of you, there's no point talking to you."

"This from a man who wants me to believe all that hogwash about a storm of the century. It cost me a lot to live my life out here, Tate Walker, the way I want to live it."

He looked her square in the eye, and Cleo felt that sore spot over her heart begin to throb when he said, "Well, I can't argue with that."

When he left, the cottage was quiet and still, the way she'd always preferred it, and when she went to rinse her brushes at the sink, the rain started in earnest and she thought of what he'd said about life repeating itself. She wondered why no matter how she twisted and turned that thought to have a better look at it, it worried her so. The truth was, she'd seen what he'd seen in that photo he'd brought, and she was miserable to see Tate Walker go.

She did not think this time he would be coming back.

Chapter Twenty-Two

FABLE

CLEO WAITED ALL NIGHT, ONLY SLEEPING FOR A FITFUL FEW hours before dawn. Joanna did not return to her room, furious and full of accusations as Cleo had anxiously hoped. None came with the morning light either. Cleo had no idea where they might be keeping Joanna in such an enormous house and had no time to search before Mrs. O'Dowd appeared to send her to the main hall. Dr. Johnston had arrived late the night before.

It was obvious that Mrs. O'Dowd understood something about what had happened, but so far as she knew, Cleo had not been at the pool house with the rest of the party. Cleo kept quiet and went downstairs to face questions or expulsion, praying things had been set right by some miracle.

But there was only breakfast and four of the young men at the table like chastised children, quiet, their eyes cast down. Morrie Johnston was among them, but he did not come at Cleo as she'd expected after hearing his comments the night before when he'd wanted to get their story straight and make a witness out of her as Joanna's delinquent companion. Cleo sat trembling, waiting for some explanation for their silence. There was no sign of Dr. Johnston, Joanna, or Ellis.

When the boys trooped off with fishing rods loaded into a truck, it felt like nothing so much as an escape. The weather had turned after the pristine day before. For the first time since waking, she realized this was the night for the bonfire. The skies were overcast and winds were high, and anyone would know the men wouldn't be catching anything on the creeks. She doubted they would even take a skiff out on such rough water. There was no excited chatter nor the expected jostling and anticipation of the festivities to come after nightfall, and Cleo wondered if it would be canceled. She felt conflicted, disappointed, and also relieved. It seemed so inconsequential now, such a silly, childish thing to have pinned her hopes on impressing these young men and Dr. Johnston, thinking she would live some sort of romantic life out at Woodbine Cottage making watercolors of children's stories.

She was given instructions by Mrs. O'Dowd to pack up what Joanna had in her room. She felt bereft as she folded the rose-scented things into Joanna's luggage, worrying about what had become of Joanna and of Ellis. She thought of the story of the siren and what Joanna's mother had believed about the stupid decision to trust her father rather than using the pearls to set her own course. Cleo's pulse drummed in her ears.

What had she thought she'd been doing when she dosed Joanna's drink? She'd been rash. She'd been careless. She'd only meant to embarrass Joanna, but who would care about that after the accident? It made Cleo sick to think of how much worse the outcome had been than she'd ever intended, and she hurried to the sink in the pretty bathroom down the hall to vomit, then stood there cleaning up after herself, one more thing to hide.

Her heart lifted with some relief when she heard Ellis's voice carry up to the corridor from the hall below. He was conversing with an older man and Cleo guessed it must be Dr. Johnston. Whatever Joanna's condition, surely their host would care for her. Cleo crept down to the landing to eavesdrop.

"It's a shame, but there's no sense in the boys missing out on their fun tonight," Dr. Johnston said. "You'll see her off and when anybody asks, you'll say it was an awful misadventure. She's glad to go home. There's been another fellow, it seems. Lucky to know before you married her and lived to regret it."

And so, somehow it had worked. Cleo's plan to ruin Joanna had ended with her fall from the rings and the men or Ellis had taken it from there, concocting their own story of the kind of girl who can only blame herself when she's sent away.

Dr. Johnston said, "I'm just sorry it came to this. I blame myself for not having been here earlier to keep an eye on things. Morrie speaks well of you, and that will go a long way. Your daddy will take care of the Burton family. There's nothing at all that's going to follow you around when you leave here. You've done your best by her."

Ellis thanked him. He groveled, in fact. She had to move farther down the stairwell for a clear view of Ellis's face, stark white and blank, as Mrs. O'Dowd appeared in the hall. Cleo saw a man in a suit who carried a doctor's bag—so this must be Dr. Marius E. Johnston—while Mrs. O'Dowd had one of Joanna's smaller cases. Cleo got only a glimpse of the famous scar that marred the side of the doctor's face. And she felt a twinge of disappointment before she even knew why, then felt sad, realizing they'd likely never sit around and reminisce about Dooley.

Joanna walked between them.

Or something of Joanna. This person was barely a shadow of the girl who had walked into Plum Orchard only days before. Cleo's heart slammed hard in her chest as she watched. Joanna's yellow hair hung lank; her skin seemed flushed, her eyes hollow. She cradled her arm next to her body and her feet shuffled. But her expression was fierce, her lips a red slash. Cleo's impression was of a feral thing, cornered. Tate Walker walked to one side of her and she understood then that he was meant to help her along, if needed.

The sound of their shoe heels was swallowed up by the worn rugs until they stepped into the foyer and across the parquet floor toward the main entrance. She could hear Joanna grumbling, belligerent. Part of Cleo was hoping she wouldn't go without a fight. She heard her say, "I want my pearls back. You'd better send them. Some of us need our choices. My dad will know you stole them if you don't send them and he'll press charges."

Cleo heard the awful echo of the Lorelei's betrayal in Joanna's threat. She tried to swallow the bile that rose in her throat. She forced herself forward, down the last steps so she stood in the hall, but she stopped, still yards behind the others, to witness Joanna descend the wide front steps and climb into a waiting car with Dr. Johnston. She stayed frozen where she was and let the car pull away. She did nothing. After all, what could she do now that would change anything?

The others dispersed. Ellis strode directly past Cleo and never even looked at her. She could only stand there staring across the lawn to the place where the car had disappeared, to the sky where the clouds gathered thick and low. Then Cleo took one of the bikes left in a heap from the day before. The wind pushed her hair off her face. The weather did not bode well for a bonfire or for storytelling. Stories told in weather like that might never even be heard.

———

The Casino was silent and the pool was dark and still. The rings hung from their ropes with no memory of Joanna Burton. Cleo left her dress on the side of the pool. In only her underthings, she dove in and swam down to the bottom, running her hands over the concrete floor, surfacing to catch her breath and descending to do it all again. The pearls from Joanna's broken necklace still littered the bottom of the pool, all those hard little choices. One by one, she brought them up and left them on the side until she had over twenty of them, some slipped loose from the silk thread and some still knotted together on the string. She remembered Joanna counting them out like beads on a rosary, sixty of them. She was exhausted and paused to cling to the side, gasping, muscles burning, head aching. She wiped her eyes and waited for her vision to clear. On the far side of the pool she saw Tate Walker kneeling there, removing his boots.

If she'd had enough air in her lungs, she'd have told him to go. As it was, she accepted his help and watched him quietly undress and then dive in at the other end of the pool. He'd been watching her, it seemed, long enough to gather what it was she'd been doing. Or maybe he'd thought of it, too, since he'd been a witness to Joanna's fall and then her dramatic parting words. Whatever his reasons, he added the pearls he gathered to the ones Cleo had already found. In less than half the time it would have taken her to find them all, she counted the full amount recovered. They'd found every one.

She thanked Tate. He turned around to save her modesty. She got dressed while he waited, then climbed out to do the same.

"I'm not going to keep them," she said, her back to him.

"I never thought you would."

"Well, I'm not going to split them with you either."

He didn't argue. He'd finished dressing and Cleo had turned to face him. They both stood there, dripping through their clothes, and she felt she might suffocate from the humidity and heat and the sulfur-scented air. She dared to ask in a voice that did not sound like her own in the strange echo of the pool house, "Where are they sending her?"

"Her daddy's been told what happened, that she's had her shoulder dislocated in a game on the rings over the pool after a falling out with Piedmont. Dr. Johnston's taking her over to Revery, then they'll get her home up to North Carolina where they'll know better if anything needs to be done."

"Done?" she said.

"She's had some trouble with her nerves in the past."

"There's nothing wrong with her nerves. I didn't know her that long, but I don't think that's true. And I don't think she did the other things Ellis says with other boys here either."

Tate nodded. "Maybe so. Dr. Johnston's a good man. He'll make sure she's all right."

"This is my fault. All of it. I need to talk to him. I need to tell him what I did."

Tate's expression remained distant and Cleo understood he didn't want her to say more. He didn't want to be any more involved that he already was, and she didn't blame him for that.

"Well, you won't be talking to him today," he said. "Anyway, he knows about the glory. Everybody knows. But nobody's going to be talking about that. He's not going to want it getting out, not when he's the one who invited you here and then failed to be any kind of chaperone. Plenty goes on in the Casino that never gets talked about, and this is going to be just another one of those things. Let it lie. Just a piece of advice—things like this get sorted out by the families and none of us has a say in it."

Cleo noticed he was wearing the railroader's watch again.

Surely it no longer kept time if he'd just jumped in the pool with it. Lumas must have returned it to him.

"Will you still take that job with the railroad when you leave? It must be hard to be away from your family," she said, realizing too late that it was a very personal thing to mention to someone who was mostly a stranger. But he didn't seem to take offense.

"I don't like leaving my son. But it's harder to let him go without. At least this way I can provide."

Cleo knew that men like Tate Walker took work where they could get it these days. The pearls felt heavy in her pocket, like sixty pieces of lead. He could have taken those from her. He could have paid a lot of bills if he sold them, and who would be the wiser?

He did not. And he did not ask about her plans either.

They stepped outside and she mounted her bike and saw he must have walked. She wished she had some way to help him get back to the other house. But they'd done all they could for one another, she supposed. But she did ask, "Will they still have the bonfire tonight?"

"Nothing could stop them."

Cleo knew it was true. They'd have forgotten Joanna Burton almost before she left, but Cleo had other plans for them. And so back in her room at Plum Orchard, she'd wrapped the pearls in a sock in the back of a drawer with her underthings to keep them safe until she could put them back into Joanna's hands herself. And prepared to tell a story.

———

Dr. Johnston still hadn't returned and the boys gathered on the lawn after dark, dressed in suits and ties and tipping their hats to one another and laughing at the warnings of a storm after everything they'd just escaped.

In the late afternoon, Cleo had seen Mr. Meeks and Lumas Gray from the window in her room and watched them loading wood into the back of the pickup and carrying it out to the sandy riverbank for the fire. She could not see the pit where they would build the pyre, but she knew it would already be blazing by the time she arrived. She wore the dress she'd arrived in, a drab brown with pintucks at the waist, with a plain hem dropping to just above the toes of her worn black boots. But when she came to the second-story porch, Ellis met her there, full of apologies and excuses. Joanna had been right about this too. Ellis was only kind when he wanted something, and Cleo knew he didn't want her for herself. He wanted her for glory.

She tried not to act surprised or show her disgust at him, but she couldn't help her gasp when he draped a fine stole around her shoulders.

"Mink," he said, stroking the collar. Cleo ran a tentative hand over the soft fur. She wondered what he had planned for her or if they would go on like this, pretending nothing had changed. "The moths haven't got at this one yet. Heaven knows how long it's been forgotten here. One of the daughters', no doubt. It suits you, don't you think? A wild thing. Sets the mood." She wondered if he suspected she might have a plan of her own. She thought that she knew enough of Ellis to finally understand this was how he liked things. He wasn't bored now.

"It's too hot for this thing," she protested, but she didn't remove the mink.

She had to admit that had been exactly what had drawn her to Ellis from the start. She'd loved their secrets. Even if she should have been offended, Cleo found there was still something thrilling to their charade. These young men did not know she was the one who had dusted Ellis and then Joanna. Only Ellis knew, and Tate. And Dr. Johnston. But none of them were going to speak up tonight. By morning, she knew she'd be just like the mink stole, left behind as these young men set out for home. But she had a tale to tell that was truly horrible, just as Ellis had hoped, and she meant for them to take it with them.

He left her there to follow the party after a time, a surprise guest, while he joined the others. She watched them below as they scattered across the lawn, black smudges that disappeared into the dark beneath the oaks. She knew the path to the river well enough and wasn't afraid to walk it alone even though it would be midnight before the stories began.

The air was heavy and florid. A storm on the horizon threw heat lightning down to earth. A flood tide was rising and the river was running high.

———

Plum Orchard loomed behind her, lit from within, casting a shadow over the flat plain until she stepped beneath the grove of oaks nearer the shore. Cleo could see the swollen water lit by the leaping flames that reached higher than she'd dreamed, spikes jumping and crackling, sending smoke and sparks skyward, and the river looked like the shining and undulating body of some great creature.

"Wonder," she whispered without thinking. A fire like this one was built to draw words from even the most reticent lips.

"That's what everyone says when they first see it," Lumas answered, stepping up beside her, keeping his voice low.

"My granddaddy used to tell me old folk stories about these

four other worlds. To get to the third world, the Land of Wonder, you have to cross fire."

She could see his face, even though he wore a dark cap low over his eyes, also dark, and kept his gaze focused straight ahead. The enormous bonfire cast strange flickers on the landscape, so it was hard to tell where the marsh grass ended and the river began.

"I should have listened to you," she said, stopping a moment before the others saw them. "When you told me to stay away from the bone orchard and I said you didn't know what you were talking about, you were right. And I wish I could go with you to catch that circus train. I bet that's where it goes, the Land of Wonder."

"You want to go back to the house, I can take you," he said. For the first time, she could hear urgency in his voice and maybe the hope that she would agree to go. "Tate's watching that Piedmont. Ellis is up to no good. He's not your friend."

"I know." Cleo wished she could explain, but in that instant Ellis had crossed to them. Before she could so much as take Ellis's arm, Lumas had turned to face him.

"She says she's not feeling good," Lumas said. "I told her I can walk her right on back."

Ellis did not look at Cleo. He looked straight at Lumas with a smile that did not reach his eyes. "You told her that, did you? You told her?"

Cleo spoke up. "He offered, Ellis. Don't be an ass."

Ellis was entertained that she'd come to Lumas's defense. The return of his arrogant manner made Cleo nervous. "I forgot you were old friends with the boy. You're fine, though, aren't you?" He took her hand but Cleo stood fast. She watched Lumas until he finally lifted his gaze to meet hers.

"I'll keep an eye out. In case you change your mind," Lumas said.

"I won't. I know what I'm doing."

"You just watch for that cat," Ellis said to Lumas. "That's what you're here for, isn't it?"

Cleo let her next words sound the first warning in this cautionary tale. "It's the water you should watch tonight. Don't stand too close to the shore."

Ellis laughed then, throwing his head back, believing this was all part of the game he'd set in motion and enjoying Cleo's teasing, convinced she was back by his side. Hearing what he wanted.

Chapter Twenty-Three

FRANCES

FROM THE FOYER, THE GRANDFATHER CLOCK CHIMED SEVEN o'clock and Frances stood in the doorway to the kitchen at Gilbreath House watching the astonishing girl who had quickly become her friend. Audrey Howell was a force. That's what Frances thought, watching her prepare dinner like it was any other evening, like nothing at all had happened just hours ago. Frances had seen her there in the street, soaked to the bone in the spot where she'd taken her stand until Rosey came to her. This thin blade of a girl, whose secret was not going to keep much longer. What a mother she was going to make.

Her black hair was in a long, thin braid now. Jimmy Walker had done that. Where he'd learned it, who knew. When Audrey had woken and come out from her room, there he'd been with her. Her brows made sharp lines in her pale face, and her color was high again. Amanda Buie had assured them that Audrey was well, but Frances was still anxious to get her to a licensed doctor. There'd be no waiting until Monday to go all the way over to New Canaan. Come morning, Rosey would take them to see the local doctor in Revery.

"Did you rest?"

"Sure," Audrey said.

Frances thought maybe she should insist that Audrey go back to bed but doubted she could make the girl do anything she didn't want to do just then. "What are you doing?"

"Making dinner." Audrey looked at her like it was obvious. "It's vegetable soup and cornbread. There's a lemon pie in the fridge."

"When did you have time for all this?"

"I prep in the mornings. Most of it was ready for tonight. I just had to throw it together."

Frances supposed she hadn't ever really given any thought to how the meals appeared at the inn or when or how Audrey was getting it all done. There was enough for an army tonight. She almost said she thought Audrey shouldn't be on her feet, but Audrey was already coming to take a seat at the table and they settled for their dinner. Frances tried to be appreciative, even when the soup had been oversalted, but she barely had an appetite. "Did you want to talk about what happened?" Frances asked. She wanted to talk about it.

Audrey stood and put their dishes in the sink. "What's to talk about? Unless you changed your mind and you're staying."

"That's not what I meant."

"I know what you meant. You don't have to stay now. Rosey will take me to the doctor."

"No, I promised. I want to be there with you."

Audrey held up her hands in surrender. Frances felt hurt by the gesture. Maybe they had both seen and said enough for one day. And so Frances wandered into the front room and put one of Freddie's records on the turntable to fill the silence.

Rosey had gone back to the Marvel, worried Will Tremmons had seemingly disappeared. Amanda Buie had explained that Will had left without a word as soon as she'd gotten them safely back to the house. Jimmy had come back wearing the jacket from Will's usher uniform, much too large for him, which he flat out refused to take off.

It was another hour after Frances and Audrey ate before Tate Walker came in carrying the basket from Cleo Woodbine. In it, he brought the commissioned painting rolled up in a leather tube.

"This is it?" Frances said weakly, taking it from him. She hadn't expected to have to contend with the painting here.

"Seems so."

Tate had not heard about the day, so Frances put aside both the painting and her own distress to explain the scene in the street. They agreed to leave Audrey alone while she scrubbed the kitchen spotless. And when another knock came at the door, Frances was grateful that Tate had made it back to answer it, as it was Glenn standing there.

"Jimmy here?" he asked. Then, more softly, "She okay?"

"Mrs. Howell's fine. We're all fine here. Come on in, sit down with us," Tate said. Frances might not have extended the invitation, but she did feel sorry about Glenn and the whole situation.

Glenn said, "No, sir, thank you, but not tonight. I won't keep you a minute. There's some concerned citizens going around checking in on neighbors. I'll let them know I've been by here and save them the time."

"They looking for Tremmons?" Tate asked.

He spoke up so she could hear when he said, "They'll want to have a word with him after what happened at the theater today."

It was not lost on any of them that no one had come for a word with Audrey, who had also helped the Buie kids get away from the people in the street.

"You expect trouble for the Buies?" Tate asked.

Glenn shook his head. "Not from me. But looks like Harl Buie's gone out to his post on Cumberland. There's bound to be some who want to get hold of him after what he pulled today. He's just given them an excuse to set him straight after all the names he's been naming for poaching on the island. I'd as soon he stop it, too, but I don't want anybody getting hurt. I just need somebody to keep an eye on Jimmy for tonight. He shouldn't be out wandering. People are riled up. He's here with you, I know. Rosey told me."

Tate spoke, working his words through his teeth like he was pushing them through a sieve. "You know that's why I'm here, for Jimmy and you. Are you sure you won't come in with us?"

"I need to get going."

Tate was worried for his son, as he should be. Frances was suspicious, but hoped for everyone's sake that Glenn could do what he was saying. It would be a lot like changing teams at this stage, but he'd been a famous quarterback in his day, so maybe he had it in him.

"I figure those men will listen to me if they're going to listen to anybody. If I can get out to Harl before them, anyhow. They don't know the Buies. I'm going to try to head this off at the pass. Rosey thinks that could be where Will Tremmons has gone, to hide out at Dungeness or maybe try to protect Harl, and I say it's bound to make things a whole lot worse if they catch that Indian."

"You'd be right about that," Tate agreed. Frances's stomach knotted.

"I'm going for Harl," Glenn stated bluntly. "That Indian's on his own. Things were good here before he came and started pushing ideas." Glenn's voice rose and Frances knew it was for her benefit, so she couldn't miss what was being said. "Maybe you don't know this, but used to be, we were all friends, us and the Buies and everybody else in Revery and over on the island. Fished these same rivers together and we got along. What happened to that? I'll tell you. People who come down here to start stuff and have no idea how we live, that's what. People who don't know us, don't know this town, don't understand us, standing up in community meetings like they know better than us."

Tate tried to take the temperature down a notch, but even Frances knew he'd blown it when he said, "You can't make this personal, son."

"This is personal. This is about *my* son and what kind of world I want him to grow up in, the kind where I grew up. I want to protect that. Protect him. Whatever happens tonight, it's on Tremmons. And somebody ought to tell Archie to get that grandson of his under control. That's what I'll be doing if you're looking for me. Trying to put a lid on things."

Glenn stepped off the porch and Tate followed, pulling the door closed behind him. Frances stood there alone, trying to think what to do. She was already packed. She had no role, it seemed. She had never felt so powerless to help the people around her, or herself. Her anger flared, anger at her mother for her secrets, anger at herself for spending all her years trying to understand something a child could never understand, and in the process never growing up. She realized now just how protected she'd been, what a life she'd been living, lost inside academic studies of stories, almost as removed from the real world as Cleo Woodbine out on her island.

She felt aimless, avoiding the painting Cleo had sent for Joanna and instead wandering through the house, peering more closely at Cleo's illustrations on the walls as if they might somehow prepare her for the new piece. The characters she drew, her tagalongs as Cleo called them, were always embedded in a swirling tangle of forest, almost completely obscured, hidden figures that had to be searched out but once seen seemed so alive they almost burst out of the scene. She appreciated the effect now in a way she hadn't before, remembering how it felt to walk the lanes on Cumberland beneath the ancient oaks with their hanging moss, how the understory dwarfed her and her voice had been dampened so she almost felt herself invisible.

She lingered in front of the drawing of the little ghost girl nestled in the limbs of one such tree, then moved on to look at the painting of a black dog, its eyes devoted and watchful from the shadows. There was a fiddler perched on the roof of what was obviously Woodbine Cottage, behind him a swirling sea and a far horizon. And the final figure was not a figure at all but the space where he should have been. Between the shadows and light that filtered down through the trees and tangled vines, there were only the deep impressions in the sandy earth, marking where he'd passed.

Maybe that's when things changed for Frances, in that moment when she wasn't thinking of or searching for anything owed to her. Maybe after all she'd beheld that day, the terrible and the beautiful things people could do to one another, her eyes were opened in a way they never had been before. For in that moment, she suspected she understood what her mother had truly asked of her—to look up from the pages of her folktales where she'd lived in her own imagination for so long and finally consider someone else.

Frances had believed Joanna wanted her to learn what had happened to her in the summer of 1932 because the result had been her birth. She'd looked at that portrait of Ellis Piedmont in the library and tried to search it out the way she was searching for tagalongs now, as if she would see something that would suddenly give her irrefutable proof that she'd come from him and Joanna and their tragic time here. But there'd been nothing, only a stranger, only a coy expression and a thousand traits and none of them the least bit familiar. Seeing Ellis Piedmont's face had only made Frances miss the man and woman who had raised her. She'd longed for them then so fiercely she'd run straight into trouble in that alley. She'd feared she wasn't the same person she'd been only a week before when she'd arrived in Revery.

She didn't open the painting. She decided to wait until she was back in Asheville, when she'd be able to see things more clearly. When the phone rang, she was pulled out of her thoughts. The house was quiet. Audrey must have gone out to the carriage house with Jimmy.

On the line, a familiar voice asked for her by name. "Mrs. Mae?" Frances said. The librarian insisted that Frances hurry to the theater if she wanted to help Rosey Devane. "We know you weren't planning to leave Revery until Monday," she said, her voice sounding hushed, hurried. "But pack what you have and bring it with you, honey."

Frances stood staring at the receiver when the line went dead. She had no idea what the librarian could mean by any of it, but she hurried to get her things together, only a single suitcase and the painting, then hesitated. Not knowing what to expect at the theater but feeling certain she wasn't meant to involve anyone else, she struggled with leaving Audrey this way. But if Rosey was in trouble, she couldn't ignore Mrs. Mae's request.

Frances had always expected that having choices meant freedom, but in reality, they tethered her to this very real world. And she suspected this was what Joanna had intended, what she'd hoped would be her final act of motherly love, to show her daughter how stories connected her to these people in ways she'd never dreamed. And to give her the opportunity to decide what she would do about it. If Frances had come to Revery hoping to learn who she really was, who she wanted to be, then she felt certain this was a moment that would decide that.

———

An unimpressive fire was lit in a burn barrel outside the Marvel, with fewer than two dozen people loitering around it, Mrs. Mae among them, her arm linked with that of a man who appeared to be her husband. Frances stood as she had that day in the alley between the library and the theater, hidden and watching. She could see a few other adult men, mostly elderly, and two ladies with little kids at their sides. Frances had a bad feeling. She lurked there to decide if what she was witnessing was any cause for alarm. But then she saw someone step up to drop a book into the lit fire. At first, the men around the burn barrel appeared reluctant, but one after another, they stepped up, as if by agreement that each one should participate. Mrs. Mae looked resolute. Frances was confused. The children huddled close. It was a quietly defiant few minutes as the flames crackled and smoked. All in all, they burned only a half dozen books or so, but Frances felt she might be sick at the sight.

At that point, Rosey came busting out from inside the theater to join Mrs. Mae and the man at her side, but Frances couldn't overhear what was being said. It was clear all were upset. Rosey gestured to the theater. Frances could not fathom the meaning of any of it. She waited in the shadows, appalled, until the little crowd began to move on up the street. Rosey stood there, arms crossed, shaking his head. No one spoke to him as they walked away.

Only then did Frances cross to him. That's when she saw the awful graffiti painted across the front entrance to the Marvel. Lit by the flames, she could read slurs too hateful to repeat. Words used against people like the Buie kids. People like Will. People who weren't allowed to sit in the bottom-floor auditorium for a movie or have access to the Piedmont Library unless they were the cleaning staff.

"Who was that? What's going on? I saw Mrs. Mae," Frances said. "I can't believe what I'm seeing."

"You don't know what you saw." He cursed under his breath. But so far as Frances could see, he was unhurt, only furious. "It's just councilmen. Piedmont Library board members. Concerned citizens making a statement. They say they're protecting the youth of the town from unethical and immoral and un-American ideas. They want Will out of town. He won't be working at the library anymore. They wanted to make a show of it, and I gave them his books."

Something was wrong with what he was saying. She couldn't make sense of why he'd let it happen. "Did they vandalize the theater?"

"Nah. That was here before they showed up. Whole town's stirred up. Today confirmed every suspicion they ever had about Will when he ran out of the theater with those Buie kids. Leading an outright rebellion in broad daylight. Far as they're concerned, Will's skipped town and left me to clean up his mess. I said I was sorry I hadn't realized what was going on right under my nose but I'd seen the light now. I said I should have listened to Glenn."

The horrible sentiments painted across the theater's entrance made her dizzy, but she knew better than to believe a word coming out of Rosey's mouth, that he would believe any of those things about Will. She kept her voice low when she asked, "Where is Will?"

He hesitated, then said, "I didn't figure I'd see you again. Didn't know if you'd come. But Mrs. Mae said you would."

Something was strange about the way they just stood there in front of the theater by the light of the fire, her with her suitcase sitting at her feet. "She said you needed my help. She said to bring my things. But I don't understand what's happening. I saw her at the fire. Why would she do that? Burn Will's books? Why would she call me here to see that?"

He leaned close and lowered his voice. He pressed his forehead to hers in an intimate way that made a soft sob escape her throat. "It's more that we want them all to see *you*."

"What are you talking about?"

"What you saw here was too upsetting for you to stay. You don't want to wait on any bus. Frances, you want to leave. You want to leave right now."

Frances didn't have to pretend to be upset or confused. And the smoke was making her eyes burn.

"Just follow me inside and I'll explain. Don't look happy about it. You're about to be out of here and shut of this whole thing."

Frances stiffened. She didn't move. "I promised Audrey I'd be with her at the doctor. I can't go until Monday. I don't want to leave her like this. I'm not scared because of today, if that's what you think."

He considered her answer and Frances waited, half expecting he might ask her to stay. She wondered if he did ask right then, what her answer would be. But he only took her elbow and forced her to follow him inside the theater.

She was truly angry then. When the door shut behind them, she said, "Tell me what is going on."

"I am telling you. There's something I need to show you. And when I do, you're going to understand some things and maybe you'll have even more questions, but for this to work, right now I won't be able to answer them. But the first thing to get straight is you're not here to help me; it's for Will." By then he'd led her back through the lobby and along that same hallway where she'd found Jimmy hiding in the lower storage room. They stopped there. "You can say no. We can turn around and walk out of here right now."

Frances was shivering from the adrenaline. "You said it's for Will. Then that's not really a choice, is it?"

He gave a short nod of agreement, then explained, "There's men looking for Will. Far as they know, he's already halfway to Timbuktu, left all his things behind, even his truck. Now, I've let them come inside and go through his things, take what they wanted. And if people see you leave here with his truck, if they know I gave it to you, it'll just be a great bit of gossip, won't it? They'll say I've come to my senses and good riddance to the Indian. And you'll head home with a new Chevy instead of having to take the bus all the way back to North Carolina. That's it. I'll tell everybody you left me with a broken heart."

Frances could see he was serious. She tried to understand all the implications.

"Look, I'll take care of Audrey. But you have to go now. That's the deal."

Rosey looked upset. He reached out to push a tall mirror to the side and turned a heavy knob that opened a door Frances never would have known was hidden in the basement wall. She saw a tunnel open there and gaped at it, then at him. Standing there, just on the other side of the door, was Will Tremmons, holding a flashlight.

"Shit, Rosey," he said. "What are you doing?"

"Now you know," Rosey said to Frances. Both men looked at her.

"Whatever this is, you ignore him," Will said.

But Rosey was the one ignoring Will's protest. "You've got to take him now, drop him wherever he says. Then just keep going till you get home. I'd have asked Glenn to do it, but he's gone out to Cumberland to deal with Harl. Frances, these men are looking house to house for Will right now, and they aren't looking to talk with him. Do you understand? The burn barrel was Mrs. Mae's idea. She figured they'd all be feeling satisfied. It's a hell of a smoke screen. She gave Will a chance. But it's up to you. Now, I've got to get back out there to be seen cleaning up what's been done to the front of the theater. Frances?"

She could only nod. Rosey was right. Now that she knew, there really was no choice. And one day she'd have a chance to explain that to Audrey, she hoped.

It was harder to know what to say to Rosey. There was no time. He didn't kiss her or give her any reason to believe he expected to see her again, but before she let him leave, she said, "You never did say what happened to the last Wandering Merry."

"Oh, well, you know. Those Merrys, they like Revery for a short stay, but it's only a stop on the way to someplace else."

She'd been listening to him tell stories for days and she knew his voice. She could hear in it now that he'd hoped things would be different this time.

———

Will lay in the bed of the truck beneath a thin blanket until Frances got them almost an hour outside of Revery, then she pulled over so he could climb into the cab with her. From there, Will drove for the next few hours while Frances tried to sleep. He woke her when they'd reached the North Carolina state line, stopping the truck along a pitch-black roadside where tall corn crops grew on either side.

"Here?" Frances asked, anxious. "What do I tell Rosey?"

"Nothing," Will said. "Better the less anybody knows. It's a straight shot to the main highway if you keep going that way. You'll make good time."

"But what will you do, really?"

"Lay low. It'll blow over," he said. "But Rosey might be right. I came home from Korea fighting every fight anybody would put in front of me."

"That's not a bad thing."

"No, but it makes you enemies. Hard to live in a dream if you keep trying to wake everybody up."

She felt it was all wrong, leaving him this way. She couldn't bring herself to simply drive away. "He respects you. But he's afraid for you."

"Rosey wants the world to be like his theater, a place where people sit in the dark and listen to stories and believe they're all friends. That's not the real world. That's not how things change."

She couldn't say he was wrong. But stories could change people. Otherwise, Frances knew she never would have been out in the dark with this man. Frances could see he was uncomfortable taking too much time before he set out, and it was perhaps a useless conversation anyway.

He reached inside the duffel bag he had slung over his shoulder and pulled something out. When he handed her the script, she recognized it as the same one she'd read with Audrey that night in the carriage house. "Can you get this to Audrey? Maybe drop it in the mail with a note. Tell her I said if she has the time, she ought to do some more stage work. She's got a real presence."

"Why don't you just give it to her yourself? When you see her again?" Will pushed the script into her hand. "All right, but I'm only taking care of your truck until you come take it back."

"Sure thing," he said. "And where am I going to find it?"

She could barely believe he had it in him to tease her now, but Will was a sweet man. "I'll get it back to Revery and to Rosey. I'll take your script to Audrey myself."

Frances couldn't avoid seeing the parallels between the story of the kids in 1932 and their situation now. She thought how Rosey was right about history overlapping and repeating.

Before he stepped off the road and into the cornfield, Will put a hand on top of hers where it rested on the window frame of the door. She was surprised by his touch, the warmth of it, the comfort given to her when he was a man on the run. If she hadn't been heartbroken back in Revery as they'd hoped any witness would believe, she was now.

"Bye, Merry," Will said. "He loves you, you know. You're his favorite tale to tell."

She sat there a long while looking at the place where he'd disappeared. It struck her how like the moment was to Cleo Woodbine's paintings as the night gathered round the rows of tall corn with their thick foliage curling up and out, her last glimpse of the man who might have been stepping into another realm as he slipped between the shadows and light.

Chapter Twenty-Four

AUDREY

AUDREY HAD BARELY SLEPT THE NIGHT BEFORE, LYING AWAKE with the scene at the Marvel playing out in her head. Now early the next morning, waiting for the doctor who had opened his clinic specially as a favor to Rosey, she sat in an antiseptic little room in a thin hospital gown tied up the front, shivering and bouncing her knee. Rosey and Jimmy waited in a room outside. She'd been confused when Rosey had shown up at the inn and brought her out to Amanda Buie's Buick in the driveway, then explained this was their ride for her appointment. He'd trusted Audrey with the truth of what had happened the night before and passed along Frances's apology for leaving without being able to tell her why. Audrey was still trying to sort out all the details in her foggy mind. She was realizing how alone she was, and it was not unlike the feeling she'd had standing in the street outside the Marvel.

She'd been grateful to have Jimmy's warm, thin body beside her on the short drive over. She'd leaned to whisper in his ear, "Did you know I'm going to be a mama?"

She saw the lightning-fast flash of delight in his eyes.

"Will I be Uncle Jimmy?" he whispered back.

"Oh yeah, you will." She'd needed to share her secret with someone who would love it, before she faced the rest.

When the doctor knocked and stepped into the exam room, Audrey tried to meet the moment and this stranger, a man older than her father, with as much courage as it must have taken for Frances to drive that truck out of town. Will's truck, it turned out. That kind of courage was there when you needed it for the sake of someone you loved.

"Let's see what we have here, young lady," the man said with an annoyed tone, obviously resenting being called to his office on a Sunday morning by a girl who had neglected her health. She'd never had an exam like this, and she felt humiliated by his blatant disapproval.

The truth was, even though she knew a hospital and a doctor were supposed to be best for a mother and child, Audrey wished right then that she could have gotten up and left. She wished she had some say in who would deliver this baby and that she could choose Amanda Buie and be back at the inn where she felt safe and in charge of herself. But she couldn't. Laws were laws and midwives had to be certified nurses, which meant a colored woman like Amanda could no longer do what the women in her family had done for generations. And so Audrey lay back and put herself into the doctor's hands. And after he rushed through the business and affirmed everything Amanda had already told her, Audrey gave him a gracious smile and took all the pamphlets about nutrition and his admonitions about good mothers who thought of someone besides themselves. She dutifully made her next appointment while he joked that when the baby came, he hoped she would not be the cause of him missing his breakfast again. And she smiled at him then the way Mimi had always taught her to do, the same way she'd watched her mother smile at her father, just before she did exactly as she pleased.

"There's a boy in your waiting room who needs a fresh bandage," she said to the doctor, who stared at her with a look of surprise at the authority in her tone. But he took care of Jimmy and sent him out smiling with a fresh boxing glove to fight another day.

And then Audrey knew she and Mimi were more alike than she'd imagined. After Rosey dropped her off at the inn, she went back to the waiting room and tied a scarf from Mimi's closet around her hair like the wild gypsy girl in the framed photo of the Gilbreath sisters.

———

Audrey got on with the day, serving brunch and cleaning up, then resting with Jimmy in her room. The temperature climbed, but Audrey had brought the rotating fan from the kitchen and it droned quietly. She turned on her side to look at Jimmy. She'd never known him to be so quiet. "Jimmy, what do you want to be when you grow up?"

"Uncle Rosey says I'll run the Marvel and give the tours. What do you want to be?" Jimmy asked.

She was already grown, about to be a mother and running the inn, but that didn't seem to be the end of it for Jimmy. He was smart like that, even if people didn't realize it. He asked much better questions of the world than she did. "I want to be like you."

He snuggled close. It was sweet. His hair smelled of sweat and heat, sweet as a puppy dog. She'd never had a sibling, but this was as close as she'd ever felt to a child. For just that moment, she wished things were different and she might have been his stepmother and Glenn might have been a man she could respect and trust and they could have been a ready-made family. But she was glad she could be Jimmy's friend, and maybe that was better anyway. She still wasn't sure she was going to make much of a mother.

"Jimmy, do you really believe in ghosts?"

Jimmy considered her question. She could feel him breathing beside her. She made herself wait and not put words into his mouth. She honestly wanted to know what Jimmy would say. She often wondered if he didn't understand life more fully than other people.

"Sometimes," he said. "I figure if I was a ghost, I'd want somebody to believe I was real. I'd want somebody to talk to me. I wouldn't want people to be afraid of me; I'd just want to know what's going on because I would miss everybody."

She listened, a little spooked by the way the conversation was going. She could see his large eyes, deep and sleepy, reflecting the thin light. His fingers played with the hem of her shirt. He sighed. "I'd just want to be friends. Like us."

It wasn't what she'd thought he'd say, but it was what she needed to hear. He turned his head then so he could look at her. His face was very close. "You talk to Freddie. I heard you in the library."

It was true. She'd forgotten that. She hadn't really thought Freddie could hear her then, but her reasons had been the ones that Jimmy spoke of now. She thought of all the things Freddie would miss and how she'd tuned out any possibility of sharing those things with him since she'd gotten here, drowned out any feelings playing his records, cooking and cleaning, watching stupid movie after stupid movie. She'd felt so out of place and disconnected from reality when she'd come to Gilbreath House that her heart had stopped right along with Freddie's. She might as well have been a ghost. But then it seemed like every day in Revery there was something happening to get her blood pumping in her veins. That first double exposure had given her a jolt. The discovery of the tunnel had reminded her she was capable of being thrilled. And then there'd been that moment in the street when she'd stopped being a shadow and become a solid person again for a reason more important than her grief. And now she felt the little thump below her navel announcing a life to come, a face she was beginning to long to see.

She thought of the photos in the darkroom waiting to be developed.

"Jimmy," she asked, "do you want to learn how to make pictures?"

Earlier, she'd worried Glenn might come asking for the old negatives and film with Lumas Gray's images, but now he had other things on his mind. And she had her own photographs of Revery to develop. She had proof of everything that made Revery both a modern tourist destination and a place with a past some called its glory days. She'd been listening to Freddie's records and she knew the way people wanted their stories to be told, the same people who believed Lumas Gray watched over this town.

Maybe she should have started with the roll of film she'd used that first day on Cumberland when she'd helped Jimmy and met Cleo Woodbine. But thinking she'd rather he not see whatever image she'd caught of him in that trap, she put that roll aside, choosing the most recent one.

Within the hour and with Jimmy's help, classic images of Revery floated in the developing trays. He delighted in watching as they came clear, celebrated as if Audrey were performing a magic trick, and was careful as they hung the paper to dry. Almost every one of the photographs turned out, most showing the sorts of scenes that would be perfect for a charming brochure. Stately houses, steepled churches, mom-and-pop storefronts, the pharmacy, the Marvel, the waterfront, fishing boats.

Only the final four shots disappointed. These were the photographs she'd taken in the confusion out front of the Marvel—random, blurred images. Audrey realized then that she was relieved the majority of them had not turned out. But in the final frame, she had captured the terrified expressions of the pleasant people she'd passed on the streets for weeks, now caught at their worst. The height of their anger and confusion in that split second before the first clap of thunder jarred them out of madness and a veil of rain spilled down and those kids jumped into that car and squealed away. Jimmy leaned close and she wished she'd remembered snapping the photos before they developed there in front of them.

But Jimmy only looked at them dismissively and said, "Not those."

"No, definitely not," she agreed. She would not destroy them; she'd store them away. She separated the pictures of that terrible afternoon and any other unclear images from the ones she would use for the brochure. And she pulled the final shot out to carry back to her room at the inn and keep for herself, a photograph of a brave young man wearing an usher's uniform at the center of it all, who seemed to be looking straight at her.

For a while, Audrey and Jimmy considered the photographs they liked and tried to imagine how they would organize them. She remembered what she'd said to Frances about how photographs could surprise a person, show them things they'd never seen about themselves. *Here*, she thought. *Take a look at yourself, Revery.* What held them all together, the mysterious element that filled the empty spaces between things that had been and would be, the only thing that could calm the fear and anger she'd seen in the street. She didn't know if that was what special relativity meant to people smarter than her, but Audrey had come to believe it was hope.

Chapter Twenty-Five

CLEO

IT HAD BEEN SO LONG NOW SINCE ANYONE HAD THROWN A PELT at her front door that Cleo startled, unaccustomed to the sound. But she stormed across the room to the door, ready to lay into one of those kids, or Tate Walker, if it was that man again and he had the nerve to show up after the way they'd parted the day before. Instead, she flung the door open to a body on her doorstep. Crouched over the crumpled form was Glenn Walker, his face an anguished mask, red from the heat and presumably the great effort it had taken to get there.

"What in the hell is this?" Cleo stared at the scene a long moment trying to understand what she was seeing. There was hardly a sound on the island. She could hear the water moving past in the river and her own breath coming too fast.

"I swear to God, Cleo, I didn't do this." Glenn sounded like he'd swallowed gravel. "It's Harl Buie. They'd already got to him before I found him like this out near Dungeness. I was trying to stop it happening. By the time I got him back to the dock, they'd taken my boat and left me. You were closest so I brought him here. But I've already seen your boat's been scuttled too. Can you do anything for him?"

"Damn it all," she said, choking back tears. "Harl?" Cleo set about looking Harl over. His face was swollen in places so it looked like a clenched fist and he had a pumpknot rising on his forehead.

She could see one of the fingers of his right hand had been broken. The boy was out cold.

"Does anybody know you're out here?" Even as she asked the question, she heard it echo her words to Jimmy only days before.

"Daddy knows. He knows I came out last night."

Cleo didn't think it likely that Tate would be out searching for Glenn, nor did she really hold out much hope that he'd be burning a path back to her door so soon, but she didn't say those things to Glenn. She tried to think. "I can keep him warm and still for now," Cleo said. "You'll have to go for help."

Glenn looked like he'd already given up the ghost. He blinked at Cleo like a blind man. "You believe me, don't you? What I'm telling you is true," he said.

"I don't guess it matters what I believe right now, does it?"

"I don't know, I don't know," he said, turning and heading back toward the river, running by the time he hit the trees.

Cleo wished the things people said about her were true. She wished she could pour something into this child that would help him stand up and walk or fly out of here right in front of the monsters who had jumped him. She'd have called out to her tagalongs if she thought they might carry him off this place and back to a land where there were hospitals and doctors and anybody qualified to handle this. All she had were jars of poison, jellies, jams, her imaginary friends, and her pride.

So she did the useless things she was able to do. She pulled a blanket over his shivering form. She sponged his face. She settled in and prayed—to whom, she wasn't sure. She hadn't prayed in so long she thought maybe it didn't matter, any old god would do. And she willed Tate Walker to ignore every last word she'd said and bring his ass back out there to fight with her this morning.

She believed he would come because there was nothing else to believe in. She willed Tate Walker to come to them until she saw what she wanted to see and he was running up from the shore and there beside her.

———

"Come on, now. Listen, Cleo. I'm here. Look. I'm here."

Tate was saying things to her, looking her over, feeling to be sure she was not hurt. It took a few minutes for Cleo to know he was not the work of her imagination. She could barely croak out what was obvious there on her stoop between them. She told him Glenn had found the boy and brought him to her before going for help—where, she did not know.

"Damn it, I knew something like this was bound to happen. Glenn told me he was coming out to check on Harl but I had a bad feeling about how it would all go. When he didn't turn up this morning, I came looking but didn't see any sign of them on Cumberland. I took a chance he might have come here."

Harl Buie's color was awful in the light of day, but his breathing was steady. Tate didn't need her help to lift him. But the boy didn't make a sound when he carried him down to his boat. She'd followed them to the water, but when Tate expected her to crawl in and go with them, Cleo balked.

"Cleo, I'm not leaving you out here today. And don't you go trying to fight me. Enough's enough."

She didn't intend to fight Tate. But there was someone who needed to know about Harl. "Somebody's got to go tell Archie what's happened. When Harl wakes up, he's going to want his granddaddy."

She could see Tate hated to let her go alone, but he was a granddaddy himself. And there was no other option. "I'll get you over to the dock to your Ford. You get to Archie. Come back with him," he said. "I'll meet you at the Fernandina hospital."

Cleo got in the boat.

———

As soon as Tate dropped her at the dock, she ran her truck through every hole in the Grand Avenue all the way up to Brick Hill and Archie Buie's place. It felt like she was on fire from the inside out. She was thinking what she'd say, working out what might have happened to Harl, knowing somebody had dragged him off from his post at Dungeness and shown him what happened to a colored kid crossing lines. Probably those same asses Glenn had been running to the island. Even if police were called out, it would be hard to make anything stick with those sorts. It was always that way when there was money. None of them would know the truth until Harl Buie woke up, and that was if the boy would even say one word about it. Worse, she thought what it would be if he did not wake.

She wondered how many times she had passed this way and never once veered off at the crossroads. She knew where Archie's house sat, but she'd always met him out at the fishing camp or the duck house or on a creek or an oyster bed. He'd been kind to her, like they'd shared the loss of Lumas Gray, but they'd never exchanged a word about it and she couldn't say they were friends when she'd only ever allowed herself to come alongside him one place or another, but it had come close to it. She'd never set foot in his home and he'd never come out to Woodbine Cottage. She'd never even thought of it.

Now, when she came up in front of the tabby cottage, she realized it wasn't at all what she'd expected. She'd had in mind that the Buies lived in some sad little shanty shack. Something like she'd seen falling down on any one of the old plantations where rows of chimneys stood in ruins in the weeds now. She'd been wrong. Archie's house was a twin to her own. And why shouldn't it be? Likely the same hands had built it. But unlike Woodbine Cottage, this house looked like it could stand another hundred years on this spot.

When Archie stepped out on his stoop to find her there, she'd have sworn he looked at her like she'd looked at those pelts. He'd seen this coming for his children and grandchildren from a long way out, maybe ages, she thought. Even after Lumas, she had never dreamed it would come right up on her porch. That was how blind she'd been.

Archie already shouldered a bag and she gave him the details.

"Tate Walker's got Harl. He's in a bad way. I set out this way at the same time they left. They'll be over to the hospital by now," she said.

Archie had a boat with a motor. He'd make a fast crossing. "I reckon you won't come with me," he said. "Weather's coming in. Feeling it in these old bones."

Cleo remembered what Lumas had told her that day when she'd asked him about the boneyard, about the people who had warned him of things bigger than his understanding of the world. He'd trusted the Buies' wisdom. This time Cleo believed the predictions of a storm that would change the course of things on the dividings. But she didn't waste his time pretending she would leave Woodbine Cottage. "No. I've seen storms before."

She wished she'd had the presence of mind to bring something sweet to eat with her. Until then, Cleo hadn't really felt her feet on the ground. She bent over and away from Archie and emptied her stomach. Archie pulled a twig of sassafras from his pocket and offered it to her. Cleo stared at it a moment before taking it from the old man.

"I came here a hundred years ago acting like my granddaddy was a hero. He wasn't anything like it. I'm still an ass, but I know better now. And I know he wouldn't have stood for this."

Cleo hoped what she was saying was true. She'd have apologized to Archie Buie for never seeing him like she should have if she thought he'd give a damn. She wanted to tell him about the photo she'd seen of Lumas and the possibility that he'd never drowned in that river, but she didn't want to hurt him one more time by jumping the gun. She wanted to be sure. So she kept quiet while she watched him cross that rough water for another boy he loved.

She'd lived on the shoals long enough to know better than to try to take a skiff out when the water looked like that, and she worried for Archie. She stood on the stoop a long while after the old man had left and considered riding out the coming weather inside the sturdy little house. But if these were the last days for Kingdom Come, that was where she wanted to be. She thought of the crack in the wall of Woodbine Cottage as she made her way back there, walking the long miles of Cumberland and then resting on the riverbank until evening, waiting for low tide. Just as Frances Flood had done that first day she'd come to Woodbine Cottage, Cleo walked over the mudflat, exhausted and sad. She would end the way she'd started here, seeking sanctuary and repeating a prayer for a boy she hoped was dreaming of far horizons and a better world.

Chapter Twenty-Six

FABLE

THE YOUNG MEN SHOWED OFF WITH RIDICULOUS, BOYISH DARES in the dark. Ellis laughed and winked. Only Tate Walker kept to himself, careful not to catch her eye. He and Lumas had been tasked with keeping watch for any trouble, most especially for the bobcat that had been heard close to the house at night and had left tracks on the shore of late. Tate had little concern about a cat coming anywhere near the huge fire, but Lumas stood with a shotgun near the truck, making Cleo remember the story of Dr. Johnston sitting ashore to watch for sharks when the children swam in the sea.

Those near the fire were passing a flask of liquor and it was doing its job. Cleo did not drink. None of them seemed to notice or care. But as the bonfire blazed higher, so did the wind and the mood, and Ellis was at the center of the gathering. He launched the storytelling with his version of Joanna's fall, leaving out any implications of Cleo's part in things.

"It's a wonder Dr. Johnston didn't skin us all alive when I said how it went, but he was going to have it out of me so I didn't have a choice. I told him I never knew anything was wrong with the girl, not right off. We were just daring her to cross the pool on the rings. She was laughing; you all heard her. She was having a good old time. You know how she is."

Cleo saw them cutting their eyes at one another.

"But she was swinging around like a wildcat, like she was drowning up there in the air. She was having some kind of fit. Then . . ."

There had been no fit. Every one of them knew it but they egged him on. Ellis ran his hands over his lank hair as he fabricated this retelling of the facts, painting a scene of female hysteria. It only made him more energized. Cleo saw the smug look of a man who believed himself to have outwitted his enemy as he returned her gaze. He'd done something terrible and she recognized the look, for she'd worn it herself.

"But then her shoulder, the way it came loose," he said. "The way she was dangling there, it didn't look right, out of joint and that acrobat's ring wrapped around her arm, like it was the only thing holding her together."

He had no shame, Cleo thought, while she felt she would burn up with it.

Ellis carried on. "But it was like it took her a minute to figure out what had happened, like she didn't even feel it come out of the socket. So how could we know? Then she was bucking and yanking on the rope and trying to get down while that swing just kept going like mad. How could we have done anything?"

The young men listened and agreed, assuring themselves they were blameless for standing by. This was the story of the night. She began to understand this was why Ellis had brought her. This was his offering to her, absolution in exchange for what he wanted. *It was out of our hands. How could we know? What could have been done?* She heard them groan and curse, and Ellis was encouraged.

"She was baying her head off like a hound and I was up there trying to pull her in. Every one of you saw how it happened. But damn it, she was naked as a jaybird and slippery wet."

Cleo drew her breath at the bald-faced lie. Ellis did not notice. He was caught up in his own fiction now.

"It was a relief when she worked loose and hit the water. Took me and Tate both to drag her out. She'd bit her tongue almost clean through. That's where all the blood came from. Nothing we did. Whatever she was drinking, she did it all to herself."

With every lie, Cleo saw Ellis, these young men, and herself more clearly. When she'd ground those seeds and swirled that powder into Joanna's tea, she had thought of these boys who had sniffed and slobbered after Joanna all week. She'd have said that Joanna was their darling and they'd have leapt to her rescue. She had imagined that they would be like hounds set on the one to blame. But now when she looked around the bonfire, their faces were lit from within. They crowed over the lucky escape of one of their own from such a lunatic bride. They closed ranks.

"The nuthouse can have that one," they said. "I bet I'll hear that caterwauling in my sleep until the day I die," claimed another. *Nervous wreck. Drug fiend.*

"What'd they do with her, anyway?" one of them asked.

It was Tate Walker who answered. "Sent her back to her family."

"Back to the auction block, more like," another said.

"I was bored of her anyway." It was Ellis again, with his final thoughts on the subject. His worst insult. Disinterest.

He took a seat beside Cleo and leaned to kiss her squarely. There were catcalls. If anyone had asked her only the day before, she'd have thought this was what she wanted. Now she felt herself curl away from him and wonder how the last hours had brought out this charisma that topped anything she'd seen from him as a result of glory. She'd only seen him this way that first day on the porch when he'd had her in his sights, toyed with her like a cat with a mouse.

"Got us a little bobcat after all? Maybe we ought to hear about that manhood of yours?"

Morrie Johnston howled at his own joke.

"Tell your story now," Ellis said. "I've got your audience all warmed up, madam."

They cheered her on. Ellis leaned close to say in her ear, "It's why you came, isn't it? To shut them all the hell up."

Then he left her side and joined the others so she stood there alone to face them.

Her face had begun to burn and she took a few steps back. It was far too hot already in late summer for a fire such as this one, but young men like this did what they wanted. If they'd wanted a fire on the face of the sun, they would have had one.

The memory of standing in the gravel road, the car in the ditch, her family gone, flashed behind Cleo's eyes. She'd believed it was the worst thing anyone could ever imagine, losing the people they loved. But she'd learned she'd been wrong: it was far worse losing herself. She was glad her parents had not lived to see what she'd done. And she prayed then, or something like a prayer, pleaded with whatever force made the currents in the river run so high, that she might turn this tide. Then she remembered the one true thing Dooley had said to her.

"All stories are ghost stories—our own ghosts," she said, so quietly the boys had to lean in.

She reached to unclasp the fur and swung the stole from her shoulders. The eyes upon her glowed from the liquor and the leaping flames. She thought of Joanna swinging above the pool, suspended forever in that golden arc. She called up the ghost of this summer, of youth, of regret, the things that truly haunt, a story none of them would ever be able to forget. She called up the ghost of a girl she'd watched walk out of Plum Orchard, only a shade of herself.

So the memory of Joanna Burton would stay with them forever.

———

"This is a cautionary tale. If you listen now, it will never leave you. So make your choice. Stay or go." The wind had died down, but the water would soon crest its banks. The tide would be high within the hour. The storm on the horizon seemed to skirt them, traveling south.

"This is not my story. It's the story of the Lorelei, told to me by Joanna Burton, and I'm telling it for her now when she cannot."

"She's here for your soul, boys," one said. There were snickers and the silly wailing of ghosts. One boy acted as though he were rattling chains.

Deep in the forest, they heard a cry. They froze where they sat, not even daring to breathe, waiting for the terrible sound to come again, and when it did, they stared at one another, eyes wide and round. Cleo had heard the sound before, of course, but except for Morrie, these men were not from a place so wild that bobcats roamed beneath their windows at night.

"Damn." It was John Oliver. "Where's that boy with the gun?"

Tate Walker said, "Nobody's shooting that cat."

Cleo looked to see Lumas leaning against the truck, rifle in hand. She wondered if Tate had even loaded it. She knew that bobcat wouldn't get anywhere near a fire like this one or a bunch of noisy young men. They just liked thinking they were holding off beasts at the edge of their gilded world.

The party grumbled about old man Tate and huddled closer to the fire and poked sticks at it to raise the flames for protection and began to giggle to stave off their nerves. Cleo thought she had never seen a group of less competent hunters. She thought of how carelessly they'd gone out to shoot turkey or hogs and of how they'd stumbled in leaving heaps of gear every evening, but she'd never seen their kill, only smelled the liquor in their sweaty clothes when they returned. Tate had managed all of that and God knew how.

The distant scream of that bobcat only seemed to her like the tolling of some wild chime, the island itself announcing the moment this summer seemed to have been careening toward since they all stepped foot on Cumberland Island.

"Along the left bank of the River Rhine," she began, "there is a cleft in a rocky cliff where a waterfall murmurs and a seductive siren's song forever echoes. It drifts over the water. It captivates the hearts of men."

Cleo was a skilled storyteller. They quieted to listen and she wove a tale for them of her own making, from the seed of the myth she'd been told, embellishing as she pleased.

"The siren was the daughter of Old Father Rhine. Her name was Lorelei, and she was beautiful, a creature so golden, so incomparable that men who heard her song lost track of time. They looked up to watch her there and could not look away, so when they realized they had lost their way, it was already too late. Their vessels crashed and she drew them down to their watery graves, only leaving her more and more disappointed and heartbroken. For she was eternal, and always lonely for love.

"Until finally one day, she fell in love with a fisherman and she spent her days helping him fish. And she was so happy for a time that she did not sing her terrible song. Every day she filled his boat with a catch that seemed miraculous. His family and friends were never hungry and he was celebrated amongst them. And it seemed Lorelei would never be lonely again. But it wasn't long before word reached her that her fisherman had betrayed her. There was another young girl who had caught his eye, one who told him things he wanted to hear, who made him forget what Lorelei had done for him.

"In her jealous rage, Lorelei dragged him away and drowned him with all the love in her heart. And in her grief, she became a fantastic horror, far more powerful than she'd been before. And this is the warning I bring to you."

They ribbed one another quietly, but they'd lost their raucous energy. They were not such a soulless bunch that they did not hear the echo of Joanna Burton's memory in this song.

"It might have gone on like this forever—the siren's call, the senseless drownings that brought her no peace—except for the son of a powerful king who heard of the siren and went to see her with his own eyes. Like all of the others, he was smitten in a trance, causing him to lose everything, including his life. And this moved his mighty father to vengeance, a man who believed himself the equal of the siren, high on her lonely rock. He knew something Lorelei did not.

"She didn't fear him because to her, he was just one more man. And even when she was surrounded by the king's army, she laughed, high above them. And they quaked with fear and wondered at the nightmare she'd become. But their king urged them to plug their ears so they could not listen to her songs. He told them that given time, they would forget what they had seen and heard. He told them that whatever terrible fate awaited her, it would not be their fault.

"Lorelei believed with all her heart that Old Father Rhine, the king of the river with all its power, would protect her. And so, into the water she dropped a string of priceless pearls from around her neck, beckoning him in her need, believing his golden chariot would come to carry her to safety."

None moved. None laughed. Cleo waited so they might remember Joanna's pearls dripping down on them from above.

"But the king had already called on Old Father Rhine to beg him to intervene on behalf of his men and put a stop to his murderess daughter. And when her father's chariot finally came, it was not to save her, as the king had known full well. Not just one lover, but the world of men had betrayed her. And in that moment, she made a sound the world has never heard before or since. The terrible chariot carried her away. It dragged her down to the very depths of the sea where she was meant to remain for eternity amongst the graves of lost love. And I wish I could tell you this is where the story ended. But this story is a warning."

There was an exhalation from one boy. A hushed curse from another. Cleo felt her own guts tighten and turn.

"For although his men lived, there was a price for Old Father Rhine's favor. A murmuring forever haunted the souls of those men. And to this day, every son who ever descended from them searches for the Lorelei in his dreams. They feel her lovely arms drawing them down, down, down, forever drowning in the currents where she waits. They see her in every reflection, in the eyes of their lovers and in the trusting faces of their children. When they dare to wade into the creeks and streams the wide world over, her golden hair tangles around their ankles. And in old age, when they hope they might finally escape her, they choke up her priceless pearls as empty promises with their last breaths.

"You've listened to her story and so you've invited her here among us. She'll come on the cresting current," Cleo said, her voice rising, calling over the wild waters. "You'll hear her song rise with the tide." She extended her arm, slow and graceful as she'd seen Joanna do. She pointed toward the river, then turned her wrist and opened her hand, as if she were beckoning to something in the dark. And she was. She was calling up the cowardice of young men who had turned their backs on someone in need. She was calling on the spirit of all rivers to defend Joanna Burton. "Oh, listen. Hear her now? She will murmur to you always, until the hour she comes for you."

———

The sounds of the fire crackled and snapped. For a long moment, the story hung heavy in the air. Then came a cry from among them. Whooping and leaping to their feet, they were not ashamed at all. "She's there! Lorelei! I see her there! Get her, boys!"

Cleo's dismay felt like the weight of a hundred pounds pressing down on her. They took the story for a joke. They were drunk and high on their own youth and privilege. One had a flashlight and the beam swung over the crawl of the dark river.

Another cried out, "There! Oh geezus. She's there! What big eyes you have! Wait, are those *eyes*, darlin'? I'll be your river daddy!"

The energy was strange. Cleo could feel it was too high. They behaved recklessly, kicking, pushing, shoving. She got to her feet in a hurry, but not quick enough to stop the stole from being snatched up and swung onto the fire. It was Ellis who had done it. She reached a hand without thinking and felt the heat lick at her before grabbing her fist closed and watching the fur catch fire and crinkle and blacken, lost in the cinders.

Ellis came after her, taking her elbow roughly, separating her from the others. They stood nearer to the rushes at the river's edge. She saw that he was angered by the story. He hissed in her ear, "What was that supposed to be? Some kind of joke?"

He'd always sounded like a man who had run a far distance, as if he could barely catch his breath, but now he bore down on each word. Pushing them out like he was spitting rocks at Cleo.

"I'm sorry," she said. "But I'm not going to lie about what happened. I'm going to tell Dr. Johnston everything tonight. It's all been my fault, Ellis."

Ellis's face was lit from the bonfire, even though they'd moved away from it. His expression changed from one of intense focus to disbelief. "Tell him? Why the hell would you do that? He already knows what you did, Cleo. He doesn't want you confessing. He wants you to keep your mouth shut."

Cleo's thoughts raced in a confused jumble. "Because he should know the truth. Everyone should know nothing is wrong with Joanna Burton. And no one should blame her for any of it. Or any of you, Ellis. Only me."

"Forget that. It doesn't matter."

"How can it not matter?"

His breath in her face was sweet with liquor and bitter with tobacco. She tried to pull away, but there was no solid ground behind her, only the rushes and the tide washing up over her shoes. He turned her so her back was to the others. To anyone who might have looked their way, Cleo and Ellis would have appeared to be locked in a lovers' embrace or having a quarrel. Neither was something the young men would interrupt. She tried not to breathe.

"You make me better, Cleo. You make me what I want to be. Everything was good until Joanna came, remember? And we can go away. You and me, Cleo. We can just go, wherever you want. Or we can stay here. But you have to help me."

He was shaking. She could feel it through his whole body. Sweat ran down her back beneath her clothes and she knew she'd started to cry, but she didn't dare wipe her face. She didn't look at Tate or Lumas, who stood near the truck, vigilant with the shotgun, watching for signs of trouble with the rollicking men.

She'd seen the look Ellis now had, his searching eyes, the tremor in his hands. Dooley's hands had done that sometimes, but she'd forgotten about that, how glory could eat a man up, when all she could think about was having Ellis Piedmont for herself. Now she remembered her grandmother's voice in another room, could hear her gentle coaxing, talking Dooley down when he'd come off the glory. Every time he'd gone back to it. But she'd fought his monster with him because she loved him.

This was different. Cleo had created this monster. And she knew it was not love that had caused her to lose all her sense and take desperate measures to hold on to Ellis. She hadn't truly wanted to help him any more than she'd wanted to help Joanna Burton. She'd wanted to make them see her as something special. She'd wanted to feel needed, chosen, the glory of someone's days as she'd only felt before her parents had died. Now, all of Ellis's desperation came at her at once, and she felt the tension of his body and her own as she watched the river roaring past, choppy and black, watched the light of the fire as it stabbed at the dark sky.

"I'll help you. Ellis, I'll help you," she promised, trying to think what to do. "But you don't need it, Ellis. Look at you tonight. You don't need it."

"If you loved me, you'd give it to me," Ellis argued weakly. She was beginning to understand why Ellis Piedmont had operated on the fringe of this crowd, why he'd been alone on that porch at Plum Orchard while the others were out.

"It will only ruin the best parts of you."

"Why won't you listen to me?" he yelled. "If you won't give it to me, tell me where to get it. Take me there. Show me."

"Stop it, Ellis. They'll hear you."

"Do you think I care? They already know!"

He tried to force her forward, as if he'd march her out in front of everyone. Now she faced Tate and Lumas.

"I do think you care. I know you do." Cleo stared into the last glow of the embers. "But glory won't ever give us what we want. It just poisons everything."

"Glory? *Glory?*" Ellis spat, confused, anxious. "You really are crazy, aren't you? Maybe that's what I'll tell Johnston. Maybe he'll cart you off too. Maybe that's what I should have said about both of you."

He shoved her away and she stumbled backward and fell in front of Tate. Lumas stood just behind him, still holding the rifle at his side. Tate reached to help her up.

"I'd feel better if you'd stop making threats, Ellis," Tate said. "Now, let's just call it a night and go dry out."

"Come on, Mr. Piedmont. Let's just walk it off, back to the house," Lumas said, as if he was just there to help after a day fishing.

"Shit, I see it again! Look there! I'm not lying. There's something there," one of the men yelled. "Get that gun, Tate!"

"Holy hell!" said another. They were pointing and staggering. The water writhed and there came the sound of a sharp splash, once, then twice, and then again. Every time the sound rang out, the men became more frantic. The beams of their lights flashed over the water, searching for the source of their fears. Cleo's story—*No! Joanna's myth!*—had come to life.

It happened so fast that in their drunken frenzy, not one of them could be sure what they'd seen. When they were asked later, details of the events were disorganized in their memories. But all would agree they'd seen something in the water, a flash of something menacing, terrifying enough that they couldn't trust their own eyes. Some things, however, were clear. They called for Tate's rifle, the one Lumas Gray was holding. Everyone would agree on that. And Ellis Piedmont tried to take it from him.

"Don't shoot her!" Ellis screamed.

If he meant a river siren arriving on the whitecaps of the rushing river, if Cleo's story had truly brought her up, no one could say. If he meant Cleo Woodbine, his warning was swallowed by the din of noise from the panicked boys.

"It's not her, Ellis! It's not her! It was only a story," Cleo yelled back.

But even Cleo thought she might have been seeing exactly what she'd meant for him to see, for all of them to see: the mythical champion of a girl like Joanna, like herself, the ones they'd used and broken, come to take a terrible revenge. She heard the others calling out. But in the end, no one could say who'd pulled the trigger, which of those two boys, Ellis or Lumas. Only that the rifle went off.

————

Cleo never heard the shot ring out over the sounds of the men and the river.

Later, she only remembered Ellis, hysterical, screaming, blaming Lumas: "That boy shot her! He shot her!"

She couldn't be sure what had happened as she clutched her middle, going numb to her fingertips, still on her knees. Even the end of her nose seemed to go cold and unfeeling. She watched Ellis leap on Lumas, the two of them struggling and staggering, splashing into the rushes. Tate was there, easing her onto her back, pressing both palms hard against her middle. She turned her head to see the river, driven by the winds and tides, dark but for the firelight and the beams of flashlights that swung in all directions, reflecting off a swell traveling across the inky water.

There, behind Lumas and Ellis, something altered, grew still and slick and then convulsed; a wave that had gathered itself up all afternoon with the outgoing tide now rushed back in and bore down on the shore, rushing over the reeds at the tide's height.

Ellis was there one moment, then gone. He sank below the water, or it swept over him, took him, pulling him off his feet so that he disappeared and there was no sign of him in any direction. They all watched in disbelief, this betrayal from the river that had been nothing but a benevolent force in the background of their wild summer days. They called his name and scanned their lights over the surface, but the water gave nothing up, only carried on downstream.

"He can't swim!" Cleo heard Wally yell. "That son of a bitch can't swim."

She saw Lumas disappear into the water then, going after Ellis. "Lumas, no!" she yelled. It seemed to her that with those words, every bit of life within her slipped close to some edge.

Cleo tried to focus, tried to breathe, horrified. Something displaced the water. For an instant Cleo was certain she'd glimpsed a familiar green and iridescent glimmer. The sleek, dark body of a scaled creature surely five feet long, wielding the power of a muscular tail that cut through the water, fierce and fast, there and then gone.

Cleo felt dread like a cold breath curling near her ear, a horrible remorse and no hope of redemption.

Her name was being called as if it were coming from the bottom of a well as Tate lifted her and carried her past the men who all staggered around on the shore. Tate ran with her down the dark path and across the great expanse of lawn, back to Plum Orchard. And she cried and begged him to go back, but she didn't think he heard her.

Dr. Johnston and everyone in the house met them before they even reached the porch. They'd heard the gun go off. He put Cleo on the long dining table and set to work removing her dress and staunching the wound while she screamed. Dr. Johnston spoke to her, reassuring her that he had seen gunshot wounds before, not the least of which had been his own. Cleo wished she had come to him before any of this. She wished so many things were different. Tate Walker stood behind the doctor while he worked and Cleo watched his face, drawn and pale, until she gave out or gave up and the horrible night faded and her eyes fell shut.

Chapter Twenty-Seven

FRANCES

THE HIGHWAY UNSPOOLED IN THE REARVIEW, AND WITH THE dawn, the road climbed into the foothills of the Blue Ridge. Frances could almost believe Revery and everyone in it had been nothing more than another story she'd read from her collection, that she'd fallen asleep and dreamed herself there. As she pulled into the familiar streets of Asheville, all she could think was that it was too late for brunch back at Gilbreath House and wished she was still back at the inn.

The mountains were beautiful here, familiar and green in their full foliage, but not long from now autumn would bring crowds for the fall color. Today was calm. The skies were clear. Nothing about Asheville had changed. But Frances felt disoriented. And she'd been studying folktales long enough to understand that when the main character made her return from foreign lands, it was not her home that had changed. For the first time, she wondered about the Lorelei, where she'd gone after she'd dropped all her pearls and what her life had been then. The stories never said.

First thing, she drove out to the cemetery to see that her mother's stone had been set correctly. It was white marble, pristine and pretty as her mother had been, standing up beside the markers for her grandparents and Owen Flood. Frances stayed there above the French Broad River watching the water slide away, deep and languid, said to be the oldest in the country. Frances said aloud, "All rivers lead to the sea."

It was the closest thing she knew to a prayer. Her heart broke a little, thinking of Rosey Devane as she'd last seen him, disappearing into the dark near the same spot where they had looked out at a different river. She hadn't even known the man existed a week ago, and now she couldn't look out at the water without wishing she could let it take her right back to him.

On Joanna's stone, she'd had a poem engraved, one inspired by the myth of the Lorelei. But that's not what caught Frances's eye. At the foot of the stone, a surprise memorial was growing, cards and letters from the mothers and children who had known Joanna over the years. Here was further proof that a story could start in one place and end in another in unpredictable ways. You could be a silly girl and grow into a woman who turned a house into a home, a lonely fisherman into a father, a fable into forgiveness.

She walked down to the water and along its banks, following the trails cut by fishermen who came out long before dawn and dropped their lines for catfish or redeye or a rare sturgeon. When she came upon such a man, she did not disturb him, but he raised his hand and she did the same, the neighborly gesture Owen Flood had taught her. She thought of the seamen waving to Rosey Devane and exchanging predictions for a mythical summer storm, men who believed in signs and wonders. She'd thought her preoccupation with such things had come from her maternal line, but now she believed it had also been born of Owen Flood. Owen had loved her so well she'd believed only a power of mythical proportions could have separated him from his daughter, from her. Whatever Ellis Piedmont had been to Joanna or to her, Frances carried in that single memory all the proof she needed for what mattered. It had been the truth then and now, even knowing Joanna's story had, perhaps, been more complicated than she'd ever known. But to Frances, her daddy would always be a man she remembered standing beneath a Blue Ridge canopy of pine and oak and ash, suited to muddy boots and khaki pants.

She thought about what happened to the history of a place—or a person. Stories sank deep into the roots to grow something new. They floated on the night breeze or flew upward in the spout spray of some legendary and impossible creature. She liked to think that was the case for her parents now, some of their love story fact and some of it mystery, and because she carried them inside her, perhaps that meant she would wake one day to realize she was just such a fantastic creature.

She thought of the dividings, the place in the East River where the tides ran both ways, and she knew Rosey Devane would understand this about her. She knew she could tell him about it, and maybe they would sit on his houseboat and drink tea and he would talk about himself again. Those were the stories she wanted to hear now. She was saying her goodbyes to the frightened little girl she had been, no longer fighting the nature of life, which could sweep away everything she'd believed, but instead trusting the current to carry her.

———

The late afternoon sun was slanting long and low when she pulled up to the curb in front of the little clapboard house where she and her parents had lived, and where dozens of children had spent their childhoods over the years at Mother's Helper. The house would soon be removed to make room for something new, a cluster of modern homes for modern families. She parked to look at it, thinking it seemed smaller than she remembered. The house already felt like part of a distant past, like her grandparents. She hadn't been the least interested in learning who they had been, only thought of them if she passed Burton Antiques, Fine Art and Collectibles and saw the sign with their name. Now she wanted to go through what she had chosen to keep before all those connections were gone. But there was no rush, she reminded herself. She could manage one thing at a time. She leaned her head back, exhausted from the long drive, letting her mind wander through so many memories. When the sound of a passing car woke her, it was approaching dusk and she'd been fast asleep for almost an hour.

She pointed the truck back toward town and the boardinghouse where her rented rooms were waiting. She barely took the time to look around at the boxes still sitting full where she'd left them. Too tired to eat, she didn't even bother to unpack her suitcase but climbed on the twin bed, the one thing she'd brought from her old room. She pulled the quilt over her, comforted by its familiar smell and missing her mother.

Frances drowsed and thought of the things she'd boxed away—a few pieces of Joanna's clothes, her jewelry, the heirloom silver—all in a storage room at the antique store. As she'd told Audrey, she'd also saved a few of the child-care items from the day care in a strange turn of optimism on her part, in case she might have a family of her own one day. She remembered there were Irish linens that had belonged to Owen Flood's grandmother. There were cookbooks with recipes in German. There was an old winter hat she had seen her daddy wear, and now she wondered if it had come with him from Ireland. There were bedsheets with embroidered stitching on the pillowcases, and Frances wondered whose hands had done the work. There was a silver brush that Joanna had used for her hair, a birthday gift to her when she'd turned sixteen, and Frances thought of the story of the Lorelei. When she was small, Frances remembered she'd watched

Joanna brush her hair with that brush countless times. When had she stopped paying attention to her mother like that?

Here was the answer. She'd pushed Joanna away and taken refuge in notebooks filled with her own thoughts and reactions to the stories she'd studied. She had maps and travel plans for all the places she wanted to see. She considered the thing she loved most about folklore, the way it connected the whole world. The stories were being told again and again from all four corners of the earth, universal tales of lives, loves, and dreams. She could study them all the days of her life and never grow tired of them, but she found herself thinking what she'd most like to do now was share them. She thought of all she could have shared with her mother but hadn't. As she drifted to sleep, she thought of the friends she'd made in Revery and what it might be to spend every day there. She thought of Cleo Woodbine and the characters she painted over and over again while she lived alone, and how funny it was that maybe they were not so different after all. Maybe her mother had known that.

———

Frances slept well into the morning on Monday, and it was closer to lunch than breakfast when she finally left the boardinghouse to find something to eat at the pharmacy counter, but her stomach was nervous from all the change. She settled for sipping on a soda while making notes in her field notebook, listing everything that would need to happen if her idea was going to be a success. She'd need to make arrangements to transport her personal belongings, and also her collection of folklore and research, back to Revery. There were calls to be made, contracts to write up for academia and artisans who might be interested in being benefactors or in the opportunity to have their work displayed. And as she dreamed up her plan, it seemed to

Frances that her whole life had been nothing but an exercise in accumulating the knowledge and material for this sole purpose: to set up a folk center. She hoped Audrey would think the same when she presented the idea. She should have called the inn by now, but she'd wanted to get her thoughts straight before she got her hopes up, or Audrey's. She'd considered trying to reach Rosey at the theater, but felt nervous about calling there, not knowing if he'd want her to wait in case there was still any danger to Will. She'd settled on a compromise and decided to call Gilbreath House tomorrow after signing the closing papers; maybe then she'd be sure her plans would work and she'd be ready to tell Audrey she was thinking of returning to Revery.

She didn't want to go back to the boardinghouse to sit for the long hours left in the day. She thought of picking up a copy of a *True Romance* magazine as she walked the sidewalk window-shopping, then spotted the movie theater marquee and smiled. She ducked inside to catch a matinee of the same monster movie that had been playing in Revery. She ate popcorn and laughed with the others in the audience, but they didn't know her, and Frances's feelings only confirmed what her business plan had already decided. This was no longer her town. She still wanted to travel, but she knew where she belonged now.

Back at her rooms at the boardinghouse, the empty walls echoed and she dug out a little radio and switched on the local station. She missed the music at Gilbreath House, the records Audrey played from poor Freddie's collection. She'd kept a bottle of Joanna's favorite perfume and she put it to her nose and inhaled, then dabbed a little of the fragrance on her wrists and neck and danced alone in the room. If there was any real way to call up a ghost, Frances thought that might be what she was doing.

She'd waited until now, when all the rest was managed, to take a look at the painting from Cleo. At first, before she'd left Revery with Will Tremmons lying hidden in the back of the truck, she'd thought she could leave the painting unopened, store it away and leave the past alone. She'd been afraid of what she might see if she opened it. But then she'd watched Will slip away into the shadows and realized what a coward it would make her to live in the dark, whatever it might mean. There was a note from Cleo, this one addressed to Frances. She opened it, sitting cross-legged on the floor.

Dear Frances,

My granddaddy told me all stories are ghost stories because they're the breath of life, that we carry them inside us until we tell them and then we breathe them right back in to keep us going. This is as close to everything I know about the way he taught me to see the wonders of this old world. If you look with your whole heart, you'll always see your mama there. And when you're ready, if you ever are, I'll tell you about that summer and what I saw in the East River.

Love,

Cleo Woodbine

Frances's hands were steady when she slid the watercolor out of the casing, letting it unfurl in front of her. What she saw took her breath. The colors and images were so vibrant and alive with movement that she could barely take it all in. It was a puzzle and a promise at once. It was a comfort and a challenge. She sat back on her heels and wondered at the intricacies of the ink outlines and the dreamy quality of the paint—a rainbow, a revelation, a secret. She felt she had the viewpoint of some great bird looking down on the shoals and yet she felt embraced, the same way she'd felt the first time she'd set foot on Cumberland, that old place with its old gods.

Here were the saltwater creeks, rivers, marshes, and islands that made Cleo's world, a small kingdom, lush and wild. The palms and palmetto, the ancient limbs of live oak, the shadow and light that streamed through hanging moss, the glistening water where the tides turned at the dividings, the river smooth as glass, choppy as scales. Everywhere Frances's eye fell, mysteries waited to be discovered. She could find them if she was patient, the characters from Dooley Woodbine's stories. The shadow of Dungeness mansion fell over the land; the white walls of Plum Orchard rose bleak; the bonfire on the shore seemed a beacon. She saw bleached bone. She saw the fruit of every tree and plant. Winding through it all, she saw a tangled vine. But there, too, was the distant town of Revery, perched seemingly at the edge of another world, the marquee of the Marvel Theater, the rooftop of Gilbreath House. And a soft border between those worlds, where the sea or the river kissed the coast and the sand gleamed, iridescent as pearls.

Cleo had outdone herself. This work was astonishing and far beyond the original illustrations in the book her grandfather had made. But as the hour grew late, she felt her eyes grow tired from searching. She had not found Joanna anywhere. Her last thought before sleep was that come morning, she would go to Burton Antiques, Fine Art and Collectibles for the envelope Cleo had mailed with the string of pearls, and something else she'd thought of that might surprise even Cleo Woodbine.

Chapter Twenty-Eight

AUDREY

FRANCES SHOULD HAVE BEEN BACK IN ASHEVILLE FOR A FULL DAY and a half but still had not called when Audrey used the number for Burton Antiques, Fine Art and Collectibles on Monday afternoon to see whether she had gotten home safe, but the phone only rang and rang with no answer. And it seemed she'd only have more questions after yesterday morning when Tate had gone out because there'd been no sign of Glenn. Audrey had been selling sack lunches as usual to the men in the side yard when one of them told her the news of gunshots fired on Cumberland.

"One of those men that come up from Florida to hunt on Cumberland got shot in the leg on Saturday night," the worker explained. *"But they say he'll live. Nothing serious."*

He'd gone on to explain that word was the men were swearing they had chartered their excursion through Glenn, which was exactly what Audrey had been afraid they'd say. The man named Morrie Johnston, whom she'd heard Tate and Glenn mention days before, the owner of Plum Orchard these days, had had them all arrested on trespassing charges. Glenn and the rest were sitting in the Nassau County Jail in Fernandina.

By lunchtime, Rosey had called to tell her a worse story: Harl Buie was in the hospital, unconscious from an overnight assault.

Audrey was stunned to learn that it had been Glenn who'd found the boy. Audrey truly hoped that meant Glenn had not played any part in the shooting or the violence against Harl. For both his own sake and his family's. *"Maybe let's not say anything to Jimmy about Glenn and Harl yet,"* Rosey had said.

Jimmy had spent the day happily playing records until Tate wandered in looking like he'd crawled home from Fernandina. Today she'd kept Jimmy working alongside her until Tate had recovered enough to take over. Whatever he wanted his grandson to know about the goings-on, she'd left that up to him.

Just before dinnertime, Audrey decided to go for a walk to get out of the house. She stopped behind the library and leaned against the wall. She felt anxious, as if she could feel everything, all the time, all at once now. The air on her skin was heavy and strange and still and smelling like steel. The glare of the light was almost blinding, the clouds hanging low. She was starving every minute, but she felt full and empty at the same time. She was tired, yet she couldn't rest.

She wished there would be good news on Harl Buie. She was glad Jimmy was none the wiser and Tate had taken him for a milkshake at the pharmacy. In so many ways, it felt like time had reset to the days before Frances had come to the inn, before the ghost photography, before the Buies had come down from the balcony. Except her belly was growing. A baby was coming. She'd have to set up a nursery. She had no idea what else. She'd have to call her parents. And when this child was born and she presented it to Freddie's parents, would they look at its sweet face and feel the way she'd felt when she'd looked at that first double exposure? Would they find the love they'd lost staring back at them?

Audrey wandered through the tall grasses and the old cemetery where all the Devanes were buried and her aunt Shirley and uncle Henry and her Gilbreath great-grandparents too. She couldn't help thinking about *Our Town*. She considered that her own parents would not be buried here but in Macon with her daddy's family, near the Howell plot where Freddie was, a near perfect stranger. Audrey had never once considered she'd be buried there beside him. The thought shocked her. Not just the thought of her grave but the thought of her death. And she realized it was because she fully expected to have a long life, a life that would include a family and love that did not end with that train accident. But what if she died in childbirth? It happened. Forever with Freddie seemed like too long now, and she realized that already she had moved on. She noticed that she'd come to stand in front of a marker that stood several yards outside the cemetery fencing where the grasses were never mowed. She knelt down to run her fingertips across the crudely engraved name: *Merry*.

There were so many stories about Merry that it didn't seem she ever could have been a real person. But here was a marker that said she'd existed. Maybe none of the stories were true, only the name. Maybe the best thing about Merry was that she got to be whatever she wanted to be and answered to no one for it. Not even now.

Thinking of where she'd be buried naturally made her consider where she might live, whether back in Macon with her parents and in-laws, or here in Revery. She'd not stopped thinking about that since she'd developed the photos for her brochure. Up until then, she'd only been busy hiding, afraid that all her choices would be taken from her the minute her family knew about the baby. Now she was starting to believe that her choices had less to do with what she wanted for herself and everything to do with the person she was toting around. It made her head ache. It made her feel bad for keeping her mother at arm's length, even if that's what she'd believed Mimi wanted.

She put a hand atop Merry's stone to help get back to her feet.

That's when she saw the small group that had gathered even farther from the fence line, beneath a grove of oaks. Friends and family of Harl Buie, she could guess, holding a prayer vigil. Audrey didn't dare move closer to join them, but she bowed her own head and sent up all her fervent wishes for that poor boy. He hadn't deserved what had happened to him. She knew everyone was hoping he would wake up, waiting to see what he would say, who he would blame. He probably knew it too. Audrey thought it would be easier for him to sleep.

She felt a hand on her shoulder and looked up to see Tate Walker looking down at her. He was holding Jimmy by the hand. She could see a resemblance between them and wondered how she'd missed it until now.

"Come back to the inn with us," Jimmy said. "Grandpa Tate's going to tape the windows." His feet seemed to have a better hold on the ground beneath him with Tate around.

Tate explained, "As if we've not had enough excitement, it looks like there's some actual weather coming in."

They did what they could to prepare, checking the windows were locked and shutters closed, filling bathtubs with clean water. By tomorrow, she told herself, things could be better in Revery. The storm would pass like so many others and wash everything clean. Harl Buie could wake up. Misunderstandings could be made clear. Old hurts could heal. She told herself this was the moment when everything could change for the better.

———

When Audrey was wrong, she was dead wrong. But sometimes she was right. Before midnight, it was obvious this was the storm everyone had predicted. And while the wind howled outside, they set up camp in the living room. They'd carried blankets down, creating almost a duplicate of what Jimmy had put together in the carriage house. They had a little transistor radio, but the batteries went flat too soon. The extra ones they had they were saving for the flashlight. Now there was no news, only what they could hear and see out their own windows and doors, which they kept shut tight.

Tate had a little surprise he'd brought downstairs: a guitar he could play fair to middling, something Audrey had not known about. She remembered what he'd said about Freddie and music being a good indicator that a man was soulful. When she looked at the Walker boys with her, she agreed. She wondered if Glenn might have benefited had someone ever given him a harmonica.

They had sandwiches and fruit and crackers and cheese. They had leftover cornbread and milk that they ate in bowls. But when they were fed, there was nothing left to do but try to keep from worrying about all the things they could do nothing about. Audrey had the thought that if the roof came down, they could be buried alive. She kept that to herself. And she was grateful Jimmy was not scared, but instead was enjoying the opportunity to entertain them.

He began with recitations. Poetry first, mostly little snippets of *Paradise Lost*. She only recognized it because she'd had to read it in school. She had no earthly idea how a twelve-year-old boy could crank it out like he ought to be on the stage. But she thought if that was what Will Tremmons had been teaching him, he was the best thing that had ever happened to any of the Walkers.

Audrey and Jimmy were delighted when Tate stood to recite Keats.

Jimmy followed this up with a verse of "Danny Boy," and they were all too sad to go on until Tate broke out in a ridiculously fast rendition of "Who's on First?"

Their laughter made the walls shake as hard as the storm and helped them forget their nerves.

Tate played on his guitar some more and told stories of what he'd seen during his days on the Southern Railway railroad. Audrey tried not to think about the trains and found herself thinking about Freddie. When Tate talked about the circus train, she wanted to hear about it almost as badly as Jimmy.

"Did you ever see the circus?" Jimmy asked. "Did you have the time of your life?"

"I think this is the time of my life," Tate said.

"Me too," Jimmy said. "But I still want to see the circus."

"I guess we'll have to go do that."

"And Audrey too," Jimmy said.

"And your daddy," Tate said.

Jimmy barely seemed to register Tate's suggestion. He had not asked where his father was during the storm. Glenn Walker sure had a ways to go with his son. Lord, she hoped he would. Everything in her really did, for the sake of these two who loved him. For Glenn's sake too.

Jimmy finally coaxed Audrey into singing "Walking After Midnight." Then they played cards, because there was no way to sleep. Mostly spades. Tate lost every round. Audrey thought it was on purpose. She was getting tired. Her mood had turned sulky.

But Jimmy wasn't slowing down. Elvis was a favorite. There was no power for the record player, but he sang an entire catalog. "All Shook Up," "Hound Dog," "Love Me Tender," the list went on. When Jimmy was worn out, they listened to Tate play some quiet tunes, and then he did something Audrey wouldn't have expected, telling tales he'd made up about two young boys and an old houseboat.

"Glenn and Rosey took that houseboat down the river like old Huck Finn."

Jimmy curled up with his head on Audrey's lap, entranced, while the storm carried on outside. Audrey had not thought of Glenn and Rosey as boys together, and maybe these weren't memories but how Tate had hoped life might have been for his son while he was away.

When he'd run through his houseboat tales, he turned to those of Cleo Woodbine.

"She can walk the whole length of Cumberland in a day.

"She can talk to mink and coyotes and bobcats.

"She knows old folk magic that can turn trespassers to hogs till the dawn.

"She can tell a story and bring it to life.

"Cleo believes we all carry our own living, breathing library inside."

Jimmy cut his eyes at Audrey and she knew he was thinking of the tunnel, but he wasn't giving up the secret.

Tate said, "She'd like this here, sitting around together with you."

"Is she lonely?" Jimmy asked.

"Loneliest soul I know. But we're going to change that when this weather clears."

Tate was worried about Cleo, Audrey knew. Maybe they would both go with him, her and Jimmy, to see Cleo Woodbine, but Audrey was grateful that for now, they were snug inside Gilbreath House. And when the storm finally blew itself out, it seemed they'd been in that living room together for ages, even though she knew by the time on the grandfather clock in the foyer that it had only been a few hours, not even time enough for the sun to come up. But when they found their way up to their beds, Audrey honestly hated to go.

Chapter Twenty-Nine

CLEO

IT WAS A BAD STORM, BUT SHE'D LIVED ON THE SHOALS TWENTY-seven years now and it seemed to Cleo it wasn't the worst to have hit the coast. The old guard would laugh over this one. She knew, too, that in spite of that, it would be enough to bring the change the locals had long been predicting. She knew that by morning, her sanctuary would at last be joined to that strange kingdom of Cumberland. But to her great pleasure, Woodbine Cottage had stood firm. The roof held. That little snake in her wall didn't creep even one inch higher.

She'd watched the first streaks of the dawn from her stoop. The heat settled heavy and thick in that awful farewell of a summer storm, after the sky had let loose its hot breath and earned its rest. Cleo, on the other hand, had had enough of rest. She walked out to see the new world and did not stop walking until she came to the place where a dock had once been, now carried off someplace down the East River. She was glad to see at least her truck remained where she'd left it. She climbed in and went to check on the neighbors she'd once promised to avoid.

There were limbs down, but Cumberland had fared well so far as she could tell. Standing water was washing out parts of the Grand Avenue, but she cruised around those with little trouble. She knew the way to Dungeness so well she could have navigated it blind. None of the old trees or vines she checked in their thickets or stands had suffered. She filled her pockets with glory. She spoke to the plants and told them her plan. They sent down roots and dropped fruit and seed and lifted their leaves and did not need her at all. She might have felt they were her children if she was another sort of woman, but she was not. She might have been proud at how prettily they had grown, as if what they were had anything to do with her, but Cleo thought it was more likely the other way around. She had not brought her basket with her today. She'd taken enough from this place.

She shot north on the island then. All signs at Greyfield were good. She'd never swung around the long drive in front of the house, but when she did so today, a woman stood on the upper porch of the stately house and Cleo knew she was Lucy Ferguson, called Miss Lucy by the locals these days, the granddaughter and namesake of the first Lucy Carnegie, who had built Dungeness and then each of the grand homes for her children. Cleo recognized Miss Lucy by the jaunty kerchief on her head. She looked at the eccentric and infamously stubborn current matriarch of the Cumberland Island Carnegies and recognized a kindred creature. She thought that in another life, where she hadn't let her regret rule her days on Kingdom Come, she might have come here sooner and she and Lucy might have been friends. Today it even seemed like such a thing as that might still be possible. It might be she would bring the woman a basket of fruit sometime. Cleo felt certain Lucy recognized her, too, and was glad when the woman raised her hand and gave a sharp wave. Cleo did the same and moved on.

She saw the same storm damage near Stafford, with plenty of folks out clearing debris or kicked back under the shade of ancient trees, grateful to see them still standing. Some folks she recognized;

most she did not. But she saw they knew her and were stunned to watch her whiz by them and throw up a hand when she'd never before looked their way. There was an unexpected pleasure in that.

Every other little spot she cruised past was part of the overall decline of Cumberland, either empty or collapsing. She knew Archie Buie had gone into Brunswick, but she'd go farther north and see what was left of the north end past Brick Hill, where she'd never ventured since she'd seen it with Lumas Gray.

Finally, she headed for Plum Orchard. It was still midmorning when she came up the lane to the imposing, palatial home. She supposed she'd hated it all those years ago on sight. She found her feelings had not changed. She pulled right near the front and considered leaving her truck running, wanting only proof of life for Morrie Johnston. She had no intention of setting foot inside. She cut the motor only to save on gasoline.

She knocked, then pounded on the front door. As she stood on that porch, a thousand memories came at her, but she was surprised how small they seemed, like some old movie reel flickering in her mind. The specter of young Ellis Piedmont did not leap from her head and stand before her to waggle his eyebrows and taunt her. Instead, it was the idea of him that bored her now. She thought of Frances Flood and Audrey Howell and hoped the inn had kept its roof. She thought of Rosey and those Walker boys and the messes men could make of their lives when they were scared. She was done with being scared. She was done with giving up her time.

She should have noticed the flies right away, but she'd been so preoccupied with the nonsense inside her own head that it took that long for her to hear their low drone and turn to see the pelt of the bobcat, hung over the low limb of an oak a few feet off the porch from where she stood.

She opened the door and let herself inside.

———

Cleo Woodbine thought she had never seen a ghost until she looked at Morrie Johnston, only a shade of the young man she remembered. If he'd stood there wrapped in his burial cloth with jangling chains, she wouldn't have been more struck by the ruin of him. Once a beautiful youth, he'd grayed and thinned and puckered and sunk into himself in all the ways a man will do when he's being eaten up from the inside out. Really, it was only his eyes she recognized.

"Morrie Johnston," she said. She saw his little grin widen. "I thought maybe you and your fiddle might have gotten thrown up in a tree last night, but you look alive enough."

"Only enough to wish I weren't," he said.

She did not doubt it. It smelled like somebody had already held the funeral. The air was stale. Even the lilies, crammed by the dozens into every corner of every room, had died in their vases. Once, this man and this house had been glamorous, frequented by the likes of movie stars and renowned politicians. Of all the Carnegie homes on the island, aside from Dungeness, nine miles south on the river, none could match this marvelous house. Cleo remembered a story about how a French count, the husband of the former Carnegie occupant, had stripped the house of nearly everything that wasn't nailed down, and so most of what was brought to the house for the Johnstons had come from Dungeness.

Cleo recalled that there had been prizewinning delphiniums

and hollyhocks so the gardens looked like something out of a story-book. She remembered pipe smoke and bourbon, tweed coats, khaki hunting pants and plaid wool shirts, monied grace. Now there was a musty room with a Steinway baby grand with yellow-ing keys, and it felt to her like a glimpse of the consequences of bad choices, like the ones in tales of old just before the character made better decisions and all this sadness was whisked away to reveal beauty restored. But in real life, time didn't work that way.

"I see someone got that old bobcat," she said.

"Enough of them out there now that they're a damn nuisance." This was not true and Cleo knew it; it was only something to say from a man who wanted to shoot something. His mind wandered and Cleo waited. Morrie looked around as if he'd misplaced some-thing. She said his name twice until he focused on her again, and she wondered how long it had been since he'd been sober.

"Nobody that comes around here now remembers anything about us from back when," he said. "Might as well be talking to myself. I can tell folks anything, they believe it. Told Glenn Walker about that bore wave that came through in '32 and he didn't believe me, but you remember that."

"I do." Cleo remembered the wave. How could she forget it? She remembered watching Ellis and Lumas disappear, there one minute and gone the next. She remembered hearing talk of the unlikely occurrence, a natural phenomenon on tidal rivers but one that had never been seen on the East River before or since. A bore wave, it was called. Some people still didn't think it could have happened that way off Cumberland Island, Georgia. Cleo had never made up her mind about what she'd seen.

"I guess we're all thinking about that since we got that obituary for Joanna Burton from your daddy," she said.

"Who's that, you say?" She could see Morrie was trying to pull up the name from his addled memory and then she knew that he had not been so affected as she and Tate had been by the news. Joanna's passing had hardly registered with him. He said, "Daddy's getting along. He'll be eighty come this spring. The day he's gone, I don't know if I'll be able to stomach this place. You know, I still have a ticket of Daddy's, that one he kept. He had a bad case of the flu and was unable to get out of bed. He missed the boat. But he kept his *Titanic* ticket just to be able to look at it and be thankful he never used it. If I didn't have that ticket, I don't know that I'd have believed him."

"I never saw it."

"Well, it's here someplace. I can tell you that. I can tell. You. That."

"Well, I'm glad to see you're still afloat out here. I just wanted to let you know I'll be moving over to Revery."

"Not surprised, not surprised. Looks like that's how it's going with just about everybody out here. We'll all be gone and there'll be nothing left."

It wasn't true. Cumberland would barely register this man's passing, she thought, pleased. "I'll keep painting out there if it's the same to you," she said, "as long as it's standing."

"The same?" He grunted. "Nothing's the same. Times are changing, Cleo. They're changing. Isn't it a shame?"

She had only one real question for the man. "I wonder if you still have that copy of Dooley's little book anywhere around here. I'd like to buy it from you, if you'd part with it."

He laughed then, a sort of strangled sound like he was having to learn how to do it again. "I'll look around here for you, but it's liable to have walked off with one somebody or another. I remember . . . Lord, those were the days listening to Dooley and Daddy."

He glanced around like he wasn't even sure where they were. "We used to love it, listening to them tell those stories. We'd sit up at Montrose."

Cleo knew he was talking about the Johnston estate in Kentucky. She had an understanding that Dooley and Morrie's stepfather had been friends there, in the hills of Appalachia. But as Morrie talked, she put more pieces together, maybe more meaningful than what she'd come for, how Dooley had come to the island after he'd married her grandmother and had been unable to keep a job anywhere else. Much of the man Dooley had wanted Cleo to believe him to be, it seemed, came from his own imagination. Even more of it had been inspired by Dr. Johnston, a friend who had given him a second chance. Dooley had taken it and turned himself into a hero. Morrie confirmed all Frances Flood had told her, that the book had become a rare collector's item, being that it was the only thing Dooley Woodbine had produced.

"My stepdaddy always liked taking in a stray," Morrie announced, slurring his words. "Your granddaddy, you, that Lumas Gray. Wonder whatever happened to that boy after he left here."

Cleo's mouth went dry. They'd both been there and seen as first Ellis, then Lumas disappeared into the river. "I always figured he'd been haunting every glen and glade these last long years."

He huffed. "That's about as true as that old siren story you told everybody. You had us all going. I still worry about it if I'm out at night and start letting my imagination get the better of me."

Cleo knew then that the news clipping Audrey Howell had found was the revelation she'd believed it was. There was something Morrie knew that she did not about what happened after that night, after the bullet, after the river, a part of the story kept secret from her and from Tate Walker. She thought of the day, after her recovery, when she'd stood in this same room at Plum Orchard and Dr. Johnston had handed down his benevolent proclamation for her life. He'd done that for all of them. He'd sent Joanna back to Asheville, and Tate away, too, off to that railroad job. Now her fingertips tingled the way they had when she'd gathered glory in desperation only a little over a week ago. She brought them to her lips to cover her mouth, afraid to ask what she longed to know. Who else had Dr. Johnston sent away?

Morrie, somehow lucid in that moment, saw these things occurring to her. He looked at Cleo with understanding dawning in his rheumy eyes.

"You didn't know. Daddy put Lumas Gray on a train down to Florida after Archie brought him here and it was all decided. Daddy just wanted to help. I thought you knew it all this time."

Tate had been right. This life really was just chance after chance and everybody bumbling through, lucky if they learned a damn thing.

"Archie knew that Lumas was alive?"

Morrie nodded. "He and Daddy come up with it together, got the boy out of here."

A long moment passed and Cleo couldn't say if she really had a name for the feelings she had.

When Morrie spoke again, he said, "So you'd really go from here? Give up paradise?"

"I don't believe I can take any more of this perfect world of yours."

He looked mildly offended, as if she'd really just thrown a favor back in his face. "Well, then, darling, go on. Make what you can of the other."

Cleo wasn't there to ask his permission to go. She wasn't even sure she believed there was anything out there worth having. But she'd made up her mind. It would be worse to stay here and hide and never know.

Morrie's thoughts had turned inward again. "Did you know that the Timucua had a custom that when their king died, they burned his house up rather than have it go to ruin with him gone? I'd sure rather see this place leveled than watch it sit and rot like they've let happen to Dungeness."

Cleo thought she wouldn't be sad to see any of it go, however or whenever that day came. "I guess you know what happened to Archie Buie's grandson, the one who's been woods runner for your family this summer?"

"I do, and that's just what I'm saying. It'll all come down on our heads one of these days. Things can't stay the way they've been. If it's not the government, it'll be the poachers that get us." She was glad when he did not ramble on with any more lengthy conspiracy theories about the end of their era. "Anyway, that's what I always heard about those old Indian giants," he said. "Daddy told it that way. Maybe they'll dig us up that same way out here one day and tell stories and such about us."

"That may be true."

Something deep in the canopy of live oaks stirred and sighed. *Boom.* The tide would come in. *Boom.* The tide would go out. *Boom.* Cleo would cross the shoals to Revery. Turtles would nest. Horses would graze. Mink would move along the riverbank; coyotes would slip through the gloom with their young. It would not matter they had been there. It would not matter when they had gone. The realization might have horrified some people, but it calmed her now.

She'd turned to let herself out but found there were men arriving from the dock. Coast Guard come to check on the families. Morrie came to the door for them, pulling himself up into some

semblance of a man, like a person made out of coat hangers. They
brought news from the rest of the island and the mainland. She was
glad to be the one sending word this time to Tate Walker, saying
she'd be coming into Revery in the morning.

Morrie invited the men inside for a cocktail, as if this was a
friendly visit and it wasn't only ten in the morning and they weren't
in the middle of a weather disaster. Clearly he had no fear of rev-
enuers. Even Cleo knew plenty of them sat out here with him on
weekends, shooting the breeze. The men waved and left them and
Cleo thought what oddities she and Morrie must seem to them.
And how odd she seemed to herself these days.

But she smiled when she saw that black lab come down the
hallway, her paws pattering softly. She took her seat beside Cleo,
leaning there. Cleo had been reticent to be too friendly with that
dog, someone else's dog, another shadow of her granddaddy,
she'd first believed, haunting her mind. Now she saw the animal
was desperate for affection. She saw she was a bag of bones, looking for a home, for a gentle hand, for anyone to claim her.

"Is she a stray?" she asked. Morrie grunted, still hovering
somewhere in his mind and not quite with her in the hall. There
was hardly any chance at all that this man would go looking for
Dooley's old book, and Cleo knew it was even less likely he'd find
it. She saw a better investment for her money. "Would you take
something for her?"

"That damn dog? She don't hunt, I'll tell you that. So I had her
walk through every one of these rooms all summer so she'd take
the fleas with her when I kicked her out. It never did work. Take
her if she'll go with you."

She did.

Chapter Thirty

FABLE

A LONELY FIDDLE TUNE CAME ON THE BREEZE THROUGH THE window in the second-floor room at Plum Orchard where Cleo convalesced for weeks after the bonfire. She woke to overhear what had happened from conversations between Dr. Johnston and others who looked in on her, having only a hazy memory of the gunshot and what had followed. She had not been taken to the hospital in Fernandina but kept on the island where Dr. Johnston had continued to tend to the wound himself. Cleo remembered lying on the dining table. She had been lucky, everyone said. The bullet from the rifle had missed her heart. It had passed to the left of it and traveled cleanly through her, barely skimming her left shoulder blade on the way out.

Cleo asked after Joanna, but no one could tell her anything of the other young woman. She pleaded to know of Ellis Piedmont and Lumas Gray. Mrs. O'Dowd finally told her the awful truth. Both boys had been lost in the river. She'd wept until she'd cried herself dry.

But after Cleo was awake and sitting up, the staff were asked not to talk about what they'd seen. Somber guests had all long since departed. Cleo remained alone in her room with questions no one would answer. She'd seen something move in the water and she'd tried to warn the others, something that had been inevitable after the story she'd told, after what she'd done to Joanna Burton and Ellis Piedmont. *Lorelei.* She'd named it. She'd known it. Her haunting. But now she wondered if she'd only been hallucinating. Cleo knew all too well about what the mind can dream up to comfort itself. It didn't seem to her that it would handle torment any differently.

She wasn't sure she was completely sane anymore. She heard whispers from the porch, a voice she remembered from her childhood, Little Hannah, one of the tagalongs from Dooley's tales. And on the roof, the fiddler played his constant tunes. Ellis himself might have been a hallucination, another ghost she'd conjured out of her imagination. She couldn't be sure. He'd come in through the window from the second-story porch, complaining the current had carried him all the way out to Little Cumberland before anyone found him and now he was no longer welcome at Plum Orchard, so it would have to be their secret he'd been there.

"Did you see? The big story's all about your river siren hokum," he complained. She'd seen the headline in the Fernandina paper. Ellis quoted it back to her: "'Heartsick Monster Haunting the East River: Mysterious sightings reported by young men following tragedy on Cumberland Island.'"

He sighed. "When they interviewed the Flemmings, the both of them were still out of their heads, crying like babies that they'd seen something dreadful in the water. Now all anybody and his brother will be talking about is your monster. They'll charge a fee to take people out on boats and make a fortune on the tourism. At least until somebody comes up with something better." Ellis sat on the floor of her room, his back against the wall. "And who'll remember me?"

Cleo's head was swimming. She couldn't decide if Ellis was alive or if he was haunting her like the Lorelei. Either way, she'd begged him to shut the window and stop Little Hannah's chattering. She had too many ghosts to account for. But Ellis only rolled his eyes and ignored the request. "You're not even listening to me. They'll call you crazy if you aren't careful, then your luck will run out, like mine." There was a tone she didn't like in his voice. "I can't stay. I'm not supposed to be here at all. Looks like you'll live, anyway, so I'll rest with a clear conscience. But damn if you didn't get what you wanted, Cleo Woodbine. Look at you, laid up here like a princess. Dr. Johnston will never be able to shoehorn you out of here now."

But he was wrong.

"I don't want to stay here alone. I could go with you," she suggested, still hopeful he'd realize that was what he wanted too.

He made a snort like one of the rooting hogs on the island. "You're trying to bargain with your own imagination." He looked down at her as if he'd never seen her face, as if he'd forgotten what silly idea had ever brought him to the room in the first place. Outside, Little Hannah's snickering had gone silent. The fiddler's tune had faded away. Ellis dusted his hands on his thighs as though he'd done an honest day's work, already dissolving as he smoothed his hair and straightened to his full height, not so tall as Cleo had once thought.

Before he'd evaporated completely, she'd noticed other things that she'd missed only weeks before—how could it have been only weeks?—the arrogance of his too-long nose and the transparency of his skin. It seemed she could see right through him. He left through the window just as he'd come in, climbing out to the porch where she'd first met him. Her last glimpse of him, that put-upon expression. And when he'd gone, she wondered if he'd ever really been there at all.

But she knew one thing. He was forever bored of her. She'd never see him again.

———

The table at Plum Orchard wasn't set for dinner as it had been when the guests had filled the house. Now it was only the family at one end in front of the great, empty hearth. It gaped like a maw when Cleo looked at it, and she wondered how she'd never noticed that before. But the great hall smelled just as sharply of tobacco and tongue oil today, and the same sickly sweet fragrance of lilies as when she'd arrived. She thought she'd never be able to smell one again without wanting to die.

Dr. Johnston sat at the head of the table, flanked by a few older men from the island, Carnegie family members who lived in some of the other fine houses in that same strange transitory way, coming and going with the seasons or their own whims. Cleo looked at the men slung back in their seats, waiting to see what she would say. At the far end of the table, Tate Walker was the only familiar face. She was surprised to see him still there.

Dr. Johnston was watching her and he frowned. "What can we do for you, Ms. Woodbine?"

"I thought it was high time I should speak with you." In fact, these were the first words she'd said to the man. Cleo stepped forward with Dooley's book. "I brought this for you. It belonged to my granddaddy, Dooley, and he told me that if I ever came here, I should bring it as a gift. He thought highly of you and he always told me if I came back to Cumberland I would be welcome. I don't know if I believe that's true."

He reached for the little book and flipped through it casually. "That old dog was my friend, all right. And my deepest regret has been I could not save him from himself, if we're telling truths today."

He leaned to note something to one of his companions. The men watched her. They frowned and smoked. Dr. Johnston was not unkind, but she did not feel easy with the rest of them.

"Dr. Johnston," she said, "it was me who made Joanna Burton act like that. There's nothing in the world wrong with her mind. I know you've probably already guessed it was glory, or maybe Ellis told you, but I just want you to know that. I want you to tell her family that, and please tell them that I'm sorry. Or tell me how to get in touch with them so I can say it myself."

Voices at the table dropped. She couldn't say if Morrie looked up from his plate because she didn't dare turn her eyes his way, but if he did, all the better. "I was jealous of her. I never meant to hurt her, only embarrass her. I never meant for those boys to die. But what I did, I did out of spite, and I deserve whatever punishment's coming my way."

She'd expected to be sent packing, or at the least made to apologize to the Burton and Piedmont families. Even more likely, the Burtons would bring charges for what she'd done, poisoning their daughter. Cleo waited to be carted off to stand trial. But Dr. Johnston only filled his cup.

"What we'd like," he said, his tone letting her know that this was not a request but something that had already been well and truly decided, "is for you to keep this to yourself, for everyone's sake and for your own. No need to cause any more confusion or heartbreak."

Cleo stared at him. "Dr. Johnston, I did it. With my own hands. None of it would have happened if it weren't for me."

If he wouldn't let her take responsibility, how was Joanna's family to know she shouldn't be blamed for the string of events?

How were the families of the boys to understand? She looked at Archie Buie, whose eyes swam with tears although he did not make a sound.

"I should have listened to Lumas," Cleo said. "He told me that weed is cursed, and I should have listened. I'm sorry. I'm so sorry, Mr. Buie."

She looked to Tate beside him, willing him to speak up and confirm what she was saying. "Tell him it was all me."

Tate only lowered his eyes and gave a jerk of his head meant to quiet her, so slight that she might have imagined it.

"Listen here," Dr. Johnston said, sitting up in his chair. "Let me stop you there. There're some facts we need to get straight. Tate has already come to us and made clear that it was an accident, that the stories had everybody seeing things and that old bobcat spooked Ellis. We certainly can't be any more sorry for what happened to you, Ms. Woodbine, for all of it. Mr. Buie's sorry about it. Ellis's folks are sorry. But our families have been friends a long time and we're going to come together around this and comfort and support one another. Now, we all know you're heartbroken. It's a sad situation, but there's just no sense in you blaming yourself. And I am not going to let what happened between me and your granddaddy repeat itself. I'm going to do my best by his grandchild."

All the blood drained from Cleo's head, and Dr. Johnston stood and led her to a chair at the table. He poured her a little of the wine they were drinking and let her adjust to what she'd just learned.

"If you want somebody to blame," he said, "you can blame the two of us for ever getting this thing started. We used to have competitions, Dooley and me, for who could tell the best stories. Did you know that? It's how that whole bonfire tradition came about. Back in Kentucky when we were just young bucks, everything was a competition. Then when he came to Plum Orchard, it started up here again."

"I didn't know that, but this isn't like that," Cleo tried to say, but he did not pause. He raised his voice to talk over hers.

"Sweetheart, I'm glad you've come down so I can tell you where things stand." The others at the table were beginning to look at her with the same boredom she'd seen from Ellis. "Now, Tate's getting ready to head out for his own work, aren't you, Tate? He's been waiting to be sure you'd be well. He's felt responsibility for you after running you back to the house, so you see, we understand why you'd feel that way about the others. It's only human."

Cleo looked at her hands in her lap. Tate thought he was doing her a favor by sitting there with his mouth shut. He didn't know how the hole Ellis Piedmont had put inside her burned worse for the shame than the pain of knitting itself back together.

"We're all a little concerned that your recent injury has got you mixed up and we just want to do the right thing here. That's what we're talking about, us and Mr. Buie."

She looked up. "I'm not mixed up about anything."

He leaned forward with his elbows on his knees as if he were talking to a very small child. "Well, all right. We've talked with the doctors and we've talked with the police. There's nothing anybody doesn't know about your situation, and we've come up with what we think will be the best medicine in your case. Here's what's going to happen, Cleo, and you have to agree that if anybody ought to have a say in this, it's the families of those boys."

Cleo nodded.

"We're going to set you up out at Little Marsh Island, just like we wrote to one another about, where you can have a good rest. Art is a great healer, I think. It's going to heal some old wounds for me and some new ones for you. You can stay as long as you like."

He saw her hesitate.

"Darling, this is not a negotiation. You understand what I'm saying?"

She'd come here to tell them what she was, but these were not people who were ever told anything. They did the telling. They'd spoken with authority on her behalf and now they told her about herself. It didn't matter what she thought about it. It never had.

She thought of Lumas Gray, lost forever out in that wide river, and her throat closed up. She thought of Joanna Burton and what she was going through now. She could not imagine her circumstances. She thought of Ellis Piedmont in those last moments before the water closed over him.

————

A week later, when she stood at the shore near the ash of the bonfire before leaving for Kingdom Come, she watched the peaceful turning of the tide and found it hard to imagine the river as it had been that night of the bonfire. But she remembered it, something powerful and old, maybe the spirit of the river itself. Maybe it was too old to have a name. But she would carry it inside her, Cleo knew, her whole life.

She looked over the water for any sign of Lumas Gray and wondered if he would ever come to her as Ellis had. And as she searched the horizon, she had a single thought of gathering all the glory her hands could hold and swallowing it down, enough to stop the endless stories she imagined for him so he had not ended there, so senselessly. She wondered if that was what had finally happened to Dooley, if it had been his choice.

She had Joanna's pearls. She'd thought she would ask Dr. Johnston to send them back, but standing before him she'd known better. And then it had become clear, the only thing she could do. She would keep them safe for Joanna Burton. She would believe that one day Joanna would come for them, for all the choices she had lost. And they would be there, right where she'd dropped them.

Chapter Thirty-One

FRANCES

THERE WAS NO FOOD IN THE CABINETS IN HER KITCHENETTE. Frances woke regretting she hadn't taken the time to buy any groceries since she'd been back. It was barely seven o'clock in the morning when she walked down to Burton Antiques, Fine Art and Collectibles to use Joanna's key to unlock the door, something she'd done throughout her life, knowing at least she could put on a pot of coffee there.

Frances loved the shop early in the morning before business hours when the light was still dim and filtered through the windows. She stood in the space, shelves rising around her, and ran her fingertips along the glass counters and watched dust mites float like some old magic in the air. Above her, objects hung suspended from the high ceilings. The shop smelled dusty and dry as paper, sweetly of leather and oil. Some of the items in the store had been there since the first days of her memory, some longer than her, and her heart hummed with contentment to be among them.

She waited a moment to let that feeling sink in, and as she looked around in the shadows, she thought she could be standing inside one of Cleo's paintings, tucked safe and secure among these beloved objects that held so many memories of the people and places they'd come from, now waiting for what came next. Not unlike herself, she thought. In a little over an hour, she would meet the lawyers to sign the closing papers.

She walked to the back wall and flipped on the lights so she could better see to find the envelope addressed from Cleo, shuffling beneath the main counter until she came upon it. It was addressed to the shop, just as Cleo had said. When Frances picked it up, there was no doubt what she'd find inside. The seal had been broken, given there'd been no name on the outside, but the contents that had been waiting for her were there. She tipped the envelope so the pearl necklace slid out into her open palm and she read the hastily scribbled note that had come with them.

> *To whom it may concern, these pearls belong to Ms. Joanna Burton Flood and have been in safekeeping for her until such time as they may have been collected by herself and only herself. Now I send them for someone appointed by her estate, as she has passed from this life and no longer has use of them. Please note that they were recovered from the Dungeness pool and are all accounted for here.*

Frances stared at them in her hands, strung and individually knotted on a silk thread but missing the clasp at each end. Sixty of them, the size of small peas. The shopkeeper who now ran Burton Antiques had done her the favor of having them appraised by a jeweler at a value of several thousand dollars. But to Frances, they were priceless. She took a soft velvet bag from a nearby drawer, the ones used for customers who purchased these sorts of pieces, and dropped the pearls inside, then tucked them and the envelope with the note inside a larger canvas tote to carry with her. Sixty gleaming little blessings, she thought, from her grandmother and mother, to remind her of them for the rest of her days until she might pass those pearls to a child of her own.

An antique register sat for show on the main counter where Frances looked for another key. There was something else in the shop that she wanted, a showpiece that had been there since she was very small, one of the most valuable items in the store. She'd called ahead this morning, waking the man who was now the sole owner of the shop since Joanna's passing, her grandfather's old business partner. When she'd tried to set a price, he'd insisted she take it in honor of her mother, who had always loved it.

Frances unlocked the glass-front cabinet that held rare editions.

Displayed on a pedestal, she could see the cover of the book she wanted with the title embossed in gold filigree. This was a first edition, number sixty-seven of two hundred printed copies of *Woodbine's Treasury of Glories and Grims*, the book Cleo's grandfather had written and illustrated, published through a vanity press that had been financed by Dr. Marius Johnston of Plum Orchard.

Frances lifted the small hardcover book and carefully handled it as she flipped through the thick pages. She was struck by the simplicity of the illustrations within. The images seemed surprisingly dim to Frances now, two-dimensional and all too obvious compared to Cleo's work. But having spent hours the night before gazing at the commissioned painting, Frances was all the more convinced that this book belonged with Cleo Woodbine.

She held the book carefully against her chest with one arm as she stepped back to close and lock the cabinet. As she turned the key, she looked through the glass into the cabinet at the empty pedestal where the book had sat almost all her life. In the dim light of the shop, her vision shifted so her own face came into focus, a watery reflection in the old glass. Frances gasped softly. For a moment, she'd mistaken the face for her mother's. But it was only an instant before she recognized herself. And once she'd realized the trick of her mind, no matter how hard she looked, she could only see her own face. She smiled at herself then and thought of what Cleo had said about the painting and seeing wonders. Frances thought she understood what she'd meant as she locked the door behind her.

———

With the formalities of the sale complete in a blink, Frances had a little money in the bank and all the debts were settled when she walked out of the lawyer's office before lunch. She'd worried the signing might make her sad. Instead, she felt invigorated.

Frances stepped into a favorite diner, feeling truly hungry for the first time since Joanna had died. She was looking over her choices on the menu, ready to tuck into a real meal, when she heard the news reports of the storm that had skimmed the northern edge of Florida, then come up the coast of Georgia and South Carolina. The scenes being reported were of a fierce event that had come in the night. Trees were down, streets flooded; there'd been property damage, although no deaths had been reported. But it was hard to learn anything specific to Camden County or Revery. The news report was only a blip before the coverage moved on to other topics and left Frances's mind rushing to the worst of conclusions. She abandoned her table and went to the phone booth on the corner to try to call the inn again but couldn't get through.

Even as she rushed to grab her things at the boardinghouse, she worried she was overreacting, that she'd simply spent too many days in Revery listening to those old seamen cracking jokes about a storm that never came. Only now she feared one of them might have truly won the bet. She could think of nothing but how to get back to those who might need help. All the plans to take her time and make practical decisions went out the window. She filled cans with diesel and kerosene and packed everything helpful she could fit into the bed of the truck: blankets, flashlights, batteries, work gloves, tool sets, and a chainsaw that had belonged to her daddy. She'd packed the book of folktales into her own luggage alongside the script for Audrey from Will, and put the velvet bag with the pearls in the glove box where she could pull them out to look at them if she needed encouragement.

The tarp she'd strapped over everything rattled in the wind on her way down the highway, so loudly she could barely hear herself think. She watched in the rearview as Asheville disappeared, folded into the bosom of the old Blue Ridge. Only a few hours before, she'd been dreaming of how she might convince Rosey Devane to go with her to see the Rhine River and that statue of the Lorelei. There were so many things she wanted to tell him now. Somewhere in the bed of the truck she had packed her father's tackle box, and she would show that to him and tell him about early mornings on the French Broad.

She thought of Audrey and the night they'd spent in the carriage house loft, just being girls. Frances felt young when she was with Audrey, not childish but her own age. She wanted to be that person, the one who believed in myths and legends and played rock 'n' roll records late at night. She wanted to read schmaltzy plays and watch silly movies. If that was life at the inn, that was the life she wanted now. And she wanted to dream about true love and weddings and travel and a future that rolled out at her feet with no limits.

Joanna had done the best she could with their lives. She'd made a home out of a house and filled it with children who needed care, making sure they never felt left behind by the ones who loved them.

She'd tried so hard to do that for Frances, too, after Owen Flood had died. Frances wanted to honor both her parents and she knew they'd have approved of what she was doing now.

It was just after noon when she followed a power truck carrying linemen out of Asheville for six hours, stopping only to fill her tank when needed and grateful for the boys at the stations who checked her tires and cleaned her windshield and told her she had a classic chassis. She listened to farm reports, national and local news, and even a gospel hour as she passed through different towns. She stopped at a diner for a meal sometime in the late evening, and the music from a jukebox reminded her of the record player at Gilbreath House and she hurried to get back on the road.

There was more traffic than she had thought there'd be when she'd started out, with everybody seeming to be going toward the trouble. But the line of vehicles had thinned out when she got into South Carolina, and dwindled more as she came into Georgia. She was running on coffee and adrenaline and shaking from it like a drunk who needed a drink. Her head was pounding from the sun in her eyes all day and now the dying light. She drove with the windows down, but if it hadn't been for the radio, she wouldn't have made it the last thirty minutes. She was singing country western music when "Kaw-Liga" came on and she heard it differently than she'd heard it before, thinking of Will Tremmons and how she'd left him on that dark roadside. She sent up a prayer for him.

It was late when at last she pulled into Revery. Debris littered the roadsides, but her headlights showed the main thoroughfare had been cleared. As she rolled slowly through mud that would surely take ages to wash away, she could see the Marvel Theater still standing. She saw that the great oak had fallen and made a sound of dismay at the sight of the devastation of the Piedmont

Library. But all was not hopeless. When she finally arrived at Gilbreath House, she saw the house was lit and the yard and porches were full of busy people. Her senses were met with grill smoke and the sounds of community. She parked the truck and made her way into the front foyer, forgetting she was dead on her feet, looking for the faces she loved.

When Rosey Devane turned around, he looked like he'd been dragged backward through hell. But she imagined so did she.

"Did you miss me?" She grinned.

"How'd you get back here so fast?" He was already in front of her and she'd have sworn she hadn't even seen him cross the room.

She shrugged. "I brought some things you might need."

The men in the yard lost no time helping her and Rosey unload the supplies. She hadn't seen Audrey yet, hadn't even made it to the kitchen. She was so tired she could have leaned against a wall and slept standing straight up, and it was hard to even focus when Rosey pulled her next to the house to tell her how things had gone. Part of her had imagined this place would have disappeared with the storm, or maybe she'd return to discover it was only something she'd made up in her own sad heart and it had never existed at all.

"You look like you fought the whole world to get back here," he said.

"I drove straight through. I couldn't tell from the reports how bad it might be. Is Audrey okay? Jimmy? Do you know if Cleo's all right?"

"They're all fine. There'll be some hard weeks to clean this up, but it could have been worse." He looked at her in a way that made Frances think he might do anything. She couldn't be sure he wasn't angry with her.

"How can I help?" she asked.

But the feel of Rosey's kiss then told her otherwise, and the way his arms came around her made her lean hard into him, a shelter. He smelled musky as the river and his hands were strong at her back. She'd have followed him anywhere as he led her away from the crowded house and along the familiar street. He was the current that had brought her all this way.

"You need to sleep," he said. "And believe me, there's no room at the inn." She laughed and he smiled. "Let's find somewhere quiet."

When they stepped onto the old houseboat and he led her below deck to the little berth, she felt the water rock beneath them just as she'd imagined it would, urgent and tugging at the tethers that held the boat in place. She crawled onto the bed where he made room for her, a place where she fit snug. He held her and touched her and looked at her, setting her glasses aside and kissing the tip of her nose, her eyes. His breath was sweet and warm on her neck. She put her hands in his hair, the thick pelt of it, and pulled him close. He did not rush or pry at her clothing, only held her there, but Frances could feel the promise of what might come next between them. And as much as she wanted to forget herself, she was astonished to realize that she felt safe to rest.

"I didn't think you'd come back," he said.

She felt their breathing rise and fall together and the boat shifting softly, and soon she was sleeping in Rosey's arms.

————

When Rosey woke Frances, it was almost dawn.

"I'll need to get back out there," he said.

But they lay there, not moving, to talk quietly. She explained what had happened after she'd left Revery with Will Tremmons in the bed of the truck. She tried to tell him how it had felt to see Will disappear into the shadows and how it made her think of Cleo's paintings, how it frightened her to leave him that way.

"And you really have no idea where he was planning to go?" she asked, hoping Rosey was just trying to keep it secret and that he might tell her now.

He shook his head and pressed a kiss to her hair just at her ear. "He wouldn't want us to know. It's better if someone asks that we have nothing to say."

"But he'll come back when it's all cleared up, don't you think?" she said. "He didn't do anything wrong." But she thought of Will's books and the burn barrel.

"I think maybe he's got bigger plans than Revery. I hope so," Rosey said.

He explained all that had occurred on Cumberland, about Harl Buie and the hunter who had been shot. "I was stuck in Fernandina when the storm happened," Rosey said. She groaned when he related the accusations against Glenn, both for chartering the boat and for being involved in what had happened to Harl.

"Glenn saw Tate early Saturday night and told him he was going out there to try and stop anybody hurting Harl. I know. I overheard them. Surely Glenn wouldn't—"

Rosey interrupted before Frances could get too upset and rushed to reassure her that Harl had woken up the day before and cleared Glenn of suspicion. "It's the other that may catch up with him, whether those men are lying or not. And if Morrie Johnston's just looking to make a point, I don't know if he's going to care too much about whether Glenn was involved this time around. He knows good and well what Glenn's been doing, and he's tired of it." Rosey shrugged and told her how he had put the theater up as collateral for Glenn's bail.

Frances could only say, "Glenn doesn't deserve you."

Rosey said, "He's my friend. He's an ass a lot of the time but he's tried to do the right thing now. Jimmy's proud of him for helping Harl and I'm going to do what I can to keep it that way. I'm just hoping if he gets out of this, he'll make something of his second chances."

But Frances thought those chances were dubious, given that with his next breath, Rosey explained that Glenn was already on his way back out to Cumberland to have a word with Morrie Johnston, convinced he could talk him into dropping the trespassing charges. He was in Rosey's sights one minute and nowhere to be seen the next. Frances thought Glenn had something in common with Jimmy after all.

"I should go see Audrey," Frances said. "I tried calling. I was imagining the worst. I really want to see her."

"Well, hold on to your hat, lady. Because she's my mama made over. Audrey's running this whole show now."

Chapter Thirty-Two

AUDREY

GILBREATH HOUSE WAS STILL NOTHING BUT NONSTOP PEOPLE wandering in and out since the morning after the storm. Some had slept on the porches or in the front rooms of the inn, grabbing naps at all hours, then setting off to rescue what they could of their own lives and homes. They'd worked together like ants and they'd consumed everything Audrey could put in front of them. Hour by hour, they'd begun to restore order from chaos, along with a little of Audrey's faith in the people of Revery. It felt like a miracle yesterday, when Harl Buie had woken up.

She'd tried to be thankful while she was emptying every last thing from the freezer and some from the pantry. A strange sort of bounty had amassed like some sort of holy holiday in the side yard, and it made her wonder if this was what it might have been like when the waters receded and Noah and the animals beat their way off that boat to charge back into the world.

She'd been surprised the first day to open the door to a street looking like the river. Amanda and Nan Buie had come in a john-boat, ready to grill and fry and feed the masses, some of whom had already gathered in the yard, looking as if they'd been working for hours.

"*Better get some food started. Everybody's out of power, but you've got that woodstove,*" Amanda had said. They'd brought with them a couple of kids, nieces and nephews, a boy and a girl, both grade-school age. Marlin and Crystal Buie. They'd zoomed out to the loft in the carriage house with Jimmy, who, for once, looked the older of the bunch.

Gilbreath House had been lucky, with almost no damage, while all around Revery the salt waters had submerged vegetable gardens and flower beds and carried fences away. Trees had fallen; elegant oaks that had been standing for centuries had turned upside down so their roots reached for the sky and their sad crowns lay crushed.

One such tree had come down on the Piedmont Library, its great arms outstretched. The roof had fallen in, now a pile of rubble beneath it, the sodden books ruined. Tate had gone to check on the Marvel Theater, just yards away, and reported back when he'd come to rest at the inn. It remained unscathed, the beautiful marquee washed clean. But he'd been surprised to discover the remnants of a tunnel, formerly unknown to him. It had collapsed and pushed mud into the storage room, probably saving the Marvel, bracing the foundation and the wall against the oak's heavy crown.

Audrey and the Buie women had been cooking nonstop over the charcoal grill in the side yard and looked at the faces of folk who came to pick up the plated meals they were doling out, some of whom she'd seen that awful afternoon in front of the Marvel, the same people who had walked past her when she was standing alone in the middle of the street. Reports had rolled in that the shoals had reached out one long arm and grabbed hold of the skirt of Cumberland, closing what had once been the dividings and moving the water several yards east, as if a kink in a long rope had been picked up and dropped down again by some colossus.

Boats had carried news from neighbors, and Tate had gotten word very early that Woodbine Cottage was still standing and Cleo with it. More surprising, she had been seen running that truck of hers up and down Cumberland, checking on her neighbors. Tate, however, had not gone far from Jimmy for one minute, and Audrey was impressed by that. In the middle of all this, she supposed no one was looking for Will Tremmons when they had alligators on Main Street. Most places had begun to dry out now, but the yellow jackets swarmed, chased out of the ground. The pavement had disappeared beneath the silt carried inland and brackish water still stood in the ditches, buzzing with mosquitoes and flies in the heat. They watched for snakes and avoided low spots.

Phone lines were still down, but crews had come from all over to restore power and clear the roads. There were even some National Guard filling the air with the sounds of chainsaws. She'd sent a note by mail to assure her folks that she had her cousin and friends and that the house had stood strong, with promises to call when the lines were up again. She'd sent a note to Frances, too, addressed to Mother's Helper in Asheville. She was glad her friend had gotten out before the weather hit.

Amanda and Nan worked alongside Audrey. Whatever she needed next seemed to magically appear, diced or washed or whipped or separated. Fish were gutted and boned, oysters roasted and stewed. Bacon was always crisping in a pan. She thanked them and kept at the work in order to push the food into waiting hands. Sentiments began to echo through Gilbreath House, a refrain repeated again and again. "Taste of home," they said. "Just like Shirley made it," they said. Audrey figured under the circumstances, anything at all would taste good to the exhausted people. "Runs in the family," they said.

That's when it had dawned on Audrey, for the first time since coming to Revery, that she felt at home in the old house.

"Now look here," Amanda had said to her the evening before, stern but kind. "You're tuckered out. Why don't you go have yourself a cool bath? You just go clean up."

"I can't leave all this."

"There's going to be plenty to do when you get back, but you've got to take care of yourself, sissy."

Audrey was surprised by the intimacy of a nickname, as if Amanda had read her mind, or her lonely heart. "I wish I could do something for you."

Amanda turned and picked up a stack of clothes and pushed them into Audrey's hands. "Well, honey, the situation is getting ripe in this little kitchen. You want to do something for us, go have a good wash."

Audrey couldn't help laughing. Amanda smiled.

After a short bath, Audrey had dragged her sore body up from the warm water, unwilling to give in to exhaustion. She'd pulled on the clothes, glad to be out of the pedal pushers that were getting difficult to fasten, then found these cotton pants had been cleverly altered. The zipper had been removed and stitched closed. At the seams of the waistband, someone had inserted elastic material so they could easily be slipped on and off. And most importantly, she could breathe. She turned to look at her reflection in the standing mirror of her bedroom. Her condition was a secret no more.

"Feel better, sis?" Amanda asked when Audrey returned to the kitchen, throwing only a quick glance in her direction.

"Thank you," Audrey said, trying hard to meet the woman's gaze.

She leaned and pecked a kiss on Audrey's cheek. She touched the scarf where Audrey had taken to wearing it tied around her hair as Mimi had done. "You're the spitting image of your mama."

Audrey's breath caught. "You knew my mother?"

"Mimi? Well, sure. Mimi and Shirley both. Mimi nearly grieved her sweet self to death when we lost my cousin Lumas. He was a child my aunt and uncle took in, but I don't know who didn't love that boy. But Mimi, well, I thought she'd never leave this house again, and when she did, we didn't see her after that." She smiled down on Audrey now. "But it's good to have her girl here now."

———

In a funny way, Audrey felt she was hitting her stride in the middle of this challenge. It had been a stretch of hours unlike any she'd known, but she welcomed the sense of purpose. With the power out, Freddie's records had been silent and she had not even noticed or missed them until, without warning, the power was restored and Jimmy started up the music. Surprised, that's when Audrey looked up to see Frances, the music rang in her ears, and all the tears she'd been storing up came in a rush.

"How are you already back?" Audrey shouted. She squeezed her friend in a hug, and when they stepped apart, Frances raised her eyebrows at Audrey's new look. "Cat's out of the bag. I couldn't breathe in those pants."

Overwhelm turned to smiles, the way it always seemed to do when she was with Frances. She had a thousand questions, some of them to do with Will. When Frances gave her the script of *Our Town* from Will, she wanted to run out to the carriage house with Frances like the kids and spend the rest of the day telling each other everything that had happened. Instead, they took care of what was put in their hands until the hour grew late and people started to wander off to their own homes, some of them still stretching out on the porches, fewer of them inside the house now.

The children begged to stay overnight in the loft with Jimmy, and Frances loaded them up with blankets and popcorn. Audrey heard Jimmy telling tales and knew that he'd adopted some of what Tate had been telling of houseboat adventures and the magical isle of Kingdom Come. It would have been hard to drag them away from that. Amanda agreed to let them sleep over. Audrey insisted she do the same and set up a place for her to sleep in the front parlor of the inn, making room between the stacks of books Mrs. Mae had been able to pull out of the rubble from the library.

It was funny to think how Harl and Nan had been sneaking through a tunnel to get to these same books and now they surrounded their aunt. The books lay open so that the damp pages could dry. If Glenn or anyone else had shown up to make a stink over any of it, Audrey was ready to give them a piece of her mind. She said as much to Frances while they walked out to the street corner where Frances had parked the truck. She'd forgotten something in the glove box, a velvet bag holding her grandmother's pearls.

Frances smiled at her. "I guess you're the new library in town."

Audrey hadn't thought of that, but she liked the sound of it. She thought of Will's books, how they'd been a sort of sacrifice, and it made her feel like she had a reason to look over these books in her care now. She hoped he'd come back to see them one day.

"Actually, when everything's dried out a little," Frances said, almost reading her thoughts, "I wanted to ask, did you ever think this place could be more than an inn?"

"Like what?" Audrey tried not to let herself hope this meant Frances had decided to stay in Revery for good.

"Well, I have some thoughts. We'd have to talk about what we'd really want to do."

"I'll tell you what I want to do," Audrey said, unable to hide her joy. She took one look at Will's Chevy and started planning road trips. "We're going to the beach. I mean it." She felt bad about Will. She thought of his kind, dark eyes and the way he'd talked about the special relativity of time and wondered if he'd find a way to slip into that in-between space. She wondered if there'd ever be a day when he might turn up again to take care of that clock.

"I've been hiding out all summer because I didn't dare wear a swimsuit," she said. "Well, forget that. When this mess is cleaned up, I'm shutting that kitchen for days and we're going to go lay out and fry ourselves."

Audrey leaned on her friend as they walked back toward the house, and Frances told her she'd opened Cleo Woodbine's painting and been overwhelmed by a beauty she could barely describe. It seemed just then that the worst of everything had passed, that it really had.

Until they smelled smoke. And this was no small fire.

———

"It's Dungeness that's burning," Rosey explained. He'd come running from the theater with word. "Folks are heading over, but it's past trying to stop it. Now they're just keeping it contained. It's been burning since about dinnertime. Whole thing will be gone by morning."

Tate said, "Well, I guess somebody's finally done it."

"Do they know it wasn't just an accident?" Frances asked.

"Not yet, they don't. I imagine it may be a while before the truth is sorted out."

"At least they can't say it was Harl," Audrey said. Amanda had come to stand beside her to hear what had happened. "Or Will."

"They'll say anything." It was Amanda who said what they were all thinking, and no one argued it was likely true.

Tate spoke to Rosey. "I ought to see about Glenn. He went out to have his say with Morrie today and might still be over there. They might need men to help."

"I don't believe there's any help to be had. What I'm told, people are just watching it burn now. But if you want to go, I'll take you over."

Audrey had already grabbed her camera from the front table. "I ought to take pictures."

"Somebody needs to check on Cleo," Frances said.

When the kids came inside to find out about the smoke and heard the news, they weren't going to be left out of seeing such a sight. Rosey said, "Well, we can't all fit in my johnboat."

The answer was obvious. And nothing could have thrilled Jimmy Walker more than all of them stepping aboard that old houseboat.

Audrey wasn't so convinced this would be a joyride given the circumstances, and the party grew solemn as they crossed the river and hugged the shore of Cumberland. She held her camera tightly in the murky air, thick and humid and acrid, black smoke choking them. Helpless to do anything else, Audrey took photos all along the approach, bearing witness to the apocalyptic scene. There was no danger to them from a distance or even as Rosey docked the boat, but she had a sinking feeling as they watched the old mansion being consumed. The kids peered out from a huddle near Amanda, dumbstruck and unsure whether to feel excitement or dismay.

Frances said to Tate, both standing at the railing, "The timing of it can't be random."

"It's not the first Carnegie house to burn," Tate said. "But it's sure the heart of them."

Audrey took photos of everyone on the boat, their faces lit by the disaster. The burning timbers made a terrible hiss and an occasional moan of something snapping in half with a crack like the sound of a gunshot. It was as if the house were burning alive and not giving up without a fight.

At the dock, there was nothing but confusion. While Audrey and the rest stayed aboard, Rosey and Tate spoke with other men to see what they could learn. People wore handkerchiefs tied around their faces to cover their noses and mouths and couldn't be recognized as friends or family. The fire raged. There was no water. No fire-fighting equipment. Only men chopping down trees, a horrible, jarring note of sacrifice felt in the bones of the onlookers. The trees closest to the house had already gone up like Roman candles, exploding and sending sparks into the canopy and undergrowth, threatening to burn the entire island. Overhead, the Civil Air Patrol flew over the inferno, but there was nothing anyone could do.

The kids held hands with Audrey at one end and Frances at the other. Only Amanda stepped off the boat to see about her daddy. It seemed Archie Buie had been there since before anyone else arrived, carrying out anything of value still left inside the old house. Audrey listened to a man explain that Glenn and Morrie Johnston had arrived on the scene to join the effort. Audrey saw Tate's face when one of the men rushed to say what had happened.

"Archie and that Woodbine woman pulled Glenn Walker out of the house, carried like a sack of feed. His leg was in bad shape. Can't say what the fire did to him. Somebody got him on a boat down to Fernandina. Only thing I know is that he was breathing last I saw him."

"Get me to him," she heard Tate say. They were having to yell to be heard over the fire.

"All right, let's find a fast boat," Rosey said.

Jimmy was hearing all of this at the same time and Audrey pulled him close. Rosey was searching the faces around him to be sure the rest of them had a way back home safely and Frances was urging him to go, insisting it didn't matter, that they'd be fine. And then they'd all stopped to look at a small figure, a woman so black from soot and smoke she was barely recognizable, stepping on board the houseboat. Cleo Woodbine.

"You go on," she said to Tate, her voice strong and clear even in the din of noise and panic. She looked over the little group and came to stand beside Frances, turning a steady gaze on Audrey. "I'll carry these ones home."

Chapter Thirty-Three

CLEO

WHEN TATE'S EYES HAD LANDED ON HER, SHE'D WANTED TO GO with him. She'd wanted to throw her arms around him and say, *I'm here. I'm here, Tate Walker.* She'd wanted to make apologies and promises. *We're alive*, she'd wanted to say. *We've got so much life left in us.*

Instead, she'd yelled, "Go!"

And now here it was, the moment she would leave this island. She'd have followed that sweet railroad man right off the end of this old world, she supposed, and that's about what it felt like to take Rosey Devane's houseboat out on the river while Dungeness burned.

Only hours before, Cleo had decided this would be the last night she'd spend in Woodbine Cottage. She'd been trying to make peace with the decision, wondering how long it would be before she'd be able to sleep in a strange bed at Gilbreath House. How unnerving it would be to lie in the dark and listen to unfamiliar noises. To wake to the smells and sounds of a house full of life. How would she walk the streets of Revery or into the mercantile when after all these years, she felt more kinship with that bobcat than most people? But Tate would be there, she reminded herself. And that had been her answer to all her doubt.

Thinking how she would share with him all she'd learned from Morrie, she'd gone walking Cumberland, hoping she'd wear herself out so when dark came, she'd stand some chance at falling asleep. The black dog had trailed her heels. And then, out of the deep forest, two coyotes had run past without regard for them, almost soundless. They'd taken both Cleo and the dog by surprise. Cleo had grabbed the dog by the scruff while she whined. Coyotes coming so close was a sure sign that something was wrong.

She regretted then that they were so far from her truck, but the first whiff of smoke reached them and she knew by the direction of the wind that it was coming from the south. They hurried on foot. The smoke grew thick down the lane. Had she not known it by heart, even she might have lost her way in the darkening haze along the Grand Avenue. She remembered what Morrie Johnston had said about the Timucuan tradition of burning the king's house, but she hadn't thought he'd truly burn any of the old mansions. Even if she hurried, she knew there'd be nothing she could do; it would take her more than half an hour for her to reach Dungeness on foot.

When finally the flaming monstrosity came into view, she'd been forced to drop to the ground to draw a full breath where the air was clearer. Only then had she seen the familiar figures of two men. Morrie Johnston was gesturing wildly, and Cleo watched Archie Buie turn and then disappear inside the burning structure. She'd called out to stop him, but he couldn't hear her over the sounds of the fire, its roar growing louder even as she crossed the lawn.

Morrie stood, hands covering his face, everything but his eyes, which were squinting to see against the heat and smoke. On the ground around him, Cleo saw several pieces of framed art, a huge vase, and such random paraphernalia it looked like he might have been preparing for a yard sale. Cleo had understood then that there had been some attempt to salvage what might be inside the house, but she couldn't imagine Archie Buie would have wasted a good piss on it to put out the flames, much less risked his life. Morrie answered her question with the one name he had spoken then.

"Walker."

She'd run after Archie then, screaming Tate's name until she was choking and gagging and couldn't scream at all. It had been impossible to see inside the house. The fire had roared like a freight train and the smoke hung heavy over everything, but the main floor had not yet begun to burn. She dimly understood that the fire must have started upstairs and she rushed along the familiar corridors and through the rooms, searching for the two men.

Cleo thought then that this was how their story would end. And she'd been angry, fighting for her life and for Tate's. But then she'd seen Archie through the smoke. He'd come across the grand foyer, dragging someone draped heavily across his back. Cleo helped to hoist the weight beneath her own shoulder, terrified they'd been too late, relieved they were getting the man out of the house. Only after they bore him outside and laid him down far enough away from the blaze to be safe did she see her mistake. She'd recognized Glenn Walker by his Red Wing boots.

"He ain't burned bad—it's the smoke in him," Archie had croaked, wheezing and coughing. *"He must've fell down them steps. Ruined his leg and tried to drag his self out."*

Cleo had barely been able to force a breath down into her lungs and rubbed at her watery eyes, but she'd seen the angle of Glenn's leg was all wrong. She pressed the side of her face to Glenn's chest long enough to feel it rise and fall. Then she shoved herself to her feet and flew at Morrie.

"You're an idiot! You sent him in there? For what? This junk?"

People were showing up by then, a crowd gathering. Behind them, the blaze had risen to lick up the turret.

Morrie had stood there shaking. *"Is he dead?"*

Cleo didn't think he deserved an answer.

He'd had to yell to be heard and it came out something like a howl. *"A man came to Plum Orchard to tell us what was going on. We got out here soon as we could. I just couldn't sit home and let it go. I said there's got to be something we can save."*

Helpers had fallen over Glenn, leaving Archie and Cleo to watch as he was rushed down to a waiting boat and away for help. Cleo's teeth had chattered then and she'd pulled her thoughts together, that Glenn was alive, that he'd gotten here after the fire had started, that he'd tried to save something for Morrie and Archie Buie had gone in to pull him out. And it had not been Tate. She waited, making herself breathe, knowing he would be on his way to find her beside this fire just as he'd found her once before. And she'd have to tell him about his son.

Neighbors from the island, Carnegie family members and those from farther afield, had come to stand around and gawk and rage and cry. Some of them, people she hadn't seen before and some she knew to look at, brought her and Archie water and handkerchiefs to tie around their noses and mouths. Men started working to clear trees away with chainsaws. She'd stood through all of it, alone after Archie left her to find a place to rest. Cleo hadn't moved. Not until she'd seen the old houseboat dock. She watched the group of kids pile out, Jimmy's head above the others, Nan Buie with a woman Cleo didn't know, then the two girls from Gilbreath House and Rosey. And Tate.

She'd started toward him but watched someone else reach him first. She saw him lean close to hear what they had to say, then watched the confusion and fear on his face and Rosey gesturing back toward the dock. She'd have yelled his name if she could have drawn a deep breath, but the pain in her chest called up that night she'd been shot. That hard knot had burned near her heart, and it was not the life leaving her then. It was something fiercer even than the fear she'd felt when she'd called something up from the deep river. It was her love for Tate Walker. And it was what finally moved her.

————

Now here she was, captaining the old houseboat that had belonged to Henry Devane. Cleo had never seen it before now, only heard Rosey talk about it like it was a floating palace. She could only hope the thing stayed afloat long enough to get them back to Revery. It was not the crossing she'd imagined with Tate at her side on a sunny day, where they could take their time and she could appreciate seeing the town come back into view with its pretty waterfront and busy little streets. She'd thought they'd step onto the dock together, normal people, walk along to get her bearings, see where her parents had lived and her grandmother had made fruit syrups, before she'd gone looking for a place with the old gods. She'd even imagined going back along that road on the outskirts where her parents had died and where she had first walked away from death. She felt like she was doing it again. Maybe that's all life was in the end.

Jimmy Walker was standing up so close to her while she tried to navigate that she thought he might climb up on her shoulders. He asked again and again for her to tell him how she'd saved Glenn. He'd decided she was something like an angel, knowing she'd helped Harl only days before. Tate had filled his head with nonsense. But she looked at the bandage on his hand and thought of the day he'd gotten caught in that trap, how he'd been braver about that pain than a lot of people would have been, and she told him what she could, only leaving out the worst and hoping it wasn't a lie to say his daddy was alive. She thought about Dooley and how he'd told his stories to her when she was small, when she needed reassurance and hope, and she forgave him a little more for only being human.

"All right now, who here knows a story?" she said. "A good one. The best one. It takes a lot to impress me."

Frances and Audrey sat with the other kids and a Negro woman Cleo didn't know but who seemed to belong with Archie and the Buie children. Not one of them spoke up. What they'd seen had shocked them. The boat chugged along. It was going to be a long, slow ride. And Cleo saw what needed to be done. She had lived too long in the ash and she did not want to see these ones do the same. She had grown one sure wisdom from that charred ground and she shared it then. "Fires do one thing for stories. Do you know what that is?" Jimmy and Nan exchanged a glance, shaking their heads.

"I'll tell you," she said. She hadn't properly told stories like this for decades, but she hadn't forgotten how. Cleo guided the boat along the shoals, inching toward Revery, and the night gathered round them. "Fires set stories free on the world. That's what stories like best. And every one of us has a library we're carrying around right inside us," Cleo said, touching the place where the shot had gone through her. "All those stories are just waiting for a night like tonight, and sometimes they get lucky and somebody builds a big old fire and they get to ride on a breath because that's when they come alive. Did you know that's why all stories are ghost stories? They're our ghosts and we give them life to walk this earth and keep us company."

"How do we give them life?" This was one of the younger boys.

"You tell them," Jimmy said, clear as a bell. People said he was simple. Cleo knew he was clever.

"You tell them," she agreed.

And so they did, slowly at first. Each one braver than the last, they told stories of that summer in Revery, the ghost stories from Rosey's tour, the stories from books they'd borrowed after hurrying through the tunnel to the Piedmont Library. Stories of brave souls coming down to sit in the whites-only auditorium at the Marvel and racing away in Amanda Buie's car. Tall tales of an alligator swimming down the flooded streets of town, scales and teeth glinting and disappearing, ancient and monstrous and beautiful too. Of their dreams and fears of the coming autumn when the school bell would ring and change would come, some mysterious kind of world they imagined for the future. Something they dared to hope they'd see.

But it was Jimmy who won the night before they pulled up to the dock, when he told the tale he'd heard from his granddaddy on the night of the storm, a story of Cleo herself.

"She can walk the whole length of Cumberland in a day.

"She can talk to mink and coyotes and bobcats.

"She knows old folk magic that can turn trespassers to hogs till the dawn.

"She can tell a story and bring it to life."

They moved across the water with the engine pushing hard, and Cleo thought of all the penance she'd done, all the miles she'd walked over Cumberland, all the years Tate had ridden those rails, neither of them ever getting home. Tonight the smoke from another fire gathered over the moon and Little Hannah still drifted nearby. A fiddle tune still whistled on the wind. Somewhere deep in the bone orchard, Cleo knew that old giant king was kicking up his feet for a well-earned rest. And she sent up thanks to Dooley, wherever he might be.

Chapter Thirty-Four

FABLE

IN ALL OF DOOLEY'S MEMORIES, KINGDOM COME HAD BEEN A storied place. Fish had jumped on the hook or into the nets. Fruit had fallen ripe from the tree unbruised. Storms washed the air clean. Sunshine dried all tears. From the trees, stories whispered and ghosts gathered, old friends and loves. The cries of the seabirds were a secret language understood by the terrapin, the fox, the bobcat, and the Spanish ponies that wandered wild in the dunes. Woodbine Cottage, however, was nothing so fanciful, and exactly as Dooley had always described it, a tabby house with a little stoop, with one main living space that included a kitchen. There was another room for a bed and a bathroom with all the necessities, but just. In all, there was no space to spare, even for one person. She could not imagine that her grandparents had shared the house with her father, but Cleo liked it immediately. The furniture was sturdy and plain and decades old, and the wood had been polished to a shine. The linens had all been cleaned and the bedding was fresh. Someone had prepared everything ahead of her arrival. She knew it was meant to make her want to stay there.

With every comfort found, Cleo felt a twisting self-loathing growing within. She knew she had done nothing to deserve Woodbine Cottage. She knew, too, what she had cost Joanna Burton, Ellis Piedmont, and Lumas Gray. And this was no punishment. It was a golden sanctuary. When she thought back on Dr. Johnston at that dinner table with the other men and considered the distant Piedmont family, she began to understand. This benevolence was not entirely about her, but a graceful way to keep the peace between the titans, for the sake of steel mills, iron works, railroads, and whatever other means by which they conjured wealth. The scales must remain balanced. A girl like Joanna Burton might be whisked away, labeled as fragile or unbalanced and unfortunate, and that was nothing out of the ordinary. But they could only afford so much of that. So for Cleo, they would say, *See there, we have ourselves an eccentric, the granddaughter of an old friend. We've had the likes before. We know how to keep them.*

And so they did.

What surprised her most were the shelves in the kitchen and pantry that still held jars her grandmother had left behind, ready for canning. Tears sprang to Cleo's eyes at the sight of them and the overwhelming feeling of comfort. She had never expected to miss her grandmother, but she ached for her grandmother and her practical determination. Her mortar and pestle were there, chipped from use. Cleo wondered if Dooley had used it to grind glory. A long table waited for Cleo's paints. The light from the east windows was clear and bright. The breeze through the west windows was salty and sharp. The house suited her every need.

It was hemmed in by dunes to the west, and beyond that, she could catch a glimpse of the sea. The cottage was eastward facing, and out the front door she saw only scrub for yards and then a deep maritime forest where a path disappeared, leading down to a dock on the river. From there, she could look across the water and see Cumberland, an easy quarter-mile over the mud when the tide was out. But it might as well have been a vision of some lost world for all she was welcome there now.

When Dr. Johnston had checked her wounds for the last time before she left Plum Orchard in a little johnboat (captained by Tate Walker until a new boy could be hired), she'd been told without exception to keep her distance. She had been given the johnboat, and also the use of the pickup truck that remained parked near Dungeness dock, conveniences Cleo did not refuse. She could take from their abandoned gardens as she pleased and fish from the creeks and estuaries, but she was not welcome in their homes. Tate had looked sorry to relay the message, but he was headed off for the railroad job himself and he'd wished her luck. The Carnegie ferry had taken Tate away and she'd felt sorrier to see him go than she could have imagined. She'd felt as if he were the only person left on the earth who really knew her, and she'd watched until the ferry was out of sight. Then never watched for it again.

Until that first night in Woodbine Cottage, she had never truly understood what it meant to be alone. The hours after nightfall were not passed with confidence. She'd lain awake, listening to the sounds of some animal on her roof and, later, a wild yelping far out in the dark forest. She'd imagined all her worst fears just on the other side of her door, a wild dog scratching to get in, nightcrawlers and palmetto bugs climbing the legs of the bed, trespassing poachers who had heard of the addled young thing on her own and were devising how they would have her. What could she have done about any of it? All her power was in those seeds in the bone orchard, miles away on the other side of a river. All she would have been able to do that night was scream, and Joanna could have told her what good that would do.

The night had seemed endless, but when the thin light of dawn began to creep into the rooms again, she stood. Unharmed. Outside, there were no signs of claw marks or paw prints in the sandy yard.

No slide marks of an alligator near her stoop. And instead of feeling like a regular nitwit for all her trembling, she felt she had survived something on some elemental level. She looked out at the dense forest that only the day before had loomed terrifying and tangled and made her feel small and deserted. Now it occurred to her what Joanna had known when she'd first told her of Woodbine Cottage, what it meant to have no one to answer to, no one coming for her, no one expecting a single blessed thing. The door was open and she stepped through it.

———

The johnboat was a great satisfaction, and she slid through the river like an arrow, cutting through the water with nothing to stop her. She found the truck waiting at the dock, just as it had been promised. Time belonged to Cleo. All time, it suddenly seemed. She had expected it would be awful to confront Dungeness, its wide eyes watching and judging her, knowing what she'd done. Or the Casino, just beyond. But she only strode past these places, completely unmolested. She swam, alone, in the sulfur waters of the pool. If no one else would, Cleo would remember. She lingered in her favorite spots, a luxury she had not known before. She sat down on the sandy shore of the river and watched the water where she'd seen something unexplained. The day was all sparkle and blue sky. There seemed to be nothing in that world that would take a toll on a person, not even one as guilty as Cleo.

It was coming on dusk before she noticed she was hungry and remembered that filling her belly would be up to her too. She chose an orange from the basket and ate it at her table, juice dripping down her arms and off her elbows onto the floor. In the quiet of her solitude, she heard Little Hannah snicker from the window.

Cleo crossed to the door and jerked it open. Perched on the stoop, a little figment girl in a white gown blew her a kiss. Her blonde curls gleamed, even in the low light. She'd kicked her shoes off so her feet were bare and pink. She beamed when Cleo rocked back on her heels as if taken by surprise. The child clapped her hands.

"Little Hannah," Cleo said. "I am a grown woman now. Too old for fantasies."

But soon enough, the fiddler took up on her roof most mornings. And occasionally an old black dog trailed at her heels. She had her old troupe of devoted hallucinations. And when she slid through the estuaries in her johnboat, she could see the water quake when the Timucuan giant walked the shoals, the character she had added to Dooley's illustrations. Over the years, she would paint their pictures hundreds of times.

"I'm not supposed to need you," she told them, mostly out of habit, for they were the only company she kept and she had all the time in the world to spend with them.

For decades, Cleo lived in this way. Not much changed. But she imagined the lives Lumas Gray or Ellis Piedmont or Joanna Burton might be living a thousand different ways. After the first year, she'd gone out to find Archie Buie gigging for flounder and he hadn't run her off when she'd taken up with him. She'd done the same anytime she'd seen him pulling in shrimp or crab. She learned to cast a net at his side. They did not speak of Lumas, and she could not take his place. But Cleo thought maybe it counted a little for Archie to know she hadn't forgotten.

Boys grew up catching mink, leaving the pelts on her stoop, tests of their courage, until the Second World War came and many of them went with it. A camp of soldiers was established on Cumberland Island to watch for dangers in the waters far greater than any water siren, but Kingdom Come remained untouched. For her part, Cleo collected basket after basket of fruit for those at the camp and contributed to the effort in this way.

If there was a lesson to be learned from living as she had, she'd been shown over and over just how inconsequential she truly was. Fruit grew without needing her to toil or plan for it or coax it. She felt her existence barely left a mark. Even her footprints were wiped away by wind and tide. In all, she'd lived so freely that her life had become purposeless, a consequence even Joanna had not foreseen. Cleo could see her days stretching before her, longer and longer, along with a little crack in the foundation of her cottage. Just one more summer storm would change the landscape. Kingdom Come would be no more. There was no locked door. There was no chain holding her there. But what then? Could she simply walk away?

On the day the envelope came, she'd wrapped Joanna's pearls in a handkerchief and tucked them alongside the fruit in her basket with a note to their owner. She'd spent the morning on the river in her johnboat before she'd gone to fill her pockets with all the poison she could carry, then looked over the East River from the shore beyond Plum Orchard.

She'd lived long enough to finally understand the cost she had paid for her gilded cage. In the stories, the isle of Kingdom Come had been paradise, but setting foot on it, she had been silenced. Where her voice—the one thing that was her own—had once been, she had a pit from which she feared nothing good could ever grow. The old gods had shown her that her words did not matter, and so she'd swallowed them down and made her friends from stories she'd been told, who never changed, never questioned, never loved.

So she'd filled her hands with glory and gone out to the water where her story had ended long ago.

Add that to your drink for colorful thoughts, more for walking dreams, a lot more for no dreams at all. Cleo wasn't sure what result she would get when she ate the seeds, but anything would have been better than being alone. With luck, it would stop her pointless wandering of these same seventeen miles of barrier lands, on a river that ran both ways to a horizon that never altered, while she became a waste. Once, she'd been young and believed she had no choice, but given enough time, even she had come to understand that only shame had brought her to this place and held her there still.

She'd bent at the river's edge, ready to drink.

Cleo believed in that instant that for all it was cursed, glory had given her two terrible gifts: all the time in the world and, finally, the choice to stop it. She'd believed it was the most power anyone could hold.

But then she had seen something that stayed her hand and made her heart turn inside her.

Only a glimmer. In the ash from the old bonfire, something solid. Something real. The unexpected twist.

Grace.

She'd dropped all her pearls. She'd been carried away. But perhaps this was only how the story began.

Chapter Thirty-Five

FRANCES

THE DAYS HAD COOLED AND THE SUN SET EARLIER IN THE FIRST days of September. Weeks had passed since the storm and the fire. Audrey Howell's baby was due any day. Frances had just dropped her at Gilbreath House after her latest doctor's appointment and now drove toward the dock, past the theater where the marquee announced *Darby O'Gill and the Little People*. Jimmy Walker was likely enjoying a private viewing from the center balcony seat. Tate had moved back into the house at the edge of town with his boys. Glenn had just started back at the mill. He'd met a nurse at the hospital who was keeping him hip-deep in homemade casseroles, and Frances knew that Audrey was much relieved.

Rosey continued to struggle with the summer's events. *"They'll tell stories about Glenn running into that fire,"* he'd said.

"In Greek or Latin?" Frances had chided, only because she knew Rosey didn't need an education on the making of heroes or monsters. Will Tremmons had not come back to Revery.

Neither did she ask if Cleo Woodbine or Archie Buie would feature in these new legends, for they wouldn't have stood for it. Perhaps the best that could be said of it all was that Glenn seemed more open to reconciliation with his dad, and that he didn't seem so desperate to prove himself in some way. There'd been an effort on the Piedmont mill's part to address concerns about the runoff, and although it hadn't made everybody happy on both sides, shifts were picking back up so Glenn and some others were back to work. He would always walk with a limp, not the battle scar he craved, but she'd heard him joke that a ruined knee was what all old football players showed St. Peter so they'd be let in at the pearly gates.

The Federal Bureau of Investigation sent agents to the area and the Coast Guard had a hearing on the matter, but no one was ever charged with torching Dungeness, although it was clear that the fire had been deliberately set. There was no insurance on the property. As stated in the *Fernandina News-Ledger*, 24 June 1959, "The fire had apparently begun on the third floor of the mammoth structure around 6 p.m. and was discovered by a worker on the island while they were eating supper. It burned furiously until around 12 midnight."

Locals, including Morrie Johnston, held firm in their belief that the same disgruntled poachers who had caused trouble all summer were the ones responsible for the blaze. In the end, the results were the same. Tourists flocked to see the ruin now, more eager than ever to see the crumbling remains of that gilded age.

Revery was a resilient community, just as Rosey had always said. So much had recovered since the storm, although some things were forever changed. Harl Buie would be part of the first integrated class at New Canaan High. Frances had moved in to live with Audrey, and Cleo Woodbine was staying in the carriage house. They were no longer taking in boarders, but Audrey continued to serve brunch and sell sack lunches to workers. With the money from Joanna's estate and part of Cleo's savings from the tagalong series, the three women had reimagined a purpose for the house as a nonprofit. Invitations had gone out to everyone in Revery, including one sent to the Piedmont family of Philadelphia, and tomorrow there would be a reception to celebrate the opening.

Frances had not asked Cleo if she knew the truth about Ellis Piedmont and whether he might be her father, but even if she never knew the facts, she knew her feelings. She was a Flood, but that didn't mean she couldn't remember the boy who had drowned in the river that summer after seeing a river siren, right along with everyone else who visited the folk center to see the tribute to that local lore.

Frances was nervous, but her dream for the center had come together with almost no effort at all. To start, on the main floor, anyone could read from the Piedmont Library collection. The board had considered restoring the Piedmont Library, but it would have meant rebuilding and a new public library was already planned for Camden County the next year. Frances's extensive assortment of mythology and folklore literature and art would be on display, including many variations of siren legends from the world over, with a nod to the local sightings in '32. By request, one would be able to see a first-edition copy of *Woodbine's Treasury of Glories and Grims*, and guests would be greeted by the permanent exhibition in the front foyer of Cleo's latest painting, *A Summer Revery*, in memoriam of Joanna Burton Flood, Ellis Piedmont, and Lumas Gray.

Just as Frances had done, visitors to the center would be able to stand for hours, searching out the hidden figures in a full gallery of Cleo's work. She knew they would be charmed by familiar landmarks like Dungeness and Plum Orchard, wonder at the twisting turns of the river and the broad horizon at the edge of the sea, and walk away in a golden haze, said to be because of the secret ingredient Cleo swirled into her water when she painted. And they would delight in the characters that had kept them all company since childhood—the little ghost girl, the fiddler, the black dog, and the giant.

Frances never doubted there was a sort of magic that went into that painting, but stories had always had that kind of power in her life.

There were future plans for music programs, theatrical productions, oral storytelling, and even classes on fishing, boatbuilding, and other regional crafts. Audrey couldn't stop coming up with new ideas. But tonight, before moving forward, Frances was looking back. She was meeting Cleo to go out to the shore behind Plum Orchard, to look over the dividings.

When she reached the riverfront, she could see Rosey there, looking much the same as the day when she'd come to Revery—tattered shorts, boat shoes, T-shirt. She wore her own shorts now, a pair of Keds like Audrey's, and she'd pulled her hair up in a ponytail. She looked younger but felt older. She pushed her glasses up while Rosey watched her climb in beside him and cocked his head the way any sailor knows to set his eyes on the horizon to get his bearings.

"You ready for this?" he asked.

"I think it's past time."

She thought about kissing him and did. They looked like an old married couple, but that was far from the case. They'd only just met months before, even if it felt like a lifetime ago. Love was like that.

He said, "Speaking of time, with Tate and Jimmy at the helm, I'll have some on my hands."

"What do you mean?"

"Will's signed his half of the Marvel over to Tate Walker. He'll manage it till Jimmy's older, then it'll go to Jimmy. And I'll be around if he needs a right-hand man."

She could imagine Jimmy Walker in his dotage, sitting up in the theater, looking out over Revery from above those marquee lights—the best view in town.

"You heard from Will?" She knew he would always be ashamed of what had happened to William Tremmons in his town, and how he could not stop it. "Where is he?"

"Oklahoma. Said he realized he needed to go home and see what he could do there. He asked after Audrey."

"Really?" Frances couldn't say she was surprised.

"And his truck."

Frances laughed.

"I was thinking about doing some traveling myself," Rosey said. "Maybe Europe. Somebody put in my head about this river that haunted her grandmother and I thought I might like to set my eyes on that. Got to be some good ghost stories over there."

He pushed his cap back from his eyes and tilted his chin up so he could gaze on her. He smiled and it was not the smile he'd given to her that first day, not the flash and fun of a carnival barker. It did something to her deep inside. She could see herself in his eyes, a girl standing at the riverbank, waiting to see what might rise.

She pushed her glasses back up her nose. "You could just ask me to go with you, Rosey Devane."

He gave a soft whistle. The sleeve of his white T-shirt rode up and she could see the mermaid tattoo, her scales a vivid blue, her eyes dancing. "Aw, I've been asking," he said. "I've been asking and asking. Did you not hear me, Frannie?"

Chapter Thirty-Six

AUDREY

WHEN CLEO RETURNED TO REVERY, SHE HADN'T WANTED THE room that had been waiting for her on the second floor of Gilbreath House. Instead, she'd chosen the loft in the carriage house. Audrey had shown her the darkroom and spread all the photographs out, thinking Cleo might remember the town that way. The older images showed Revery as it had looked when Mimi had been Audrey's age. Mimi had stood in the same place where Audrey had stood when she took the shots of the kids in the street, out front of the theater. Mimi had made a choice to leave her camera and everything she'd seen in Revery for a different life. Audrey believed she understood part of the reason why: that Mimi had loved Lumas Gray.

Cleo had reached to lift a particular photo off the table.

Audrey said, "You see it too? It's just this one that bothers me. It's the shot I got of Jimmy that day we first came to your house. I know it's only another double exposure."

"This is the photo you took that day Jimmy was stuck in that trap on the creek? This summer?" Audrey nodded and Cleo said, "Well, aren't they a pair."

"I know it's Lumas Gray. This is going to sound insane, but doesn't he look different to you than in the other photos my mother took? Different from the photo from the news clipping? Maybe I'm seeing things. Just tell me if I'm crazy."

"Honey, that doesn't sound crazy at all and I'm an expert."

"I guess I got a taste of my own medicine, is all. I shouldn't have been making those fake photos. It was all in my imagination." Audrey was looking at Cleo and holding her belly in her hands. She admitted, "I thought if Freddie would just give me a sign, I wouldn't have to be so sorry to be alive. I could be happy. About this."

"Yes, indeed. That's what we're all looking for. Permission to live a little," Cleo agreed.

"I don't think it was even real, or not what I thought love would be. He didn't know me. And I didn't know him. Or his family." Audrey knew it was going to sound stupid, but she asked anyway. "How am I supposed to raise a child that's half his?"

Cleo said, "We're all just going to have to get to know one another, aren't we? Give each other a chance."

Later, when Audrey chose prints to hang on the walls of the upstairs room that would soon be a nursey, she didn't choose Cleo's tagalong illustrations. She was afraid of what Cleo would think. But Cleo laughed when she saw the Beatrix Potter illustrations and said, "See, I knew I'd like you."

———

The photographs she'd taken of the Dungeness fire ran in national papers, showing up on the doorsteps of America, and of Will Tremmons. He'd called her at the inn the day he'd signed over his rights to the theater to Tate. She told him about the baby and he told her about the job he'd taken, working on the preservation and restoration of a place called Hunter's Home, once the family home of a woman named Jennie Ross Cobb. She was Cherokee and had been a photographer in her youth. She'd used a box camera, and her photographs from a half century earlier made him think of

Audrey's pictures. Audrey wished she could see the photographs. She wished she could see Will Tremmons. She kept the picture she'd taken of him tucked away.

"I guess I've thought a lot about that space in between the ticks and the tocks, like we talked about that day," he'd said. "That's where I've been trying to live since I came home from Korea. But I'm not a ghost, am I?"

He said he'd avoided going home, hoping like Rosey had that they were coming back to something new, an integrated country, and he'd been afraid to go back to the way life was before. But he'd missed the people who knew him and the places he'd loved.

"That day I saw you in the street, taking that stand with your camera," he said, "I realized something. You were where you were supposed to be. This town is your town. You were home and you were going to be part of the reason things were changing. And I want to be that too."

"You can't be that in Revery?" she asked.

"One of these days I'll need to come back for that truck," he said. They'd both laughed. But they both knew change wasn't happening fast enough for a man like him and a young woman like her. Of course, Will Tremmons was only eight years older than her, Audrey told herself. In a few years, when she was in her midtwenties, he would still only be in his thirties. And it would be a whole new decade by then. Maybe that would be their time. Maybe one day, Audrey hoped, this town would be their town.

————

When it was time for the circus train to pass through on its way back to Florida, Audrey had waited above the railroad tracks. Tate was with her, and Jimmy. She felt time was full in so many ways.

She was sweating and the mosquitoes were bad, but she stood her ground. She smelled the creosote from the crossties and listened to the grasshoppers sawing in the tall grass near the rails. Then she felt the rumble in the ground beneath her Keds as the locomotive approached. They watched the train cars flash past, their sides marked in bright, swirling colors with a promise painted in tall, clear letters. *The time of your life.*

On the same morning that Jimmy got his bandages off and proudly showed the scar across the top of his hand to anyone they saw, they'd taken Will's truck and rode down to Fernandina Beach to see the circus.

"I knew it would be like this!" Jimmy declared. Audrey worried about him a little, he was so overcome. But Tate always had hold of him now with a strong, soft hand.

They'd gotten hopped up on cotton candy and Coca-Cola and candied apples. They screamed their heads off at the pig races, one of them looking a lot like Glenn to Audrey's eye. Jimmy shot a cowboy pistol water gun to win a stuffed gorilla as big as he was. Audrey had her fortune told. Tate Walker pounded a contraption with a railroad hammer and rang a bell announcing his strength. They all had a corn dog with mustard.

She'd snapped photo after photo of marvels and monsters, animal and human, impossible acts. Death-defying feats. Tigers, elephants, trapeze artists, a strong man, and more clowns than should fit inside one car. "Freddie Howell, you should've seen it," she said with every shot.

She'd smelled the grease and heat and something like lightning as the wind blew over the rattling, grinding, greasy carnival rides and her skin. It had blown the scarf back from her hair, the hot breath of life that would not slow down and left everyone gasping.

Audrey felt the changing of an inner tide as the baby in her belly stretched and turned, ready to be born. And she understood she was a young woman, a widow, an innkeeper, a friend, and almost a mother in a cheerful cotton top with daisies on it, and it suited her. A little bit wild, a Gilbreath.

And when she got back, she called her parents and her in-laws with the news of a new life. "Come see us," she said. "I'll always have a room waiting for you."

Chapter Thirty-Seven

CLEO

CLEO BELIEVED A LOT OF THINGS AGAIN, THE WAY SHE HAD WHEN she was a child. Like the fact that people never outgrew their stories, a living repository of the soul of humankind, all our beauty and sorrow, without end, right inside each of us. And there were worlds inside worlds on this earth. To reach the Many-Coloured Land, water must be crossed. Next came the Land of Wonder, and fire had to be faced. Beyond that lay the Land of Promise, and no one knew what must be crossed to reach those shores.

But Cleo was no longer facing that crossing alone. A few days after the fire, when Cleo had waited alongside Tate while Glenn underwent surgery on his knee, she'd looked at Tate's sad, dark eyes and given him something better than glory for colorful thoughts, for walking dreams, better than anything she could have imagined.

"Lumas Gray did not drown in that river," she said. "Dr. Johnston sent him away, the same as he sent me and you. Morrie told me."

She watched his eyes widen as he tried to take it in. She'd heard it said that men looked like that just before they died, beholding something beyond the world they'd known. She knew the world Tate was seeing because she was seeing it too.

She said, "Lumas went down to Florida on a train, just like he said he would. It's true."

Little Hannah, the fiddler, and the giant, ever present at Cleo's back, had leaned in to hear how the story would end. She'd been glad to tell it.

Frances had called around until she'd found the full article, Cleo explained. They were waiting on a mimeographed copy being mailed to Gilbreath House, confirmation of what Morrie had claimed. The article in the paper was from 1945, part of an obituary, although the photo was captioned "1932, Ybor City, FL." The headline read, "Cuesta Rey Cigar Factory Remembers Soldier, Last Lecture."

Tate had lost weight, she thought, and looked paper thin, and every mile seemed to show on him. He was quiet a long while before he said, "He always told me he was going to get to Ybor City."

"That's right. Archie made sure he got there." Cleo put her hand on top of his. He turned his over and held on to her. "Based on this, it would seem he lived another thirteen years. But then he enlisted in the Second World War and died overseas."

More than a decade after the bonfire.

"Somebody must have known to send that obituary back to Revery," Tate said. "Lumas must have talked about this place to at least one person. They must have figured somebody at the inn would want to know he'd died."

Everything clicked into place as Cleo reflected on the things she knew.

"It says he was a lecturer. That's a reader, isn't it? Audrey's mama taught Lumas to read when they were little, when she lived in that house. Maybe he talked about Mimi Gilbreath to somebody."

Tate said, "That camera was Mimi's. Audrey found the clipping in with Mimi's film. I guess somebody must've sent it to Mimi and she tucked it away and never showed it to anyone else. Just kept it for herself."

It would have been the only part of Lumas she could have kept,

Cleo thought. Mimi had left Revery a long time ago, married another man, taking that knowledge with her and whatever feelings she'd had about it all. What else could she have done, if they'd been friends, a white girl and a colored boy in Revery? Why would she ever have been compelled to let anyone know the news of Lumas, let alone Cleo?

But later, Cleo would think often of Audrey's photo rather than the news clipping, an inexplicable image of an older Lumas Gray standing on the shores of the river behind Plum Orchard, looking over Jimmy when he'd been caught in that trap. There was no earthly explanation for that last exposure on a brand-new roll of film, a photo showing a full-grown man who had led a long life. A photo that never should have existed, unless Mimi had seen him again.

Tate said some people believed love could exist for a split second where time overlapped, unaccounted for, held in light. Or, Cleo figured, maybe she was just seeing things.

Maybe that photo was like Tate's watch, which he had found just a few days after the Dungeness fire, tucked inside the pocket of that ruined pair of pants she'd tossed away weeks ago, there all along. Some things were never really lost.

———

Almost as soon as Kingdom Come had become part of Cumberland, people had begun to talk about it like it had only ever been something out of one of Dooley's tall tales, as if her living memory of what had happened there was only another fable. But Cleo still swirled the last of the summer's glory into the water where she dipped her brush.

She'd spent so many days with nothing unexpected breaking

up the routine until this summer of visitations. Now with autumn on her doorstep in Revery, she loved the predictability of her days. Tate wore a fisherman's hat and it gave him a comical look. She could count on him to always reach to take her hand and help her into her boat, even if she never needed it. And the hours would run in and out and over one another with Cleo settled on the little seat the same as she had that day when she held the mink on her lap. The boat would pitch and bob with the weight of the black dog. She'd turn a full circle and settle herself, tongue out, smiling up at Cleo with all the love in the world, as if she liked it that Cleo had named her Grim.

"You're a good dog," Cleo would say and wrap her arms around the dog's neck, proof of life. "That's my girl."

If Cleo knew anything, she knew that there was a fine line between what people dreamed and what was real in this world. She'd seen her share of figments and she'd come face-to-face with hard truths too. When she thought of that night in '32, she knew she'd seen something both true and fantastic, even if she'd been unwilling to trust her own eyes and later attributed what she'd seen to some trick of the moonlight or an addled mind.

The memory had begun to fade as soon as she'd spoken it aloud to the men who had decided the truth for her, blurring into something both fact and fiction. In the weeks and months after she'd first been sent to Woodbine Cottage, she'd walked the shoals carrying a hole inside her the size of her youth, where faith in wonders had once been. And Cleo had accepted their version of things down to what she should think of herself. A full year passed that way before she saw a miracle again. And then she saw it every summer since. Before the visitations of Tate Walker, Frances Flood, or Audrey

Howell, another came to her shore, a flash of green, the glimmer of scales.

Tonight, beneath a sky of stars over the East River, Cleo took Frances Flood out in her johnboat. They moved silently over the dividings and down into Cumberland Sound.

Cleo didn't embellish the facts. She only told Frances everything as she remembered it from the summer of 1932—Joanna on the rings at Dungeness, then bundled into a car and sent away; how she'd spent an afternoon searching the pool with Tate Walker to find all sixty pearls; what it was like telling the story of the Lorelei, believing she'd called up something from the deep on the night of the bonfire, and the horror of the drownings; how they'd heard something and then seen it glimmer in the water before the river swept Ellis Piedmont and Lumas Gray away; what it was like to lie shot on the grand dining table at Plum Orchard. Told altogether, it could hardly sound true. But Frances accepted every word.

"That was a long time ago," she said.

"It does sound like it," Cleo admitted, but it still felt like yesterday. "It was a tidal bore, they say, that took those boys. There's never been one here, but a wave like that can come up a river like this one, and that night, they reckon it did. I don't know why. That, I can't tell you." Cleo looked at the young woman with a steady resolve. "I tried to tell them what I'd done. No one would listen. I thought if I stayed here, your mama would come back to take her pound of flesh. I prayed for it for a long, long time. And when I heard she had died, I thought that was the end of it. I'd have no peace. I came out to that same shore. I was going to eat up every last bit of the same thing I gave to her and Ellis, guzzle it down, put a stop to my pointless self. But then life just kept knocking at my door. Again and again. Joanna sent you. And I realized I owed Joanna something more than death."

"The painting?"

"Lord, no." Cleo shook her head. Maybe that painting would be the best thing she'd ever make. Maybe it had given her a voice again, a way to look back and forward at the same time. She'd put everything she knew into it, every technique she'd learned from her granddaddy, every color she'd seen on the shoals. When looked at closely, what might have seemed a shadow could be a friend. And in it, Cleo had finally seen herself.

"Don't you know," she said, "Joanna sent me her most precious pearl. That's how I know she forgave me. She sent you here because she knew I would love you for her when she was gone. That I would be your tagalong."

Frances cried quietly. And Cleo did not reach to comfort her, but let her come to the end of her tears.

"Audrey told me you've been worried Ellis Piedmont might have been your daddy. But that's not true."

Frances sucked in her breath and wiped her face with both hands. "I didn't want to ask. But how do you know?"

"Because she never slept with him. She told me. She never even wanted to be here with him. That was an idea her parents had. She said they were pushing the match, but there was some-one else before Ellis. She told everybody that when they were at the pool that day, and I heard Dr. Johnston talking before she left. I think she just wanted to go home to your daddy.

"Maybe you can tell me some about her life," Cleo said. "I've had a pretty good one myself. I wish I'd been able to tell her that, but I'm not sure I knew it at the time."

There came a shuddering sound, like a newborn thing drawing its breath and finding air instead of water. "Look here," Cleo said. A change came over the river, a swelling a few yards away. "This is what I saw that night. It's what I wanted you to see."

The water's surface broke with a sigh and a shining, ebony skin shone slick, huge as a barrel and moving toward them. Then a burst of air and a soft spray rained over their skin before the animal disappeared just as swiftly. They sat there in the hush. But they'd seen it with their own eyes. They'd heard it. They'd felt it. Cleo looked to Frances to see she was alarmed but smiling, teeth white in the dim light off the water.

"That's a sturgeon," Frances said, excitement in her voice. "Daddy talked about them jumping in the French Broad. It's massive."

"Hold on. She's not gone. They jump at the light this time of year. You'll see them other times, but mostly at dawn. They can knock you right out of your boat," Cleo said, smiling. "Scared me to death the first time I saw them. Until Archie Buie told me they migrate through here every year."

She knew, too, that what monsters we make of our loves and our lives might be unmade.

They waited and only moments later a large shape cruised so near the boat that its body bumped the side. Cleo feared they would tip over. But just as it slid past, silent and impossible, she reached as if in a dream to touch the bony ridges along its back. She felt she might as easily reach from this life and touch the next, a thing she should never be able to do. But instead of being met by death, she was instantly reminded of life and the fear of losing her own. And Cleo wanted this life. The thrill of it almost broke her heart.

The moment was over in less than an instant. The great fish was gone, leaving the boat to rock along into the inky night with only the memory shared by two women who both should have been home in their beds. Cleo knew they were no different from many who had come before, that they would have no proof of the wonder they'd witnessed, except for the sharp sting of a cut as she lifted her hand to her lips to taste blood and salt on her fingertips. An old fiddle tune came on the air. With her other hand, she reached to take hold of Frances's and they sat together on the river.

Her granddaddy's voice came to mind, a few lines she remembered from one of the ancient tales, and she spoke them aloud like a prayer. A promise.

"*The green tides of ocean rose over me and my dream, so that I drowned in the sea and did not die, for I awoke in deep waters, and I was that which I dreamed.*"

Cleo watched the tide's turning, and a new day broke over the dividings.

A Note from the Author

If time is a dream, Cumberland Island, Georgia, is its landscape. This gentle wilderness holds sway over the imaginations of those who've encountered its unchanging landscape throughout centuries and I'm just the latest to fall under its spell.

When I began to scribble notes for what would eventually become *The Fabled Earth*, a trip to Cumberland Island was where I started. I wasn't sure what I was hoping to find there. For our twenty-fifth wedding anniversary, my husband and I traveled to stay at the Greyfield Inn, one of the nineteenth-century homes built by relatives of famed philanthropist Andrew Carnegie converted to an inn in the 1960s. It's now the only hotel accommodation for guests on the island. I was breathless as the ferry that carried us along the island's shore passed miles of tangled maritime wilderness and long white beaches. I knew that in 1996, only a few months after my own wedding, JFK Jr. and Carolyn Bessette had been married there in a secret ceremony, and I couldn't help thinking of that, and how that sweet story was made more precious some years later for its tragic end. *What brings us all here*, I wondered. I felt time slipping around us. Serenaded by cicadas, we slept in a room that was once part of a second-story porch. We ate at the dining room table where the Carnegie family once ate, then wandered the island almost completely alone. It was easy to be captivated by the remnants of the past, but I felt conflicted too—enchanted and lucky to be there but also voyeuristic and aware of every footprint I left in my wake. Over and over, my conscious whispered, *Take care*.

Did I see things that I write about in this story, even the ones that seem mostly impossible? Yes. Arriving with my diphthong and stories from the foothills of Appalachia to stand in the long shadows of robber baron mansions, did I feel a longing to find my way as an artist? You bet. Did I feel the hair on the nape of my neck rise as I stood in a quiet boneyard beneath ancient oaks with drifting moss and surrounded by resurrection ferns, or as I walked on an endless beach, gazing over waters where sharks or larger mysteries are ever at play? Oh, absolutely. Cumberland Island was a basket of plenty. And it fooled me. I believed from the very start that after the trip, this novel would be easy pickings, and I left the island with a head bursting with ideas.

When I came home, I read everything I could about the area. I pored over photographs with the kind of obsession that writing novels requires. With every era, there were events that entertained or angered me. The names of famous individuals piled up beside the names of unknown figures, each as interesting as the next. But pretty soon, I started to see the trouble. Every time I turned an idea to see how it might catch the light, hoping it would lead the way into this story, the images in my mind shifted like pieces of colored glass inside a kaleidoscope. I asked myself what *one thing* I could say about Cumberland Island that mattered. Experiencing the island firsthand only complicated my feelings about its conservation and exploitation and ultimately its mystique. I stalled out, convinced that I'd never be able to capture any of it in words.

But here's what happens to an unwritten story: it walks a storyteller's dreams. I couldn't forget about it; the haunting ran too deep and wouldn't let me sleep. For a long while, I was aimless, wandering Grand Avenue in my mind, with my own ghosts trailing my heels. More than once, I thought I never should have gone there. But then one night, along came Cleo Woodbine, yearning to make her mark and betraying herself. There was Frances Flood, more comfortable with monsters than men. And Audrey Howell, raising ghosts and raising hackles in a town where she felt like a stranger and so many lonely people longed to find home. And eventually, I concluded that this book would not be about the history of Cumberland Island or even the famous Carnegie family. I wasn't even really writing about the natural splendor of the place, although that is the backdrop. Nor was I writing about the complicated and embittered history of the island or our mythical dividings, although that fragility is clearly on the page. Ultimately, I came back to that question I'd asked myself about the one true thing I'd learned from my trip to Cumberland and finally, I knew the answer. My story was about how in this world we ever arrive at hope, a place that refuses to be found by latitude and longitude. It's not a place we must reach, but one that we carry within. It's a gift we offer to one another, the storm party we host through every season of this life.

So, here are some scattered truths in this fiction. The fact is, while it may do little for your painting, if you mix morning glory seeds into your drinking water, they are known to be an effective hallucinogen. The myth of the Timucuan Indians as giants is thought to originate from early engravings by artist Jacques le Moynes, who traveled to Florida with explorer Jean Ribault in 1568, in his attempt to portray depth. Look that up. Dr. Marius Johnston makes an appearance in the novel. While his is a fictional account, he was a true figure and beloved member of the Carnegie family. I like to imagine that he would have been as benevolent and practical in his dealings with the young guests in my story. His son

Morrie was truly known to frequent Plum Orchard after he was older, remembering the glory days, listening to "Some Enchanted Evening." And drawing from historical reports, it was easy to see that the antagonism between the Carnegie family and poachers did finally reach dangerous levels in the summer of 1959. Where I chose to deviate from known history to fit my fictional narrative, I apologize in advance to historians and scholars.

The circus did indeed winter in Sarasota, Florida, although I took some creative license in routing such a train in a way best suited to the story. The Cuban-owned cigar factories of Ybor City, Florida, truly existed, as did the men knowns as lecturs, who would read aloud to the others at work in the warehouses.

When the first photographs were developed, we learned how to capture an image of people who would have otherwise been lost to us. We were able to witness an event without actually attending it or look into the face of someone who was no longer alive, sometimes resulting in a manipulation called Ghost Photography. I was grateful to also mention the important work of Jennie Ross Cobb, the first known indigenous woman photographer in the United States, known for her photographs in the late nineteenth century among relatives in the Cherokee Nation in Tahlequah, Oklahoma.

As for sturgeon, these creatures are as close to dragons as anything I have ever encountered. They do migrate in the summer and, especially at dawn, these jumping fish can be dangerous, known to knock fishermen overboard or capsize their boats. I love the mystery of their centuries-old journeys to return and be reborn where they began.

From personal experience in my former career as a teacher, I learned of a rare condition known today as Williams Syndrome. In 1959, it was still commonly referred to as Elvin Face Syndrome.

Those diagnosed with Williams Syndrome have unique characteristics but their lived experiences and challenges are widely varied, and thankfully medicine and society are evolving every day toward a better understanding of this population. When I was teaching children with significant learning and behavioral differences, I had the privilege of working with a student diagnosed with the syndrome, meaning I had the good fortune to spend time with one unique individual living her distinct life. Every good and hard-won lesson I learned from that time about personhood and perseverance, I hope is honored in this work. That is how I hope the character of Jimmy Walker will be received, with Williams Syndrome presented as merely a detail in the whole of his multifaceted story.

While the Piedmont family, private library, and the paper mill in this novel are only fiction inspired by true history, sadly, the story of the Wanderer as Rosey relates it is drawn directly from historical record. And while the last year of the 1950s may not have gone down in history as an especially significant one, I found it to be particularly poignant. In this story set in the wake of Brown v. the Board of Education, the culture of our country and region was changing, often painfully and slowly. Those changes, and what people believed about personal freedoms, was being reflected in art, music, and books. The same old monsters and marvels have always entertained people, soothed or threatened them. I believe our commitment to one another survives in these narratives we have in common and that our stories can lift us to our better selves. I hope the careful choices I've made to portray the relationships and the language within this community of 1959 in an honest light, and the complicated moments that characters face in this fiction, ultimately inspires courage and hope in readers in the times in which they live.

The Fabled Earth is really just a fable about an island with a history that's very real. And a reminder that you don't have to leave your armchair to gather round some faraway fire to tell your stories. Be brave where you are. Don't be afraid of monsters or men or ghosts, but find courage in love and see the light it will throw across the faces around you so you can know them better. When you find yourself in a place where the tide runs both ways, turn to one another, like every character who comes to Revery dreaming of home, of community, of a place to be cherished and accepted. And if you ever do come to stand on Cumberland Island, I hope you'll protect that splendid and precious reminder of the wild and wonderous, our common dream.

Take care.

Acknowledgments

To begin at the beginning of this book is to reflect on the first conversations about attempting a new novel, something akin to sharing a dream. Danielle Egan-Miller, you get me. You cry when I want you to and you laugh at my jokes and my foibles and you encourage me to kill characters without apology—everything a Southern writer needs in this world. You named the town of Revery and it's absolutely right that it should be so, since you are my dream literary agent. Thank you to the entire team at Browne and Miller Literary Associates for all the work you do to help a creative mind manage in a business world, not to mention the hours spent helping me to untangle plot and theme and sort through my own psychology. Thank you to Mariana Fisher for reading and reading and then reading again.

Thank you to my brilliant publishing team at Harper Muse, who are incomparable in their kindness and enthusiasm for my work— Kimberly Carlton, Amanda Bostic, Nekasha Pratt, Margaret Kercher, Taylor Ward, Caitlin Halstead, Savannah Breedlove, Patrick Aprea, and Colleen Lacey. You have my eternal gratitude for making everything in my imagination into an actual book.

Thank you to Julie Monroe, the line editor with the sharpest eye and best sense of humor! You straighten everything out and never, ever break a sweat, even when there's math.

I can't articulate how much I appreciate the support and enthusiasm from my team at Kaye Publicity and how much I admire each of you. Thank you, Dana Kaye, Eleanor Embody, Kaitlyn Kennedy, and Jordan Brown, for embracing me and *The Fabled Earth* and for doing the magical work of guiding stories into the hands of readers.

Reaching back a few years, thank you to my students in Washington state at The Children's Institute for Learning Differences for the experience of teaching in my early days out of college and for relationships that enriched and expanded my life in so many creative and beautiful ways. I learned as much or more from you than you ever learned from me.

When it comes to writing setting and history, sometimes a writer is lucky enough to travel to the places that inspire their stories. Thank you to the staff at the Greyfield Inn for welcoming my husband and myself into your gracious space and to the guides from the National Park Service who carried us on tours, answered questions with patience and enthusiasm, and shared their love for Cumberland Island with us. I hope you'll find that love and desire to protect the place you cherish reflected in these pages.

There were particulars I had to suss out for the writing of this book. Thank you to my daughter, Claire Brock, as well as Benita Van-Winkle, for patiently answering questions about photography in the 1930s and 1950s.

Thank you to my son, Paul Brock, for the inspiration for Cleo Woodbine's paintings, drawn directly from your own beautiful artwork, and for your gift of Arthur Rackham's illustrations and James Stephens' collection of *Irish Fairy Tales*, which informed Dooley Woodbine's fictional work.

To my son, Morgan Brock, thank you in the first place for the inspiration following a Charleston ghost tour with Buxton Books years ago, to write a story about ghost stories.

Thank you to my mother for teaching me to love the Georgia

coast and to my father for reminding me of that tunnel connected to The Wink Theater in Dalton, Georgia, where I saw my first movie, and the inspiration for the Marvel Theater in this story.

The thing that makes me the most nervous when I try to express my thanks after years spent working on a particular book is that I am absolutely bound to forget a name. There have been countless writers who have come alongside me while I've worked on this novel, some from years ago when I first began to conceptualize the setting and later, those that helped me work through iterations of the story. Here are a few of you: Those who attended a Tinderbox Writers Retreat many moons ago may not know that just sitting in the beach house with you as we quietly worked gave me the first bit of inspiration to start this story, and so I thank you, Reta Hampton, for offering your cozy little house to us.

Much later, Gina Heron and Heather Adams, you read a very early draft of this book and cheered me on when I was still lost in the woods. Emily Carpenter, you keep me from wandering off on tangents or tag along for good trouble. Katie Crawford, Carmen Slaughter, Ann Hite, Joy Callaway, Aimie Runyan-Vetter, Renea Winchester, Marybeth Whalen, Adele Myers, Colleen Oakley, Lynn Cullen, Kimbelry Belle, Tori Whitaker, Angela Jackson-Brown, Robert Gwaltney, Melanie Sue Bowles, Jeffrey Dale Lofton, Eden Robins, and Alicia Bessette, you are the touchstones and encouragers when I'm being wimpy. Constance Sayers, no two introverts on a plane ever got luckier to be seated together. Lynda Loigman, you are my sister of the heart. Thanks to Yvette Corporon, Joy Callaway, T. I. Lowe, Pam Arena, Heather Webb, Jamila Minnicks, and Paulette Kennedy for pondering possible titles. Jonathan Haupt, Mary Green, and Bren McClain, you brought me to Beaufort and gave me the gift of morning on a marsh. And to the army of lowcountry locals who, when asked for their memories, rallied to Mary Greene's call and inspired dreams of storm parties and community and alligators swimming down the street.

Thank you to Jon Mayes and Linda-Marie Barrett for your friendship and to the Southern Independent Bookseller's Alliance for welcoming all stories, setting crowded tables, throwing open wide doors, and for the tireless hours you spend faithfully keeping lanterns lit in our communities.

To the authors of Gutenburg's Angels, we have weathered storms and cheered one another on these last few years and held one another through losses and triumphs. I treasure each of you, and especially Amy Sue Nathan, to whom this novel is dedicated.

To the extraordinary Adriana Trigiani and to Robin Kall, your early support for my writing kept me believing in myself as I started this novel. Kristy Woodson Harvey, Kristin Harmel, Patti Callahan Henry, and Mary Kay Andrews of Friends and Fiction, your generosity has been boundless and that of the community of book lovers you have helped foster, especially Lisa and Brenda Gardner and Ron Block and the members of the official book club. There are no words to fully express what your support has meant to me or how it fills me with gratitude to see your smiling faces at my events. In particular, Annissa Armstrong, Dawn McCurry, Bubba Wilson, Allison Burns (and Nora), and the Atlanta crew have been incredibly good to me. You are the very best part of this journey.

To all booksellers (especially to the staff at Foxtale Book Shoppe, in particular Karen Schwettman and Gary Parks), book club members, festival coordinators and attendees, and librarians who dedicate their lives to reading and sharing stories, this one is absolutely for you.

And thank you to Daniel, my husband, who knows all my ghost stories better than anyone and isn't afraid one bit.

Discussion Questions

1. Great emphasis is placed on stories, myths, and legends. What is your favorite myth or legend? Is it one you read or one that was passed down to you by family? Why do you like it?

2. What did you think of Cleo using the morning glory concoction on Ellis and Joanna? Do you think she deserved her exile to Woodbine Cottage? Why or why not?

3. How would you have handled living alone for decades in Woodbine Cottage like Cleo did?

4. The book touches on many of the issues facing the United States, and particularly the South, in the first half of the twentieth century—racism, gender inequality, classism. Did any particular narrative on one of these issues affect you more than the others? Did you notice any parallels between the events in the book and events in the world today?

5. What did you think of Dr. Johnston, who did not have much dialogue in the story, yet whose presence and authority weighed heavily throughout the book?

6. Who was your favorite character, or which character had the most affecting story arc and growth, in your opinion? Why?

7. Frances believed that "stories could change people." Do you agree or disagree with her? Why?

8. Do you think Will Tremmons will ever come back to Revery and to Audrey? Why or why not?

9. What do you envision for the future of the characters in this book?

LOOKING FOR MORE GREAT READS? LOOK NO FURTHER!

HARPER MUSE

*Illuminating minds
and captivating hearts
through story.*

Visit us online to learn more:
harpermuse.com

Or scan the below code and sign up to receive
email updates on new releases, giveaways,
book deals, and more:

@harpermusebooks

About the Author

Claire Brock Photography

Kimberly Brock is the award-winning author of *The Lost Book of Eleanor Dare* and *The River Witch*. She is the founder of Tinderbox Writers Workshop and has served as a guest lecturer for many regional and national writing workshops including at the Pat Conroy Literary Center. She lives near Atlanta with her husband and three children.

Visit her online at kimberlybrockbooks.com
Instagram: @kimberlydbrock
Facebook: @kimberlybrockauthor
Twitter: @kimberlydbrock